GREED

Book One of

The Death of Money

By

D. Thomas Jewett

GREED

Book One of

The Death of Money

Certain public figures – both individuals and corporations – are represented herein. In representing these figures, the Author has, wherever possible, shown these figures according to information recorded in public records. Where the Author depicts private conversations and/or behavior by public figures, the Author hereby states that these depictions are fiction, and are derived solely from the Author's imagination. Aside from those public figures depicted herein, all other characters and corporations are fiction, and are a figment of the Author's imagination – and any resemblance to real people or corporations is coincidental.

DISCLAIMER: The Author hereby declares that he is not an investment adviser; and that nothing contained herein should be construed as investment advice. For investment advice, the reader is encouraged to seek a competent investment adviser.

This book previously published under the title: Edge of Darkness; Book One of the Bankster Chronicles, by David Jewett and Dave Jewett.

www.davidjewettauthor.com
www.jtmediapublishing.com
www.whenmoneydies.com

ISBN-13: 978-1790732463

ACKNOWLEDGMENTS

I do not know how anyone trying a first novel can do it without sympathy, help, and faith of friends. No one who has tried has had better friends than I.

I especially want to thank Linda and Kate. For without their encouragement, I might not have finished this story, or brought the story to this point in its evolution.

Cast of Characters

Episode 1

Henri Aleman	Proprietor of *Olde Skippers Pub.*
William Martin	Dry goods proprietor.
Colin Martin (child)	Son of William Martin.
Joseph Crispin	Respected landowner.
Ian Williams	Goldsmith.

Episode 2

Aaron Silverstein	Goldsmith.
Jason Silverstein	Aaron's son.
Arthur Griffin	Dry goods proprietor.
Meredith Griffin	Arthur's wife.
Mary Griffin	Arthur's daughter.
Jonathan Merchant	Peasant.
Nathan Goldman	Goldsmith.
Colin Martin (adult)	Bookkeeper and historian.

Episode 3

Lord Basil	Ultra wealthy banker.
Lord George	Basil's father.
Lady Jessica	Basil's mother.
Lady Diana	Basil's cousin.
Swenson	Basil's butler.
Daniel Elsbach	Lord Basil's strategist.
Dwayne Jeffrey	Rare coin and precious metals dealer.
Patricia Jeffrey	Dwayne's wife.
James Jeffrey	Dwayne's son.
Joshua Lindt	Commodities Trader for AB Jorday.
Stephanie Walker	Joshua's administrative assistant.
Dave Palmer	Commodities Trader.
Kirk Kincaid	Expediter and hatchet man.
Buck Fuller	Kirk's right-hand man.
George Hammond	Owner and operator of Metalworks, Inc.
Brandon Payne	Owner and operator of Rheingold Fabrication.
Bailey Keating	Administrator for Jacob-Mortenson.
Bill Ford	Former engineer and Freedom Dollar Partner.

Brandy West	Former banker and Freedom Dollar Partner.
Murray Hofstadler	Chief Engraver of the Golden Mint.
Alan Greenspan	Chairman of the Federal Reserve (by himself).
Robert Rubin	Secretary of the Treasury (by himself).
Lawrence Summers	Deputy Secretary of the Treasury (by himself).
Arthur Levitt	Chairman of the SEC (by himself).
Brooksley Born	Chairman of the CFTC (by herself).
Jim Martin	Chief Economist at the Federal Reserve.
Joe Miller	Just an average 'Joe'.
Jane Miller	Just an average 'Jane'.
Mark Shannon	Aide to congressman.
Sheryl Barclay	Aide to senator.
Tim	Survivor.
Squirt	Survivor.
Jim	Survivor.

. . . And a cast of thousands . . .

"History is written by the winners."
– Napoleon

Table of Contents

GREED – Book 1 of *The Death of Money*

Prologue

> *Banking was conceived in iniquity and born in sin. The Bankers own the earth. Take it away from them, but leave them the power to create deposits, and with the flick of the pen they will create enough deposits to buy it back again. However, take away that power, and all the great fortunes like mine will disappear — as they ought to in order to make this a happier and better world to live in. But, if you wish to remain the slaves of Bankers and pay the cost of your own slavery, then let them continue to create deposits.*
>
> - - - - - Sir Joshua Stamp (1880-1941), one time governor of the Bank of England, in his Commencement Address at the University of Texas in 1927. Reportedly he was the second wealthiest individual in Britain.

THE FULL MOON cast eerie shadows and a pale light upon the urban landscape. Yet it was in the windy, cold shadows that the shivering, disheveled couple strode quickly along the sidewalk, passing store after store. Their faces nestled down into their warm woolens, they wrapped their arms tightly around their coats, holding them close to their bodies. With teeth chattering, they deftly stepped over and around the trash, the garbage, the carcasses; all strewn along the pavement.

The stores were lined up in a neat row, like cookie-cutter pastries in a bakery. And yet the security bars had been ripped from their mounts and thrown along the street. Stores were vandalized, if not demolished, and shattered display windows left a blanket of broken glass. Open to the elements, the damage from snow, wind, rain all accumulated until the structures around the windows rotted and sagged.

And the carcasses. Mostly people. Dead from starvation or violence or sickness; they littered the sidewalk and the streets. Unhuman mangled forms - with chunks of flesh chewed out. *Dogs - packs of dogs. No longer man's best friend!*

And the cars - the dead cars. Sat like hulks in the streets, the windows smashed and the insides gutted. They were left wherever the gasoline ran out - gasoline was now too hard to come by, and too expensive.

The couple made their way along the street ...

... *food,* he thought. *All we need is food!*

But they maintained a quick vigilant stride. The man, Tim, found his thoughts flashing back a few months, to a time when pandemonium ruled the streets, when gangs broke into stores and hauled out televisions, electronics - anything they thought of value. The gangs were dehumanized - thoughtless and mindless - like drones around a hive. For if they were more than drones, they'd have taken food and water, not televisions and stereos.

But they were thoughtless. And so, Tim and his partner Squirt seized what the drones had overlooked - food.

The couple continued on their way ...

Were Tim to have his wits about him, he would have thanked God for the cold weather; for that, at least, kept the rotting carcasses from stinking. But he was not thinking, for he - actually, both of them - were nearly crazed with hunger.

Squirt, the woman, strode slightly behind. Her legs moved quickly to keep up with the long strides of a much taller Tim; while she constantly glanced over her shoulder, too afraid that she would see what she feared. But Tim was alert and focused, always looking forward; seeking the prize of their desire.

"Tim? Do you think we'll find food today?" she asked.

"We've got to! We've got to ..." he replied. "I don't know that I can go much further without it." He stopped and looked at the skinny young woman; her red hair not so fiery anymore. But her green eyes still held the fire of a toughness he knew burned deep inside her. "How're you doing, Squirt?"

"I'll make it," she shivered. "Let's get going – find us some food."

They crossed a street – the mangled sign read 175th St. They continued on, passing one storefront after another, one alley after another.

And then Tim's acute hearing picked up a slight noise; maybe a groan. It was coming out of the darkness.

They froze in their tracks. Both cocked their heads, seeking the direction of the sound. Tim listened; sensing it was coming from the nearby alley. His gaze sliced into the alley; trying to separate the movement of shadows from the shifting darkness.

And then he heard it again. Louder, but still a whisper. *Help ...*

"Did you hear that?"

"Yeah," she whispered. "What is it?"

"Down there!" He gestured toward the alley.

"It's a trap. I know it!" She paused. "It's like every other damn alley sound we've passed. Traps! But no food! No help!"

"Still, I think we need to check it out," he whispered. "Follow me; but back me up!"

"Okay."

Tim pulled a pistol out of his pocket. He held it down by his side as they edged slowly into the alley. His senses scanning outward, he held his reflexes on a hair trigger – ready to bolt at the first sign of danger. Listening, watching, feeling. Squirt followed him down the alley; watching their backs.

Tim could make out a shadowy form stretched out on the ground. They approached, slowly; coming upon an old man. He laid face up on the pavement, still breathing. Tim studied the man, observing his unkempt gray beard and his gray locks, seemingly cut at random. His tattered clothing hung from his form in strips and strings, even on the ground.

Tim pocketed his pistol. He stooped and touched the old man; feeling his chest move, feeling for a pulse. The old man shuddered and then opened his eyes.

"Wha? – What!" The old man blinked. "Who the hell are ya? Where am I?"

"That's okay, mister," Tim said in a soothing voice. "We found you lying here. You're here in an alley."

"Alley? What alley?" The man lifted his head and looked around. "Get your damn hands off me!"

The old man picked himself off the pavement. Wobbling, he grabbed Tim's shoulder. He coughed. And then he gagged, tightening his mouth shut to hold down his stomach. But to no avail, he stretched his neck forward and heaved onto the pavement. He gasped, twice, and then heaved again.

He wiped his mouth on his coat sleeve. "Shit!" He spat. "God, I don't feel so good!"

"You just hang on for a bit, old man."

The old man held onto Tim's shoulder while his dizziness faded. He let go and attempted to stand unaided, wincing as he put weight on his left foot. "Damn. That hurts," he spat. "I must've sprained my ankle."

"You okay, sir?" the girl asked.

"What the hell do you want?" The old man spat through his nearly toothless mouth. He straightened up and glared at the couple, his eyes narrowing to slits. "Who the hell are you?"

"No one," Tim said. "I guess we'll be on our way."

The couple turned and began to retrace their steps.

"Wait a minute." The old man's voice was forceful. "Maybe we can trade!"

Tim and Squirt stopped in their tracks. They turned to look back at the old man.

"Maybe we can trade," the old man said again, quietly this time.

"Have you got food?" Tim asked.

"That depends," said the old man. "I'm lookin' for silver – got any?"

"If you've got food, I've got silver," Tim replied.

"Follow me," the old man said. He turned and limped further down the alley, further into the shadows. The couple followed, Tim keeping his hand in his pocket, grasping his pistol.

"Damn it hurts," he growled as he limped up to a metal door. He pulled out a key and inserted it into the padlock. *Click!* He pulled the door open, turned his head and looked at the couple with a toothless grin. "C'mon," he cackled. He limped through the door and a light quickly came on from inside.

The couple followed him through the door. Tim's hand was still in his pocket, grasping his pistol.

Tim and Squirt were a bit dazed at finding themselves in a lighted, heated living space. Tim looked around and could see that the light came from a kerosene lantern. He scanned the room, noting a bed and a kerosene space heater – and a kitchen. "You live pretty well!" Tim said. The heat was already beginning to warm them.

The old man limped over to a cupboard, opened a cabinet, and revealed a stack of canned food. He grabbed two cans and held them up next to his nearly toothless grin. "How's chili sound?"

Tim looked at the cans dubiously. "How much?"

The grizzled old man's toothless smile appeared once again. "A dime a piece."

"A dime a piece!" Squirt exclaimed. "Why, that's highway robbery!"

The old man shrugged. "Take it or leave it."

"We'll take it," Tim replied. He pulled two silver dimes from his pocket.

The man took the dimes and dropped them into his pocket. "I've got a fire. I can heat it up. Or you can eat it cold," he offered.

"Cold," the couple said at once, too hungry to wait.

The old man opened the cans, handing one and a spoon to each of his 'guests'; and then he took one for himself.

Tim and Squirt wolfed down the food, scraping the inside of the can clean.

"Water?" the old man offered.

The couple nodded, and each took a glass of water. They gulped as though it were air.

"Well," the old man said, "I've got to sit. Let's get acquainted."

"More food?" Tim asked.

"Not yet," the old man snorted. He wiped his nose with his hand. "It's best to let that sit for a while before you eat anymore." He paused and studied the couple shrewdly. "You two haven't eaten in a while."

They each found a chair and looked curiously at their host. The young woman opened the conversation. "So, who are you?"

"Me? I'm Jim. Just Jim," he shrugged. "My friends call me Jim. You can call me Jim." He paused and took in the couple, his mouth forming the shape of a crooked moon. "And who are you? How long have you been on the streets?"

"I'm Tim, and this here is 'Squirt'," he nodded over to the young woman. "Or at least, that's what everyone calls her."

"Everyone?" the old man asked. "Who's everyone?"

"Well, just me, I guess now. Everyone else we knew is dead."

"Yep," replied the old man as he scratched the stubble on his cheek. "That's truth everywhere now."

"What do you mean?" Squirt asked.

The old man gestured over to a radio on the far desk. "That's a ham transceiver rig. With it, I can pick up a lot of traffic from the rest of the country. Even from around the world." He leaned forward earnestly, "I gotta tell ya, the world has really changed! That's truth."

"How so?" Squirt asked.

The old man eyed her. "I don't think you wanna know."

Squirt hesitated. "Sure, I want to know."

"No. You don't." He looked down a long while. Then his voice took on a grim tone. "The once-great United States of America is dead! It's balkanized; reduced to city states and guarded areas. It split into a bunch of regions. Let's see." He began counting on his fingers as he listed the regions. "The New England states, the Atlantic Coast states, the Southern states, the Midwest states, the Central states, the Southwest territories, the North and Northwest territories, and the Far West region. And most of it is in anarchy, from within and without."

Even though Tim and Squirt were still hungry, they were becoming engrossed in the old man's tale...

"Technology is gone," he snorted. "Hell! Electrical appliances are just about useless, 'cause there's no grid anymore – and no way to power them. Unless ..." he gestured toward a back room, "unless you have batteries like me."

"And gasoline? Hell, it's just about dried up. That's why all those cars on the street are just standin' there – there's no damn gas to drive 'em." Again, he wiped his nose on his sleeve. "The population of North America is down to about 40 million. The world population is way down. No food, sickness and death everywhere, and marauding bands of slime preying on people in the big cities. Hell, just look at what happened to me! Just look at all the dead bodies out there!"

The old man looked down again a while longer, lifted his eyes, and gazed into Tim's.

"The entire world has changed, guys. Truth! Oh sure ... if you're lookin' down from space, the geography is the same. But look closer, and you'll see massive chaos and upheaval around the globe. Russia and China have gone back to the 18th century. Most of Europe is in the clutches of rioting mindless Islam. South America – hell, maybe back to the 17th century. And Australia – it's burning up in the sun's rays. Everywhere, people – people like you – prowl the streets scrounging for food and fuel."

The old man's voice broke with a grim quiet laugh. "Mad Max and the four horsemen have come to pass!"

Tim's mouth contorted into a gnash. And then he spat. "Why're you tellin' us this?"

The old man looked into the young man's eyes. "Because you asked," he finally said. "And because I thought I was doing you a favor. Hell, how else are we gonna avoid this in the future if people close their eyes to it?"

The room became silent. And then the old man continued. "Hell. What about your kids? Your grandkids?"

"We don't have any kids," Tim replied.

"But you will. At least, if you live through this shit you will." The old man paused and then spoke with passion. "And I gotta tell ya – this is a tale that needs to be passed down to our children. And our grandchildren. Or else we're gonna do it all over again!"

The room became silent. Tim and Squirt were on the edge of their seats.

"So," Tim finally chimed in, "How'd it happen? How'd we get to this place?"

The old man smirked as he looked at the couple.

"It's a long story. You sure you wanna hear it?"

"Yeah. Go on." Both Tim and Squirt nodded.

"Well, we'd have to go back thousands of years to start at the beginning. But it's just as good if we go back to the seventeenth century. Let's say, about 1650 A.D." The old man took a deep breath. "It was in that year that ..."

Episode 1 – The Chespik Incident

> *Paper is poverty, ... it is only the ghost of money, and not money itself.*
> – Thomas Jefferson to Edward Carrington, 1788.

Chapter 1 – Circa 1650 A.D.

A HIGH CLOUD COVER nonetheless imbued a day of lightness, a day of serenity, on the people of southeast England. For it was not raining, nor was it drizzling, nor was it even damp! And the view from the Chespik village centre was of a dirt road passing through the village, the road lined with merchants' shoppes built of white or stucco covered wood frame and brick; and their thatched roofs almost touching in their orderly formation.

Running north and south, the road had a character all its own – a coarse layer of decomposed granite, combined with finely sifted dirt – and with a soft, almost furry texture that distinguished it from its gravel cousin. Were one to hold the dirt in one's hand, it would disappear in a cloud of dust!

And beyond the village, one could see the rolling green hills of endless countryside, tapering off in the distance, expansive and plush in their form and with a palpably soft texture, they stretched out to some place of origin – somewhere beyond the horizon.

It was late afternoon on a summer day. And breathing all of this in, William Martin strode easily along the road. The lightness, the serenity, held him firmly in its grasp; imbuing his body – his soul – with the pleasure of life. With a bounce in his gait, he soon came upon a popular village location. A sign hung from a protruding overhead member: *Olde Skippers Pub.*

William stood outside and listened. The raucous sounds of male voices – laughing, shouting, swearing, talking – penetrated the walls, spilling out onto the road. He set himself facing the entrance as he stole a deliberately large breath into his smallish frame. He pushed open the door, feeling its fluid movement give way under his hand, and affording him an easy entrance. Inside, he was greeted by raucous voices, noise, shouting, and festive chaos – all carrying through the haze of tobacco and the smell of ale and unwashed bodies.

William's gaze was immediately drawn to the far side of the room. A dart game was going on, and the throng of ale-drinking men were jostling each other for the best view. William heard a cheer go up as the players walked up to the dart board and collected their darts. *They be wagering on the game*, William thought. *And Joseph is playing! I wonder 'ow he's doin'?* Weaving his way over to the dart game, he stood among the throng and shouted, "Joseph, 'ey Joseph!"

Joseph was a burly, bearded man, accustomed to consuming large amounts of ale. Without saying a word, he held his glass high in a greeting to William, tipped his glass up, and swallowed another gulp. He turned his focus back to the game.

As William made his way toward the bar, he heard a familiar voice ring out through the din. "Greetings, William!"

William scanned the room, his eyes keying on a lean raw-boned man standing behind the bar. "Henri," he shouted through the noise. He made his way through the throng and reached the bar, smiling. "Henri, it does me good to see you!"

"As do I," Henri replied as they shook hands. "Get you an ale, I will." And Henri turned to the tap and drained some brown ale into a pint-size mug. He turned and handed the glass to William. "And there's plenty more where that came from!"

Another cheer went up from the dart game.

"Your family is well?" William asked.

"Aye, mate," Henri replied with a smile. "And yours?"

"Aye. Keeps me busy, they do!"

Then Henri's expression turned serious. "And what are ye 'earing these days?"

"War," William replied, a disheartened tone in his voice. "Rumors, mostly. But during my life there's been much war, there 'as. And I 'ave no reason to doubt that more is coming."

"Well," Henri interjected, "I 'eard a rumor, I did." Henri leaned over the bar, closer to William's ear. He whispered in earnest. "I 'eard the King is planning to take all of the merchants' gold and silver on deposit at the Mint, I did."

William looked at Henri with a frown. "The King would not do that, would 'e?"

"Aye," Henri replied, "the King would do anything to fund his wars, 'e would!"

William's shoulders and neck stiffened. "But I 'ave my gold, my silver at the mint!"

"As do I, my friend!"

"And it's all I own!"

"Aye. I do also!"

William peered at Henri through tightly-drawn eyes. "How many know of this?"

"Few," Henri replied. "So far, just a few!"

"Keep it quiet, my friend?"

"Aye. But it won't stay quiet for long!"

William nodded. "Well, get my gold out of the mint, I will. Before the King can steal it!"

"Aye, my friend. As will I." Henri frowned. "But where shall you keep it?" Henri asked.

Just then, a cheerful Joseph stepped up to the bar next to William. "Greetings, gentlemen – and I use that language advisedly," he chortled. "William, it does me good to see you."

"As do I," William responded. And then William's face lit up. "Joseph. If I may be so forward to ask ... per chance, do you keep your gold at the goldsmith's depository?"

Joseph began the process of lighting his corncob pipe. He peered at William out of the corner of his eye as he took several drags, and then he answered. "Aye, William. I do indeed keep my wealth there; what little I 'ave. An honest man, the goldsmith is – I've 'ad many dealings with 'im."

"In fact," Joseph continued, "I leave my gold and silver on deposit with 'im, and 'e gives me receipts. I can use the receipts to claim my gold at any time, or I can use 'em for trading. It's much easier than carrying the 'eavy metal, and the receipts make it easy to split up a piece of gold into smaller portions."

"Good," William replied. "I shall leave tomorrow to retrieve my money from the mint."

"As will I," Henri chimed in. "In fact, I propose that we travel together. After all; strength in numbers, there is."

"Aye," William assented.

Thus, William and Henri departed for London the next morning, returning three days later with their wealth in hand.

*   *   *

On the morning following their return ...

Henri was up and out the door early – with barely a kiss even to his wife. *I hope Elizabeth forgives me,* he thought. He hit a quick stride on his trek to the goldsmith. Walking purposely through the village centre, he nodded cursorily to several of the merchants who were just opening up their stores. He continued on toward the north side of the village. *I wonder what time the goldsmith shoppe opens?*

He walked past a vendor who had an early customer.

"... I will accept a note for 6 pieces – my final offer, it is!"

"Done," was the reply. The buyer turned over a piece of paper – a claim on silver held at the local goldsmith – and the vendor gave him his merchandise. People felt like they had extra money to spend, and few noticed that prices seemed to be rising.[1]

Henri continued on his trek...

*   *   *

---

[1]   Rising prices are frequently an indication of monetary inflation – an increase in the amount of money in circulation.

Built on a mound overlooking the village, the goldsmith's office was the largest and most prominent structure in the village. With a sweeping view of the town and the surrounding countryside, it was built from stone and mortar, with granite steps leading up to the entrance. Interestingly, the stone, granite, and setting lent a palatial feeling to the site; as though the King was soon to appear.

Henri reached the goldsmith's office just as an aide was opening the doors. He waited at the bottom of the stairs; taking in the sight of the building and the guards posted at the entrance. And then he gazed at the sign posted over the main entrance. It read simply, *Goldsmith.*

When Henri entered the goldsmith's realm, he was immediately overwhelmed by the wealth on display. For as he gazed around the chamber, he could see several exquisite pieces hanging from the walls, in various stages of creation. *Wealth,* Henri thought, *a long time to acquire, it did! How did 'e collect all of this!* Henri shook his head in wonderment as his eyes shifted from one display to another.

The goldsmith broke Henri's concentration. "I'm Ian," the goldsmith said simply, "Ian Williams."

"Aye, mate," Henri replied. "And I'm Henri – Henri Aleman."

"Greetings, Henri. How may I help you? ..."

* * *

Henri departed the goldsmith's office, with a smile on his face. He felt around in his pocket, feeling the texture of paper receipts – receipts that represented the gold and silver that Ian now held on deposit. *All right!* He thought. *Much easier to handle, these are, than heavy gold and silver coin!*

Henri thought back to his conversation with Ian ...

"These days, I'm sure you've noticed that most people trade with the paper, rather than with real coin. So, it is good that we all come into the 17th century." Ian

paused and then continued. "And at the pub, I'm sure you see receipts from the mint, as well as from various goldsmiths – so, it doesn't matter where the receipt comes from. And," he paused, looking at Henri, "you don't have to carry around all that heavy coin ... And you can break a gold coin into smaller portions; so it gives you more bargaining power when you negotiate."

"... And if you want your gold returned, you need only endorse your receipts – I will immediately redeem them for gold or silver."

Henri bounded down the stairs, paused, and glanced back. My *wealth is secure.*

* * * * *

Lugging a bucket, Colin Martin struggled with the added weight as he trudged along the road. He stopped and placed it on the ground, allowing his heavy breathing to recede as he scanned the countryside.

From his vantage, he could see only grass extending north and south. But he was traveling west on a well-used dirt road, and he could see his destination in the distance – a small clump of homes. And just beyond the homes he could see a small town dotting the landscape. He didn't bother to look behind him, for he had already traveled that stretch of road and knew that it led downhill toward the sea.

Colin was growing up. Now at the tender age of 12, the blonde-haired blue-eyed boy was old enough to catch fish for his family's dinner – at least a couple of evenings a week. Colin's family could enjoy the fish because his route from the grammar school to his home took him near the ocean. And thus he needed only a fishing pole and a small detour to obtain the fish, bringing them to his family – about a mile inland.

He looked down at the bucket – it was wooden, and with a cover across the top to keep the water and fish inside. He hoisted it and resumed his trek home.

* * *

Colin soon approached the house, walking past a chicken shed and garden to his right. It was a small house; built of stone, brick, and mortar, and covered in a thatch roof. The windows were small and sparse, with many panes of thick glass distorting the view into the interior.

He walked up to the door and reached for the handle. And then he heard Claire's voice from inside the house say, "Mother, when is Colin to arrive? I'm hungry."

Colin pushed on the door and stepped into the house. He had a sheepish expression as he looked down to the dirt floor. "Late, I am. Sorry."

William placed his quill on the book in front of him, and then looked at Colin. "What happened?" He asked.

Colin sighed and said, "The fish were not biting at first, Father."

William nodded his disappointment and then asked, "And the catch, my son? How was it?"

"I got flounder – four big ones."

William smiled and said, "Aye, Master Colin. Wonderful!"

Marion stopped her dinner preparation and made for the bucket. She took the bucket from his hand and said, "Give 'em to me, dear. I'll clean and put 'em on the fire."

Colin sat down at the table next to William. Feeling the warmth radiate from the hearth, he looked around the room. He didn't really notice the white stucco walls, adorned as they were with homemade tapestry and hanging curios. Nor did he notice the floor – dirt, with home-weaved rugs covering the traffic areas. But he did notice his older sister Claire, preparing dinner on the countertop – which to this point consisted only of vegetables.

He looked down at the tabletop, made of rough-hewn pine and smoothed by whatever means only his father knew. And then he noted the dishes and dinnerware – and that there were four place settings arranged on the table. *We always use pewter for dinner,* he thought. *Mother says it's the best we have.*

William looked at Colin and said, "And 'ow was school today?"

"Fine," Colin replied.

"And what did you learn today?"

"Numbers, Father. And bookkeeping."

"Bookkeeping?"

"Yes, Father. So we may keep our money in order."

"And what else did you learn?"

"Writing, Father."

"Good," William exclaimed.

William picked up the quill and continued to write in the book.

"What is that, Father?"

"Tis my diary, Master Colin."

"What is a diary, Father?"

William leaned back in his chair and stole a deep breath. And then he said, "A diary is a place where we write our thoughts, our experiences, of a very personal nature. It is where we write about ourselves."

"And what are you writing today, Father?"

William gazed at his son and smiled. And then he replied, "Writing about the King and the Goldsmith, I am. As you know, Mr. Aleman and I just returned from London, where we withdrew our wealth from the mint. Well, today I deposited our wealth with the local goldsmith, Ian Williams, for safekeeping."

"But why did you withdraw our wealth from the mint?"

"Because there's rumour that the King was to take all the people's wealth from the mint and use it to finance his war."

"That sounds bad," Colin said.

"Indeed, Master Colin, it is bad. Because today, I've 'eard that the King did indeed take the people's wealth from the mint!"

The door opened and Marion brought flounder into the house. The family said grace, and then they proceeded with their dinner.

Chapter 2

Two years later . . .

It was yet another raucous evening at Henri's pub, and a throng of men were seated, standing, or weaving amongst the crowd – but all were partaking of ale. And with the smell of ale wafting through the tobacco smoke, Henri was busily serving up drink to yet another customer. The customer grinned and raised his newly filled quart mug. "Thanks, Henri – and cheers!"

Henri raised his own mug. "And cheers to you, mate. Bottom's up!" Henri brought the mug to his lips and took a swallow.

Like so many times that evening, Henri pulled out a cleaning cloth and began wiping down the bar. Just as he was finishing, Joseph Crispin stepped up. "Henri, it does me good to see you," he said. "Ye doing well, I trust?"

"Aye, Joseph. All is well. And with you?"

Joseph was bubbling over with excitement. "Aye, Henri. I just returned from Essex, and I've decided to buy some property there." Joseph smiled broadly. "I'll be moving there as soon as the deal is done."

"Aye. Sounds grand, it does."

"And grand it is, Henri. Tis good for my children – there's lots more children for them to play with. And the land," he paused with a gleam in his eye, "the land 'as forest. And it 'as lots of space for cultivation and grazing. And there's a great water source!"

Henri looked across the bar into Joseph's eyes. "Ye will be missed, my friend. Ye will be missed!"

* * *

The next morning, Joseph was waiting at the entrance to the goldsmith's office when it opened. He wasted no time approaching the goldsmith's desk. "Greetings, Ian," he said.

Ian looked up from his work, his mouth shifting slightly as he attempted a smile. His square jaw barely moved as he spoke.

"And greetings to you, my friend Joseph. To what do I owe the honor of your visit?"

Joseph placed a stack of receipts on Ian's desk and smiled. "These are receipts for 54 troy ounces of gold and 76 troy ounces of silver. I'd like to withdraw all of my coin, please."

Ian looked at the stack of receipts and slowly placed his quill down on the desk. His meager attempt at a smile dissolved as his forehead furrowed. He looked up at Joseph. "That's quite a sum. Are you certain you wish to withdraw all of it?"

"Aye, Ian. Certain, I am."

"Are you not aware that you can trade with these receipts as though they were coin?"

"Aye. Aware, I am. But I am buying some land over in Essex. And the agreement requires that I pay coin. Also, I wish to take all of my coin and deposit it with an institution closer to Essex."

Ian grasped the receipts in his hands and examined them one by one. Ian stroked his chin and then looked up at Joseph, a somber expression on his face. "Well, they all appear to be in order."

Ian stood up from his desk and walked over to the vault. He pulled on the vault door. It creaked as it opened, and then Ian entered.

Standing by the desk, Joseph could hear some rustling inside the vault; but his angle in relation to the vault inhibited his view of the interior. Finally, Ian came out of the vault wearing a frown.

Ian ran his hand through his brown hair. "I'm sorry," he confessed, not looking at Joseph. "But this is a large quantity of gold and silver. I will need to go to my hidden off-site vault and retrieve the gold that you require." He took a deep breath and then continued. "If you return tomorrow, I shall give you all of your coin."

Joseph stood at the desk – his expression was one of confusion. "Wait," his voice quivered. "You agreed to give me all of my coin on demand. And now – you tell me I must wait!"

"It is only a day," Ian said as he looked directly at Joseph. "I know our agreement. But I had no idea that anyone would withdraw this quantity all at once and without notice. I do not keep that much wealth here; so it will take me some time to obtain it. I promise I will have it for you tomorrow. In the morning."

Joseph's face was now red. "Very well," he hissed. "I shall return in the morning!"

* * *

Early evening found Joseph at the pub, sitting across the table from William ... "Fit to be tied, I am. Fit to be tied!" Joseph blurted out. "Something tells me that damn goldsmith has been playing fast and loose with my money. Ye should have seen the look on his face when I asked for my coin!"

William listened. He looked over at Joseph and then shifted his eyes to his pipe - watching a trail of smoke wafting up from it. Finally, he spoke. "Maybe Ian is being truthful - maybe he really does have most of the coin stored elsewhere. This seems wise and prudent to me."

Joseph seemed to relax a bit. "What you say is logical." Joseph's voice was steady but stern. "But so heavily guarded his office is; why would he store it elsewhere? No sense, this makes to me. And even so, he should stand by his word and pay me at the time of my choosing. After all," Joseph spat, "that I could have my money immediately, he committed. And now he has reneged!"

Joseph was getting even more worked up as he continued. "The look in his eyes, bastard that he is ..." And in his most profane language, Joseph went on to describe his encounter with Ian.

But in the middle of his diatribe, Henri came up to the table. He listened; his face turning red as Joseph continued his rant.

And soon, still more villagers moved close to the table – listening all.

Finally, when Joseph stopped talking, Henri spat, "Crook, he is! I 'ear ye Joseph – I will be gettin' my coin back tomorrow with ye!"

"Here, here!" shouted some of the other listeners.

William spoke up quietly. "I too will be there in the morning. Let us all see what happens."

* * *

The next morning, a throng of seven – William, Henri, Joseph, and four others – stood at the base of the steps of the goldsmith's office. The guards stood rigid – out in front of the entrance as the crowd gathered.

Ian soon pushed open a door, preparing his office for business. But he did a double-take as he looked down at the crowd. His expression took on a frown, and Henri could've sworn his face turned pale. Ian paused, and then he stepped up and announced to the throng, "The goldsmith's office shall be open in 10 minutes."

As murmurs and chatter grew louder from the crowd, Ian turned and walked back into his office. The door closed behind him, and the crowd waited.

Minutes later, the door opened and Ian reappeared. He stepped out and stood at the top of the steps. The crowd was larger, and they booed as he stood. He raised his hands, gesturing the crowd to lower their voices.

"My fellow villagers," he began speaking as the shouting diminished, "your money is safe, it is. Secure, it is – in a very secret cache. If you will please come back tomorrow, I shall have it for you."

Joseph stepped forward. With a shaking voice, he shouted, "where is my coin, Ian? Yesterday, you promised you would deliver my coin. Where, Ian. Where is my coin?"

The crowd seemed to get bigger even as Joseph stood out in front. Joseph shook his fist at Ian.

And then, old James Shipstead stepped forward from the crowd. "Ian," he shouted, "you shall pay me my money, on demand, for my receipts. Where – is – my – money !"

And then several other people stepped out from the crowd. "Here, here!" They shouted. The din of voices grew still louder.

Ian gulped. And everyone could see his face turn ashen. He yelled a command to the guards and then he closed the door. And for the remainder of the day, the goldsmith's office remained closed.

* * *

The *Olde Skippers Pub* was a favorite place for villagers to meet over ale or spirits. It was a fixture – having stood its ground near the centre of the village longer than many could remember.

On most any evening, a visitor to the pub would be greeted with a happy, festive atmosphere; and the villagers looked forward to a relaxing good time after a days' hard work.

This evening was different. Joseph, Henri, and William were assembled around a table near the centre of the room. And many other villagers were also gathered around the table – most of them standing. The murmur of voices from the gathering was like the buzzing of bees around a hive.

"Worked hard, I 'ave. My whole life I 'ave saved my coin." Joseph's voice was loud and shaking. "Thievery of my coin, I shall not accept!" Joseph was becoming blind with anger as he hunkered over his ale. "I think that bloody bastard Ian has taken my money to enrich his own pockets." And then he looked around at the other people in the gathering – he said to no one in particular, "does anyone know what 'e is doing with the money?"

"Buying land, I've seen 'im," old Shipstead piped up. "I was wondering where 'e was gettin' the money." The murmur from the crowd became louder – and angry voices came to the fore.

A voice rang out from the gathering. "You don't suppose he's lost our money. Do ye?"

"What would that mean if 'e did?" Henri posed.

For just a moment, the room went silent.

"It would mean," William answered, "that we be poor – the whole village be poor!"

"Right you are," Joseph chimed in. "For these paper receipts are of no worth. Just paper, they are."

Henri stepped forward. "I will be at the bastard goldsmith's tomorrow to demand my coin!" He shouted. "Who will join me?"

Henri's words were greeted by loud and angry shouting from the gathering.

* * *

The next morning, a large crowd formed at the base of the granite stairs – a raucous, vocal, angry crowd. Again, there was a guard stationed on each side of the entrance. The mob watched as the entrance opened a crack and Ian peered out.

Henri stepped out from the crowd and shouted. "Where's our money, Ian! Where's our money!" It was not a question.

But even as Henri stepped forward, the mob took their cue and stormed the doors, pushing the guards aside. Ian attempted to close the doors, but the guards and the doors were over-whelmed by the speed and intensity of the mob as it swarmed through the entrance and into the building.

"Wait! Wait!" Ian shouted as several of the mob grabbed him – first pushing him to the floor, and then dragging him outside. The crowd was chanting, "We want our money! We want our money!"

Henri stepped forward and gestured the mob to quiet – the shouting subsided. Henri looked sternly at the goldsmith, and said, "Our money, Ian. Where is it?"

"I don't have it," Ian squirmed as he whimpered. "I bought land over in another county. They demanded coin. So I spent it. I've – I've been living off receipts," he confessed.

The noise, the shouting from the mob increased, louder and louder. Ian's face turned ashen; his lips, his hands, quivering with fear.

Henri held up his hands, gesturing the mob to quiet. "You 'ave been living off receipts!" Henri shouted, his voice quivering with anger. "Counterfeiting our money, you 'ave!"

Hearing this, the shouting from the crowd again rose, louder still. Ian's fear was palpable, and it seemed to make the crowd even more aggressive.

Henri held up his hands, gesturing the mob to quiet. The shouting from the mob subsided.

"What will we do with him?" Henri shouted.

Someone from the crowd yelled, "hang 'em." A crescendo of cheers arose from the mob, and then they began to chant: "hang 'em, hang 'em ..." The chant went on and on as several men dragged Ian to a nearby tree. Someone produced a rope, and it was quickly tied around his neck. Someone else slung the rope over a stout branch.

"Hang 'em. Hang 'em ...," the crowd continued their chant as Ian stood with the rope around his neck, his face ashen, shivering in fear, and standing in a puddle of his own urine.

Several members of the mob started to pull, raising Ian's feet off the ground. The angry voices of the mob became still louder, cheering at the sight of Ian's kicking, his struggling, his thrashing. Ian's eyes were bulging as he held his hands between the rope and his neck – trying with all his might to delay his impending death. But soon, his strength gave out and his feeble kicking gave way to a thick fluid dripping from his legs. The angry voices diminished as Ian lost consciousness.

The mob turned away, leaving Ian's corpse to swing in the breeze.

* * *

Somewhere out of sight, the Sheriff listened. He knew what was going on; and yet he did not intervene. But sometime later, after the crowd had dispersed, he made the trek to the goldsmith's office. He cut down the corpse and turned the body and effects over to the proper authorities.

* * * * *

That evening . . .

His eyes wide open, Colin again turned over in his bed. *Not to be, sleep is*, he thought. *There's a light coming from under the door!* Colin arose from his bed and walked out into the great room.

He found William at the kitchen table, writing into his diary. "Hello, Father," Colin said.

"Hello, my son," William replied.

"I can't sleep," Colin said simply.

"Nor can I," William replied. He put his quill down and gave his attention to Colin.

"What are you writing, sir?"

William sighed and then said, "I am merely writing down the day's events and what they mean for us, and for the townspeople."

"And what does it mean?"

"The Sheriff informed me that Ian lost the wealth in risky investments. And so, Ian's passing means that the townspeople are now poor." William sighed again and continued, "Stole the people's money, he did. And paid with his life, he did that too."

"But why are you writing it down?"

William looked into Colin's eyes and said, "My son. This can happen to anyone. It can happen in any place and at any time. And thus we should record these events, so that we remember, and so these memories are passed down to our descendants, ... with hope and prayer that others will not allow goldsmiths this much power."

"Does that mean you want me to tell the story too?"

"Yes, son. Tell your children and grandchildren, and everyone else you meet throughout your life." And then their eyes met as William grasped Colin's shoulders. His voice quivered as he said, "My first born son, you are. As such, I shall someday pass this diary to you. We must always know, Colin. We must always remember."

* * * * *

"Damn!" Tim interjected. "They sure did him in!"

"But how sad the village lost so much of their wealth," Squirt chimed in.

"Yep," the old man snorted, "there was a time when counter-feiters were executed by hanging. Even in the United States. Hell, it was considered a crime against the people; not just against an individual. And that's truth!"

"So why would people even use a goldsmith or a banker to store their money?"

The grizzled old man frowned. And then he said, "They go into the deal because they're looking for security. In this case, people wanted to keep their valuables safe. But they didn't be-lieve they could do it themselves, and so they got the goldsmiths to keep it safe for 'em." The old man's toothless grin spread from ear to ear. "But everyone has to learn – you really can't trust anyone except yourself."

"So," Tim interjected, "I'd have thought an episode like this would put a stop to money printing. But that must not be true since we just had a major collapse."

The grizzled old man nodded. "That's right, sonny. For some of these people, it's not easy to change their stripes. Hell, some are just plain evil through and through."

"So, what happened next?"

"Next? Well, the bankers had quite a few tricks up their sleeve. And so, just 40 years later, in 1690, they began to use 'em . . ."

Episode 2 – An Incident of England

> *Whoever controls the volume of money in our country is absolute master of all industry and commerce...when you realize that the entire system is very easily controlled, one way or another, by a few powerful men at the top, you will not have to be told how periods of inflation and depression originate.*
>
> - James Garfield, 20th President of U.S. Assassinated 1881

First Interlude . . .

THE BLAZING FIRE dances in the massive brick fireplace, sending its tentacles out into the room. And with the dancing flames, we catch a glimpse of the room; a room with a low ceiling, with a pine floor made of rough-hewn planks. And the walls ... well, the walls are an indeterminate color, an indeterminate texture ... they are walls distant from the light; lost in the flickering shadows.

And arranged in a semi-circle facing into the dancing flames are four chairs. Upholstered in leather, the chairs are occupied by men. There is a fat man, puffing on a cigar. There is a thin man, waving a snifter of brandy under his nose. There is a tall man - maybe 6 feet tall - scratching his ear. And there is a short man, sitting unperturbed.

A gleam in his eye, the fat man wheezes as he begins to speak. "Well, gentlemen. I believe we are nearing our objective." He looked to the thin man, and then continued. "Do you have a report on the formation of the cartel?"

"Yes, my Lord," the thin man sniffed and then responded. "We have contacted all of the goldsmiths and presented our proposal to them - explaining how a cartel can benefit us all." The thin man frowned, and then continued. "Our proposal has been well received for the most part. But we have also encountered resistance."

The fat man's eyebrows raised. "Oh? From which quarter?"

"Aaron Silverstein. He is the most prominent, I think. Althhough there are a few less prominent who also resist."

"Silverstein ... Silverstein ..." The fat man's voice trailed off. "Oh yes. He owns the goldsmith shoppe on the outskirts of London - Bexleyheath, I think."

"That is correct, my Lord."

"Well," the fat man addressed the thin man. "How shall we handle this – this Silverstein character?"

"Well, my Lord. We have infiltrated his operation. I think we should see how that proceeds."

"Very well. Now, on to our other business ..."

Chapter 1 – *Circa 1690 A.D.*

Seated behind his desk, Aaron Silverstein was going through the month's transactions; checking his bookkeeper's work and scratching notes where appropriate.

He paused. Looking up from his desk, he glanced around his office. But preoccupied as he was, he didn't notice that he was surrounded by books, all arranged neatly and in rows on their respective bookshelves. Nor did he notice the mahogany wood-work – the trim around the entrance door, and the crown and baseboard moulding. Nor did he notice how the woodwork's colours complemented and enhanced the look of the red-oak floor, adorned as it was with plush woven rugs imported from some far away Asian land.

No. He was not at all aware of his surroundings. Instead, Aaron wore a frown. A frown borne of thoughtfulness? Curiosity? Who knows ...

What we *do* know is that Jason entered the room at just that moment. *I hope my grooming takes hold*, Aaron thought, as his son approached the desk.

"Hello, Father," Jason offered, his deep brown eyes looking at Aaron expectantly.

"Hello, son. What is on your mind?"

"Father. I want to take over the Depository operations."

Aaron put down his quill and leaned back in his chair, looking into his son's eyes.

"My son. We have previously talked about this," Aaron replied. "My answer is still 'no'. And that is my final answer."

"But Father," Jason continued as though he had not heard Aaron's answer. "I'm ready – as ready as I will ever be."

"What did I just say?"

Aaron watched as Jason's face turned red; but he nonetheless stood firm in his resolve.

"Bastard, you are!" Jason's face turned crimson as he shouted, "I know I can do it!" And then Jason paused, tears welling up in his eyes as he looked at his father. "A good job with the Depository, I will do. Please, Father. I want to run it. I want to run it now," Jason pleaded, tears streaming down his young face.

Aaron remained resolute, watching as his son worked through a tantrum.

And when the tantrum was finished, Jason looked at his father, forlorn, with tears rolling down his cheeks. "Well, Father? Please. Please let me do it –"

Aaron patiently interrupted him. "But you still refuse to adhere to the Depository's guidelines for loan approval. How can I trust you?" Aaron paused and then continued, "And you have no understanding of our metals trading program. France and Germany are important customers, and I don't want to lose them because of your lack of experience."

Aaron looked back at Jason, his chiseled square jaw now firmly set. "You may think you are ready to run the Depository, but your loan policies and your inexperience will ruin this business."

With these last words, Jason's face turned beet red. "Go to hell," he spat. "If you won't let me run it, then I shall find another way." Jason stormed out of the office, slamming the door behind him.

Aaron's pent-up tension flowed out of him as he exhaled. *I just do not know what to do with him. Twenty-three years old, and he is yet a child!*

Aaron did not sleep well that night.

* * *

The next morning, Aaron Silverstein arrived at the *Olde Guardsman Goldsmith Depository.* Built of brick, stone, and mortar, and with granite steps leading up to the entrance, the Depository was a monument to Bexleyheath - a smallish village situated east of London.

Damn, I'm tired, he thought. He pushed the unkempt strands of hair out of his face as he walked purposely up the steps. *I wish I knew how to work with Jason - make him a true partner,* he thought. *But so irrational, he is!* Tall and gangly, he moved through the small throng of people waiting for the Depository to open. His narrow lips and wide mouth formed a jagged crinkle as he said, "Excuse me," and then he nodded with a reserved English smile, his hair again falling into his face.

Reaching the door, he nodded to the guards stationed at the building's front corners. Then, he turned and addressed the throng. "Open in just a few minutes, we shall." Aaron turned and entered the Depository.

When the doors opened for business, Aaron was stationed at a teller position. In short order, his first customer of the morning stepped forward - Helen Farnsworth.

"Good morning, Mrs. Farnsworth. Are ye well today?"

"I am," she said in a hurried manner. And then her voice diminished to a whisper as she leaned over the counter toward Aaron. "I wish to deposit some of my silver."

Aaron just smiled. *As usual, Mrs. Farnsworth was secretive about her affairs,* he thought. *Well, perhaps we should all be a little more secretive!*

Mrs. Farnsworth laid out several silver coins. "That will be fine, Mrs. Farnsworth. Let me write out a receipt for these."

In short order, Aaron gave her a receipt for the coins and deposited the coins in his teller's drawer.

He looked up from his drawer and nodded to her. "My wish is that you have a fine day, Mrs. Farnsworth."

"Ugh!" She replied. She turned and walked away from the window.

Next at the window was Arthur Griffin. "It does me good to see you, Aaron." Aaron and Arthur had known each other for some time.

"Hello, Mr. Griffin. How are you today?"

"Wonderful. A fine day, this is. And you?"

"I'm well, thank you," Aaron replied. "What can I do for you today, Mr. Griffin?"

Arthur's face took on a sheepish expression. He paused and then began speaking. "I am looking at buying Darlington's Trading Post, and I'd like to obtain a loan."

Always avoided debt, Arthur has, Aaron thought. *This must be very important to him!* "Certainly," Aaron replied. He put out his *Window Closed* sign and caught Jason's attention. "Jason, please help my customers while I attend further to Mr. Griffin."

Jason nodded his understanding.

Addressing Arthur, Aaron continued. "Will you please step into my office?"

Aaron and Mr. Griffin moved off to Aaron's office.

Aaron closed the door and turned to face Arthur. "May I examine your plan for the business?"

Arthur handed Aaron a package of notes, and together they examined Arthur's financial summary.

Aaron was conservative with his loans. And he took seriously the fiduciary responsibility that his depositors and borrowers entrusted in him. Although he created the loan amount by printing up extra receipts – that this was done was well-known in his profession, but was not divulged to customers – he was careful to create only that amount of money that was justified by the value of the assets and expected revenue.

Aaron was impressed with the documents Arthur presented. "You have certainly done your homework, Mr. Griffin. I especially like how you've summarized your cost of goods and fixed expenses."

Arthur was encouraged. "The monthly payment of the loan should come in about here," Arthur pointed at a number on the document. "This is based on the interest rate that I calculated here," he said as he pointed at still another value on the document.

Aaron scratched his head; and in his usual conservative manner, he did some arithmetic on Arthur's summary. "You should have no problem making your revenue and profit projections. Happy I am to provide a loan for the amount you request – and under the terms you request: 30% down and 11% interest. My only stipulation is that the promissory note be secured by the business and property."

This last statement gave Arthur pause. "What? ... What do you mean?"

"I am saying," Aaron answered patiently, "that if you fail to make payments in the amount and schedule specified in the note, the Depository will assume ownership of the business."

"But that's not fair," Arthur replied. "After all, we are investing substantial funds of our own. And besides, this is paper money you are loaning. It is far different than real gold!"

"But – but it is not paper money," Aaron lied as he turned a shade of pale. "It is receipts backed by real gold and silver."

"Then," Arthur replied with a smirk, "you should provide the loan in gold and silver, rather than dispensing receipts!"

"Well, s-sir," Aaron was still stuttering, "Darlington may certainly cash his receipts for gold or silver."

"And you will cash his receipts at his bidding?"

"Ya – yes! Absolutely," Aaron lied again.

Arthur looked at Aaron shrewdly. He hesitated, and then seemed to make up his mind. "Well in that case, I accept."

Aaron extended his hand. Arthur was tentative when he grasped Aaron's hand, but then he smiled and they shook with some enthusiasm.

Aaron addressed Arthur as he was heading out the door. "It seems, my friend, that you will be a businessman of means. Please give my best regards to Meredith."

Arthur waved just as the door was closing behind him. "That I will, Aaron. That I will."

Second Interlude . . .

As though a fly on the wall, we are privileged to view the activity in a room; a nondescript room, with elegant appointments and chairs covered in leather. Seated next to the fireplace, there is a mature man; leaning forward in just such a chair, stirring and sniffing and tasting from a snifter. And there is a young man, a man of smooth features and youthful black eyes; sinking deeply into a leather chair, obscured by the shadows.

The older man's hair, what there is of it, is shaggy – unkempt. And his face, wrinkled; his mouth twisted into a sneer, and his eyes – gray eyes of steel – penetrated the flickering shadows toward the young man.

His manner uncertain, the young man sank further into the chair under the steady gaze of the shaggy man.

And so we listen ...

"... there are but few goldsmiths who still resist our overture; who resist abiding our guidance. But when we bring them into our fold – and bring them we shall – we will move forward."

"Forward with what, my Lord?"

"With our plan, my young apprentice." The man replied with a smile – a smile borne not of happiness or joy, nor of humour, nor of laughter; but instead, a smile borne of nefarious subterfuge, of anger, of hate.

"And so," the man continued, "we are counting on your help. And in return," he paused, looking into the young man's eyes, "you shall receive great wealth!"

"But, my Lord; receive great wealth, I shall. I need only be patient."

"Ah, but impoverish your father, we can; and then you shall inherit nothing!"

The young man's expression changed to a frown. He withdrew into silence.

The wrinkled man continued. "More goldsmiths, we need for our common benefit. Bringing them into our, ah - group is the proper way."

"And how does this benefit us, my Lord?"

"In time, you shall know more. For now, just know that it allows us to move the masses in a direction of, ah - our choosing," the older man smiled.

"My Lord, you suggest that you can control the people?"

"Yes, my young apprentice. Yes."

The young man remained silent.

The wrinkled man continued, "the larger question is - how do we convince the remaining goldsmiths to join us?"

"Persuade them, my Lord?"

The wrinkled man smiled, a gleam appearing in his eyes. "Now, my young apprentice, you are learning."

Chapter 2

Whistling a happy tune, Arthur was working in the wheat section, stocking still more bags of wheat on a mid-level shelf. He looked to the shelves above, appreciating that they were mostly stocked - ready for still more customers. *These bags have really been selling well,* he thought. *I need a way to get more of them; faster, and cheaper!*

Arthur was pleased with their new Trading Post business. Like most buildings in the downtown area, it was constructed of brick and stone; but unlike most buildings, it was large and modern - enabling it to house 8 rows of shelves. Of course, the ceilings were still the standard 84 inches high, and heat from its single fireplace did not easily spread throughout the store.

As he placed yet another two packages on the shelf, Arthur glanced down at the wood plank floor. It was dusty - dusty enough that Arthur noticed the tracks ... *Mouse tracks! Damn, not again. Where's that cat!*

"Hi, Father!"

Arthur looked up to see his young daughter running toward him from the store entrance. He squatted down and smiled, inviting her into his arms. "Hi, Mary. How was school today?"

She came into his arms. Panting, she replied, "Oh, Father. School was wonderful today. And you know what?" She continued breathlessly, "Jenny's mouser just had a litter of kittens. Can we get one?"

Great! Arthur thought. *All we need is another worthless cat!*

"How nice, Mary," Arthur said as he smiled. "But we need a mouser that will take care of these mice – right now."

Mary bowed her head. "Oh."

"So," continued Arthur, "maybe you could find Mittens and see if you can coax her into hunting the mice?" Arthur paused. "And in return, we will get you another kitten."

Little Mary's face lit up with joy. "Wonderful!" She ran for the door, yelling over her shoulder, "I'll go find Mittens."

Arthur's expression softened and his smile widened as he watched her run out the door.

It was then that Arthur felt a poke in his ribs. "Ouch!" Arthur yelped. He turned around and embraced his wife. Without words, they enjoyed a long, passionate kiss.

And then Meredith ended the kiss and smiled, saying, "I heard you tell Mary that we are getting another kitten?"

"Well, only if Mittens and Mary get going on these mice." Arthur laughed, shaking his head.

"Well," Meredith replied. "I found mittens. She's sleeping in a corner atop a stack of grain bags. I also watched a mouse enter into a crevice between the bags." Meredith was grinning ear to ear.

"Damn cat," Arthur said, shaking his head with a wry grin.

Third Interlude . . .

Again, we peer into a nondescript room, with elegant appointments and leather furnishings. A mature man is seated in a leather chair; soaking in the warmth from the fireplace, his gray eyes of steel boring into the black youthful eyes of a man seated across from him. Alert and attentive, the youthful black eyes shift from the gray eyes of steel to the blazing fire; and then back again. Watching. Listening.

The man with gray eyes was speaking, "... we now have most of the goldsmiths in our little, ah - group. And it seems that only Aaron is in doubt."

"Help with that, I can my Lord."

"Oh, really? Doubt it, I do!"

"Why?" The black eyes blinked. "Why doubt me?"

"You're too young to know," the old man sniffed. "That's why?"

"Know what?"

"That you don't have the guts to do what is necessary."

The black eyes pleaded, "what do you mean by 'necessary'?"

"A path is there for you, if you choose to take it," the old man whispered. "You need only discernment to follow it."

"Is that part of the plan?"

"No. We have not yet discussed the plan. Distinct from Aaron, the plan is."

"What is the plan?"

"Reclaim our wealth, our birthright, from the peasants - that is our plan," he chortled. "Enslave the peasants, our plan is!"

"How?" The black eyes blinked again. "How will you do that?"

"By seduction," the wrinkled man smiled as he said it. "By seducing them into buying real assets - land, property, business - and taking the assets from them."

"And how will you seduce them?"

The man's steel grey eyes bored into youthful black eyes. "Money," he replied. "By loaning them an abundance of money at a very low price. This will make them prosperous, for a time. And they will sell their souls to borrow the precious money – to buy their precious land and businesses."

"But how will that make you wealthy?"

"'Us', my young apprentice," the wrinkled man chided. "You are one of us."

"Okay. 'Us'. So how will that make 'us' wealthy?"

"Because the people who sold their souls to borrow our money will not be able to repay."

"And?"

"And when they can't pay, we shall foreclose on their assets and we shall hold their very souls in our hand," the wrinkled man chortled, an evil gleam in his eyes.

"But why would they not pay?"

"My young fellow. They will not pay because we shall withdraw the money from the economy. We shall slow the economy." The wrinkled man looked into the fire as he chortled. "And we shall make them poor!"

"But how will you slow the economy? How will you make them poor?"

"As I said, by taking money out of circulation. And when we do this, they will not have enough money to pay their debts – for money will be scarce!"

"You have that much control?"

"Indeed."

The youthful black eyes receded in thought. And then the eyes lit as the young man posed a question. "From where will the money come to create loans?"

The wrinkled man smirked as he framed his answer. "We shall create it, my young colleague. We shall conjure it out of nothing – with little etchings on paper – and the peasants shall believe it has value!"

The wrinkled man began ranting ...

"Because we control the goldsmiths, we control the amount of money in circulation. Collectively, we can increase the amount of money in circulation; and we can decrease the amount in circulation."

Talking ceased for a moment.

"Of course," the wrinkled man wheezed as he continued, "the goldsmiths must create much more money in receipts than we have in actual gold and silver. But the peasants will not know, since we will confiscate their money along with their property. And the peasants will be none the wiser, as they have come to believe that paper receipts are money; and gold is some barbarous relic!"

Chapter 3

Toiling under an overcast sky, Jonathan and Frances rolled the last bundle of wheat along the ground and then tied it off. Wiping the sweat from his brow, he stepped back to survey the bundle. "Whew! Hard work, it is!" His large frame breathing heavily, he glanced toward Frances and smiled.

Frances shook her fiery red hair and wiped her brow. Meeting Jonathan's gaze, she said, "Aye, Jonathan. It is indeed!" Her smile grew wide across her face as her eyes lit brightly.

Jonathan looked up at the sky. "Store these bundles, we should. Before rain comes." While Frances watched, Jonathan went to the barn and returned leading an ox hitched with a wagon. They loaded the wheat onto the wagon, hauled the load to the barn, and stacked the wheat in a storage bin.

Mist began to fall just as they came out of the barn. "Go back to the house, we should," Jonathan announced.

Frances smiled and moved up close to Jonathan. She put her head up to his chest and said, "Aye, my love.

Holding hands, they walked across the field toward their quarters – a brick and mortar structure with a thatched roof. Sauntering along, they paid no mind to the rolling green hills or the low hanging clouds in the distance. Nor did they pay any mind to the nearby hill lined with trees. Newly married, their thoughts were only of each other.

Frances hummed as they walked. But then she broke off her humming and posed a question. "How long will you continue working as one of Lord Mallory's peasants?"

"I do not know. Save more money, I'd like. And then, perhaps, purchase a business in the village."

"Business? Hmmm ... What kind of business?"

"I do not know. I can do blacksmithing pretty well, or maybe something else ..."

"But are there enough people wanting a blacksmith?"

"Again, I do not know. But no matter. If we buy an existing business, then we can see the money it receives. Then we can figure our offer accordingly."

Frances stopped walking, pulling Jonathan toward her. Her expression took on a coy grin as she engaged him. "I'm carrying your child, Jonathan."

"What?" he gasped. "What did you say?"

"I 'ave a child inside of me," she said simply.

Jonathan's expression became one of wonderment. "Really?"

"Yes, my love," she looked at him and smiled. "Happened right after we married, it did."

Jonathan jumped in the air with glee, He shouted "Wow! A father I will be. WOW!"

He grabbed both her hands and they moved together; fluid, easy movements of happiness and joy.

Jonathan's voice quivered with excitement. "Is it a boy, or a girl? Can you tell?"

Frances giggled as she replied, "No, my love! I can't know. I only just found out yesterday. Or at least, I talked with mother and she told me the signs to look for. And signs I have!"

They held each other close as they walked toward their hut, oblivious to the mist falling around them.

* * *

Heat radiated outward from the fireplace, spreading its warmth throughout the one-room hut. The hut was cozy, furnished as it was with homemade throw rugs dispersed across the dirt floor. The coziness was a tribute to both Jonathan and Frances – for they were young, vibrant, and full of energy. The kind of energy it takes to make a home, and create a family.

Jonathan placed his mug on the mantel and looked down at the blazing fire. Surrounded by the white brick walls, he listened. Listened as Frances' impassioned plea filled the room.

"... Jonathan, I beseech you to move away from this – this 'peasant' slavery you're trapped in."

Jonathan began pacing the floor, running his hand through his long brown hair. "But Frances," he pleaded, "we need a secure, stable life. Especially with the baby coming." He paused and then continued his pleading. "And I don't 'ave enough money saved to go off into business. What would happen if we 'ave an emergency? We shall 'ave no extra money!"

"Jonathan," she replied, "how long will you continue to be a slave to Lord Mallory?" She paused and then almost shouted, "sucking the lifeblood out of you, I swear 'e is!"

For a moment, the room fell silent. And then Jonathan replied. "But we 'ave stability 'ere! At least we have a place to come to – with food and shelter."

"But Jonathan. There may not always be enough to raise our family. Surely, you can see that! Farming is risky – what with the weather and pestilence; and that Lord Mallory can throw us off his land as is his whim! After all, we cannot own this land – it shall forever be owned by his Lord and family!"

She paused looking squarely at Jonathan. "Yes, our labour can support us when times are good. As we already 'ave – we can even continue to put some money away. But when it comes to raising a family, we won't 'ave enough! And you will break your back working 'ere as a slave!"

"But Frances. Enough money, I do not 'ave. And if I borrow from the goldsmith, then I'll be a slave to 'im!"

"Oh, my darling Jonathan. We can always pay back the goldsmith. But Lord Mallory – you'll ne'er see a penny from 'im!" She paused and then continued. "So I ask you, Jonathan. Again. Please seek a business, or employment, at least, in the village. Please, Jonathan. Please!"

"Oh my darling Frances. I shall leave tomorrow morn for the village."

"Aye, my love. Come with you, I shall."

* * * * *

And the following morning, Jonathan and Frances drove their horse and buggy across the green rolling hills, arriving at the outskirts of Dartford by mid-morning. Their travel was smooth and uneventful. Even the weather cooperated, as they were blessed with a bright sun shifting in and out between the clouds.

Jonathan brought the horse to a halt and stood overlooking the township - watching the bustling throngs of people milling around on the street, each seeking his desired commerce. Although situated in a valley and intersecting with the River Darant, the town nonetheless stood as a prominent display to the people of the area. To the north lay a large marsh; and it was rumoured that the settlers were originally attracted to the marsh - containing, as it does, rather large and spectacular deposits of London clay.

Jonathan smiled as he glanced over at Frances. "A beautiful day it is."

Frances' eyes were sparkling with anticipation. "Aye, it is, my love."

Jonathan parked the wagon and tied the horse to a rail. They proceeded to enter the village, merging into the mass of disorganized and scurrying people.

Holding hands, the two weaved their way through the crowd, approaching the town centre along High Street. Along the way, they scanned the shoppes lining the street, seeking any business that might be for sale. They passed a dry goods store, a pub, a food market, and others. And there were many smaller shoppes - artisans and craftsmen - jammed all together and extending out into the street. They investigated those as well.

Imagine a street, surfaced partly in dirt and partly in stone, ramshackle shoppes lining both sides of the street, with scores of people weaving their way in and around the crowds, with voices shouting over the din of other voices. For this is the scene that presented to Jonathan and Frances.

They pressed on, reaching the village centre and continuing through to the west side of the village. Sauntering along, they walked and weaved past still more shoppes; fish, brewery, blacksmith shoppe, and others.

Frances noticed it first – a sign posted on one of the blacksmith's vertical columns. The sign read: *For Sale.* "Jonathan," she called, gesturing toward the sign. "Look over there."

"Aye, my love – I see it. Shall we inquire?" It was not really a question since Jonathan was already walking toward the entrance.

Jonathan came to a halt in front of the store. He looked at the sign, and then perused the front of the shoppe – seeing that the posts and stone walls were weathered with varying shades of grey. The thatched roof was in good repair, and the door to the stable was solid and functional.

Frances waited outside while Jonathan stepped into the shoppe. A shorter man wearing a blackened apron and trousers was hunched over a furnace. He was working – his back and shoulder muscles flexing, gleaming as the light from the furnace reflected off his sweating skin.

Shouting above the din of outdoor activity, Jonathan addressed the blacksmith. "How much do you want for your business?"

The blacksmith turned; he looked at Jonathan through his blackened face and red hair. "All what?" he spat in a sharp grizzled voice.

"I say again," Jonathan replied, "Your business. How much do you want?"

The man rose up and approached Jonathan. He stood in front of Jonathan, sizing him up with one eye squinted. "And who might ye be?"

A full head taller, Jonathan looked down on the man's red locks. "I'm Jonathan. Of the family Merchant."

"I see," the blacksmith nodded. "And what do ye seek?"

Jonathan heaved a sigh and then answered. "I seek to acquire a business."

"Do ye 'ave money?"

"I 'ave yet to get it – but get it, I can." Jonathan paused and looked at the man. "How much do you want?"

The man rubbed his chin; his sinewy arms flexing with the motion. "Well, that depends ..."

"Depends? Depends on what?"

The man looked up at Jonathan, one eye squinting. "It depends on what you want to do with it."

Jonathan was distracted by the sound of horse and buggy passing outside.

The blacksmith continued. "I am looking for a buyer who will do right by my customers."

"Huh? What did ye say?"

The blacksmith continued. "I am looking for a buyer who will do right by my customers." He paused and then continued. "I mean good quality work, good service, and fair prices."

Still another horse and buggy passed by.

The blacksmith peered into Jonathan's eyes. "Were you to own this shop, you would quickly be out of business," he paused, squinting, "... unless ye give the customers what they want."

"Hmmm," Jonathan frowned, putting his hand up to his chin.

The blacksmith continued. "My customers are also my friends and my neighbors. These are people that I care about, and that is why I want this business to continue and to thrive."

"Sir," Jonathan was resolute, "my wife and I will be using most of our savings to buy a business. I think that a blacksmith business is well suited to me, as I have proficient metalworking skills – skills that I learned while working on a farm. We want to buy a business and continue to make it a thriving business – we want this because we need enough income to raise our family."

"Well," the blacksmith paused and then replied. "I can show you 'ow to be a successful blacksmith."

"My name is Jonathan," Jonathan extended his hand toward the blacksmith.

"I am Jeffrey," he said as he smiled, "of the Blackman family."

"So," Jonathan asked again, "how much do you want for your business?"

"One 'undred and twenty-five pounds," was the reply.

"Do you 'ave records on the business - income, costs? Can I look at 'em?"

"Aye, mate. Here they are." Jeffrey paused as he handed over a tattered folder of notes. "Now, mind you, these are very conservative. Ye are certain to make this or better it each month."

Chapter 4

Stunned, Frances stood in front of Goldman & Sons Goldsmith and Precious Stones. Built of granite, and with a facade consisting of an archway supported by four pillars, and with five granite steps leading up to the entrance, the building was indeed an imposing structure. Several tapestries hung from upper-story windows, and statuesque figures appointed the corners and around the entrance.

"Amazing," Frances exclaimed. "Wealth lives here. Like nothing we 'ave ever known."

"Aye, my love," Jonathan replied. "I've 'eard much about this goldsmith. I've 'eard that lately, 'e is quite accommodating with 'is loans."

They walked up the steps and into the building. Inside, they were greeted by plush appointments. There were silk and velvet tapestries, decorations, and large pieces of jewelry made of gold and precious stones, all embellishing a palatial chamber made of granite and marble. And the tall ceiling was adorned with murals, adding to the feeling of expansiveness throughout.

Off to the right was a teller's window. They walked over to it.

"Greetings, mate," said the young man behind the counter. "May I 'elp you?"

"We wish to inquire about a loan," Jonathan replied.

The young man smiled and pointed to a desk toward the back corner. "Please see the receptionist. He will 'elp you."

The two strode over to the receptionist's desk, their footsteps clicking on the granite floor as they walked. Their clothing was distinctly out of place in the palatial chamber; but neither Jonathan nor Frances cared.

The receptionist greeted them. "May I 'elp you?"

"Er – aye," Jonathan replied. "About a loan, we wish to inquire."

"Aye. Have you been 'ere before?"

"I 'ave not," said Jonathan.

"Then I shall fetch the bookkeeper. Just wait one moment." He hurriedly stood up and walked into one of the offices. Soon, an older man emerged, dressed in a business suit and with grey hair and blue eyes. He was followed by the young receptionist.

The bookkeeper's eyes scanned Jonathan and Frances as he approached. He extended his hand as he came forward, "Greetings. I'm Colin. Colin Martin."

"And greetings to you as well," Jonathan said as they shook hands. "I am Jonathan, of the family Merchant. And this is my wife, Frances."

Colin nodded to the couple and said, "Please come into my office."

The three entered his office, where Colin gestured to two chairs. "Please be seated." As Colin sat down, he closed a leather-bound book sitting open on the desk. He moved the book to the side.

"Now," Colin continued, "How may we help you?"

"We wish to take out a loan, sir."

"Oh, please do not call me sir," Colin said. And then he frowned. "For what purpose do you want the money?"

"To buy a business. A blacksmith business."

"Can I look at the revenue and profit projections?"

Jonathan pulled out the tattered folder of notes. "These are the numbers."

"Oh my," Colin responded after looking at the parchment. "And 'ow much is the purchase price?"

"One 'undred and twenty-five pounds," Jonathan replied.

Colin folded his hands together and looked across the desk. "You realize, of course, that the loan will require that you provide collateral – and that you may lose all your collateral should you fail to pay."

"Yes, but, we don't 'ave much now."

"How much do you have?"

Jonathan pulled some coins out of his pocket and displayed them to Colin. "Just this," he said.

Colin looked at the handful of coins and said, "That's not very much, Mr. Merchant. What else do you 'ave?"

"Nothing," Jonathan replied as he looked down. "We are just simple folk."

"Hmmm," Colin rubbed his chin while looking across the desk at the young couple. And then he came to a decision. "I believe that Mr. Goldman – he's the owner of this institution – will allow the loan using only the business as collateral. I'm going to recommend that he allow the loan at 100% financing."

And then Colin's eyes fixed on Jonathan and Frances, and he said, "I strongly – *strongly* – recommend that you save those coins for a rainy day, and that you not offer the coins for collateral under any circumstances." Colin paused and then asked, "Am I clear?"

Both Jonathan and Frances nodded. And then Jonathan asked, "But why?"

"Because bad times are coming," Colin replied grimly.

The room paused in silence.

"Now," Colin continued. "Presently, we are loaning at 1% interest, re-calculated monthly."

Jonathan and Frances looked at each other, hesitating. And then Jonathan looked at Colin, a question beginning to form on his lips. "What's 're-calculated monthly mean?"

"It means," Colin replied, "that we calculate the amount of interest owed based on one-twelfth of 1% each month."

"And what will the payments be?"

"Hmmm ... I will have to work out the details; but it will be approximately ten schillings a month."

Jonathan and Frances glanced at each other; then Jonathan replied, "we will need to talk and think about this."

"That's fine. I will notify Mr. Goldman of your interest and provide him with your information. You should see him if you decide to move forward."

* * *

Soon after, Jonathan and Frances sat next to each other at *The Bursting Cow*, a local eatery.

"Well. What ye think?" Jonathan asked.

"Concerned, I am, about the high monthly payment. So long as we are able to keep our revenues at the present level, or even create more revenue, success we shall 'ave." She paused and then continued. "But we'll 'ave problems if our revenue drops very much from Jeffrey's revenue numbers."

"Aye, my love. My sentiments exactly."

"So, what shall we do?"

"Let us go forward with it."

"Aye, my love."

* * *

The following day, the two entered the goldsmith's sanctum and strode up to the receptionist's desk.

The young man behind the desk greeted them. "May I 'elp you?"

"Aye," Jonathan replied. "We are 'ere to speak with Mr. Goldman about a loan.

"Just one moment," he replied. He hurriedly stood up and walked into an adjacent office. A man soon emerged, dressed impeccably in a three-piece suit and with his hair combed in a fastidious manner to complement his hawk-like nose and features. He was followed by the young receptionist.

His sharp eyes scanned Jonathan and Frances as he approached. He extended his hand. "My name is Nathan, of the family Goldman."

"I am Jonathan, of the family Merchant. And this is my wife, Frances." And then he smiled and said, "With child, she is."

Nathan seemed momentarily flustered. He regained his composure and asked, "how may I help you?"

"We wish to take out a loan. We spoke yesterday with Colin."

"For what do you want the money?"

"To buy a business. A blacksmith business."

"Ah – yes," Nathan replied. "Colin has already provided me with your details." Nathan paused and then said, "But 'e also said you 'ad no collateral to provide, save the business itself."

"That is true, Mr. Goldman."

"Are you sure you 'ave nothing else for collateral? Maybe your money for food or lodging?"

The two looked at each other, and then Jonathan turned and said, "We 'ave nothing else to provide."

"Well, it is not our usual custom to give a loan without the borrower providing additional collateral." He looked at the two shrewdly, and then came to a decision. "But Colin believes your revenue will be more than sufficient for your payments – as do I."

"Willing to make the loan, we are."

With that, Jonathan and Frances looked at each other and smiled.

* * *

In the goldsmith's office, Jonathan, Frances, and Jeffrey all watched as Nathan counted out the loan amount.

"...Twenty-One," Nathan continued counting the receipts, "...Twenty-Two, Twenty-Three, ..." Finally, Nathan counted off the last receipt. "One hundred and twenty-five pounds," he announced.

"Hmmm," Jeffrey squinted an eye at Nathan and put his hand to his chin, "but this is all paper. Where's the gold?"

Nathan was taken aback by the question. And then his posture became resolute as he answered. "With all due respect, sir, everyone trades with receipts these days. I assure you that you will have no difficulty redeeming these receipts for gold, or for anything you wish to purchase." Nathan paused and then continued. "After all, there is no reason to use gold, since all the receipts are backed by gold anyway."

"Hmmm." Jeffrey rubbed his grizzled chin and frowned. "Well, let's go ahead and finish it. Fill out the papers, I shall."

Fourth Interlude . . .

Wrinkled face and grey eyes of steel stared into a sneering expression with cold, dead eyes.

"I am concerned about this goldsmith – Aaron Silverstein is his name. He runs a goldsmith operation out in Bexleyheath. I want you to watch him – and in particular, the way he structures his loans. Do this for two weeks and then report back to me on what he does."

"Yes, my Lord," said the sneering man. He departed.

A young man was seated in a chair, obscured by the shadows. He watched the interchange in silence. Now that the sneering man had left, he spoke, "help with this, I can. What information do you seek?"

The wrinkled man's grey eyes of steel looked into the young man's eyes. "I seek evidence that Aaron is with us, or against us. And I don't think you are in a position to know."

The young man nodded and grew quiet ...

* * *

It was early evening with overcast skies – it was time to go home. Aaron Silverstein locked up his depository and walked down the shallow granite steps, humming a tune.

Aaron lived close by – one of the benefits of inheriting a very wealthy goldsmith business passed down through several generations.

Aaron sauntered down the street, without a care in the world.

Were Aaron to look behind him, he would have seen a man with cold, dead eyes following him. He would have recognized him as someone who came into his depository to open an account earlier today. And he would have recognized him as someone who talked with two of his depository employees just last week.

But Aaron had not a care in the world. Aaron did not turn around ...

* * * * *

Keeping a record of the day's withdrawals and deposits, Jason flipped back his long brown hair as he wrote yet another entry in the books. With a flourish of his quill, he leaned back in his chair and placed the quill in front of him. *It's been a long travel for father.* He mused. *I hope he was able to come to an agreement with the French gold trader. I shall know the answer when he returns – tomorrow, I think.*

He put his head down and continued writing.

He was just about finished when Thomas, his aide, stuck his head through the doorway. "Aye, Mr. Silverstein. Edgar Robinson is 'ere and wants to inquire about a loan." And then he looked at Jason and smiled. "You've given many loans this week past, sir."

"That I 'ave," Jason nodded to Thomas. "Please show Edgar in."

"Yes, Mr. Silverstein."

Thomas quickly ushered Edgar through the door, closing the door behind him.

Jason rose to meet him with his hand extended. They shook hands as he said, "Edgar, my friend. It does me good to see you!"

"And you as well," Edgar replied.

"To what do I owe the honor of your visit?"

"Aaaaaaye, Mr. Silverstein. I want to borrow some money. Expand my business, you see."

Jason seated himself and gestured to Edgar as he said, "Please sit down and tell me your circumstances."

Edgar seated himself across from Jason in a leather chair. He began to speak in his characteristically hoarse voice. "Well, Mr. Silverstein. Ruth and I want to expand our crafts and artisan business. We see a lot of new business coming along, and we want to take advantage of it."

"Do you have a written plan or notes you can show me?"

"No, Mr. Silverstein. We don't do much writing."

"Well, how much increase in your business do you foresee?"

"We think it will double, Mr. Silverstein."

"And why do you think it will double?"

Edgar smiled and said, "Because we will add more space." Edgar leaned forward, his voice quivered as he said, "Mr. Silverstein, if we create more space, customers will come. We are certain!"

"That's fine, Edgar."

They proceeded to talk about the details of the loan. When they finished, Jason said, "I will let Thomas know to draw up the promissory note." He paused and then continued. "Please know that the loan will be secured by your present business."

"What? What does that mean, Mr. Silverstein?"

"It means, Edgar, that the goldsmith firm will foreclose on your business should you fail to make a scheduled loan payment." Jason then looked into the man's eyes and said, "Is that acceptable to you?"

"Oh yes, Mr. Silverstein." Edgar shook Jason's hand. "Thank you, sir."

"Have a good day, Edgar," Jason responded.

Jason leaned back in his chair and smirked. *There's no way that he can afford to repay the loan,* he thought. *The Depository will own his business soon enough!*

Chapter 5

His back to the shoppe entrance, Jonathan was working on a two-horse rigging; attempting to fasten a leather strap to a metal connector ring. He turned to grab another tool just as Frances entered. She was carrying their child, Paul. "Greetings, my husband," she said with a smile. A broad smile came over Jonathan's face when he spotted her. *Love the way she moves, I do. Relaxed, flowing, sensual, even when carrying our son.*

She held up a bag and showed it to him. "I 'ave lunch for you," she said in a teasing voice.

He chuckled. Smiling, he reached for the bag as he asked, "what 'ave you brought me?"

"Chicken. I 'ave chicken and carrots," she said with a smile. She pulled it away from him, but dangled it in his face. "Tempting. Is it not?"

"And what must I do for this 'lunch'?" He asked dubiously.

"Make me a promise," she responded.

"Yes?"

"Make me a promise that you will be close with me – tonight."

"And if I refuse?"

"Then, I will seduce you," she said in a coy voice.

"And what do you call this?" He said, his voice mellow with a soft laugh.

"Ah, um – a proposal?" She snickered.

"Oh ...," his voice trailed off. "Well, my dear, gladly be with you tonight, I will. In whatever way that you want."

* * *

Meredith Griffin packaged up still another order. *We're selling out on many things; but these food items are just flying off the shelves*, she thought. *Hard work, it is. But people are spending a lot of money and our business is successful. Times are indeed good!*

In the next aisle, she heard Arthur's voice talking to a customer. "Yes, Mrs. Reynolds, we can have that for you on Tuesday – although I do not yet know the price because my supplier has been raising prices on me."

"Well Arthur," she replied, "return on Tuesday, I shall. Until then, I offer my payment for today's purchases. I trust that these receipts are satisfactory."

"They will do quite well, Mrs. Reynolds."

Amazing how little gold and silver coin we use in commerce these days, Meredith's thought flashed through her mind.

"Thank you very much Mrs. Reynolds," Arthur said. "I look forward to seeing you on Tuesday."

As Mrs. Reynolds walked out, Mary brushed past her on her way into the store. She was carrying a new kitten and said, "Father, Father, how do you like my new kitten?"

Arthur sounded impatient. "Mary, you just got a new kitten last year. Who gave you permission to bring home another kitten?"

"But Father," Mary pleaded. "Mother said that I could have another kitten. Mother wants to get rid of the mice."

Arthur's voice was stern as he said "I just walked by Mittens and Pumpkin this morning. They were both sleeping just as a mouse was walking down the aisle. I think you're feeding the mousers too much of that feed!"

Meredith, overhearing the conversation, dropped what she was doing and joined the exchange. "Arthur," she said in a stern voice, "I think we need another mouser. And so I asked Mary to bring one home. I promise that we will stop feeding grain to the mousers so they will instead hunt the mice – and with three mousers, we shall be rid of our mouse problem."

"Aye, my wife. Whatever is your wish."

* * *

A few months later . . .

Mr. Reynolds walked up and down the aisles of Griffin's Trading Post. Seeking food and food items, he scratched his head at the half-empty shelves. And he was even more perplexed at the high prices for the in-stock items.

"I tell you Arthur; too high, prices are. I can barely afford to feed my family – it seems like all we eat are beans! Beans, beans, beans!" Mr. Reynolds' voice was becoming louder. "You must find a way to get us some decent food, and at prices we can afford!"

"I am so sorry, Mr. Reynolds," Arthur replied in a somber voice. "I have talked with my suppliers, but they insist that their production and raw material costs are going higher still. They tell me they have no choice but to raise prices."

Tight-lipped, Mr. Reynolds glared at Arthur. "Are you taking more profit for yourself?"

Arthur was taken aback. Never before had anyone accused him of exploitation; and for a moment, a tense silence intruded between them.

Then Reynolds bowed his head and said, "I am sorry, Arthur. I know you are doing your best. Please forgive my indiscretion."

Arthur glanced at his empty hands. And then he replied, "Mr. Reynolds, I will try my best. But please remember I too have a family, and I care about all my customers."

* * *

And a few months later . . .

"I am amazed, Meredith. It's like no one has enough money. If I could buy a full selection of goods to sell to our customers, our customers would not be able to afford the prices we must charge. Prices continue to go up all around, and the prices are too high now."

"I know, Arthur. I talked with several wheat suppliers yesterday. They all tell me that they may go out of business because their cost of production is higher than the price they can obtain for their products." Meredith was shaken at what she was finding.

"But, but ...," Arthur's voice trailed off. "This means that people may starve."

"Look around, Arthur. People are already starving. Prices are too high for many people." Then, Meredith's eyes widened as she looked at him.

* * * * *

Frances and Paul stopped by the blacksmith shoppe. "How is business today?"

"Not well," Jonathan replied. "We received one new job this morning." He paused and looked at Frances. "At this rate, we shall not make our payment this month."

Frances shifted her weight and looked down at the ground. And then she said, "but what has happened to cause business to slow down?"

"Nothing that I can see, my love. Except that ...," he paused and then continued, "... people are complaining they have no money to spend. Many times I am hearing that."

"But how can that be?"

"I do not know, my love."

Frances looked down to the floor and said, "We must pay the goldsmith. But how can we?"

Jonathan frowned. "I don't know. But I shall think of something. At least, I hope that I think of something."

Chapter 6

Pouring over the books - especially the more recent loans in the portfolio, Aaron shook his head.

With a grim expression, he stepped out of his office and shouted, "Jason, please come in here!"

Jason entered the office, looking directly at Aaron. "Yes, sir?"

"I just went over our loans, Jason. Disappointed, I am." And then he spat, "no - I am angry!" Aaron glared directly into Jason's eyes. "Son, your decisions to ignore our loan policies are putting us at risk of insolvency."

"In fact," Aaron was now jabbing his finger at Jason. "You are putting the well-being of this family in peril!"

Jason fidgeted as he looked down at the floor.

"Damn it! – what do you have to say for yourself?" Aaron snarled.

"But - but, Father." Jason looked up at Aaron. "Secured with property, these loans are. If the borrower defaults, we assume ownership of their assets."

Aaron sighed with exasperation. "But wrong this is. Can you not see it? To make loans they cannot repay is wrong!"

"But Father, why is this wrong? After all, the borrowers are adults. Think for themselves, they can."

"I – I – I don't know." Now it was Aaron's turn to look down. And then he looked up and said, "Can you not see this is wrong?"

"But Father, is it any more wrong than loaning paper receipts instead of gold?"

An awkward wordlessness descended into the room.

"I – I – I don't know," Aaron muttered. And then he looked at Jason with resolve. "It is clear, my son, that I cannot count on you to follow our loan guidelines. So from here on, you are confined to the teller window – AND NO WHERE ELSE!"

Jason was still looking down at the floor. His head was shaking as he lifted his eyes to look at his father. "Yes, Father. I understand."

Aaron glared. "What did you say?"

"I understand."

"Now, get out of my sight!"

Jason left the room, closing the door softly behind him.

* * *

It was morning, and Meredith walked the streets with Arthur on their way to the Trading Post. Typically cool and damp, the overcast sky cast a dim illumination on the scene before them - a scene filled with people lining the street, shivering, huddled in old tattered rags. Some were standing, some were sitting, and some were lying on the ground – but all had the look of despair, of suffering.

A wrinkled old woman appeared out of nowhere, crouching in front of Meredith and blocking her forward progress. She clasped her hands, holding them out to Meredith as she looked up and pleaded, "Help me. Please, help me. Please give me food..."

Meredith turned away, muttering, "I can't. I can't help you." She stepped around the poor old soul and continued along the street with Arthur.

They walked. And as they walked, she felt their eyes following her – stooped, grizzled old men and wrinkled old women. And then Meredith noticed the buildings. Rotting, and sometimes tilting in places; with dilapidated 'for sale' signs hanging ... *but there are no buyers, and owners no longer have the money to keep them up*, she thought.

They walked by a grizzled old man. He was shuffling along, huddled in a torn and tattered coat. He stared at her through empty eyes. *Don't look at him*, she thought.

A cry arose again and again. "*Can you spare some food?*"

They arrived at their store and noted that the doors were broken inward – again!

A note was left by the Sheriff:

> To: Mr. and Mrs. Griffin;
>   I apprehended the thieves. Please call on me when you get time.
>
> With Best Regards,
> Sheriff Wilson

Arthur took down the note and looked at Meredith. "Put a stop to this, we must," he hissed.

"Yes," Meredith replied. "It seems we shall be sleeping here from now on."

* * * * *

And in Nathan Goldman's office . . .

"I'm sorry, Mr. Merchant. But you have violated the terms of our agreement. I have no choice but to foreclose on your business."

"But Mr. Goldman. Surely you can give us one more week to raise the money for the payment. We're doing everything we can – Frances and I are eating only one meal a day!"

"I'm sorry, Mr. Merchant."

"But if you take the business, you will take our life savings. We shall have no place to go. We shall starve!"

"Please, Mr. Goldman," Frances chimed in, "just a few more days – please! What do you want? Do you want me to beg? Do want me on my knees? Pleading?" She clasped her hands and held them out to Nathan. "Please, Mr. Goldman. Please!"

Nathan sat in his chair listening. Unmoved. At Frances' last pleading, he turned in his chair and faced the wall. "Please leave," he said.

Heads stooped, the Merchants rose from their chairs, turned, and walked out of Nathan's office.

Colin Martin appeared at his office door as they walked past. With a somber expression, he watched as they shuffled across the lobby toward the exit.

* * *

"The Court hereby decrees that ownership of this property be assumed by the honorable goldsmith, Nathan Goldman. The Court further decrees that all assets of the property, including metal-working equipment and tools, shall be transferred to the honorable goldsmith, Nathan Goldman. By order of the Court, this decree is effective today."

With this, and using the force of law, the Sheriff proceeded to evict Jonathan from his blacksmithing business.

Jonathan's head was bowed – but his face was a mask of anger and despair as he looked across the room toward Nathan Goldman. And in response, Goldman met Jonathan's anger with a baleful gaze – his eyes hard and gleaming. And Frances – she took no notice of the exchange; but she nonetheless stood close to her husband, tears welling up in her eyes as she held their child.

They shuffled out the door and into the murky street – a street filled with desperate, destitute, poverty-stricken souls. They continued walking, passing a line of suffering people at the local soup kitchen. The line stretched around the corner.

Jonathan stopped and looked deeply into Frances' eyes. "I love you, my darling. Somehow, we shall survive." And then Frances began to sob, her belly rolling in spasms as Jonathan held her close.

At just that moment, Jonathan felt a tap on his shoulder. He turned, surprised to find Colin Martin standing next to him.

Colin smiled and said, "Help many people, I cannot. But ye I can 'elp." He grabbed Jonathan's hand and shoved something into it.

"Take this," Colin whispered, "And go to America!"

With those words, Colin disappeared like a wisp of smoke.

Jonathan looked down at his hand as he opened it, and was still more surprised to find a gold piece. His smile spread ear-to-ear as he looked at Frances and exclaimed, "What shall we do? Shall we go to America?"

Frances wiped her tears as she nodded her head. "Aye, my love. Let us book passage now!"

They turned and began walking, now with a bounce in their step. But intruding into their consciousness was the vision and stench of poverty surrounding them. The streets were crowded as they walked, and there were sad, hungry kids in the street – unwashed and stinking.

"Money? Can I have some money?"

"Food? Can I have some food, honey?"

They could hear a bell ringing in the distance; and the call, *"Soup! Soup!"*

Fifth Interlude . . .

Once more, grey eyes of steel meet youthful black eyes. The young man listened intently.

"... and pulling the money out of the economy is an effective means of control, is it not?"

"Yes, my Lord. And yet, I am amazed at how easy it is to steal the people's property."

The older man's smile faded. "You must understand – we are not stealing; we are taking what is rightfully ours. As soon as the borrower signs the promissory note, we need only print up the money and pay the seller. The fact that we conjure this 'money' from nothing is of no consequence – because no one is any the wiser."

The man paused and then continued. "And then, when the day of our choosing arrives, all we need do is withdraw money (as if these paper receipts are anything close to real money!) from circulation. The economy crashes, and the borrower freely – well, almost freely – gives us his business, his property."

The younger man nodded, and the gleam in his eyes shone brighter still.

The older man continued. "I am, however, concerned about Aaron. He has not prosecuted our plan with sufficient enthusiasm. While we were liberal with our loan activity, his loans were much too conservative. And while we have aggressively foreclosed on the peasants, he has offered too much forbearance. It seems Aaron is a threat to our power."

The younger man frowned. "So, what do you intend to do?"

Just then, a knock on the door announced a caller. "Enter," barked the old man.

The door swung open. In the doorway stood a man; seemingly with a perpetual sneer pasted on his mouth. And his eyes – his cold dead eyes.

... and despite the blazing fire, the room took on a chill.

* * *

Darkness was descending just when Aaron and Jason locked up the Depository. Nodding to the guards, they proceeded down the steps and struck out on their usual route home. Walking the streets, they weaved their way among the wretched homeless and destitute – people wearing dirty, tattered clothing and begging from passers-by.

"Do you see what I mean about being too liberal with our loans?" Aaron asked.

"What do you mean?"

"Just look around. This is the consequence of easy credit. It creates an economic boom; but then it necessarily collapses as the credit is withdrawn. These people – they are the victims of the credit withdrawal."

"I guess I do see that, Father." Jason said this as though he didn't care.

They continued walking, with Aaron closest to the buildings and alleys lining the street.

"You see, son," Aaron looked over at Jason as they walked, "it is especially difficult for people to maintain their business and make payments when the economy collapses. And even though we can foreclose on the property, these people need our help. They need a loan they can live with."

As they continued talking, they came upon a dark, murky alley. At just the entrance to the alley, Jason stopped and grabbed Aaron's shoulder; talking earnestly to his father.

"I do know how to run our banking operation, Father. And I promise I will –"

But just then, Jason moved his hands down and grabbed Aaron's wrists. Simultaneously, a second man stepped out of the alley and threw a thin silken cord around Aaron's neck. The man snapped the cord tight as Jason held onto his father's wrists.

But Aaron reacted instantly, his body slipping off to the side as he tried to twist away. It was all Jason could do to hang on; but he held both of the wrists in a vise grip, pulling Aaron still more off balance as the man pulled the cord tighter still. Aaron's face quickly turned a dark purple, and the strength in Aaron's arms drained away. In mere seconds, Jason could easily hold Aaron's hands; and he began to sob – tears were streaming down his face.

But the man behind Aaron continued to pull the cord, tighter and tighter, as the ground became wet. Aaron's muscular system was no longer under his control. His legs buckled, then folded as his body sagged. Sobbing, Jason let go of Aaron's hands. Watching as the man with cold, dead eyes stayed with his victim – crouching and then sinking to his knees as he followed Aaron's body to the ground. By this time, the cord was drawn so tight that it had disappeared into Aaron's neck; causing Aaron's eyes to bulge out of his head. And when the man let the cord go slack, Aaron's bulging eyes remained. Aaron was dead.

* * * * *

Soon after . . .

The Palace was exquisitely appointed. Gold engravings and gold statues adorned the upper perimeter of the walls, and were complemented with still more gold engravings and statues around the lower wall perimeter. Underneath the gold adornments; or rather, framed by the gold engravings, could be found chiseled and sculpted marble.

Large and elaborate candles were held within gold candle holders. The candles illuminated the entire chamber; their flames flickering off the walls and appointments with startling luminescence.

A fat man entered the chamber and walked the textured marble floor. Wheezing, he took in the exquisite adornment of the chamber; and as he approached the King's throne, he bowed gracefully. "Thank you for taking time to see me, your Highness."

Sitting erect and self-assured upon his throne, the King welcomed him with a smile and a nod of his head. With his curly brown hair and his softly-chiseled features, he exuded an air of privilege as he gestured an invitation to be seated.

The fat man sat down; and grey eyes of steel looked into eyes of royal blue.

Silence descended on the room.   And then the King's eye twitched as he spoke, "Your message spoke of a source of funds that can help me to grow and maintain my empire."

"That is true, your Highness."

"Did you arrange our, ah – economic 'event'?"

"Yes, your Highness.   I was part of the group that arranged it."

"A very telling act that you performed."   And then the King's expression became stern as he continued, "some may call it treason."

"With all due respect, your Highness, there was no intention to undermine your rule.   Nor did we."

"In due time, I desire to know more about this."

"Of course, your Highness.   I shall gladly explain to whatever depth you desire."

"Fine," the King responded.   He paused and then continued. "About your proposal to help me grow and maintain my empire – I want to hear more about this."   A wry smile crossed the Kings features, and then he continued.   "It seems the people become restless when I raise their taxes to fund our wars.   So I seek a way to wage war without alarming the people; and I am informed that you can help."

"Well, my Lord.   I represent a group that can provide you with monetary resources and loans with which to arm and maintain your armies.   This will give you – give England– the opportunity to consolidate empire throughout the far reaches of the world."

"And what do you want in return?"

"Oh, your Highness.   We desire very little; a mere trifling."

"Go on ..."

"... And that's how the banking cartel came about." The old man snorted, wiping his nose with his finger.

"So, you're saying that the bankers and kings joined together?"

"Yep. The marriage of rulers and bankers is as old as the history books. The rulers like war, but they need bankers' money for their armies."

"And the bankers?"

"Hell! The bankers make money from war; and that's truth!"

"Shit," Squirt exclaimed. "I guess that explains all those damn wars we were in at the time of the collapse. Huh?"

"Yep," the grizzled old man responded. "And if you look close, you'll find the bankers behind 'em all."

The old man looked down at the floor and sighed.

Squirt piped up. "So how do you know all this?"

"The diaries," the old man replied as he wiped his nose.

"Diaries?"

"Yep. There's boxes of 'em in that closet over there." Then the old man tilted his head and said, "Why don't you get one of 'em out of there?"

"Over there?" Squirt said, pointing to a door.

"Yeah. Let's see what we got."

Squirt opened the door and dragged out a large cardboard box. And then another. She left still more in the closet.

"Yep," the old man sniffed. "That's the diaries!"

She opened a box, revealing a curious collection of books – their covers and bindings tattered and dry, with pages loose in many of the older books.

"Wow," Squirt exclaimed. "What is all this?"

"That's truth!" And then Jim's voice was subdued as he said, "That's history – the way it really happened."

"Huh? What's that supposed to mean?"

"You know the first story I told ya? The Chespik incident?"

"Sure. But what's that got to do with these books?"

"Do you remember me tellin' you about William Martin and how he recorded the Chespik events in his diary?"

"Yes, but –"

"Well. His diary is in there – somewhere."

"You're kiddin' me."

"Nope. And so is Colin's diary."

Squirt looked down at the boxes and said, "But there's a lot more than just that here."

"That's correct," the old man replied. And then he took a deep breath and said, "What you're seeing here are diaries from descendants of William and Colin, as well as diaries from other families."

"So what's in all of these?" Tim interjected.

"Truth, sonny. That's truth!"

"What's that supposed to mean?"

"Sonny, in there you'll find the recorded history of the bankers for the last 350 years – but not the way the bankers told history, but instead the way history really happened!"

"Like what?"

"Well. See that book with the red cover?"

Tim picked up the book and turned it over.

"That's the civil war – or part of it," the old man said. "It talks about how the English were lined up on our northern border and the French were positioned down at the Rio Grande – and how the bankers had planned using 'em for a pincer maneuver to split the U.S."

"Huh?" Tim exclaimed. "You can't be serious!"

"I'm deadly serious, sonny!"

A moment of silence descended into the lair.

Then the old man pointed to a gray-covered book. "And that there's the lead up to the war for independence."

Tim picked up the gray-covered book and turned it over. He opened it to the middle, and read aloud "... the King declared that we (the colonists) could no longer print our own money ..." Tim stopped reading, his eyes widening as he looked at the old man. "Holy shit!"

The old man pointed at a book and said, "This one here talks about the bankers' takeover of Europe." And then he pointed at yet another binding. "And then this one here covers the creation of the Federal Reserve."

"What's the Federal Reserve got to do with anything?" Squirt asked.

The old man eyed her and smirked. And then he said, "In 1913, the Congress passed the Federal Reserve Act. It created a private banking cartel with monopoly power over the money of the U.S. Since that time, the dollar has lost 98% of its value – due to inflation." And then his voice quivered as he said, "That's truth!"

Silence again permeated the lair. And then Squirt asked, "What's this book here?"

"That?" The old man eyed the book cover. "I think that covers the bankruptcy of the U.S."

"Bankruptcy?" Tim asked incredulously. "But I've never seen THAT in the history books."

"Most people haven't. But it's there. It's in that book you're holding. And it's all in the public records – House Joint Resolution 192." The old man's voice dripped cynicism. "But they don't want you to know about it – they've hidden it."

"So, I don't understand." Tim interjected, "How could the U.S. go bankrupt? Why didn't the U.S. just pay the debts with their gold reserves?"

The old man's voice quivered as he answered. "Because the U.S. had been paying out the gold as interest on the debt to the Federal Reserve. And when the gold ran out – voilà – the U.S. was bankrupt."

"So, the gold in Ft. Knox wasn't owned by the Federal Government?"

"Hell no. If there's any gold in Ft. Knox, it's owned by the bankers, not the American People." The old man looked at the couple. "Frankly, the collapse you're seeing now is because the U.S. was broke."

Silence descended as Tim and Squirt looked at each other.

"So. You were telling us how this happened ..."

"Yeah. I was, wasn't I?"

"So what happened next?"

"Next? God, you keep asking that!"

"Well?"

"Well, that's where we get to the story – the story of how the world went bust. But first, let's get you some more food."

The old man stood up tentatively, shifting his weight onto his good leg. "Damn it hurts!" His frame jerked to the side as he limped over to the counter.

"Hey, old man," Tim said. "You need to put that leg up."

"It'll heal," the old man replied in a hoarse voice. He pulled out two more cans and cut them open.

Tim held out two dimes. The man looked at the proffered dimes and then looked at Tim. "You keep your money, sonny. Here, take these." He handed a can each to Tim and Squirt.

The old man snorted. "You were right, Squirt. It was high-way robbery."

He limped back and lowered himself onto his seat. "Now. You two listen to what I have to say ..."

Episode 3 – Quest for Empire

We have, in this country, one of the most corrupt institutions the world has ever known. I refer to the Federal Reserve Board. This evil institution has impoverished the people of the United States and has practically bankrupted our government. It has done this through the corrupt practices of the moneyed vultures who control it.

- - - Congressman Louis T. McFadden in 1932

Part 1 – Ascension

For we are opposed around the world by a monolithic and ruthless conspiracy that relies on covert means for expanding its sphere of influence–on infiltration instead of invasion, on subversion instead of elections, on intimidation instead of free choice, on guerrillas by night instead of armies by day. It is a system which has conscripted vast human and material resources into the building of a tightly knit, highly efficient machine that combines military, diplomatic, intelligence, economic, scientific   and   political   operations.

Its preparations are concealed, not published. Its mistakes are buried not headlined. Its dissenters are silenced, not praised. No expenditure is questioned, no rumor is printed, no secret is revealed.

- - - Excerpted from John F. Kennedy's Secret Society Speech, April 27, 1961

Chapter 1 – Circa 1950s

REGALED IN A GOLDEN CROWN, sparkling multi-colored jewels, and a silken robe, He glowingly sat on His gold and silk throne, receiving the adulation of the crowd, the throng chanting in unison, "Your Highness! Your Highness! Your Highness!"

He levitated above the crowd, gliding through the air above His adoring subjects. His arms extended outward – taking in the crowd's applause – and knowing that He was special; that He was their ruler and their savior. And all the while, each person in the crowd bowed to Him on bended knee.

He looked down. And there in the crowd he spied Mother! And Father! They were together, and they too were in adoration of Him.

And then, He lowered Himself to the ground – slowly – making sure that the crowd had ample chance to adore Him, and acknowledge Him as their special savior. And as He landed, the crowd circled him. And in their circle, they moved around Him in a clockwise fashion, chanting, "King Basil! King Basil! ..." And then Mother and Father emerged from the crowd. They came forward and knelt at his feet, bowing, with their faces resting on the ground, and kissing the ground He had just occupied.

Your Highness!

And then the dream ended ... or was it a dream?

* * *

Young Master Basil awoke in his oversized bed and gazed up at the off-white ceiling – adorned as it was with engravings, seemingly chiseled into the surface as if made of stone. The sun was streaming through the balcony windows, creating dancing shadows and reflections on the opposite walls.

Empty, he thought. *What is this emptiness I feel inside?*

He sat up. Then putting his legs over the side of the bed, he slid down off the bed to the marble floor. He was not yet tall enough to touch his feet to the floor while sitting on the side of the bed. But at 10 years old, he didn't care.

Summoning the butler, he pushed the button at the side of his bed. *It looks like a nice day,* he thought. *I think I'll see what's on the balcony.* He sauntered toward the French doors and pulled them open, stepping out onto the balcony.

The palace – because it was much more a palace than a home, or even a mansion – stood on a great hill with a magnificent view of a river and surrounding countryside. Master Basil scanned the lands around him; taking in the hundreds of acres of pasture and forest. To Master Basil, the expansive manor and the flowing countryside had always been his home. He could not imagine anything different.

As Master Basil leaned against the railing, his butler entered the suite. "Good morning Master Basil," Swenson said. "May I draw your bath?"

Master Basil appeared to ignore Swenson's greeting at first. Swenson shuffled and cleared his throat, yet he waited patiently. Then, Master Basil turned to face Swenson. "Hello, Swenson. Yes, I'd like a bath this morning."

"Very well, sir." Swenson went into the bathroom and began running the bath water. While the bath water was running, Swenson returned.

"What is Master Basil's desire for breakfast this morning?"

"I want eggs benedict, Swenson."

"Very well, sir. I will inform the chef."

Swenson then went into the bathroom and turned off the faucet. "Your bath is ready, Master Basil." Swenson announced. "Is there anything that I may do for you, sir?"

"Where are mother and father?"

"Lady Jessica is getting ready for her bankers' wives social gathering. And Lord George is traveling out of the country and will return Friday."

"Is there anything that I may do for you, sir?"

"Yes, Swenson. I want you to lay out my clothes for today." Master Basil said with a haughty tone. "I desire the gray suit."

"Very well, Master Basil. As you wish."

"After you lay out my clothes, you may go, Swenson."

Swenson bowed; then went to the Master's dressing area, where he retrieved a handsome gray suit, a red bow tie, appropriate underwear, and shoes. He hung or placed all of these next to the Master's bureau.

Then, with a robot-like precision and posture, Swenson withdrew from the suite.

Master Basil walked into the bathroom. It was as elegantly appointed as the rest of his suite; with marble floors and a rich, exquisite walnut trim throughout the chamber. Master Basil walked past a mirror and looked back at himself. He spent a few moments in front of the mirror, admiring his regal posture and his dignified features. *If I hold my head like this,* he shifted his head ever so slightly, *then I stand like a king.*

Master Basil dropped his pajamas, and stepped into the bathtub; proceeding to wash his fair, unblemished skin.

He reflected on the day's coming events. *That science tutor was coming today. He was too pushy and too demanding; and I never seem to get the right answers. I think I might fire him and get Mother to get me another one.*

And then he grimaced when his thoughts turned to Mother's Social. *I hate it when those women make over me!*

In his mind, he pictured Lady Humphries' big mouth. *"Oh, Jessica darling - he's such a handsome boy, and such beautiful curls!"*

But Basil hated his curls. *They make me look like a girl!*

The social gathering was accompanied with tea and crumpets; and frilly, frumpy women sitting around and talking like magpies about nothing important. As he closed his eyes, he could picture those old women, their mouths moving incessantly as their shrill voices grew louder and louder. Their gossip just went on, and on - and on. *The old bags!*

* * *

Master Basil wore a suit every day; and he wore it well. But he looked especially good, especially elegant, in his gray suit. As Master Basil walked into the dining room, his butler held out the Master's chair for seating. "May I provide you anything, sir?"

"Yes, Swenson" Master Basil replied. "Please get me some orange juice and some water."

"Very well, sir." Swenson was a model of efficiency. Magically, the orange juice and water appeared; and then Swenson rushed off to get the Master's breakfast.

"Eggs Benedict; as you like them, sir." Swenson bowed and stepped back and behind Master Basil. He waited on the Master's next command.

Swenson was still waiting when Lady Jessica walked into the dining room. Master Basil looked up and into her eyes. "Good morning, Mother."

Beautiful as always, the corner of Lady Jessica's mouth crooked up slightly in greeting. "Good morning, Basil. How did you sleep?"

"My sleep was satisfactory." Basil said.

My but this is the first time I've heard him say that word, Swenson thought.

"Are you ready for your science instruction this morning?"

"No, Mother." Basil blurted out. "I do not like the science teacher. He asks hard questions and he doesn't tell me the answers!"

"Well, dear, I will speak with him," Jessica replied.

"But Mother." Basil's face was turning red now. "You have already talked with him twice, and he still won't tell me the answers!"

"Well, dear." Jessica's voice had a cold, distant quality. "Perhaps he wants you to find the answers for yourself."

Basil's face turned an intense crimson. "No, Mother! I want you to fire him!"

"But dear. We've already fired two teachers this month."

"No! No!" Basil was out of his chair and screaming at Jessica now. "I won't go! I won't go!"

Lady Jessica shrugged. "Basil, you must go."

"No, Mother. No!" Basil sprung out of his chair and ran out of the dining room.

They heard a door slam shut.

Emotionless, silent, Lady Jessica remained standing.

She glanced over to the corner where Swenson watched the unfolding drama. Swenson felt his body *tight, tense,* as though he were a spring under pressure. But then he sensed relaxation beginning to wash through him.

Lady Jessica's face – especially her eyes and her mouth – looked sad; and then out of nowhere her eyes sparkled and her smile emerged. She nodded to Swenson. "Good morning my dear Swenson. Are you well?"

"Very well, My Lady. And you?" Swenson looked at her with his head crooked to one side.

"I am fine, my dear Swenson. Please – carry on." She turned to leave and then looked back at Swenson. "Oh. Will you please help Brewer with the preparations for my social?"

Swenson came to attention. "Of course, My Lady."

With that, Lady Jessica turned and walked out of the room, while humming a song.

Swenson shook his head and went off to find Lady Jessica's butler, Brewer.

* * *

In the circle of English socialites, a Lady Jessica 'social' was not just any event. It was an event to which invitations were highly sought.

So one might ask, what attracts the female upper crust to Lady Jessica's social gatherings? The reasons were varied – as varied as the guests themselves. Some women wanted to establish a network with other women, so they could help their husbands advance. And others wanted to show off their latest gown, their newest shoes, their exquisite jewelry, or their new found wealth. But the primal desire of each of these women was privilege – to hobnob with the elite – to be the crème de la crème. And since the women were competing for status, Jessica's Socials tended to reveal the womens' claws.

And strange as it may seem, many socialites found this – the claws and the snarling – to be an entertaining activity.

Each socialite was announced as she entered. Many walked as though they'd (indeed!) been trained. With head held high, shoulders back, and spine erect, each socialite walked as though she were floating above the marble floor.

Master Basil stood over to the side of the room, watching each woman enter in all her fluffy, frumpy glory. He waited. Waited for the one woman he had eyes for – Lady Diana.

Finally, the announcer called out, "Lady Diana." And in that moment, Master Basil's eyes sparkled as he smiled broadly, excitedly. He watched as Lady Diana entered the ballroom.

Many described The Lady as stunning, glowing, radiant, with bright beautiful eyes and – and *dimples*! Tall and regal in her own right, she had an unpretentious smile and a free-flowing manner that stood in stark contrast to the petty shallowness of the other socialites.

Lady Diana had a standing invitation to Jessica's social gatherings. And she was somewhat of a fixture at the Manor; which is to say she visited quite often. And with her visits, she would fuss over Basil in a grandmotherly sort of way. But Basil didn't mind. He liked the attention she gave him.

Unlike his mother Lady Jessica, Master Basil was drawn to Diana – even though she was just his second cousin. Sometimes she seemed to awaken in young Basil some long-ago feelings of closeness. And yet Basil was aware of painful feelings – as though he had experienced a deep and painful loss. And with these feelings of pain, Basil learned it was better not to feel.

Lady Diana walked up to Master Basil and smiled at him. "And how are you today, Master Basil?"

Master Basil's eyes lit up and his smile was broad. "Fine," he said.

Master Basil clasped the Lady's hand. She pulled him to her, and they hugged. Finally, Lady Diana ended their embrace; holding Basil at arm's length.

"So," Lady Diana continued, "what have you been up to?"

Master Basil looked down to the floor as he responded. "Oh, nothing." He paused. "Just school."

And then he looked at Diana. "I'm bored."

Lady Diana laughed. "I've got news for you my young Basil. So am I."

Just then, Lady Jessica interrupted them. "Basil my boy, it's time for you to have your lunch."

"But Mother," Basil pleaded, "I just want to talk with Lady Diana for a little more."

She took Basil's hand and marched him toward the kitchen. "I'm sorry dear," she glared back at Lady Diana as they were walking, "But Lady Diana is busy and you must have your lunch."

Master Basil stopped walking and looked up at Jessica. "No!" He shouted. "I want Lady Diana!"

"No, Basil. You come with me," she replied in a firm voice.

With that, Master Basil pulled away from Jessica and dropped to the floor. He thrashed on the floor; hitting it with his hands and feet as he screamed and shouted, "No! No! No! I want Lady Diana!"

Lady Jessica stood her ground, watching young Basil throw his tantrum. "Basil, dear. You let me know when you're done with your tantrum - you will, now, won't you?"

At that moment, Lady Diana came up. "Is there anything I can do?" She asked Jessica.

Jessica turned and looked at Diana. Her voice was pure venom as she said, "Haven't you done enough?"

Neither had noticed that Basil had ceased his tantrum and was watching the two.

Lady Diana was taken aback. "What do you mean, Jessica?" Lady Diana really did not understand Jessica's insinuation; and her innocent and curious voice attested to that fact.

Lady Jessica's eyes bored into Diana. "Stay away from him," she spat.

"Stay away from him?" Diana paused. "Who do you think you are?"

"Who I am, my dear Diana, is his mother!"

"Bullshit," Diana spat. "Why don't you tell him the truth!"

"What - what," Basil interrupted with a pleading voice. "My Lady, what's the truth?"

But Jessica grabbed Basil and pulled him behind her. She turned and glared at Diana. "You stay away from him, damn it! Stay away," she hissed.

She turned and dragged Basil toward the kitchen.

* * *

"Mother, when can I see Lady Diana again?"

"Basil honey. Lady Diana has moved away," Lady Jessica lied. "It will be some time before you can see her again."

"But why? Why? Why did she leave, Mother?"

"She left because of an emergency," Jessica replied.

"But Mother, she would have told me that she was leaving."

"Basil, darling. Lady Diana was called away with no notice," Lady Jessica lied again. "I'm sure she will contact you when she has time."

Master Basil wiped away tears.

"Basil, honey," Lady Jessica continued. "You should not cry. You should never cry. It does not become you – the next King of the world."

"Yes, Mother."

Chapter 2

Master Basil was standing on his balcony when he heard still another limousine drive onto the grounds. Off to the left, he watched the limo drive through the wooded, shaded grounds and toward the front entrance to The Manor.

Master Basil knew there was much more activity than normal. But he neither knew nor understood what it was about. Nonetheless, he was curious, if not intrigued. *This is very unusual for the middle of the week,* he thought. *I think I'll investigate,* he smiled at himself at his use of a new word.

Basil walked – actually, ran would be a better description – along his usual path from his suite on out to the palace foyer. Just in time to watch two men in suits walk into father's office.

Oh wow! Who are they?

Swenson was holding a door open for the men when he spied Master Basil. "Keep low," Swenson mouthed at Basil; and then grimaced in a way that told Basil to lie low and keep some distance. Basil put his finger to his mouth in a gesture to 'be quiet'; then he responded by receding into the shadow of a pillar.

Swenson quickly finished with his doorman charge and wandered over to where Master Basil was 'hiding'.

"Hey Swenson, what is going on?" Basil whispered.

Swenson looked down at the young man, whispering. "Your father is conducting some rather important meetings."

"What about?"

"What about?" Swenson mimicked. "You're too young to know about this!"

"I'm twelve," Basil announced.

"Twelve," Swenson repeated. "Master Basil, that's too young."

"Aw c'mon, Swenson," Basil pleaded. "What's going on. Please?"

"Well, I don't really know what's going on. But even if I did, I'm sure I couldn't say." And then Swenson's voice turned to a whisper. "I heard them talking about the 'Federal Reserve' and 'President'. So, it must have something to do with the United States."

Master Basil nodded. He knew that the U.S. and the President were a common topic of discussion in father's circle. But he also knew that this was uncommon – to have so many of Father's high-level associates assembling – with hardly any notice.

Basil retreated to his suite, where he began plotting to find out what father's meeting was about.

Once he had a plan, he again walked toward the palace foyer and father's adjoining office. But this time, he snuck up on the rear office door – the door that no one but the servants ever used.

Putting his ear to the door, he overheard fragments of the conversation – "Batista" ... "Cuba" ...

Master Basil could barely make out any words, and it left him still more curious and intrigued. Just then, Brewer came walking up from behind with a tray of refreshments. Basil was intent on his eavesdropping and did not hear Brewer's approach. Brewer tapped Basil on the shoulder.

"Huh?" Basil shuddered and almost fell over.

Brewer looked at Basil in a condescending manner. "You had best not stay here, Master Basil. Or your father may hear of it!"

Master Basil retreated to his suite.

* * * * *

That night, after Basil had fallen asleep . . .

Basil opened his eyes to the sound of a woman's voice. "My dear Basil. You are so handsome, my dear. You so warm my heart."

Is that mother? He thought. *Still dark.* Basil felt himself begin to shiver. *Not again!*

"Hel ... hello, Mother."

He could sense her breathing, and feel her close by his bed. "My dear Basil," she cooed. "I'm cold. Could you warm me?" Without asking, she lifted the covers and came into the bed with him.

Basil knew instinctively she was naked. He felt heat pouring from her body. She drew closer; and drew him closer to her – so that their bodies touched along the contours of hers'. *Oh my God,* he thought, *this feels so good.*

"Oh Basil, darling," she whispered as she began removing his clothes. "You must be so hot. Here, let me help."

"But Mother." Basil cried.

"Oh, Basil. Your mother needs you. She needs to be close to you." He felt his pajamas sliding down.

Then Basil felt her hand down on him. "Oh Basil, you still have shorts on. Please," she cooed still more, "let me help with those."

He felt his shorts slide below his waist. Felt her hand touching him. Then he closed his eyes. His body writhed even more intensely as he responded to her soft flesh against him – *this is so wrong! So wrong!!!* Basil thrashed in his confusion – both shame and pleasure washing through him. *Oh my God. I'm gonna die!*

And then his young body became hard; impervious to any feelings from within or without.

Basil turned over and warmed his body to hers. His eyes gleamed, and a smirk grew on his boys' lips. Pulling her closer, he said, "Come here, Mother. I can take care of you."

Chapter 3

Gazing across the expanse of forest, pasture, and river, Master Basil was leaning against the balcony railing when he heard a car drive on to the grounds. He looked to his left and watched the limo drive through the estate grounds, finally pulling up to the Manor's front entrance.

Master Basil did not know who was in the limo. *People come and go all the time*, he thought. *Why should I care?* Nonetheless, Basil was bored and curious; and so he decided to investigate.

He strode quickly along his usual path from his suite on out to the palace foyer. He reached it just in time to see a woman walk into father's office. *Is that Lady Diana?* He thought. *Oh, how I've missed her!* Basil made a movement to intercept her, and then he thought better of it. *I'll get to see her when she comes out.*

As Swenson held the door for The Lady, he caught a glimpse of Master Basil. He grimaced toward Basil, in a way that told Basil to lie low and keep some distance. Basil crossed his mouth with his finger. *Quiet!* Then Basil receded into the shadow of a pillar.

Swenson quickly closed the door and sauntered over to Master Basil's hideout.

"Hey Swenson, what's going on?" Basil's whispered voice had just a hint of intrigue.

Swenson grimaced. "If I did know, I could not tell you. But, I do not know, Master Basil." And then Swenson put his face close to Basil's and whispered, "I know only that Lady Diana wanted to speak with him."

Swenson glanced at his wristwatch. "I have some important duties to attend to." And then Swenson looked sharply at Basil, and said, "You watch out for yourself."

Swenson departed, leaving Master Basil to wonder what his next action should be.

I think I'll just go back to the service door and mill around – see if I can hear anything, he thought. He walked softly around to the office service entrance. *Only the servants use it,* he thought. *No one's going to see me.*

He could hear fragments of conversation inside the room.

" ... but, George, he's mine ..."

"... I know, I know, ... but Jessica ... wanted him to be hers ... how do I? ..."

The more Basil listened, the more it aroused his curiosity, and the more confused he became. He listened more.

"... Damn it, George," Basil heard Diana's voice resonate with anger, "he's my son – not that damn witch Jessica's ..."

"... I know. I know ..."

As Basil listened, his face became red. His jaw already tight, became contorted; and his eyes – his eyes lit up as though on fire.

Basil withdrew from the door and returned to his suite.

Chapter 4

Expansive and plush, Lord George appreciated his office and all its appointments. Walnut woodwork with gold inlay, an intricately carved mahogany desk, paneling, and bookcases – all reeking of obscene wealth – surrounding him whenever he worked.

George's desk stood near the back-center of the room, with bookcases adorning the wall to the right of the desk. Much of the remaining space was taken up with leather upholstered lounge chairs and two sofas. On the wall to the left of the desk was an unobtrusive wet bar; well stocked with brandy, very old scotch, and other means of liquid respite. Off to one side, a doorway led into a meeting room – a large meeting table was visible through the doorway.

Master Basil took all of this in as he stood in the office doorway. "You wanted to see me, Father?"

Lord George was seated at his desk, looking over some documents. He looked up at his son and smiled, clasping his finely-manicured hands together. "Thank you for coming, Basil. I have so much to discuss with you." He gestured to a leather chair and said, "Please, come in and sit down."

Master Basil walked tentatively into the office. He seated himself in the comfortable leather chair across from his father.

At this stage in his life, Basil's features were youthful, his lips thin and tightly drawn, with light brown hair combed straight back, and deep-set eyes that looked everywhere except at his father. "What did you want to discuss, Father?"

"Well," Lord George hesitated, "I have an engagement coming up. I will be traveling for a few days."

"Okay," Basil replied. "Is there anything else?"

Lord George frowned. He hesitated and then began speaking. "Son, you are now seventeen years old. And although I have previously made suggestions about your future, it is now time that you know what your future will be."

"Yes?" Master Basil thought to himself, *this idiot doesn't know what he's talking about!*

"Master Basil," George continued. "You will become Lord Basil. You, my son, will inherit my position and become the leader of the western world."

Basil unconsciously became erect in his chair, holding his head in a regal fashion. And then Basil slumped, shaking his head. "But Father – there is The Queen, the United Nations, the United States, the European countries."

Lord George smiled. "Ah, my young Basil. There is time enough to explain all of this. In the meantime, you must prepare – prepare yourself to take over my position."

Silence formed in the room, even as son and father looked into each other's eyes. Basil felt hate toward his father. Hatred at his finely combed hair, his impeccable dress, his correct manner, his detachment. *If only I could meet his expectations – maybe he would give me the attention I need – that I deserve!*

Lord George continued. "There will be education – Oxford, Harvard. And there will be education in our family heritage, and in things known particularly to our family. And there will be time enough to learn the world, and to know the world stage and the players on that stage. And of course, there will be time enough for you to create and grow your family, as a part of the family heritage."

Basil turned his head away, looking at the bookcases to his left. "Is that all, Father?" Basil's voice was flat – detached.

"Don't you want to hear more?" Lord George asked hopefully.

"Hmmm ... not now, Father." Basil looked down and away from his father, looking around the room.

Basil's appearance was sometimes deceiving – he was almost full grown and he carried himself as a regal gentleman. It was easy for George to believe that Basil was emotionally an adult. And yet Lord George sometimes needed to be reminded that Basil was seventeen years old – still very much a child.

This was one of those times.

* * *

Master Basil walked out of his father's office with decidedly mixed feelings. *I wish he would love me,* he thought. *But he doesn't want to love me. All he wants is for me to follow in his footsteps.* And then Basil's features hardened. *I guess he's not going to tell me about my mother. Liar! I'm better than him – and I'm going to do what I want! And Jessica. If Jessica's not my mother, then why should I care! I hate her!*

That same evening, Basil was confused as he roamed the corridors, seemingly at random. *Where am I going?* But soon, he found himself at the entrance to Lady Jessica's bedroom chambers. *Damn,* he thought. *Why did I come here? All those times she used me. God how I hate her!*

The door was closed. *But why should I care?* Basil thought. Without knocking, he turned the knob and pushed on the door. He walked in on her, slamming the door behind him.

Jessica was stretched out on the bed, reading a book and sipping from a glass of wine. She looked up at him. Her voice quivered with surprise. "Oh, Basil darling. You should have knocked."

Without saying a word, Basil approached the bed. He stood, perusing her form through her low-cut nightgown. Her hips, her breasts; she was full, but still quite desirable.

"What do you want?" She asked, demurely.

"You."

"Me?" She laughed. "I don't feel like it, dear. I have a head-ache." then she giggled as she looked into his eyes. "You're nothing but a boy! Why don't you go screw the maid?"

Basil's face, his eyes, hardened. He grabbed Jessica's gown by the cleavage and pulled; the gown tore and so he pulled some more. And as he pulled, Jessica's face took on a look of surprise, even shock. She flailed her hands, shouting, "Don't do that! Stop that!"

But Basil manhandled her gown; stripping it from her body and revealing her naked flesh. She tried to cover herself in sheets, but Basil yanked them off of her too, leaving her exposed, and shivering. "What – what! What do you want?" She stammered.

Basil dropped his trousers. "You. I want you." His lips were drawn tight, his eyes hard as steel. "Roll over."

She remained on the bed, shivering but not moving.

Basil grabbed her throat and choked. "Turn over, bitch – or I'll squeeze!" She moved, rolling over as he grabbed her hair to keep her on the bed. "On your knees." She followed his direction.

He moved up behind her, using his knees to spread her legs.

"Don't take me. It'll hurt!" She cried.

He pulled her hair. "Shut up," he growled.

Basil spat into his hand and lubricated. "Take this," he hissed, thrusting against her. "Ohhhh!" Jessica screamed. "You bastard!"

He said nothing, but his mouth crooked up in a smirk.

Basil pulled on her hair as though he held the mange of a horse. She whimpered as he thrust; all the while she moistened, more and more. Basil's grip on her hair served to pull her head high, even as she opened up. She was moist, even wet.

He continued; but as he did, she began ramming herself backward, meeting him. "C'mon, damn it!" She shouted. "Give it to me you little shit!"

He let go of her hair and thrust harder; too absorbed in his anger to notice her red-flushed skin. He just wanted to hurt her – and yet she craved still more.

Their anger grew more intense, feeding off each other, until he shuddered in release.

She shivered too, for her release came in the same moment.

Chapter 5 – Circa 1963

EXECUTIVE ORDER 11110

AMENDMENT OF EXECUTIVE ORDER NO. 10289 AS AMENDED, RELATING TO THE PERFORMANCE OF CERTAIN FUNCTIONS AFFECTING THE DEPARTMENT OF THE TREASURY. By virtue of the authority vested in me by section 301 of title 3 of the United States Code, it is ordered as follows:

SECTION 1. Executive Order No. 10289 of September 19, 1951, as amended, is hereby further amended - (a) By adding at the end of paragraph 1 thereof the following subparagraph (j): "(j) The authority vested in the President by paragraph (b) of section 43 of the Act of May 12, 1933, as amended (31 U.S.C. 821 (b)), *to issue silver certificates against any silver bullion, silver, or standard silver dollars in the Treasury not then held for redemption of any outstanding silver certificates, to prescribe the denominations of such silver certificates, and to coin standard silver dollars and subsidiary silver currency for their redemption*," and (b) By revoking subparagraphs (b) and (c) of paragraph 2 thereof.

SECTION 2. The amendment made by this Order shall not affect any act done, or any right accruing or accrued or any suit or proceeding had or commenced in any civil or criminal cause prior to the date of this Order but all such liabilities shall continue and may be enforced as if said amendments had not been made.

JOHN F. KENNEDY THE WHITE HOUSE, June 4, 1963

* * * * *

Lord George's office had many leather chairs; all of them comfortable. Basil was ensconced in just such a chair when his father walked in. Basil greeted his father - tentatively, diffidently. "Hello, Father."

"Hello, Basil. I'll bet you are wondering why I called you here today."

"Yes, Father. Would you please enlighten me? I've heard the telephone ringing incessantly - cars and helicopters coming and going, and men running in and out of your office."

George's face turned grim. "I have been talking with some of our highest level consultants ... We seem to have a problem, Basil. One of our important surrogates is no longer on board with our program."

"Huh? What does that mean?"

Lord George glanced at Basil as he walked toward his desk. "President Kennedy is no longer with us. He is no longer following our orders."

"But Father, what do you mean about President Kennedy? What has he got to do with anything?"

Lord George looked grimly at Basil. "Do you remember when we talked about our heritage, Basil?"

"Yes, but -"

"Well, Kennedy is a surrogate of ours - a very important surrogate. You see, the United States - and especially the Federal Reserve - is an important piece of our empire. When they do not follow our orders, they put our plans of greater empire at risk."

"Empire? But – but can you tell me more about this?" Basil was confused.

"Soon, Basil. My associates will arrive momentarily, and I will explain it to everyone at the same time."

Just at that moment, the butler escorted several men into the office. They were each dressed in a suit – tailored, groomed, and expensive.

"Good afternoon, gentlemen." Lord George held out his hand. "Please, all of you take a seat." He looked up at Swenson and said, "Please bring hors-d'oeuvre and refreshments for these gentlemen."

Swenson nodded. "As you wish, sir."

Lord George turned in his chair, sweeping the room with his eyes as he began talking. "Without delay, gentlemen. I called you here because we have a serious problem. In short, President Kennedy is no longer following our orders. He has stepped outside of our control."

George paused and then continued. "Of course, all of you know about Kennedy's executive order – the order that gives authority for the government to print silver certificates based on silver that is held by the U.S. Government." George paused and grimaced. "Well gentlemen, the U.S. Treasury has proceeded with the printing of silver certificates based on their silver holdings!"

While his audience listened intently, Lord George's eyes continued sweeping the room.

"The problem, of course, is that these silver certificates compete with our federal reserve notes. And worse – WORSE!" George's face turned crimson as he paused. "As Americans use silver certificates to pay for their purchases, we lose leverage over the U.S. economy!"

Basil was confused – he did not understand all of this. But he heard gasps and murmurings from the men in the room. He watched as the men glanced at each other, obviously upset.

Lord George continued. "It's clear that if this were to continue, it would put our plan back many years."

The murmuring in the room increased in intensity.

"But also," the room silenced as Lord George continued, "We have just recently received word from inside sources that Kennedy has ordered a U.S. withdrawal from Vietnam to commence soon, and take place over a two-year period."

Again, the murmuring in the room increased in intensity. Some of the men began talking amongst themselves. Master Basil continued to watch; but he did not yet understand the problem.

Lord George began speaking again over the din of voices. "As you all know, war is important to us – it allows us to expand our wealth and influence. And it is important that we keep the U.S. engaged in this war – and even escalate it."

George scanned the room, speaking forcefully. "With any luck, we should be able to keep the U.S. in Vietnam for another ten years. Easily enough to fill our coffers, buy off more of the U.S. and world financial system, and continue to expand our control!"

George continued scanning as the men were talking. Soon, his associates stopped talking as one of the men spoke out. "So, My Lord. What do you propose?"

"Gentlemen. I see no alternative but to eliminate Kennedy and install Johnson as the President. After all, he has been in our pocket for these many years, and we can count on him to carry on our program. He will stop this nonsense with the silver, and he'll push the U.S. further into Vietnam."

The room became still.

George continued. "We shall allow no one to get in our way!"

The men stood up and began eating on the hors-d'oeuvre and refreshments. Master Basil listened as the men talked amongst each other.

" . . . so what's the weather doing tomorrow? More overcast? . . ."

" . . . how's your daughter? Is she in college yet? . . ."

* * *

Document 100.1.3.2.0 31 of 39...

"The high office of the President has been used to foment a plot to destroy the Americans freedom and before I leave office I must inform the Citizen of his plight." -PRESIDENT JOHN F. KENNEDY (10 days before he was murdered)

* * *

Transcripts Show Senators Knew Gulf Of Tonkin Was A Staged False Flag Event

Senators hid details from Americans for fear of reprisals from power brokers that run the media and the presidency

International News; Friday, July 16th, 2010

More than 1,100 pages of previously classified Vietnam-era transcripts were released this week by the Senate Foreign Relations Committee. According to the transcripts, several Senators knew of the deception by the White House and Pentagon about the 1964 Gulf of Tonkin incident.

Thirty years would pass before the truth would emerge – that the Aug. 4, 1964 Gulf of Tonkin incident, whereby North Vietnamese PT boats allegedly attacked US warships, was a staged event that never took place. The Gulf of Tonkin 'non-incident' is widely acknowledged as the event that brought the US into the Vietnam conflict, resulting in the deaths of more than 50,000 Americans and many thousands of Vietnamese.

* * * * *

Basil stepped into The Manor, with Swenson carrying his suitcase behind him. He stopped and looked around; taking in the expansiveness and architecture of the foyer. He smiled. *God! I'm so glad to be back home,* he thought.

Just then, Lady Jessica came out to the foyer. "My dear Basil. How I've missed you!" She came up and gave Basil an arms-length hug. They kissed each other on the cheek.

"Mother," he replied. "I have so missed you. Are you doing well?"

"Yes," she cooed. "Life here has been grand!" She moved to touch her cheek to his. "I'd love if we could get together to-night," she whispered.

Basil slowly pulled his cheek from hers. He looked at her and smiled. "Sure," he whispered.

With Swenson dutifully behind, Basil began walking in the direction of his suite.

"Master Basil," Swenson offered, "your father wishes to see you at your earliest convenience."

"Thank you, Swenson," Basil replied with a smile. "It shall be my pleasure."

* * *

"Hello, Father," Basil said as he extended his hand.

"My son. I am so glad to see you." They shook hands.

"How have you been?"

"I am doing well, Basil," George smiled at his son. "Please, sit down. I was hoping we could discuss some, ah – arrangements."

Basil seated himself and began speaking. "Before we begin, I have a question."

George's eyebrows raised. "Yes?"

Basil's lips tightened. "Why did you not tell me that Lady Diana is my mother? Why did you lie to me all these years?"

George leaned back and looked across the desk at Basil. "Be-cause, my son, we did not want to hurt you."

"But, Father. You hurt me by not telling me."

"Well. I'm sorry Basil. I should have told you long ago." George paused and then continued "How did you find out?"

"I just knew," Basil replied. And then he continued. "But why have Diana as my mother? Isn't that incest? Isn't there increased risks for abnormalities and disease?"

"Well, yes. There is greater risk; although we have some technology to help with that."

"But with your cousin? Why, oh why?" Basil pleaded.

"Because," George paused. "Because, son. As you know, we have a very large empire. And to run our empire, and to foster loyalty within our empire, we place a higher value on blood relationships." George paused to let his words sink in. "The fact that Diana is your mother, means that we keep our lineage entirely within our family. And with no outsiders, there is far less chance of betrayal."

"But," Basil hesitated and then continued. "But, what does that mean for me?"

"Oh, that's very simple." George paused and then continued. "To foster your heir to the empire, you must mate with one of your cousins. Kathleen, I think, is probably your best choice."

"But I don't even like Kathleen."

"No matter. It's just for procreation. She'll understand; and she'll willingly do it. After all, it is in the best interests of the family and the empire."

"Do I have to marry her?"

"Certainly not. You may marry whomever you choose. You merely adopt your offspring from Kathleen – or whomever you choose to have your child with."

"You see," George continued with a smile, "you are heir to a very large empire. An empire that encompasses media, banking, energy, minerals, land..." George stood up and looked out the window. "Hell, Basil, we own all of the mainstream media and most of the world's governments." George paused. "We control the world through our ability to create money. With money, we buy influence, politicians, corporations, and control – all purchased through proxies, of course."

"Of course," Basil chimed in.

"So," George turned and looked at Basil. "Do you have any questions?"

"Yes, Father. Absolutely. I have so many questions I don't even know what they are!"

George smiled and nodded his understanding. "I know. I was once in the same place you are now." George paused. "I was quite overwhelmed."

"If we could, Father, I'd like to talk later."

"That's fine, Basil. Whenever you're ready."

Chapter 6 – Circa 1971

Seated at the head of the conference table, Lord George's face wore a broad smile. His eyes crinkled with joy as he engaged each man at the table. "Our plan worked!" He announced.

But it was an announcement that he need not have made; for all in attendance already knew. And most knew of its significance.

"Our timing was perfect," he continued. "The war, Johnson's great society, have given us what we want – we have again pushed the United States to the brink of bankruptcy." George paused to let his words sink in. "And as our reward, we have again given them only one way out – a way that gives us even more power, and a way by which we now will execute the next phase of our plan."

George smiled gleefully as he continued. "Thanks to Nixon, and of course Johnson for all he's done, the U.S. dollar is now completely decoupled from gold, silver, or any other commodity – we can now print money without restraint. Gentlemen," he came to his feet and raised his glass, "I offer a toast. A toast celebrating our magnificent achievement. And a toast to all that is yet to be! *le'chaim!*" And with his gesture, the other men too stood up and raised their glasses; and they drank in unison.

The men seated themselves; watching the head of the table.

James Van Der Worth raised his hand, catching the attention of the meeting. "Gentlemen. I offer a toast." He raised his glass. "A toast to celebrate the reclamation of our gold from the United States." He looked around the table. "It is now confirmed that all of our gold has been removed from Ft. Knox and is now safely stored in our vaults throughout Europe." James stood and held his glass high. "*le'chaim!*" And with that gesture, the other men too stood up and raised their glasses; and they drank in unison.

The men seated themselves; again watching the head of the table.

"Now, our next phase in the plan is two-fold. We shall create the new dollars we need to buy more influence around the world; and, we shall bring down the Soviet Union." George looked around the table. "With these two actions, gentlemen, it will set us up for the end game of the plan."

Basil was seated to the right of his father; and until now, he had been silent. Basil raised his hand. "How will the Soviet Union be brought down? Will it be by creating a nuclear war?"

George smiled. And around the table, everyone else was smiling.

"Well, Basil brings up a very good point – a point that we have discussed at length in the past." George paused and then continued. "Jacob," he said looking at Jacob Astor, "I know you have been a strong advocate for a global nuclear war. And you too, Sir Kutchner. And nuclear war certainly has merit. After all, it will help us to wipe away all of these excess people around the world; and it will allow us to impose a global order from day one."

The men at the table were watching, listening, intently.

"Unfortunately, it will also irradiate much of the northern hemisphere, and I think we all decided this was, ah – less than desirable. So, unless we can hear new objections to our plan," he paused, waiting for any objection to be offered, "we should continue on."

Basil again raised his hand. "Pardon me, sir. But how will the plan be executed?"

George smiled and began his answer. "By money, my dear Basil. After all, to control the creation of money is to control one-half of every transaction on the planet. No – power over the creation of money is sufficient to control the planet. And we now have control over the world's money!"

Part 2 – Tipping Point

Until now, the world we've known has been a world divided – a world of barbed wire and concrete block, conflict and cold war. Now, we can see a new world coming into view. A world in which there is the very real prospect of a **new world order.**

- - - George H.W. Bush – September 11, 1990, "Toward a New World Order" speech given to a joint session of the United States Congress after the fall of the USSR.

Interlude

IMAGINE A PLUSH ROOM. Appointed in gold and leather, and adorned with polished black walnut and deep, soft carpeting, and with a warm fire dancing in a massive stone fireplace, the fire creating flickering shadows across the walls. The location of this room is not important, nor is the structure in which the room exists, nor is the time of day. It is merely a room, a room filled with the finest imaginable of every comfort and convenience.

Further, imagine this room is occupied by five men, talking amongst themselves as they enjoy the comfort of a leather-upholstered chair, and a snifter of very old, very rare, brandy; and each enjoying the pleasure of a fine cigar of their choosing. All of them relaxed and at ease around the dancing fire.

Imagine these men talking, and joking, about world events. And imagine these men taking credit for their conduct of these events, and finding joy and celebration in these events, and finding joy and glee in the pain and suffering of others as they have watched these events unfold.

With this picture, touch your innermost feelings. Drive deep within yourself, and allow your inner self to feel the chill, *the cold,* emanating from these men. A frigid depth that belies the warm dancing flames.

The leader, a middle-aged man among middle-aged men – a wizened face of keen intellect, with blond hair and graying temples – is joyful and expansive in his celebration, as he draws on his cigar and exhales into the air. And then, his cold gray eyes seek out each of the men in turn. "Ah, gentlemen ... *gentlemen!*" He smiles broadly. "The collapse of the Soviet economy was stunning. My dear colleagues, this has been a fine, truly fine, piece of work."

Smiling, each man radiates a glow of satisfaction from the Leader's compliments.

The leader, Lord Basil, continued. "I propose a toast – *le'chaim* – to all of us."

"*Le'chaim*" the chorus replied in unison, as they lifted their glasses in salute, and then to their lips.

The men leaned back in their plush leather chairs; relaxed, each reveling in their great achievement. For the destruction of the Soviet economy, and of the Soviet hierarchy, was indeed a great achievement. *And it mattered not at all to these men that the object of their celebration, the collapse of the USSR, thrust tens-of-millions of people into abject poverty!*

"Now, gentlemen," The Lord resumed speaking in his deep, raspy voice, "it is time to move on to the final phase of our plan – undisputed control of the world. To this end, we shall review our master plan and develop ever-more detailed plans that will bring our strategic objectives to fruition."

Lord Basil then pushed a button on the intercom next to him. Speaking into it, he said, "Daniel, please come in."

"Right away, sir."

The door at the far end of the room opened. In walked a tall, dark, lanky man with graying temples. The man walked up to the circle, and nodded (*or did he slightly bow his head?*) at the gathering of men.

"Hello, gentlemen." Belying the man's lanky posture, the hard-set jaw seemed barely to move as it framed its greeting.

The seated men returned his nod, even as the Leader's eyes met Daniel's squinted gaze. "Thank you for coming in to talk with us, Daniel."

"My pleasure, sir." The tall lanky man nodded again.

"As I am sure you remember," the Leader continued, "we recently talked about the next objective in our strategic plan, as well as a broad approach toward our attainment of this objective. I asked you to drop by to talk about our plan and to begin its implementation. And too, I know that I speak for all of us when I say that we are all very interested in hearing your perspective."

"Of course, sir." The tall lanky man nodded.

The Leader waved his cigar in a flourish as he spoke. "Now, Daniel, in order that we achieve world domination, we must collapse the world economy into the dust heap of history. We must impoverish the world population; and of necessity, this impoverishment means the starvation and death of several billions of people. In doing this, our goal is that people suffer grievously, so that they beg for a one world government to save them. This – a one world government – we will be ready to provide."

The cigar smoke was wafting overhead as the Leader flourished his cigar still more. "Remember, Daniel, that suffering is the key. The more people suffer, and the more intense their suffering, the closer we are to our goal.

"Yes, sir." Daniel acknowledged.

With a flourish of his cigar and a studied condescension, he continued. "The first order of business is to deal with this pesky United States. They present a particular problem because they are so wealthy and free. But worse, their culture is based on freedom; this 'rugged individualism', if you will. We must tear it down."

The Leader drew from his cigar. "This will take time. Much time ..."

Chapter 1 - Circa 1992

Dwayne hit the enter key on his computer and leaned back in his seat; his clear blue eyes watching the printer as it spewed out a listing. He slowly reached both hands behind his head and clasped his hands together. Leaning his light brown locks into his hands, he watched the printer do its work.

Dwayne was seated in the back room of his store, busily retrieving listings on rare coin and precious metals market activity. The rare coin shop – located in a shopping mall on the west side of Omaha – was a dream come true; for since he was a youngster, he was fascinated with old rare coins and precious metals.

Dwayne rubbed his hand on his square jaw. *It sure would be nice to get these quotes up to the minute, rather than having to scrounge for updates twice a day,* he thought.

Dwayne heard the chimes at the shop entrance. He looked through the door out into the customer area, seeing a man who was just now walking through the entrance. Dwayne stood up and walked out to greet him. He sized the man up; about 5 foot 8 inches, youngish and slender, with straight hair falling over his eyes. The man seemed nervous.

"May I help you?"

"Hmmm ... not right this minute," the man said with a tentative smile. "I just came in to browse."

The man's eyes fixated on the display cases – stocked as they were with old and rare U.S. coins and stacks of gold and silver bullion coins and bars.

Dwayne moved over behind the nearest counter and began shuffling the U.S. proof sets. It was a pet peeve of his – he wanted the sets arranged to grab the most light possible, so that the brilliance of the coins reflected upwards to the glass top of the case. *I'm always interrupted when I go to move these,* he thought.

The man perused the display for a few minutes and then stopped at the section of silver dollars.

He looked up at Dwayne. "Excuse me. Can I see that coin?"

Dwayne moved over to the silver dollar display case. "What piece do you want to see?"

"That one, there." The man pointed into the case. "The coin with the white plastic square around it." The man was bent over the display looking intently at the coin.

Dwayne retrieved the coin from the display case and handed it to the man. The man had chosen a somewhat rare date – an 1892-S Morgan silver dollar.

The man's hands were shaking as he held the coin. He looked at the obverse of the coin; and then, glancing up nervously at Dwayne, he turned the coin over and examined the reverse.

"Do you want a magnifying glass?" Dwayne held out a magnifier.

"N-n-n-n – no thank you." Hands shaking, he handed the coin back to Dwayne muttering "that's a nice coin."

"Huh?" Dwayne held his hand up to his ear.

The man said louder, "That's a very nice looking coin."

Dwayne responded. "It's graded as 'extremely fine'. It has the plastic slab around it to show that it was professionally graded – so you can be certain of its condition."

"Can you look at this coin that I have?" The man withdrew a coin encased in a clear coin holder from his pocket. He handed it to Dwayne and said, "I'd like to sell it to you if the price is right."

Dwayne looked at the coin; turning it over to scan both sides.

"Yes, sir. This is also an 1892-S silver dollar. But just off hand, I'd say it's a counterfeit."

The man gasped and said, "Counterfeit! Are you sure?"

"Yes, sir. I'm sure."

The man peered at Dwayne shrewdly. "Are you saying this just so you can get a better deal?"

"No sir. It's a fake. And I'm not at all interested in owning it – at any price."

"So," the man looked at the coin as he talked, "what makes you so certain?"

"Well, sir, if you look at the coin's surface, it has a lot of small pock marks and the image is poorly defined. I'd say that the coin was cast from a form, rather than being struck the way coins were manufactured at the time."

"What do you mean by cast?"

"I mean that someone used a silver dollar coin and created a mold with it – then they would pour metal into the mold to make a copy. It's a rather old method of counterfeiting. And for a coin of this age and grade – the coin would grade as an average circulated specimen – it might just pass as authentic."

Dwayne paused and looked at the man intently. "Where did you get it?"

The man held his head down, allowing his face to sag. He heaved a sigh and then said, "I got it mail order. They advertised it as a great price for an 'extremely fine' specimen. So I thought I'd give it a try."

"I'm sorry sir," Dwayne replied, "but you've been had. How much did they charge you for it?"

"About $150," the man replied, his eyes looking down at the coin.

"Well, that's about right. They usually charge about $300 for a real one."

The man took the coin from Dwayne and put it back in his pocket.

"Can I help you with something else?" Dwayne asked.

The man hesitated, and then said, "Where can I find the spot price for gold and silver?"

Dwayne smiled, "You can find those in this national financial newspaper; or most of the newspapers' market quotations. Just look under commodities."

"Okay – well, thanks!" The man headed for the door.

"Uh, wait!" Dwayne exclaimed. "What's your name"?

"The man turned and smiled. "Frank. My name is Frank Meeks. And yours?"

"I'm Dwayne Jeffrey." He smiled as the man walked out. "I'm really sorry about that coin. But thanks for coming in; and please stop by again."

The chimes rang again as Frank walked out through the door.

* * * * *

With a wry smirk on his face, the news announcer's penetrating eyes and manufactured voice emanated from the TV. "And for more on this story, we go to Ted Rollins, our correspondent in Mexico."

Ted Rollins picked up the dialog without missing a beat: "Yes David. Today, President Clinton visited Mexico and signed NAFTA – the North American Free Trade Agreement. He was joined by President Bush, President Carter, and top congressional leaders of both parties. Vice President Gore and President Clinton spoke at the proceedings."

The apparently live broadcast then cut away to film.

> *VICE PRESIDENT GORE:* "*. . . The presence of three former presidents, two Republicans and one Democrat, to join President Clinton here today on this stage, is evidence of our country's ability to support what is in our nation's best interest over the long-term without respect to partisanship. . . .*"

And then, the film cut to still a different frame; a sound bite in the making:

> *PRESIDENT CLINTON:* "*. . . Today we turn to face the challenge of our own hemisphere, our own country, our own economic fortunes. In a few moments, I will sign three agreements that will complete our negotiations with Mexico and Canada to create a North American Free Trade Agreement. In the coming months I will submit this package to Congress for approval. It will be a hard fight, and I expect to be there with all of you every step of the way. . . .*" *(followed by applause)*

> "*. . . I believe that NAFTA will create 200,000 American jobs in the first two years of its effect. I believe if you look at the trends – and President Bush and I were talking about it this morning – starting about the time he was elected President, over one-third of our economic*

growth, and in some years over one-half of our net new jobs came directly from exports. And on average, those export-related jobs paid much higher than jobs that had no connection to exports."

"I believe that NAFTA will create a million jobs in the first five years of its impact. And I believe that that is many more jobs than will be lost, as inevitably some will be as always happens when you open up the mix to a new range of competition."

"NAFTA will generate these jobs by fostering an export boom to Mexico; by tearing down tariff walls which have been lowered quite a bit by the present administration of President Salinas, but are still higher than Americans. . . ."

Then, Ted Rollins' confidently smiling face returned to the screen. "Of course, this entourage of Presidents and Vice Presidents made no mention of the polls that show a majority of Americans against NAFTA. Nor did they mention Ross Perot's insurgent bid for the Presidency that would have killed this treaty."

"So there you have it. This is Ted Rollins from Mexico. Back to you, David"

The newscaster took the cue. "And for our next story ..."

* * *

... the TV voices droned on in the background.

Patricia Jeffrey removed her glasses and looked across the table at her husband. "Does this mean what I think it means? Is this what you've been telling me about?"

"Yes," Dwayne replied as he turned and stared out the window. "The NAFTA they're pushing has a commission that would set the rules for trade in North America – if you don't follow the rules, you don't get to trade. Real free trade, on the other hand, would have no rules at all."

He turned and looked at her. "No," he spat. "This commission means there's a political agenda. And that means there'll be benefits for the rich and powerful at the expense of the common man." He paused with a sigh. "So, I think that the 'agenda' will bring the American people great harm."

"How? Why do you think that?"

"Because it will send jobs to countries' whose cost of labor is lower. And it will cause investment capital to move out of the U.S. as well."

Trish leaned back and folded her arms. Shaking her head, she said, "Don't you think you're being just a bit paranoid?"

Dwayne looked at her and smiled. "I don't think so, Trish. Just look at all that's been going on.

"Like what?"

"Like George Bush's announcement of his 'new world order' right after the fall of the USSR." Dwayne's gaze was steady.

"So what?"

"So, he was the President at the time he said it. And frankly, I take him at his word." Dwayne was becoming exasperated as he continued. "You may not see it, but I see this as the beginning of the decline of our country. It won't happen all at once; nor will it happen quickly. But this is a clear move to begin merging the United States into a world order and making the U.S. subservient to world powers."

Trish frowned. "But if you're correct, what can we – what should we do about it?"

Dwayne turned and looked at Trish, the mother of his children and the most beautiful woman the world has ever known. "Well, we first need to take care of ourselves and our family."

"And then?"

Dwayne heaved a sigh, and then said, "Damn it, we need to fight."

Dwayne's face became flushed. "And by fight, I don't mean that we pick up guns and start shooting people. I mean that we look for ways to subvert these rascals – these – these P*owers That Be*. To me, the best way to fight these bastards is to go back to our Constitution; to use the rule of law to oust these vermin from our government."

Big man that he was, Dwayne was exuding passion now. "We must educate people. We must bring knowledge to people. The truth! For the truth be told, these vermin are stealing our wealth from us, and they are stealing the best and brightest of our children. They are driving us deeper and deeper into debt through their endless inflation. And they have driven us to mortgage the future of our children and our grandchildren."

Trish's pleading eyes looked deep into Dwayne's. "But are you sure? Are you really sure there's someone behind this?"

Dwayne sighed. And then he said, "I don't know."

Chapter 2 - Circa 1994

I am just saying that we need to be honest about the fact that we are transferring from the United States at a practical level significant authority to a new organization. This is a transformational moment. I would feel better if the people who favor this would just be honest about the scale of change.

I agree .. this is very close to Maastrict [the European Union treaty by which the EU member nations have surrendered considerable sovereignty], and twenty years from now we will look back on this as a very important defining moment. This is not just another trade agreement. This is adopting something which twice, once in the 1940s and once in the 1950s, the U.S. Congress rejected. I am not even saying we should reject it; I, in fact, lean toward it. But I think we have to be very careful, because it is a very big transfer of power.

— Newt Gingrich, House Ways and Means Committee hearings during June 1994. He later became Speaker of the House of Representatives.

* * * * *

Mark Shannon and George Redding were best of friends. As roommates, they could count on each other for a good time – and at least one of them was always in the mood for that! As were their friends, who looked forward to their frequently raucous parties.

But this was Monday evening. It was not a typical party night – at least, not for them. And yet the party was going great guns. The crowd noise was deafening as the booze flowed freely, and smoke filled the air. But through all the noise – the music blasting, the voices yelling, and whatever other grotesque sounds might be heard – fragments of conversation nonetheless intruded into Mark's subconscious.

> *"Hey, Buzz! How're you doing?"*
> *". . . I LOVE you, Dolly! I LOVE YOU!"*
> *". . .Oh shit! You bastard . . ."*
> *". . . so I says to this guy . . . "*

In short, the party was typical of that thrown by a 20-something year-old (aspiring) man.

His drink teetering in his hand, Mark was oblivious to the noise even as he weaved and wound his way through the smoke and the crowd. But then he stumbled over someone's foot. Regaining his balance, he looked up to see the owner of the foot – a hot young babe oozing hormones from her tight, pert body. Mark had never met her. Short, blond, and talking incoherently with a young guy, she paused and turned, peering at Mark through her bloodshot eyes. "I'm so sorry," the slurring words rolled off her full lips. Mark did not know what to say, so he just smiled and moved on.

Although somewhat intoxicated, Mark kept his eye peeled on the entrance door. Previous experience taught him to be wary of someone busting in to crash the party. A crasher could be some kids cruising around; or it might be the police. Mark spied a guy near the entrance. The guy was gesturing to him, and mouthing, *come here!*

Mark weaved and wobbled his way through the crowd, the smoke, and the noise. Reaching the door, the guy shouted into his ear, "The police are outside. They want to talk with you."

Mark nodded his head and grimaced. "Shit!"

Mark's brain fog slowed his thoughts to a crawl. Thinking ... thinking ... He finally realized, *I just don't know if there's marijuana in here. I better go outside and talk with them, 'cause it's too risky to let 'em in.* "Hookay," he said to the young guy. He opened the door and stepped outside.

"Good evening, officers," Mark slurred. "How may I help you?"

The lead officer had a stern look on his face. "Is this your apartment?"

"Yes, sir."

"What's your name?"

"Mark. Mark Shannon."

"Shannon ... Shannon ... Hey – I've heard of you! You've been a real troublemaker around here," the cop sneered.

Mark tried to keep his expression neutral; but he secretly smiled at his notoriety.

"What's that smoke in there?"

Mark assumed a look of pure innocence. "Smoke? Ah, well officer, I'm sure it's just cigarettes. After all, there's no law against smoking cigarettes, is there?" *I think he's suspicious. I bet they'll try to get in.*

"Hmmm." The officer continued. "We received a call from one of your neighbors."

"Which one?"

The cop's eyes became hard. "Never mind which one, Mr. Shannon. The bottom line is this: you need to quiet this crowd down."

Despite his intoxication, Mark nodded his agreement. He had been down this road before. "Yes sir. O-o-okay officer. I will take care of it right away."

"And one more thing," the cop continued. "If we get a callback on this, you'll be going to jail for disturbing the peace."

"Yes sir, officer."

The police officers turned and left, and Mark re-entered his apartment.

Mark knew that he'd be screwed if they came back. He chuckled under his breath, thinking, *if nothing else, the marijuana in here could get me in a lot of trouble!*

He walked over to the stereo and turned down the volume – this caused a few partiers to look over in his direction. Mark then let out a loud, shrill whistle and yelled for attention. "Hey everybody! Listen up!"

Most turned and looked at Mark, although a few voices continued talking.

Mark yelled again while waving his arms. "Listen up! Hey – you! Listen up!"

Mark waited a moment for the crowd's attention. And then he said in a loud voice, "The cops were just here. They've threatened me with jail if they have to come back."

Hearing this, some people in the crowd let out catcalls and boos.

Mark continued yelling. "Keep it down, damn it! Keep it down. The music will be off for the rest of the night!"

The crowd began murmuring and milling around amongst themselves.

Mark was watching the crowd even as George stumbled up to him. George was wobbling back and forth, seemingly ready to keel over.

"Hey, buddy. Good job, man!"

Mark felt tipsy; but nowhere near George's condition. "Shouldn't you go lay down?"

George wobbled some more; leaning forward and then jerking himself almost upright. "Yep," George slurred.

Mark wrapped his arm around George and guided him into his bedroom. He sat George on the edge of the bed and took George's drink. Mark walked over to the dresser and placed the drink on top of it. He turned back toward the bed to find George slumped over on the bed – he was snoring. Mark helped him into the bed and made sure he was facing down, just in case he puked.

His legs still unsteady, Mark wobbled back into the living room and watched as the crowd filed out the door. It was Monday night and many people needed to go to work in the morning.

Mark was swaying to the left when he felt something wet in his ear. He turned to find a blond withdrawing her tongue – and this time, he wasn't tripping over her foot.

"Hey stud," she whispered into his ear. "I don't think I can make it home." She ran her hand along his chest as she looked at him. "Do you have a place I can stay?"

Intensely sexual feelings washed through Mark as he pulled her close. Their tongues found each other in a deep throaty kiss, and the two became engulfed in lust.

They ended their kiss. Mark looked into her eyes, seeing a smoldering lusty desire. "Yeah," Mark's voice was hoarse – deep. "I think I can find a place. Just follow me."

Mark put his arm around her and they weaved and wobbled off together into Mark's bedroom.

* * * * *

With a splitting headache and red, watery eyes, Mark Shannon stumbled along an open aisle in the parking lot adjacent to a line of parked cars. He continued his wobbly path south across the street, and finally into the Hart Senate Office Building. Mark was still dizzy from last night's party – his partying didn't cease until the early morning hours. *Let's see – what was her name? Oh – right. Laura! I need to give her a call today.*

Mark walked down the hallway toward Senator Leech's office suite. As the junior Senator from California, Mark was recently hired as a junior legislative aide. But because he had worked on the Senator's campaign, they were more than just acquaintances. He had a lot of respect for the Senator, and even more respect for the Senator's views: universal health care, environmental activism, gun control, and help for the less fortunate, to name just a few.

Mark had watched the Senator fight his way through the campaign – a bruising campaign that had left the Senator damaged and licking his wounds. His opponent – a republican executive of a large technology company – dragged the Senator's family through the nasty muck of political brinkmanship. Slinging mud, insults, and innuendo all have a way of stripping a man's dignity, and the Senator's dignity was left behind in a trail of crumbs.

This morning, Mark's head was spinning without focus as he stumbled into Senator Leech's office suite. The Senator's Chief of Staff, Stacy Klinger, happened to be talking with the receptionist, but he looked up just in time to see Mark trip on his own feet. Stacy snorted and glared. "It's about time you made it in. Where've you been?"

Mark looked away as he smiled his secret smile; and then he took on a look of childish innocence as he turned back to the Chief of Staff.

"Aw c'mon, Stacy. The buses were running late."

Stacy grunted and looked him in the eye. "Bullshit! You don't take the bus, do you?"

Mark remained silent.

"The Senator wants you to go with Maggie to a committee hearing this morning." Stacy looked at his watch. "It starts in ten minutes."

"Where is it?"

"It's in the Russell Office Building – second floor."

"What's the name of the committee?"

"I can't remember. Ah – the Commerce Committee. The Chairman is Fritz Hollings. They're talking about GATT – the General Agreement on Tariffs and Trade – or some such nonsense. It's all Greek to me, kid!"

Maggie Marsden was the lead legislative aide on economic issues. Mark didn't know her all that well; but what he knew of her, he liked. She had been on the Senator's staff when he was a Congressman, and the Senator brought her along when he won election to the Senate. She was older than Mark by about 10 years, and was somewhat aloof toward him – sometimes looking down on him with disapproval.

Mark glanced into Maggie's office and looked back at Stacy. "Where is she?"

"She's already left. You better get going kid – and make sure you take good notes!"

Mark ran out of the office and sprinted over to the Russell building. Panting, he arrived just before the hearing was called to order. Standing in the entrance, he scanned the chamber looking for Maggie. There were several of these conference rooms in the building – large, expansive, and usually paneled in birch or some other hardwood. He could see the committee members seated at a long desk on one side of the room. The remainder of the room was populated with audience seating and front-row seating for witnesses' testimony.

Mark spied Maggie seated in the audience, and made his way over to her.

Maggie glanced at him as he sat down. Pursing her lips, she said, "Tough night?"

Mark's face turned red. "Yeah. It was damn hell." Then he smiled. "Actually, I had trouble with the bus this morning."

Maggie looked dubious. "I thought you drove in?"

"Oh, ah – not today," he lied.

"Well, just be sure you take good notes. They're going to be talking about the World Trade Organization. I'm gonna take notes too, but I'm especially interested in your impression of the witnesses."

"I'll be on top of it," Mark promised.

Just then, Senator Fritz Hollings called the hearing to order.

Mark suffered through the preliminary discussions. Beginning with introductory remarks, the discussion soon moved on to a couple of economists who were questioned on comparative advantage. Mark was somewhat schooled in economics, so he understood the notion of comparative advantage – that some countries could produce certain goods more efficiently than others – and therefore, each country would benefit by trading with the other. He listened, but found no reason to take notes on this portion of the hearing.

The witnesses droned on and on. The voices were low-pitched and muffled; and Mark was drifting off as he heard the name 'Sir James Goldsmith'. Mark's head jerked and he smirked from under his eyelids. *He was back in a long lost time, where King Arthur and his Knights were doing battle against the Saxons. Riding on top of his armored mount and decked out in his chain-mail armor, he held his sword high above his head.*

Then his head jerked up again. *What the hell is English royalty doing here?* He thought.

The testimony was hypnotic; and Mark became ever more drowsy as the discussion wore on. But in between his 'adventures', he picked out snippets of the discussion.

... Global free trade will force the poor of the rich countries to subsidize the rich in poor countries. What GATT means is that our national wealth, accumulated over centuries, will be transferred from a developed country like Britain to developing countries like Communist China, now building its first oceangoing navy in 500 years. China, with its 1.2 billion people, three Indochinese states with 900 million, the former Soviet republics with some 300 million, and many more can supply skilled labor for a fraction of Western costs. Five dollars in Communist China is the equivalent of a $100 wage in Europe.

Mark jerked his head up as Maggie nudged him. "Mark!" She whispered. "Take notes! I can't remember all of this!"

"K," he mumbled. Mark began taking notes but again succumbed to the incessant droning. He again nodded off ...

It is quite amazing that GATT is sowing the seeds for global social upheaval and that it is not even the subject of debate in America. If the masses understood the truth about GATT, there would be blood in the streets of many capitals. A healthy national economy has to produce a large part of its own needs. It cannot simply import what it needs and use its labor force to provide services for other countries. We have to rethink from top to bottom why we have elevated global free trade to the status of sacred cow, or moral dogma. It is a fatally flawed concept that will impoverish and destabilize the industrialized world while cruelly ravaging the Third World.

.
.
.

And this is the big point, Mr. Chairman. **What we are witnessing is the divorce of the interests of the major corporations and the interests of society as a whole.** It used to be said that what was good for General Motors–and we all believed it, probably was true– was good for the United States. That is no longer true. The trans-national corporations, Mr. Chairman, I've just brought some figures that came out recently, they now have 4.8 trillion dollars per annum in sales; they account for one-third of global output; the largest one-hundred account for one-third of all foreign direct investment. Now where do you think the bulk of that investment is going? It's going where it earns the most; there's no other way it can go. What chief executive can invest otherwise, Mr. Chairman?

So, if as you've heard today, you have freedom of movement of capital, freedom of movement of technology, and you can employ people for forty or fifty times cheaper who are skilled, and you can import their products back anywhere in the world–that's the basis of global free trade–**how can those investments, how can these trans-national companies who have 4.8 trillion dollars of sales invest anywhere other than where it's cheapest and where their return is greatest?** Because if they don't, the system that you and your

colleagues would be voting for, if you pass it, forces
them to do it; otherwise they go bankrupt.

Again, Maggie nudged him.   But this time no words were
spoken - only a stern glare.

* * *

The committee hearing over, Maggie and Mark walked back
to the Senator's office.

"Mark."   Maggie stopped and looked directly into Mark's
eyes.   "If you can't stay awake and do your damn job, I'll make
sure you're run out of here - I'll get someone who can do the
work. Do I make myself clear?"

"Ah, yes. Yes, Maggie. I'm - I'm sorry. Really, I'm sorry. I
didn't get to bed until late. I had an emergency."

Maggie was quiet as they continued walking.

Mark's defensiveness passed and he became curious. "Do you
know how the Senator will vote on this trade deal?"

Maggie looked at Mark and smiled.   "Well, I'm really not
supposed to say.   But the fact is that this global trade deal is a
terrible deal for America - it's especially bad for blue collar
workers, technology workers, and unions.   And as Sir James as-
serted, it will expand the ranks of the poor in countries such as
the U.S. Because of this, I think the Senator will vote against it."

* * *

It was 2:00 pm; and Mark was seated in the conference room
when Stacy, Maggie, and Senator Leech walked in. Mark watched
as the three pulled up chairs around the table.

Senator Leech opened up the discussion. "Well, what did you
find out at the hearing?"

"Well," Maggie began, "I can tell you that Sir James Goldsmith doesn't like it.   He argues - and I must say he provides
compelling arguments - that GATT and the WTO will bring
about the downfall of the United States, and of western civiliza-

tion. He also argues that it will wreak havoc on the third world, causing lasting food shortages, starvation, and wholesale revolution."

"Wow!" Senator Leech looked over at Mark. "What do you think?"

"Well, sir. I think that Sir Goldsmith is highly credible. I could find no fault in his arguments."

"Hmmm," Senator Leech paused. "How about the other witnesses? The economists?"

"Well, sir," Maggie answered, "they talked a lot about comparative advantage. They all believe that free trade would be best for our country and that the U.S. would benefit. There was one economist that said we could see benefits as high as $300 billion over the first ten years."

"$300 billion?" the Senator's face took on a quizzical expression. "That's peanuts!"

"Yes, sir," Maggie replied.

"Did anyone ask these 'economists' if they thought the plan actually proposed 'free trade'?"

"No sir," Maggie shifted her posture, I don't think that question was asked."

"I'm phrasing my question like this for a reason," the Senator continued. "I looked at the plan for this trade deal. This is not 'free trade'; this is 'managed trade'. The plan says trade will be managed according to some damn international committee, and it looks like the U.S. will lose its sovereignty over international trade."

"Yes, sir," Maggie agreed.

The conversation paused.

"I also talked with a finance guy that I trust. He looked at it and said it would alter the worldwide flow of capital. He said there would be a loss of capital in western countries – especially the U.S. – and it would cause a tremendous loss of jobs."

"That's my assessment, too," Maggie agreed.

The Senator ran his hand through his dark brown hair. "Shit," he spat. "I think Goldsmith is right. This is a bad deal for us."

The Senator looked at Maggie. "What do you think? Do you think this will benefit us?"

"No sir," she replied. "Honestly, I think this deal sucks. I think this will kill the United States. Not today, and not tomorrow. But ten or fifteen years from now, the U.S. would be a very different country."

* * *

Mark was working on his post-meeting notes when he looked up and spied someone walking by his door – it was the receptionist accompanied by a lanky, tall man with dark features. He could hear voices on the other side of the wall. "Senator, this is your 3:00 pm – Mr. Daniel Elsbach."

Mark heard a greeting from the Senator. Then, he heard a thud as the Senator's office door closed. He watched the receptionist as she walked past his door.

Later on, when the time to vote arrived, Mark and Maggie were surprised – very surprised – that Senator Shaun Leech *voted in favor of the deal.*

* * * * *

The TV newscaster droned on ...

"Today, the World Trade Organization has been created. This new World Trade Organization is derived from the former GATT – the General Agreement on Tariffs and Trade. The WTO is created to facilitate free trade around the globe."

"This is a direct result of President Clinton's ambitious initiative. As you may remember, President Clinton convened a special session of Congress to push through the free trade agenda."

"But as our Washington correspondent, Brett Skow reports, not everyone is happy with this."

With this, the camera switched to a live scene inside a marble palace – somewhere in Washington D.C.

"I have Congressman Fuller from Ohio here; and he has serious concerns about the WTO and our participation. . . . Congressman? . . ."

"This agreement purports to advance free trade; but it is actually a major threat to free trade. To implement the WTO means that we implement a world-wide bureaucracy that will manage international trade for their own purposes. This is absolutely opposite the notion of free trade. This form of managed trade is meant to enrich the corporate interests and the interests of government, at the expense of our working class. Mark my words ... this agreement will promote the fall of the U.S. economy and the fall of the middle class in this country ..."

The correspondent pulled the microphone away from the Congressman and continued, "and that's the word here in Washington. Back to you, Chet."

Chapter 3 – Circa 1992

Joshua closed up his office and locked the door. He glanced at his wristwatch. *It's time to call it a day*, he thought. *I've just enough time to make the meeting.*

Joshua thought back to last night's telephone call. It was a cryptic message – one that he would usually chalk up as a crank. *But I've got a feeling about this one*, he mused. *I think it will bear fruit!* And since he was weary of his present arbitrage job, he decided it couldn't hurt to listen to this guy. *What was his name? Daniel who?*

Joshua walked the corridor until he came to the elevator that quickly brought him down to the lobby. He sauntered through the lobby, nodded to the security guard, and stepped outside. He took a deep breath and coughed. *Bloody awful this London air is!*

As he walked along the sidewalk, Joshua Lindt became aware of just how upset he felt. *Bloody 'ell,* he mused. *This has been a bloody tough day!*

He thought back to his wife's afternoon telephone call ...

> *Linda's voice was more shrill than usual.* "*Joshua, I've gone ahead and filed for divorce.*"
>
> "*But Linda, I thought we were going to talk about this first?*"
>
> "*Talk!*" *She shouted.* "*I've talked 'til I'm blue in the face. I want a nicer home. Bob James' wife has a much nicer Mercedes than I do – how can I ever look her in the eye? No, you asshole, you just don't provide what I need – and I've had it!*"
>
> "*I'll be home at about 7 o'clock – we can talk then,*" *he replied.*
>
> "*Go to hell, you moron! For months I've been neglected. You treat me like I don't even exist! Hell – you haven't given me a decent gift in months ...*" *her voice trailed off.* "*Wait! Are you screwing someone else? ... I know you are – I just know it! I'm tired of this crap; and I've had enough! My lawyer will contact you!*"
>
> *Click!*

He still had mixed feelings about the phone call. He was happy that she would soon be leaving, but sad that he would now have to fight to keep his property – to keep what he had earned. He was not looking forward to the court battle. In these matters, the English courts were partial to the woman; especially when the man was a high-income earner like himself. And the

English government did not like white men who earned a lot of money. After all, they were usually the exploiters of the poor and downtrodden. And they would see Linda as a victim – a poor, downtrodden victim.

It's a good thing I stuffed some of my more liquid assets in a safe place, he reflected.

* * *

Joshua pulled on the heavy ornate door handle, feeling the finely-balanced door begin to swing toward him. But then the door opened quickly just as a couple brushed past him on their way out. "Sorry, mate," said the man. Joshua stepped back and stared the man down, even as he straightened his suit coat – a coat he had purchased from *Tarpleys of London*. Once more, Joshua stepped into the pub, pausing just inside the door to take in the layout of *The MoonDancer* – a popular (at least, popular in the financial district) London City pub.

The room – a large space with a low-hung ceiling of open beams – was perhaps half full. Through the light fog of cigarette smoke, he could see patrons dispersed throughout the dimly lit space; some standing at the bar, some seated at tables, some milling around. All of them were doing what they do – talking, sipping, smoking, bantering, flirting – or whatever. Off near the back of the room, a piano played a melancholy piece that drifted through the sultry atmosphere.

There was nothing unique about this pub. It was like a hundred others he visited before. In fact, the people looked the same. *Was it possibly the same people he had seen at those other pubs?* Quite a few of the patrons were winding down from a typically tough day of work in London's financial district. Some were brokers; and some were investment bankers, arbitragers, or traders. But whatever else, they all had one thing in common – money. They lived money, they breathed money, they smelled the fragrance of money, they would even sell their soul for money. *Blimey,* Josh reflected, *maybe they did!*

Josh looked down the bar and spied a man seated at the end; a man seated alone, holding a half-full glass in front of his eyes, and gazing past it as though it didn't exist. Joshua walked the length of the bar. As Joshua drew closer, the lonely man turned and looked at him.

"Daniel?" Joshua asked.

The man's mouth formed a tight, barely noticeable smile. "Yes, I am. And you must be Joshua."

All at once, Josh took in Daniel's 'too correct' features – his steel gray eyes and a seemingly tanned complexion, with dark hair and a touch of gray at the temples.

"Let's find a table," said Daniel, eyeing a sparsely populated corner of the pub. Joshua followed Daniel to an empty table where they seated themselves.

Daniel turned to Josh, "my name is Daniel – Daniel Elsbach. I represent –"

Just then, a perky young waitress came up to their table. "Good evening, gentlemen. May I take your order?"

Daniel waved his half-full glass; even as Joshua gazed up at the waitress. "Vodka on the rocks."

The waitress' smile grew even larger. "Certainly, sir. I shall add this to the bartender's queue, and bring it shortly."

She moved off, blending into the backdrop of clinking ice, the din of voices, and the sultry, smoky room. Ignoring all of this, Josh focused his attention on the man before him. "What do you want?"

Daniel smiled and looked down at his glass. "Mr. Lindt ... ah, Josh. I represent a group who is interested in engaging your services – your services as a master of commodities trading; and your services as a financial department manager."

Joshua's eyebrows raised up. "Oh?"

"Yes. At AB Jorday investment bank, we are opening a commodities trading department that will focus specifically on the gold and silver trade. We are looking for that spark of brilliance – that crème d la crème – to make it go."

Joshua frowned. "Well, I can certainly make it successful, but there are lots of people who can trade commodities. So why choose me? Especially since precious metals' trading is boring – there's nothing to it."

Daniel smiled as he ran his fingers along the side of his glass. This is different, Joshua. Very different –"

Just then, the waitress returned with Joshua's vodka and placed it in front of him.

Joshua was holding out a 5-pound note. "Keep the change."

The waitress beamed at the nice tip and headed off to the next table.

Josh turned his attention back to Daniel. "How different?"

Daniel smiled into his glass and continued. "We want you to work the commodities markets so as to, ah – let's say, 'manage' the price of gold and silver."

"Manage? What do you mean by 'manage'?"

"Let me be clear, Josh. We want you to drive down the price of silver and gold, and keep the prices as low as possible."

Josh's eyes widened. "You're asking me to manipulate the market? People go to jail for things like that!"

"Shhhh!" Daniel whispered. "This must be kept quiet!"

Josh looked down at his glass. He barely noticed the floating ice as he took a swig. "Why are you bringing this to me? If I were to sign up for this, it would be a conspiracy." He looked into Daniel's eyes and said, "Frankly, I don't need any trouble!"

Josh got up to leave when Daniel grabbed his arm. "Wait. Wait! Sit down. Let's talk – I can make this worth your while."

Josh stared into Daniel's eyes. "Let go of my arm."

Daniel released his hold. "Will you let me explain?"

Josh slowly re-seated himself. "Bullshit. I don't know you from Adam. Why should I believe anything you have to say?"

Daniel held up two fingers, almost in the shape of a peace sign. "Two reasons. First, I know that you presently work for Marcia Simpson at Lehman and that you know Marcia well – ask her about me. Second, the salary for this job is substantial. At a minimum, a low eight-figure number."

At this, Josh whistled.

"But there is a stipulation," Daniel continued. "We must be certain that we can trust you."

With his friendly smile, Daniel was as smooth as though he were selling free heat to an Eskimo "So, how much must we pay to secure your trust?"

"You talk to me about breaking the law; and then you want *my trust?*"

"This is really a two-way street," Daniel said. "You need to be able to trust us; and we need to be able to trust you."

"We? *Who* is 'we'?"

* * *

A few days later . . .

The *MoonDancer* was a busy place tonight. But Joshua had found a table out of the mainstream. There, he waited for Daniel while sipping on his wine.

Joshua reflected on what he knew, and what he didn't know. And he realized, shaking his head, that there was much he did not know – about Daniel, about the people behind him. Nor, did he know what knowledge they had about him.

Joshua couldn't know how carefully Daniel investigated his prospects – especially those who were to play an important role in Daniel's plan. Nor could Joshua know that he had been investigated more thoroughly than most.

In fact, Joshua did not know anything about Daniel's dossier on him – that Josh was accustomed to living high, as was his wife and his mistress, and that Josh was not making it on his six-figure salary, and that his wife and mistress were each demanding ever-more.

No. Joshua had no knowledge of any of this.

Joshua continued to reflect on Daniel's offer. Eight figures was huge – he would have no trouble supporting his lifestyle with that much money! *Blimey! It's only illegal if you get caught!*

Just then, Joshua was distracted by a young woman who stumbled by his table. She had the face of a model. And her body – oh, wow! Josh enjoyed the way she moved, feeling more than just a twitch down in his loins.

"I hope you haven't been waiting long." Joshua looked up to find Daniel sitting down next to him.

"She's something, isn't she!" Daniel couldn't keep his eyes off of her either. "I see her here once in a while. I think she works at the Bank of England, as a banking analyst. Whew – she can analyze me anytime!"

Both men were now very much at ease.

"So Daniel," Josh opened. "I am very interested in your proposal. Please tell me more."

Smiling, Daniel began talking more details.

* * *

Two months later . . .

Joshua was digging through his plans for the new commodity trading operation, when out of the corner of his eye he glimpsed a shadow in his office doorway.

He looked up to find a young shapely woman standing at the entrance.

"I'm Stephanie Walker," she said, reaching her hand out. "I'm guessing that you're Josh. And if my guess is correct, then I'm your new assistant." She smiled and looked at Josh through her clear blue eyes – eyes slightly obscured by her straight blond hair.

"Ah – oh. I'm a – Josh. Yeah, ah – Josh Lindt." Josh reached out and shook her hand. He looked at her with a quizzical expression, and asked, "How did you get here? Ah – I mean – who hired you?"

"Oh, Daniel asked me to stop by. He didn't tell you?"

"Ah, no. He didn't mention you. Come to think of it, I don't ever see Daniel."

"Well," Stephanie was almost bouncing with energy, "Daniel asked me to sign on as your assistant. With your permission, of course."

"Hmmm ... Well – okay. Will you please sit down? I'd like to talk for a moment."

Stephanie's smile was wider still as she took a seat.

By the end of the interview, Josh had made up his mind. Tall, blond, lanky, well-proportioned, and with an incredible smile, Josh immediately liked her. More importantly, he found her to be articulate, smart, vivacious, and engaging – she was the perfect assistant and hostess, and a great spokeswoman for a man in his position.

Daniel could not have made a better choice.

* * *

Joshua stepped off the elevator and strode along the hallway toward the now familiar suite of offices – a suite easily viewed on the other side of a large glass-paneled wall. On the glass next to the door, the legend *'AB Jorday Precious Metals'* was inscribed. *Blimey! What a difference a couple of months make*, he reflected.

Stepping into the suite he was assaulted by the din of printers, computers, and people talking over each other. It was like entering a beehive of industry.

> *"... hey, Dave."*
> *"Hey what?"*
> *"Did you submit that order Friday afternoon?"*
> *"Ha, ha, ha ..."*
> *"What?"*
> *"Hell – ohhhhh! I've been working on this for a week!"*
> *"How about we offer twenty million?"*

As Josh strode purposely through the atrium, he was as oblivious to the surrounding conversations as he was to his physical surroundings. He didn't see the Tudor woodwork, nor did he notice the fine English artwork lining the walls. And neither did he notice as his black wingtip shoes sank into the fine-weave plush carpet. No – as he was walking, all of his attention became focused on Stephanie as she hurriedly ran across his path.

She looked up at him and her eyes lit up. "Hi, Josh."

"Hi, Steph!" *Blimey! She's so sexy!*

"How's it going?"

"Great!"

Josh continued down the hall, hearing a giggle from Natalie's office as he passed her door. He glanced in, noticing that Mike was there trying yet again to make time with her. Josh smiled and continued apace.

Sunshine was streaming through the windows when Josh walked into his corner office. The office was large and expansive, yet felt even larger because of the two walls of windows framing an imposing view of London's financial district. Taking off his coat, he hung it on a rack next to the sofa. Too excited for anything else, he pulled up the market information on his computer display and began going through the early morning reports. As usual, Josh found a wealth of 'interesting' information. But he was particularly interested in the reports coming out of last night's Asian commodities and currencies market activities. He was watching the dollar; and it was showing a bit of weakness. He was concerned that the weakness of the dollar might prompt an increase in the price of gold. *If this happens,* he thought, *we will need to sell still more gold into the market.*

Josh knew that selling more gold meant there would be a greater supply in the market – and a greater supply meant a lower price, with a correspondingly higher price for the dollar. In fact, he knew it so well he didn't give it another thought.

Josh continued to page through the report. And he finally found what he was looking for – it was not good. The dollar showed a clear drop in value on the international indices with a comparable rise in the price of gold. Worse, the gold price did not just rise in dollar terms – it also rose against several other paper currencies.

Josh leaned back in his chair, reflecting back on Daniel's guiding words.

"Our objective, Josh, is to strengthen the value of the dollar. And one of the primary ways we do this is to keep the price of gold low. Keeping the gold price low influences the psychology of the investing public – they

will think that the low price of gold warrants a high valuation of the dollar. Of course, this also keeps the price of government bonds higher."

Josh glanced at his wristwatch, noting that it was now five minutes until his staff meeting.

* * *

His staff – Dave, Mike, Stephanie, Natalie, and Chet – filed into his office; each finding a seat on the sofa or an upholstered easy chair.

Natalie's red hair and green eyes lit up as she talked and joked with Mike. Young and impetuous, Dave looked eagerly at Josh. "Alright, Mate?"

"Yeah," Mike chimed in, "what's goin' on?"

Joshua ran his hand through his hair, shifting his posture and stroking his chin in thought. *Where should I begin?*

"Okay, team. Today marks the day that we begin to fulfill our charter in earnest."

Everyone listened attentively as Josh continued. "Natalie, you're tasked with analysis. Right now, the price of gold seems to be hitting near $400 per ounce. I want to know how much gold must be sold into the market to drop the price to $350 per ounce. And Natalie, we will need that number quickly."

Natalie nodded her assent.

"Mike, I want you to give a heads-up to the central banks to see how much gold we can lease from them. Of course, go through our bullion bank[2]."

"Okay," said Mike.

---

[2]   A Bullion Bank is an investment bank that functions as a wholesale supplier dealing in large quantities of gold. All bullion banks are members of the London Bullion Market Association (LBMA).

"Dave, I want you to stand ready to sell the leased gold into the market. And if necessary, we will also expand our naked short[3] positions; so plan for that as well."

"Chet, Stephanie. We will need you to step up and expedite all of the forms and paperwork while you coordinate with the other departments."

"Finally, doing this will help us create a process that we can replicate in the future, as need be." Joshua smiled. "So, think of this as our pilot run."

"Any questions?"

The staff members looked at each other and shifted their posture. Then Dave hesitated as he raised his hand. "Josh, what's our objective here? I mean, um – what are we doing this for?"

"Good question," Josh replied. "We are supporting the currency-trading arm of the bank. It seems that they've taken a position that will cause us to lose a lot of money unless we can maintain and increase the value of several currencies – the dollar, the pound, and the franc."

"Oh," Dave replied. "But what does the price of gold have to do with currency valuations?"

"It's a psychological thing, Dave. Gold has been a form of money for six thousand years – remember that much of the world still looks upon gold as the money of choice. So, when the price of gold goes up, people tend to lose confidence in paper currency. And when the price of gold goes down, people tend to have greater confidence in paper."

Dave's forehead crinkled around his blue eyes. "So, we're manipulating currency values?"

"Well, let's just say we're pulling the currency traders' asses out of the fire."

---

3   Selling an asset 'short' occurs when the seller borrows the asset and then sells it into the market, expecting that he can reacquire the asset later at a lower price. A 'naked short' occurs when the asset is sold into the market without the seller first possessing, holding, or borrowing the asset. Note that a naked short sale gives the appearance of an increase in the supply of the asset. An increase in supply usually results in a decrease in the price of the asset.

The room became quiet.

"Any other questions?" Josh asked. "If not, then let's get at it."

The team filed out of Josh's office.

* * *

Josh stepped out of his office for a break. As he was walking through the atrium, he noticed a figure waving out of the corner of his eye. He turned his head to see Dave, standing in his office doorway and motioning him to come over.

Then Dave disappeared into his office.

Josh didn't know much about Dave Palmer. But he knew that Dave was smart, that he was the youngest on his staff, and that he was a new graduate of Oxford Business School. Josh also knew that he was impatient and impetuous. And he knew that Dave was born into an upstanding middle-class family. But Josh could not know Dave's high standards of integrity and ethics, nor could Josh know how outspoken he could be.

So when Dave gestured to him, Josh became curious. He walked into Dave's office and looked over Dave's shoulder as he was typing. "Alright?"

Dave looked at him and smiled. "Blimey. Check this out. This is a great process you've put in."

Dave's finger pointed to a specific area of the computer screen. "Look at how our trades this past month have paid off! Selling short into the gold market has caused the price of gold to decline by $20 so far. Damn! And we're covering our short positions with lower-priced gold and making gobs of money!"

Dave gleefully rubbed his hands together.

"Absolutely," replied Josh, "that's the way it's supposed to work – especially considering the large amount of leased gold we've been selling –"

"Yeah," Dave interrupted, "I caught a glimpse of those lease rates. They are so bloody low!" And then Dave frowned, and said, "How much gold have we leased, so far?"

Josh paused before speaking. "I think we've leased about a hundred metric tons. That's one hundred tonnes, to this point. Frankly, it's amazing just how much gold the central banks have been leasing – not just to us, but to some of the other investment firms as well. Blimey, they lease it to us for next to nothing – and then they let us keep it for years. It's hard not to make money with a system like this."

"But the big question," he continued," is whether or not we can buy back the gold at a lower price. We'll need to do that so we can return it to the Bullion Bank on schedule." *Now that could be a problem,* he thought.

And then Josh interrupted himself. "By the way, have you heard from the Bullion Bank? They were supposed to have some more gold for us on a new lease – I think we'll need it so we can roll over some of our short positions into new positions." Josh paused and then continued. "I think they have some silver for us too." *Talk about a tough market to play in; silver's status as both money and an industrial metal makes it hard to predict where it will go ...*

"Blimey!" Dave interrupted Josh's thoughts, "you seem to know a lot about these markets. Can you teach me some of it?"

"Sure, I'll be glad to. Especially as we do more trading, we'll need to work our strategy. And by the way, thanks for your great work. Keep it up."

Josh walked out of Dave's office, heading out through the atrium to take a break.

* * * * *

The apartment door opened just as Josh was switching to the evening news. Josh called out, "Cheryl?"

"Hey," she replied.

"How was your day?"

"Great. Doing great," he heard Cheryl's reply from the hall-way. She bounced into the living room and onto his lap with a big smile and a long, deep kiss.

"And, how was *your* day?" Cheryl finally found a breath to ask.

Josh moved in with Cheryl – his new main squeeze – just after his wife Linda left him. Outgoing, vivacious, and sexy, Cheryl liked the lavish gifts that Josh poured on her. It seemed that Josh was attracted to women who liked expensive things, but he never gave it a second thought.

Josh was truly glad to be out from under Linda. And he was happier still because his divorce had been granted just a week ago. Josh did not know at the time, but found out later that Linda had been sleeping with some rich guy over in Manchester. He was smothering her with everything expensive – clothes, gifts, and vacations; and she was smothering him with that hot body of hers. *Linda and the guy (whoever he was) were both getting what they wanted*, Josh reflected.

"Hey, stud ..." Cheryl started rubbing his chest. "What do you want to do tonight?"

Josh smiled and flipped the TV off – he liked this kind of distraction! "Oh," he said innocently. "I don't know. There's a great restaurant just a few blocks from here. It's a brand new Italian place with a piano player ... interested?"

"Oh, yeah!" Her voice went up two octaves when she was excited. "I'd love to try it out – I sure don't feel like cooking."

"And then," Josh continued. "How about we come back here and play?"

She grinned and said, "All right! Let me clean up."

※　※　※

Later that evening . . .

Bound tightly in the chair, Josh could do nothing but watch. And so he watched as Cheryl paced back and forth, glaring down at him through her mask. And then she paced around the back of the chair, out of sight – and his eyes followed her as she came back into view. He loved looking at her in her leather mask; wearing the scant leather bustier, her black netted nylons, and her black four-inch pumps. And he especially loved her steel chain – the chain she wore as a belt – the belt she used on him when she was particularly angry.

And tonight, Cheryl was angry.

She moved up to him and placed the heel of her pump on his bare foot. She ground on his foot, ever so slowly as she looked into his eyes. Josh squinted with the pain – she stopped her grinding. And then Cheryl put her face up to his. She extended her tongue; making a motion as though she were licking ice cream. And then she used her tongue, slowly, licking around one of his eyes, and then the other – and then he felt her tongue run across his nose.

Josh squirmed, trying to free himself. But his bindings were too tight – she had made sure of that. He tried to speak; yet she had also gagged his mouth – the red rubber ball shoved into his mouth and held in place with the strap around his neck. And he tried to move his head, yet she had fastened his head to the back of the chair. So he could only sit, bound, waiting to see what humiliation she would visit on him next.

Cheryl stood back and looked at him. "Don't worry dear. We'll have a long evening of play. A long evening for you to suffer," she put her face up to his and smiled; "and a long evening of pleasure – my pleasure!"

She again came up to him. Holding him, she began to stroke, caressing him. And then she stooped, wrapping her mouth around him – he moaned through the red rubber ball. She continued with her mouth, slowly moving up and down, inflicting more pleasure upon him. But then she stopped, gazing at his member. "Oh my," she purred. "You are sooo close!"

Josh grunted through the rubber ball in his mouth.

She stepped back and gazed down at him. "How long do you want this?" She asked. Her breathing was heavy, her skin and her cheeks now flushed with passion. She watched as his arousal receded, ever so slightly.

And then she again came up to him. Bending over, she slowly wrapped her hand around his jewels. And slowly – ever so slowly – she squeezed, watching as Josh became more aroused. And then she glared into Josh's eyes, and her eyes grew wider, lusty. And then Josh felt pain – as she squeezed even more; and he could see in her eyes that she reveled in his pain. She flung back her head, her hair whipping behind her; and her body shuddered. And when her shuddering diminished, she looked into his eyes and then she slowly released her grip.

Oh my God, he thought. *I so love her pleasure – and I so love the pain!*

And the game continued ...

Interlude

A fire roared within the massive stone fireplace, sending its flickering shadows climbing the walls like tentacles clawing sheer rock. And in the shadows, there were five overstuffed leather chairs arranged in a semi-circle, each facing into the fire. In each chair there was seated a man, and each man was sipping from a snifter of brandy while indulging in a premium cigar of his choice. And they were talking amongst them – joking, bantering, and self-indulgent conversation.

But who were these men? Alas, except for one of the five, this was unknowable – for the features of the men were obscured by the darkness and the flickering shadows.

With purposeful strides, a tall, dark, slender man strode into the room. The man walked to the center of the five chairs and remained standing, even as his head was slightly bowed. "You wish to see me, my Lord?"

"Yes, Daniel," the Leader flourished his cigar. "Tell us of your success!"

Daniel bowed his head. "At your pleasure, my Lord." He then took a deep breath and continued. "We have used our leverage in the U.S. Congress to push through these 'so-called' free trade agreements – NAFTA and WTO. As you know, these agreements give us complete control over trade and capital flows in and out of the U.S.; and they will allow us to transfer jobs and capital out of the U.S. and western civilization. Of course, the President, the House Speaker, and others are all in our pocket. They have done our bidding."

"Fine, fine!" The Leader said. "This is a magnificent start. But now we must ensure that the wealth flows to our selected comrades in Asia."

Daniel's head remained bowed as he continued. "My Lord. As you know, there is strong resistance within the U.S. Congress to normalized trade with China. Nonetheless, we shall continue to work toward an on-going most favored nation trading status between China and the U.S. Until that time, we shall seek this status on a year-to-year basis."

Another man, a large burly man, spoke from out of the shadows. "This is great news indeed, Daniel. The dollar will appear much stronger, although it will actually be weakened. And a weak dollar, combined with the slave wages of Asia and India, should see capital and manufacturing leave the Western countries. And with the globalization of the Internet, we shall see many high-paying technology jobs move from the Western countries to Asia and India –"

Lord Basil waved his hands excitedly. "Yes – yes, Julius! But our weak dollar policy will be much more effective if we drive down the price of gold."

Lord Basil pointed his finger directly at Daniel. "You find me a way to increase the amount of gold in the market so that the gold price will fall!"

"Yes, my Lord."

Chapter 4 – Circa 1994

Ring! Ring! The sharp ring of the telephone destroyed the silence.

Groggy and disoriented, Kirk Kincaid rolled over and picked up the receiver.

"Hello." The words were almost incoherent as they rolled off his tongue.

"Kirk?" A scratchy voice began talking.

"Who's this?"

"This is Daniel. Daniel Elsbach."

"Oh. Hi, Daniel." *Daniel? ... Oh - THAT Daniel,* he thought. "What's going on?"

Daniel's voice sounded urgent. *"I've got a big job for you."*

"Okay. What's the job?"

"I don't want to talk about it over the phone. I'm sending you a special couriered package that should arrive at your place in a few hours." Daniel paused and then continued. *"If you have any questions, there will be instructions in the package on how best to communicate."*

Kirk was now wide awake as he glanced out his window. *Damn. Still dark!*

"Okay - thanks. I'll take a look."

Click!

Kirk ran his hand through his shaggy black hair and yawned. The clock said 4:30 am.

Shit, he thought. *A special courier job - hush-hush. I hate those jobs! And why now? Can't they let me take some time off?* He looked over at the woman in his bed - still sleeping. *It's no wonder I can't keep a woman - it seems like I always have to work - cleaning up someone else's crap!*

Alisa moved under the covers and opened her eyes. She looked at him and said in a groggy tone, "Do you have to go out of town again?"

"Probably," Kirk replied. "That's what they usually want."

"Mmmm," she moaned as she moved. "Tell 'em you don't want to go. Tell 'em I want you to stay in town."

Damn clingy woman, he thought. And then he replied, "I can't. They're sending a package to me this morning, and then I've gotta go handle business."

* * *

Following receipt of the package, Kirk looked through it and made some telephone calls. Soon, he was on the road.

Kirk's first stop was Metalworks, Inc.; a foundry located in western Pennsylvania.

It was a sunny day when he drove onto the foundry complex. He continued on toward a sleek modern building, situated on the edge of the campus. Noting that it was indeed the headquarters, he parked in a visitors slot. He paused for a moment, taking in the smooth lines and art-deco like appearance of the building.

Like other 'below-the-radar' jobs he'd done, Kirk had already engaged an investigator to screen MetalWorks and its ownership. The place was just as he had seen in the investigator's pictures; and he was pretty certain that this was the foundry that they wanted to use. *After all,* he thought, *the investigator verified they could handle the order, and that the owner keeps his mouth shut!*

Kirk walked up to the receptionist's desk and smiled at the young brunette. She smiled back and spoke to him in a well-cultivated southern accent. "May I help you, sir?"

Kirk absorbed the vision of her sexy curves – curves barely held inside of her skirt and sweater. "Yes, I'm Kirk Kincaid. I have an appointment to meet with your CEO, Mr. Hammond at 10:00 am."

"I know he's expecting you, sir." Her drawl was as sexy as her looks. "Please have a seat. I'll tell him you're here."

She picked up her telephone and hit a number on the keypad. "Mr. Hammond, your 10 o'clock is here. Yes. Mr. Kincaid."

While Kirk waited, he took in MetalWorks' lobby. Against one wall was a display of awards and product samples – prominently displayed was a sample silver bar and an array of silver coin blanks. Continuing to scan the room, he noticed how the contemporary styling and artwork of the room accented the precious metals on display. Kirk was still pondering the styling of the lobby when Mr. Hammond appeared.

George Hammond was a squat burly guy in his early 50s. Clean cut and full of energy, he strode quickly into the lobby, reaching his hand out as he drew closer to Kirk. "Good morning, Mr. Kincaid. I'm George. George Hammond."

They shook hands. "I'm delighted to meet you, George. Please call me Kirk."

Introductions and small talk complete, Kirk followed George into his office. George gestured toward an inviting lounge chair. "Please, sit down."

When they were both seated, George blurted out, "Kirk, I know that we talked a bit on the telephone about fabricating tungsten bars. So where is this going? How can I help?"

Kirk leaned forward and looked intently into George's eyes. "Before we begin, I want your promise – your solemn word – that you will not ever tell anyone of our conversation. Is that a deal?"

"Yes. Of course, Kirk. My relationship with each of my clients is very personal. I never divulge my clients' information."

Kirk stood up and began pacing. "George, I need to obtain about 1.3 million solid tungsten bars." Kirk then whipped out a piece of paper and handed it to George. "This is a list of detailed specifications."

George looked at the sheet:

Top Surface: 251.8 x 77.8mm
Bottom Surface: 232.8 x 53.8mm
Thickness: 33.8mm

"Of course" George replied thoughtfully, "this size order will take me a long time to produce; probably several years."

"I understand." Kirk nodded. "Actually, it will be beneficial if we can spread it out over, say, maybe eight to ten years."

George nodded an acknowledgment and continued. "Our contract will need to stipulate that we deliver in multiple batches of bars. And the contract needs to be structured so that you pay me up front for each batch of materials, and that we receive full payment for a batch of bars at the time we deliver."

"That's fine." Kirk nodded again.

"And we will deliver each batch of bars on a recurring schedule," George concluded.

Kirk was nodding his head. "George, that sounds good to me."

"Very well." George felt good about this. "I will draw up a contract that you can look over."

"One other thing," Kirk interjected.

"Yes?"

"This agreement is between you and me. I expect that you will keep this deal in your personal confidence even after the deal is delivered. Okay?"

For a split second, George's jaw tightened and his eyes hardened. And then his expression shifted into a pleasant smile. "Okay, Kirk. I promise you – absolutely – that no one will hear of this from me or anyone under my employ."

"Great!" Kirk smiled as he shook George's hand. "Please let me know when you have the contract drawn up. I'm anxious to iron out the details."

"I will be in touch," George replied.

Kirk noticed George's change of expression – and in light of this, Kirk was a bit concerned about George. Nonetheless, with two promises of confidentiality in hand, he departed believing that George was on board with the program.

But Kirk did not know about George's thoughtful analysis. Nor could Kirk know that George checked the specifications of the tungsten bars against the specs of gold bars from the London Bullion Market Association – and found them to be nearly identical. Nor could Kirk know that George's suspicions had been raised, and that George suspected he would be a party to the counterfeiting of gold bars.

Kirk knew nothing about George's perception of the deal. Kirk was pleased.

* * *

Once the final contract with *MetalWorks* was drawn and signed, tungsten bars began rolling off the production line in short order. The contract specified production of 1.3 million tungsten bars, about 520 bars per business day, to be delivered in a constant stream over a ten year period. The contract also stipulated a monthly payment schedule, that transportation was to be Kirk's responsibility, and that the finished product was to be transported out of George's facility on a weekly basis.

Although George needed time to ramp up production, he knew that his operation was more than equal to the task. He contacted his tungsten suppliers and placed orders for the necessary materials, to be delivered weekly. And he also added a graveyard shift dedicated specifically to the project, and hired a couple more men to work it.

George was indeed concerned about the legal aspects of the project, and the risk – especially the risk that he could go to jail. But he had dealt with these kinds of risks before. Hell! He'd worked with bankers before! And so, he was confident he could deal with those problems. *Damn, this is a great contract,* he mused.

*   *   *

The next stop on Kirk Kincaid's tour was a visit to Rheingold Fabrication and Brandon Payne. Kirk had worked with Brandon before – on 'not so savory' kinds of deals. Indeed, Kirk knew Brandon as an astute businessman; and he also knew Brandon as shrewd and unsavory. Shrewd, because he took a backwoods metal foundry and made it into a highly profitable business; and unsavory, because he would deal with the devil – if the price was right.

So when Kirk Kincaid contacted him by phone, Brandon knew there was the prospect of a deal in the works. And meeting over coffee seemed like a small investment to find out the particulars.

"So Kirk, what are you into these days?

"Oh," Kirk paused in thought, "I'm still working for the same people. And doing about the same thing."

"People? Like, what people?"

"You know. The bigwigs who're trying to corner the markets." Kirk smiled. I'm their expediter, their go-to guy, their hatchet man. I'm the man they count on to get things done."

Kirk smiled as he sipped some coffee. "So, Brandon. What have you been up to?"

Brandon shrugged as he looked down at his coffee. "Oh, you know. Just getting by."

There was a question dangling on the tip of Brandon's tongue; and he finally blurted it out. "Have you run across any good opportunities lately?"

"Yes," Kirk responded with a smile. "Maybe even something you'd be interested in."

"I'm listening."

"Well, it's pretty simple, really," Kirk replied. "I'll deliver a shipment of tungsten bars each week. I want you to stamp certain markings and distinct numbers on each bar, and then plate each bar in a 1/16th inch covering of gold. And then keep them in storage until we come to pick them up."

"Hmmm." Brandon looked down at his coffee, and then looked at Kirk. "I'm guessing that you'll want to purchase the silence of my men. Correct?"

"Yep. It's absolutely vital that nothing about this is ever leaked. Not ever."

"Hmmm." Brandon stroked his chin and then smiled. He joked, "so, should my staff plan on entering the witness protection program when this is done?"

"No," Kirk replied. "But in the future, they sure need to watch what they say." Then Kirk looked at Brandon with a steady gaze. "It could be dangerous for them otherwise."

Brandon acknowledged Kirk's reality with a sober nod. And then he continued. "And the feds. Is there any risk that the feds will get into our soup?"

"No," Kirk replied, "I don't think there's any risk of that."

"And this gold we're supposed to use. Would you be ensuring delivery of it?"

"Yes, but you'll be financially responsible for it once you sign for it; and you'll need to store it in a very secure place." Then Kirk looked at Brandon with curiosity. "You DO have a secure vault, don't you?"

"Of course. With our vault and all the security procedures we employ, I can take care of storing it."

"Great!"

"So, how much work do you have? How big is this?"

The corner of Kirk's mouth crooked upward as he looked at Brandon with level eyes. "About 1.3 million bars. And I antici- pate the job will be stretched out over 8 to 10 years."

Brandon whistled softly. And then his eyes narrowed. "What are you gonna do with all of –" he stopped himself in the mid- dle of the question and held up his hand with a wry look on his face. "I'm sorry, I'm sorry. I shouldn't be asking."

"That's okay," Kirk responded. "But my question to you is this: are you willing to go in on it with me?"

Knowing the money part of Kirk's deals were always worth- while, Brandon responded without hesitation. "Absolutely."

"Then how about we iron out the details?"

"Let's do it."

Chapter 5

It was nighttime, and it was dark. There were lamps in the park, sparsely distributed throughout, creating a dim glow. One could easily find an illuminated park bench, as there were several standing underneath a light fixture. But one could also find a bench that was not illuminated; a bench that was secluded – en- gulfed in the darkness – if one looked hard enough.

Seeking such a bench, the man strolled easily through the park, along one of the several paved walkways. He was a short, stocky man. Built low to the ground, he rumbled along slowly; as though he were a tank. He took a draw from his cigarette. Exhaling, he flicked the butt off to the side of the walkway. He continued his stroll.

The tank came upon a dimly-lit bench, occupied by a lone man of indeterminate height. The tank sized up the lone man, and sat down next to him.

One could see the tank reach inside his coat and produce a package of some kind. "Cigarette?"

"No thanks. I don't smoke."

"Don't mind if I do," the tank said as he lit up.

"Thanks for meeting with me."

"What can I do for you?" Asked the tank.

The lone man sniffed noisily, almost anxiously. "I need you to allocate some serial numbers for your smelter's gold bar run. Take those numbers out of production, and give them to me."

"Huh?"

"You heard me."

"So," Tank hesitated. "How many numbers do you want?"

"I want five hundred thousand. And if this is to be done as a 'mistake', then I want the mistake to be unseen for at least 20 years."

"You can't be serious! Who do you think I am?"

The lone man turned and looked into Tank's eyes. "I am indeed serious; and I have a high regard for you and your work. After all, we've done some great deals in the past."

"So, can you do it?"

Tank hesitated. "Hmmm. I think I can, but I may need to disappear after it's done. Not that I expect it to be discovered; so I don't need to disappear right away ..." He paused, then continued in a grim tone, "But when it's discovered, they'll know that I did it. And I don't want to go to jail."

"So, how much do you need to do this?"

"Well, I'll need to disappear. And from that moment forward, my job prospects won't be worth a pile of dog shit." Tank let out a chuckle. "So, I'll need to find a place to hunker down, live a different life and stay out of the way."

"Yes?" intoned the lone man.

Tank exhaled a sigh and threw his butt down on the ground. "Leave it to you to screw up my life!"

"So, how much do you want for this?" The lone man repeated his question; but this time, with a smile.

"Okay. Okay. I can do it for ten million. But you gotta transfer it to my Swiss bank account."

"Done." The lone man declared, without hesitation.

Tank was taken aback. The speed of the deal, and the magnitude of the price; all of a sudden this looked much larger than just some vacant serial numbers for gold bars. *Sure, gold bars* were a lot of money; but serial numbers? *What could anyone do with serial numbers?*

"I will contact you when I have the numbers."

"When will that be?" asked the lone man.

"Soon." Tank stood up. Tank was perplexed; but he knew sure as it was nighttime in the park that he'd left money on the table. But then he thought, *maybe leaving money on the table is the best way for me to stay alive!*

Tank stood up and began walking away from the bench, continuing his casually measured pace through the park. A minute or so later, he stopped and looked back at the park bench; the lone man was nowhere to be seen.

✻ ✻ ✻

Bailey Keating drove up to Jacob-Mortenson's facility and entered the high-security manufacturing area. As he navigated the shop floor toward his office, several of the men greeted him along the way – joking and smiles lit his passage. Although short and stocky like a tank, he moved easily along the walkway and past a pallet of gold bars. Bailey loved the look and feel of the gold. Glistening gold metal – each weighing in at thirty-odd pounds and 400 troy ounces – had a way of heightening his emotional energy. *It was just like driving a high-end sports car or walking on acres and acres of one's own land. Gold was substantial, and wealth.*

Bailey Keating was gainfully employed as a mid-level administrator for Jacob-Mortenson, a large smelter and refiner of precious metals. Management was smart and capable, and they had looked favorably on Bailey during his fifteen year tenure. In return, Bailey had repeatedly demonstrated his loyalty and dedication to the Company.

Bailey managed the accounting and tracking of precious metals. This included both the arrival of raw material, as well as the shipment and sales of newly finished product. In this capacity, Bailey performed flawlessly, to the credit of all concerned.

Bailey liked his office – it was adjacent to the shop, and equipped with windows that allowed him to look out onto the shop floor. And so when he was working at his desk, he would frequently look out a window and observe the final stage of gold ingot production – the actual pouring of the gold into forms that defined the dimensions (and therefore the size and weight) of each London Good Delivery gold bar.

Bailey reached his office and entered. And then he immediately turned to the window and looked out. And as he watched them pour a gold ingot, his favorite pun ran through his mind: *ingot we trust!* He smiled and chuckled to himself, *I really crack me up.*

Bailey stooped down and spun the dial on a two-drawer filing cabinet. The combination lock moved easily under his short thick fingers and the top drawer opened quickly. Removing The Book from the cabinet – for this was the book that itemized all of the London Good Delivery[4] gold bars and their dates of manufacture – he sat down to his desk and opened it to the crease with the bookmark protruding. As keeper of The Book, Bailey kept the bookmark creased at the page from which the next serial number was to be issued.

At the open page, the next serial number had already been written in. Below the entry, Bailey drew a large 'X', and wrote in *"Serial numbers 100,001 – 600,000 rescinded due to accounting changes. Next serial number begins at 600,001."*

As sole keeper of The Book, Bailey knew that it was highly unlikely that the rescinded numbers would be noticed. And if they were noticed, he could easily pass it off as an accounting change.

He copied the range of rescinded numbers on a piece of paper and shoved it into his wallet. Then whistling through pursed lips, he began working on his daily tasks.

* * *

---

[4] A standard for gold bars that assures a specific level of quality, fineness, and weight.

Bailey found the lone man sitting quietly on the park bench, secluded from the light of the lamps.

"Do you have the numbers?"

"Yes."

Like their last meeting, the night was dark without benefit of moonlight, and the lamps remained sparsely distributed – merging their dim glow into the surrounding darkness.

And like their last meeting, they barely looked at each other, barely acknowledged each other. Remaining nameless – just the lone man, and the tank.

Reaching inside his jacket, Bailey produced a cigarette and lit it. He took a deep draw and exhaled into the air.

"How do you want to be paid?"

Bailey handed him an envelope. "In here you'll find the range of vacant serial numbers, along with the account number for my numbered Swiss bank account. Please transfer the funds to this account."

"Fine. I will take care of it."

"When?"

"By close of business tomorrow."

"That's acceptable."

Tank stood and walked away from the bench, continuing his casually measured pace through the park. A minute or so later, he stopped and looked back at the park bench. The lone man was nowhere to be seen.

Chapter 6 – Circa 1996

Her mid-length brown hair blowing behind her, Brandy was running a smooth 70 mph along the Superstition Freeway. *The morning desert air feels so good*, she reflected. She looked in the rearview mirror and caught a glimpse of the sun – rising over the Superstition mountains. *Wow! So beautiful!* She pulled out her sunglasses – a perennial fixture in the Arizona desert – and fitted them over her eyes.

Still at 70 mph, she glided along the road, chewing slowly on a wad of gum. And then she shifted to a more focused posture when, up ahead, she spied an 18-wheel tractor pulling into her lane. To the right side of the shifting truck, she caught a glimpse of an 18-wheel tanker truck; the trailer was obviously moving into position to pass the tanker. *Damn they're slow!*

Few cars could match the acceleration and handling of her Porsche 911 – and she knew it. So when the truck moved over, she felt her face flush with glee – *I got ya now!* Simultaneously, she engaged the clutch, downshifted to fourth, punched the gas, and flipped the wheel ever so slightly – bringing her into the adjacent lane. Now doing 80 mph, she accelerated quickly – faster and faster toward the ever-narrowing gap between the two trucks. In a flash, she shot the gap – and despite herself, she felt her body flush with excitement! She smiled and looked down at her speedometer – 120 mph. *Cool!* She grinned as she began to scale back her speed.

She soon reached 80 when she noticed red and blue flashing lights in her rearview mirror. *Damn cops!* She pressed down on the gas – again accelerating faster and faster. *What the hell am I doing,* she chided herself. She slowed down to 65 mph, the speed limit, and watched as the cop came up behind her. He didn't pass.

Damn! Brandy pulled into the breakdown lane and came to rest. The cop pulled in behind her, his flashers continuing their spinning.

She composed herself while she waited. She knew he would first run her license plates by headquarters; and while he did, she took stock of her assets. Brown, wind-blown hair touched the shoulders of her V-necked blouse; and showing just enough cleavage to be acceptable in a business setting. She looked down at her trim waist and skirt; coming just above the knees – *but he probably won't be able to see much of my legs*, she mused.

She caught a glimpse of him getting out of the cruiser. She allowed herself to relax and let her personality come forth – an engaging smile with bright eyes and (gasp!) dimples.

The state patrolman walked up to the passenger's side. She watched as he took in the sleek lines of her car, and then fixed his gaze on her. He spoke in a somewhat perplexed tone. "Excuse me, ma'am, but do you know how fast you were going?"

A Dallas native, Brandy was no fool. So she used her sexiest Texas drawl to great advantage. "I'm sorry, officer; but I just have to make it to work. You see, I have a conference with a very important client. And if I don't make it on time," she blinked twice; her eyelashes ever so subtly telegraphing her southern bell persona, "they – well – they'll *fire* me," she lied.

"Huh!" He said, obviously unconvinced. "License and registration please."

Brandy sifted through her purse and produced her drivers' license. She then reached over to the glove box and retrieved her registration. She handed both documents to the officer, her southern belle persona again showing through.

Patient and assured, Brandy watched as the officer walked back to his cruiser and made a call on his radio. Soon, the officer returned to the passenger's side of her car. She watched him as he took in her appearance – as though he were undressing her in his mind. His face softened.

"Well, ma'am," he continued, "you were doing 80 – and maybe faster." He hesitated for a moment. "But I tell you what – I'll let you off with a warning – this time."

And then his features hardened. "But if you *ever* come through here like that again, I'll have your ass! - er, ah – what I mean is, I'll give you a ticket!"

"Yes, officer," Brandy said demurely.

And then the cop hesitated as he looked up and down at the sleek lines of her car. "And another thing," he spouted out. "This is a nice car – but it's red. And red cars carry a sign that says 'pull me over'. You best get yourself a different color!"

He tipped his hat at Brandy. "Good day, ma'am." He strode back to his cruiser.

Brandy felt a wave of relief wash through her. *Eureka!* She started her car and engaged the throttle, pulling out of the breakdown lane and proceeding down the freeway at (sigh) a meager 65 mph. Within a minute, the cruiser flashed by her.

* * *

Brandy drove into the parking garage at the First National Bank of Arizona. In her rearview mirror, she glimpsed the bright sunshine of the desert as it disappeared – replaced with dark concrete and steel. Pulling into her space, she stepped out of the car and strode across the garage toward the back entrance to the building. With purposeful strides and head held high, her long legs and smooth-flowing posture carried her down the spartan corridor where she cornered an elevator.

She entered her office and sighed – *just another day!* She was still waiting for her new office furniture and decorations. *Damn! These large corporations move so slow!*

Brandy West was a newcomer to the banking industry. With a two-year-old MBA, most of her work had been in marketing and organization – stuff that made sense to her. But this ... the way the banking industry worked ... made no sense at all. Unless, one was devoid of ethics!

Oh, sure. She understood the ledger entries. She understood the marketing of loans. And she understood the loan origination process – mostly. But what she could not understand – ethically – was how the bank could manufacture money out of thin air!

She thought back to the first day of her orientation; head-spinning as it was ...

"And this is our loan process. First, we have the borrower sign the promissory note. Then we use his promissory note as collateral for a promissory note that we create. And then we deposit the promissory note into an account under his name ..."

For a time, she spun it around in her head. *But how can this work? How can such a scheme possibly work!*

And then she thought back to the explanation her manager provided: *"Let's say that I write an IOU for $100 dollars. And let's say I walk into a store and purchase a dress priced at $90*

dollars; and that I give the merchant my IOU for $100. Well ...
the merchant will give me the dress and also give me money back
– the money she gives me will be an IOU for $10 dollars. So you
see, we use IOUs to exchange for goods and services."

Brandy shook her head in dismay as she thought about this.
This so-called money is nothing but paper. There's no value to
it!

Sitting down, she began typing on her computer keyboard.
Some data appeared on her computer monitor – the previous
day's mortgage loan activity. She perused the data until her gaze
zeroed in on a specific entry:

Patricia Bowman application; denied.

She printed it out.

Ripping the paper out of the printer, she strode down the hall
and into the office of the Vice President in charge of Loans.

Marcus was the primary loan officer. He was also a haughty
sort of man – aloof, distant, particular, and mechanical – he had
been a strong supporter of the banking system and had worked
his way up on the back of his accounting degree. Marcus had
recently hired her, so Brandy was still learning how best to work
with him.

"Marcus," she said as she handed him the paper. "I was just
perusing the loan reports and I came across this entry."

Marcus scanned the paper and paused.

"Yes?" Marcus looked at her with raised eyebrows. "Do you
have a question?"

"Yes, I do!" Brandy's eyes bored into him. "Her background
looks good. And I personally interviewed her – she really needs
the money. So why was she denied?"

Marcus leaned back in his chair, touching the fingertips of his
hands together. "As you know, we periodically receive reports
from the FBI about people in our area."

Marcus looked directly into Brandy's eyes. "We received a report about Ms. Bowman."

"And?"

"And apparently, she has been involved in some kind of right-wing patriot group."

"Is this a problem?"

"Well, yes, it is indeed a problem," he replied. "Some of these patriot-type people don't accept Federal Reserve Notes as money. They – some of them, at least – think they do not have to repay a loan."

"So, does Ms. Bowman's credit history give any indication that she won't repay?"

"No." Marcus looked away. "In fact, her credit history is impeccable –"

"Then besides this report," Brandy interrupted, "is there anything in her background that suggests she will not repay the loan?"

"No ...," Marcus replied. "The worst thing we show for her is that she bounced a check about ten years ago. But it looks like she paid it promptly."

"Then why do you give this report so much weight?" Brandy asked.

"Because the Federal Reserve has instructed us to do so," Marcus said. "As you know, we are required to conduct our business in accordance with Fed policy."

Marcus continued. "We've received previous citations from both the Fed and the FBI stating that these patriot people are on a watch list. They say they're a threat to our government and our banking system. And as you know, the list has expanded since the Oklahoma City bombing."

"So," Brandy's eyes narrowed as she looked down at Marcus, "what does the report say that she did – specifically – that was so dangerous?"

"According to the report," Marcus answered, "she entered into a contract with some kind of unregulated investment trust. The prospectus of this 'trust' says they may invest large sums of money in the 'private economic arena', whatever that is; and that returns on investment can be in the millions on just an initial investment of just $1,300."

Brandy stroked her chin, and then said, "Okay ... so maybe she's stupid. Are we supposed to assess a borrower's IQ prior to giving a loan? Besides, it seems to me that the Constitution protects the individual right to contract; so, are you saying that the government now assumes the right to pass judgment on private contracts?" Brandy was drawing on her knowledge of contract law from her MBA coursework.

"No," Marcus replied. "It's not the Federal Government that is stipulating this. It's really the Federal Reserve. Apparently, the Fed wants borrowers to completely buy into the system. And this woman has shown she doesn't necessarily buy into it."

"I don't understand." Brandy replied. "How would investment in a private trust be equated to not buying into our system of money?"

"Well, it goes further than that." Marcus continued. "Apparently, this group she invested with is also teaching about the plain language of the U.S. Constitution. And as you may know, the plain meaning of the Constitution does not allow for the existence of fiat paper money, nor does it authorize a central bank."

"The fact is," Marcus continued, "this is what they teach and this is what Ms. Bowman believes. Frankly, we can't allow people access to credit when they refuse to acknowledge the supremacy of our monetary system."

"Damn it, Marcus, this makes no sense! The woman is 62 years old. Hell, she's a threat to no one! What does the FBI think she's gonna do - blow up a building or something? Damn! I guess we better all take to the bunkers now!"

Brandy was on a roll now. "Shit! The loan would be secured by the home that she's buying. Damn it, we're creating the money for this loan off of her promissory note - the bank is not putting any of its own funds at risk!"

Marcus sat in his chair, still touching his fingertips together, seemingly unmoved by Brandy's diatribe.

"Well?" Brandy raised her voice still more.

Marcus paused, and then said, "I'm sorry, Brandy, I can't authorize this loan."

Chapter 7

The flock took off seemingly all at once, moving in a chaotic rush of feathers and wings. Bill Ford raised the shotgun to his shoulder and fired at one of the doves in mid-takeoff. He smiled as he watched it fall. *That makes two today,* he thought.

Early morning dove hunting was getting to be a habit. A habit he truly enjoyed; especially since it provided a nice prelude to his work day. He wasn't sure what he liked more; the hunting, or just spending time in the outskirts of the Valley – out in the desert, where it was quiet and peaceful.

But the habit was soon to end; or at least the 'work' part of it was ending. For his mother had passed from this world, and now her wealth belonged to him. A year had gone by since that day – a year of grief, of reflection, of deliberation; and finally a decision. And it was just last night that he resolved to move on his decision.

Bill gathered his game and field-dressed them. Then he hiked down the trail, retracing his path through the dry dusty desert – past the rocks, a clump of cholla, a barrel cactus here and there, a saguaro cactus. He soon arrived at his truck, where he stored his game in a cooler. Driving home, Bill let the cool desert air wash across his rugged features and his dirty blond hair. It was April, and the early morning desert was a sight to behold. The air was cool, clear, crisp; and you could see the mountains on the far side of the Valley – 30 miles or more away. And yet the mountains were so clear, it was as though you could reach out and touch them.

He was smiling – serene. *Damn – I love bird hunting in the early morning!* And then his mouth clenched and his eyes became hard. *But doing something like this was always a hassle when I was with Jennifer,* he reflected. *God how I'm glad to be out from under her nagging – what a bitch!* But even as the thoughts passed through his mind, he felt a wave of sadness wash through him. *I don't think I ever want to marry again!*

Bill dropped the birds and shotgun at home, then proceeded on to work. He soon drove into a vast parking lot and navigated rows and rows of cars, until he finally pulled into a parking space.

Winding his way between the cars, Bill reflected on his work and the people he would be leaving. *I must be nuts to do this! What if it doesn't work out? What if I screw it up? What if ... ?*

Bill swiped his access card across the card reader and heard the expected *click!* of the door lock. As he walked into the hallway, he was greeted by an engineering colleague – Russell Hart. "Morning Bill," said Russ, waving as he passed by.

"Morning Russ," Bill replied as he strode toward his office.

He logged on to his computer; and in no time at all, he typed his resignation into an email and sent it to his manager – Alexis Cooper. Then he leaned back in his chair and smiled. *Two weeks notice – that's enough,* he mused. And since a slack period was approaching, he was certain that Alexis and the group could bring someone else up to speed in time to handle the next schedule crunch.

Bill's thoughts shifted to his transition. *Wow! This is as big as when I split with Jennifer! I've seen a lot of changes in the last two years. Who'd a thought!*

A senior staff engineer with a large electronics company, Bill had worked at the firm for the last four years. He started in the Network Systems Division as a technical contractor; and when they decided they liked his work, they brought him on as a staff engineer. But he felt only marginally fulfilled by the job. *Working in a large bureaucratic organization was not all it was cracked up to be,* he reflected.

Bill grabbed his coffee cup and headed to the break room. He rather liked this cup – inscribed with 'IS-41 1996' – it made a statement about his area of expertise. Cellular networking.

The break room was typical of what you'd find in a technology company. Cabinets, kitchen sink, countertops, and several cafeteria-style tables throughout the room.

"... so, how do you like the real world?" Bill joked with Pamela, a new apprentice engineer.

"Oh," she grinned, "it's a lot different than college. The assignments here are bigger and more complex. And," the corner of her mouth crooked up, "the guys hitting on you tend to be older than college."

Bill laughed and then took a sip of coffee. "Hitting? Who's hitting on you?" He joked. "I hope you know that sexual harassment would make me liable for dismissal – or worse!"

"Ya – right!" She replied. And then her expression became sly – seductive. "So – Bill – you wanna come up to my place?"

Bill feigned interest. "What do you have in mind?"

"Oh. I could get you drunk and take advantage of you." She laughed.

At that moment, Alexis walked into the break room. She paused and looked at Bill with a smile – a decidedly unhappy smile. "Bill, will you please drop by my office when you get a chance?"

"I'll be there in just a minute," Bill replied.

Alexis walked out of the room.

"Uh oh! You're gonna get it now, Bill," Pamela laughed. "Have you been harassing Alexis too?"

＊   ＊   ＊

Alexis Cooper was a tall redhead with stylishly short hair. An engineer by trade, her promotion to department manager came quickly – at least, by the standards in any large bureaucratic electronics company. She repeatedly demonstrated a quick and agile mind; and considering the talent and genius of her staff, she needed it just to stay a step ahead of them.

Bill walked into Alexis' office. "So, I take it you got my message?"

Alexis smiled and leaned back in her chair. "Yes, I did. I must say – you'll be hard to replace." She sighed and then said, "Care to tell me more about it?"

Bill sat down at the round meeting table positioned across from her desk.

"So, what are your plans?" Alexis asked.

"I'm going into business. But not in technology." Bill shuffled in his chair. "No ... I'm looking at starting a business in precious metals."

Alexis' red eyebrows raised, "Precious metals? Oh my. That's quite a change. Whatever brought you to that?"

"Well, it's a long story and it's not very interesting." Bill hesitated and then said, "I think there'll be a time when precious metals will be a really good place to be. And I want to be well-established in the business when it comes time."

"When it comes time?" Alexis looked quizzically at Bill. "Time for what?"

"Well, ah – I think that gold and silver will be a good long-term investment ..."

Bill was starting to squirm. He was acutely aware that he was touching on an area that most people wouldn't understand.

"... and I want to be in a position, ah – to take advantage of it."

For a moment, both were silent. Then Alexis picked up the conversation. "Gold and silver are very poor investments – but I'm sure you know that." She paused. "Stocks and real estate are much better."

Bill smiled but didn't respond.

Then Alexis continued, her curiosity aroused, "so, what will the business do?"

Damn, she's inquisitive, he thought. "Ummm... I plan on minting custom gold and silver coins for the coin collector market. From there, ah – I plan on minting coins for some third-world countries."

"Great. So, why didn't you say so?"

Bill shrugged and then replied. "Most people aren't interested in those kinds of details."

Alexis and Bill looked across the table at each other. Alexis broke the silence. "So how can I convince you to stay here, instead?"

Bill frowned and looked at her. "You really can't. This is something I've thought about for a while." He looked earnestly into Alexis' green eyes. "And my gut is telling me I need to do this." He sighed and then said, "So, that's it ..."

Alexis smiled and nodded. "Okay. But can we at least do lunch before you leave?"

"Sure."

Interlude

The flickering shadows danced across the dark walnut paneling, casting silhouettes of eerily dark and foreboding spirits. Ensconced among the silhouettes were five men, seated in their leather-upholstered chairs; each sipping a rare, old brandy from an antique snifter.

The short thin man with the manicured mustache looked over at Lord Basil and began speaking in a thick French accent. "Do you think we should tell him?"

Lord Basil seemed to hesitate. "At some point, we shall have to tell him. But for today, let us keep it our little secret."

Just then, a tall, lanky man with dark hair and graying temples entered. The eyes in the room followed him, expectantly, as he approached.

"Gold!" Lord Basil waved his hand in elegant, yet pretentious, gestures. "Daniel, tell me about the gold!"

Daniel stood before them, his head in a slight bow of greeting. "Yes, my Lord." He took a deep breath and then continued. "We have commenced manufacturing of 1.3 million tungsten bars which we shall plate in gold and sell into the gold market. The manufacturing process shall require several years; so the gold bars will be sold into the market at a slow but steady rate."

"We have finalized our plan to swap counterfeit gold bars for the remaining gold at Ft. Knox. We shall execute this plan in the near future, my Lord. And when we are finished, all of the Ft. Knox gold will be removed - leaving Ft. Knox an empty shell."

"And, sir. We have begun a program of central banks' leasing their gold to sell into the market. This has enabled us to sell ever-larger short positions into the gold market."

"With these actions, my Lord, we will inject a large supply of additional gold into the market, thereby driving the price far below its fair market value. And because the new gold will enter the market at a moderate rate, we expect to see gold prices decline slowly."

"Ahhh ... excellent. Excellent!" Lord Basil waved his arms in a flourish of gestures.

"You may go, Daniel"

"As you wish, My Lord." Daniel turned and retraced his steps.

Julius, the big burly man that he is, turned and spoke in his high melodic voice to the group. "This is genius, gentlemen – genius. Many here in the West disregard the emphasis that the world places on gold as a form of money. In fact, the world views gold as *the premier* form of money. Driving the price of gold down sends a clear psychological message that the paper currency is strong – even as we print ever more amounts of paper to drive our agenda forward."

Chapter 8

Tungsten is a hard metal; and it's heavy – heavier and denser than lead. With a density of 19.3 times that of water, it is comparable to uranium or gold. A steel-gray metal when pure, it can be brittle when combined with minor amounts of impurities. But very pure tungsten is more ductile than the impure variety; and when pure, it can be cut with a hacksaw. In short, tungsten is an unusual and remarkable material.

Kirk did not know much about the finer details of tungsten; he left that up to George. But when it came to meeting his end of the contract, Kirk was on schedule and on task with transportation. Just one week went by before Kirk arrived at *MetalWorks* foundry – first thing in the morning – accompanied by a ten-wheeled truck and two tough, burly men. In short order, George had the truck backed into the loading dock. Then using a deft touch on the forklift controls, George's man quickly loaded the pallets of tungsten into the truck. After taking some time out for coffee and conversation, Kirk and his burly associates were on their way.

* * *

Loaded down with tungsten bars, Kirk and his burly crew drove directly from MetalWorks into the mountains of eastern Ohio. The drive was both uneventful and scenic.

Kirk reflected on his negotiations with Brandon Payne and Rheingold Fabrication. Kirk knew they were dominant in the market for custom alloy fabrication, and they could produce custom alloys in a variety of form factors. And he was also aware that Rheingold could profitably take on small jobs, or they could ramp up a production line for large contracts.

Kirk thought about Brandon Payne. He knew that Brandon and his staff would soon become wealthy, and that their accumulation of wealth would increase as the term of the contract wore on. But Kirk was clear with Brandon about an important condition of their newfound wealth – that they were to tell no one from where it came. *For whoever was to disclose the source of their wealth would meet a swift and certain end!*

It was mid-afternoon when the truck rolled up to the loading dock of Rheingold Fabrication. Brandon came out to meet it, and on his heels was his operations manager, Jim-Billy Owen.

Jim-Billy climbed aboard the forklift and proceeded to unload the pallets. In short order, the pallets were lined up inside the receiving door.

* * *

Kirk and his crew became accustomed to their transportation schedule. Like clockwork, they took on a load of tungsten bars from MetalWorks and delivered the load to Rheingold. And while at Rheingold, they would unload their tungsten bars and take on a load of the gold-plated bars. It was on a scheduled stop at Rheingold that Kirk had the opportunity to observe the Rheingold manufacturing operation. In fact, the process of gold bar plating and manufacturing was going well. Brandon was a taskmaster who managed to keep his crew on schedule; and he produced a high quality gold bar to boot.

Shaking hands in their usual greeting, Brandon's first question was, "Cigar?"

"No. No thanks."

Brandon lit up a cigar and drew from it; exhaling smoke into the air. "I want to show you our operation, Kirk. Walk with me."

The two walked the floor, with Kirk observing the operation.

"Right here," Brandon said. "You can see the process we use to stamp the appropriate devices on the bar – the manufacturer's insignia, the serial number, the fineness of the bar. Of course, each number is unique, as is the weight in troy ounces."

They continued walking the floor. "And over there," Brandon motioned with his cigar for Kirk to follow, "is one of our plating production lines. C'mon. You gotta see this, Kirk. We've put together a helluva setup."

They arrived over at the plating equipment. "Isn't this a beauty?" Brandon smiled proudly as he leaned back on his heels; holding his cigar in front of him. As you specified, we plate a full sixteenth of an inch – but no more – all the way around."

"These look great!" Kirk reached over and lifted a bar from a pallet of finished product. Hefting it in his hand, he smiled and looked at Brandon. "That's just what I'm looking for."

＊ ＊ ＊

Kirk's transport team stayed over at a local motel. And the next morning, they made their way back to Rheingold.

Without ado, Jim-Billy soon had their truck loaded. And with that, Kirk and his burly crew said goodbye and drove off.

"Where to now, Boss?" Buck asked.

Kirk looked at Buck and said, "The Port of Wilmington, Delaware. Step on it."

* * *

The Port of Wilmington was formerly known as the Wilmington Marine Terminal. A deep-water port located at the confluence of the Christina River and the Delaware River in Wilmington, it is located 65 miles from the Atlantic Ocean; and about a two-hour drive from Bethlehem, Pennsylvania.

By late morning, the unmarked armored truck rolled into Wilmington. Navigating their way through the narrow streets of the city, they soon reached Pier 35 on the Wilmington Docks. Kirk chose a parking area close to the loading dock and motioned Buck to pull in.

Kirk looked across the street and spied a man standing by the entrance.

"Wait here," he said as he opened the door and got out of the truck.

Kirk watched the man follow him as he crossed the street. The man continued to watch him as he approached. When they were face to face, the man said, "The moonlight glows brightly."

Kirk became at ease as he responded, "but only at night."

They shook hands. "Kirk?"

"Yes. You must be Bailey?"

"Yes. That's me." Bailey said as he lit a cigarette. "So, whatcha got for me?"

"Per our instructions, I did not want to talk about this on the telephone."

Bailey dragged on his cigarette as he nodded his understanding.

As he was talking, Kirk pulled the paperwork out of the manila envelope. "This is a list – a manifest, if you will – of all the gold bars we're selling into LBMA[5] on this transaction. I need

---

[5] LBMA is short for London Bullion Market Association. The **London bullion market** is a wholesale over the counter market for the trading of gold and silver. Trading is conducted amongst members of the **London**

your signature on them so that the LBMA sees Jacob-Mortenson as the manufacturer and seller of the bars. Of course, I've included the settlement account number – that's the account that will receive payment – in the appropriate box on the form."

"Can I take a look at them?" Bailey asked as he reached for the forms.

Kirk handed them over. "Sure. I just need your signature on them."

"Did you check the numbers against the bars?"

"Yep. They all match," Kirk replied.

"Because," Bailey continued, "if the numbers don't all match up, we're screwed. It will raise their suspicions and they'll start checking and maybe do an audit."

Bailey signed each of the forms, then motioned toward the shipping/receiving office. "Let's go talk with the counter attendant and get this rolling."

They walked together into the office and up to the counter.

"Hack? Hey, Hack?" Bailey called.

Just then, the counter attendant came walking out from the back room and smiled. "Tank! How're you doing, man?

"Great. How about you?"

"Doin' good. Whatcha got for me?"

"I've got some bars shipping to LBMA. Think you can handle 'em?"

"You bet. Lemme see the paperwork."

Bailey handed over a stack of papers.

Hack thumbed through the papers, then looked up at Bailey and Kirk. "Tell you what. Bring the bars around to the loading dock. We'll unload 'em and check 'em out."

Buck had the truck backed up to the loading dock in short order. After the bars were unloaded, Hack performed an inventory. He found everything in order.

Bullion Market Association (**LBMA**), loosely overseen by the Bank of England. Most of the members are major international banks or bullion dealers and refiners.

"Okay, guys," Hack smiled at them both. "I'll sign for these, and you'll be free to go."

*   *   *   *   *

Years later, this news piece appeared in the print media:

NYMEX[6] executive investigated by District Attorney and disappears ...

Manhattan, New York, February 20, 2004 (International Press) – The Manhattan district attorney is investigating a top NYMEX executive. Confidential inside sources have cited Stuart Smith, senior vice president of operations as a target of investigation; and they say he was served with a search warrant last week. A spokeswoman for NYMEX stated that the investigation was not related to any of NYMEX's markets; but she refused to disclose any details other than to state that no charges had been filed. Also declining comment was a spokeswoman for the Manhattan district attorney's office.

NYMEX's offices of the senior vice president operations are directly responsible for the records and documentation (serial number, smelter of origin, etc.) of all gold bars physically settled on the exchange. Critics of NYMEX have speculated that the records held by this office would show that the quantity of gold settled on the exchange is simply too great to have all originated from U.S. mining operations. In fact, the records would show that the quantity of gold from U.S. smelters would be much greater than could come from U.S. domestic mine production.

---

[6] NYMEX is short for New York Mercantile Exchange. This agency manages the records for all of the serial numbers of gold bars exported out of the U.S.

Following the raid on the offices of senior vice president operations/NYMEX, this reporter has been unable to locate Mr. Stuart Smith. Sources have stated that Mr. Smith took administrative leave from the NYMEX and he has not been heard from since. In addition, this reporter has found no further follow up information regarding the DA's action – neither from the District Attorney's office nor from the media.

This reporter notes that NYMEX offices were raided, and then the Sr. V.P. of operations departed on leave – for no obviously good reason.

* * *

Around the same time, this piece also appeared in the print media:

Rothschild & Sons Ltd. Withdraws from Commodities Trading.

"LONDON, April 14, 2004 (International Press) - NM Rothschild & Sons Ltd., announced on Wednesday, that the London-based unit of investment bank Rothschild [ROT.UL], will withdraw from trading commodities in London, including gold. It stated that "... it's operations are under review.""

This reporter speculates that the risk to gold investors has increased; thus motivating the Rothschild's departure from the gold market.

Chapter 9

Bill inherited a substantial sum of money – enough so that he didn't have to work ever again. He was certain he had sufficient funds to capitalize his new business, but he also knew that the biggest problem a new business encounters is insufficient capital. *I've heard of many a startup business failing because it ran out of money,* he mused. And so he decided to seek some additional investment capital to finance the coin design and manufacturing equipment that he would need ... *But what kind of financing should I seek?*

Bill was aware that the purchased equipment could be used as collateral for the loan. This fact suggested that a bank would finance such a purchase – hopefully at a reasonable rate of interest.

With this in mind, Bill walked into the main lobby of the First National Bank of Arizona. He strode across the lobby to a smiling receptionist seated behind a large mahogany desk. "I have an appointment with a loan officer at 9:30," he said.

The receptionist's smile widened still further. "The loan department is on the 4th floor, sir. Just take that elevator and turn right when the elevator stops. The loan department will be straight ahead."

"Thank you," Bill nodded.

At the loan department, Bill took a seat and opened up today's national business newspaper. But right on time, a well-dressed (and very attractive) businesswoman came out to meet him.

"Mr. Ford?"

"Yes, please call me Bill." They looked into each others' eyes as they shook hands. *Wow – is she hot!*

"I'm Brandy – Brandy West," she responded with her charming Texas accent. "Please come with me."

I like this woman, Bill thought, as they walked down the hall toward her office. *Smart, articulate, and wow – does she have a presence about her!*

They sat across from each other. Brandy's sparkling smile came through as she said, "How may I help you?"

Bill shifted in his chair. "Well, I'm planning on starting a business and I'd like to borrow some money to help fund the capital equipment purchase."

Brandy leaned back in her chair. "What kind of business are you starting?"

"I'm planning a private mint," Bill replied. "You know – minting private coins for collectors. And then in the future, moving toward designing and striking coins for other countries."

"Interesting," Brandy replied. "In fact, awesome! I've not ever heard of a business like that."

She continued. "So, what kind of market is there?"

"Well," Bill replied, "There're two primary markets – collectors' pieces, and legal tender coins for other countries." He paused and looked into her eyes. "Collectors' pieces are a specialty market with high margins. On the other hand, minting legal tender is more of a mass-production market – it comes with higher sales volumes but smaller profit margins." He paused to hand over a document. "This is a copy of my business plan. There's a full discussion of market potential along with other analysis."

Brandy looked at the thickness of the document. "So, I'm sure that all of your costs are outlined here. How big a loan do you want?"

"I'm projecting equipment costs of about $450,000," Bill replied. "I'd like a loan for $360,000 – about 80% of the equipment costs – and I will cover the rest of it."

Brandy frowned and then seemed to make a decision.

"Okay, Mr. Ford – ah, Bill. If you will fill out this application, I'll see what I can do."

"What are my chances?"

"I'd say they're really good. We do business loans all the time. The big thing we look for is an asset that will secure the loan. Obviously, you will have such an asset." Brandy paused and smiled. "We will, of course, go through your business plan. But if you've done your homework – and I'm betting that you have – then there will be no problem at all."

Brandy's face lit up with a warm smile. "I'll move on it as soon as you get me that application."

* * *

That evening, Brandy sat down with a glass of wine and began reading through Bill's business plan. She was quickly engrossed.

To negate the economies-of-scale advantage from larger competitors, this plan anticipates capital equipment costs of $450,000.

She read through the projected revenue sources and costs – they were clearly spelled out, and many other details were equally clear. *This is a damn good plan*, she thought.

She especially liked Bill's discussion of risk mitigation. Bill had taken the time to detail the risks of a decline in gold and silver prices. But he went further and detailed the costs of managing these risks through the purchase of *put options.*

Brandy searched her memories from college. *Simply, a put option gives the owner the right to sell a security (or a commodity) at a specified price, regardless of the price of the underlying commodity. This means that he's covering the risk of a decline in gold/silver prices. Very smart, indeed.*

Brandy finished her wine and packed it in for the night.

*   *   *   *   *

Another day at the Bank . . .

Brandy poured a cup of coffee and walked back to her desk. She sat down and perused her newest emails, quickly keying on a message from Marcus. The message referenced Bill's loan. Curiously, Marcus had held up the loan application for a few days, and so Brandy now was planning to talk with Marcus. *Maybe I won't have to talk with him after all*, she mused.

She opened up the email and read the text.

"Brandy, I have declined the loan as described by the attachment. Please come and see me so that we can talk about it.

- Marcus"

Brandy's face turned red. She pulled up the attachment – a copy of the loan application. But she found no statement about the denial.

She breathed deeply and leaned back in her chair. *Son of a bitch!* And then, she let go of her tension, allowing it to flow out of her. She knew Marcus didn't respond favorably to other peoples' anger; and so she relaxed, bringing herself to a grounded, rational place.

Brandy walked down the hallway to Marcus' open office door. Long ago, he had requested that she just walk in if his door was open – and so, she entered and sat down. She watched Marcus as he was finishing up a call. It sounded as though he was giving his broker instructions for a stock sale.

Marcus put down the phone and turned his attention to Brandy.

Brandy spoke. "About Bill Ford's loan –"

"Oh, yes," Marcus interrupted. "I wanted to talk with you about it. Thanks for coming down."

Marcus leaned back in his chair; looking down at the pen he was fussing over. "I know that you recommended this loan highly. And given the quality of his business plan, I can surely understand why."

Brandy sat quietly, watching him fuss with his pen.

"But," Marcus looked up at her, "I had to run this by the loan approval board – both because of the loan amount, and because of the nature of his business –"

"Nature of his business?" Brandy interrupted. "What about his business?"

"Well, ah – it seems that some of the loan board members think that Mr. Ford's business is more about investment than it is about minting coins," Marcus replied. "They are especially concerned with his use of a loan to play in the gold and silver markets."

"Huh?" Brandy was prepared for just about any excuse – except this. "What are you talking about?"

Marcus paused in his meticulous, tedious manner. "One of the loan board members produced Federal Reserve Notice 96-037. This rule states that the bank shall not fund a purchase, either directly or indirectly, of any gold and/or silver."

Someone needs to shoot this bastard, she thought, even as she sat quietly listening.

"So," replied Brandy, "is there any possibility that we can give Bill the loan?"

Marcus was back to fussing with his pen; even as the undercurrent of tension and anger raged between them.

"No," Marcus replied, "there is no way we can loan him the money with this type of business."

Brandy tried hard not to show her feelings. But somehow, her "thank you, Marcus" sounded much more like "*fuck you, Marcus.*" She got up and walked out.

That night, Brandy made a telephone call. "Bill? This is Brandy. Is this a good time to talk? No? Okay - can we meet somewhere? I'd like to talk with you about your loan." She paused and then said, "No - not at the office. How about we meet for lunch at say - Roscoe's? Is noon tomorrow okay? Great. I'll see you then."

* * *

Roscoe's was established as an upscale restaurant in an upscale part of Scottsdale. Built on a miniature mesa, the restaurant had a north-facing unobstructed view of the McDowell mountain range. Besides the really great mountain views, the restaurant was quiet - an ideal place to talk business.

Brandy walked into the restaurant and up to the hostess' podium. "I'm supposed to meet someone here. He's tall with wavy blond hair. His name is Bill."

"Oh my," the hostess giggled. "He sounds like someone I'd like to meet, too!" Then she became all business and grabbed a menu. "Please follow me."

She led Brandy straight to Bill's table. Brandy greeted him as she sat down.

"So," Bill said, smiling, "to what do I owe the honor of a lunch meeting? Do you do this with all your clients?"

"No," Brandy laughingly replied, "you're my first."

"So, what's the word?" Bill asked.

"Well. In a nutshell, they turned down your loan application."

Bill paused, his smile turning to a frown. "I thought you were sure this would go through?"

"I was," Brandy replied, "I have seen a lot of these approved – and frankly, on much slimmer grounds than yours."

"Did they give a reason?" Bill asked. He started stretching and massaging his fingers.

"They gave two reasons," Brandy replied. "The first reason they cited was the loan amount. And the second reason was the nature of the business."

Brandy paused and looked into Bill's eyes. "The loan amount is bullshit – I'm sure of it. But their second reason – the nature of the business – is, *I think*, the real issue."

"My business?" Bill was perplexed. "What about *my* business?"

"I've run across several loans that were easily qualified, but that were ultimately denied," Brandy replied. "And get this – the reason they usually give is some nonsense that it violates the Federal Reserve's rules, and –"

Bill interrupted. "What does the Fed have to do with anything?"

"That's the weird thing," her voice lowered, "a few months ago I got a loan app from a 62-year-old woman – she totally qualified, Bill! And yet they declined her because she had joined some non-registered investment trust. The FBI had sent out a report that her membership in the trust meant she could be anti-government. And the Federal Reserve put out a notice that we were not to loan money to people who participated in these types of investments. And of course, because we are a 'National Bank', we are required to follow the rules of the Fed – go figure!"

Brandy continued. "I've gotten a few of these. In all of the cases, it's like someone does some sort of background check to see if the borrower is some kind of anti-government zealot."

"Now in your case, I don't think your profile came back as anti-government. But they seemed to be really attracted to your proposed business in gold and silver coins. In fact, the specific reason they cited was that yours' was more of an investment in precious metals than creating an actual business."

Bill rubbed his chin. "Hmmm ... But why would this be an issue? It doesn't make any sense!"

Brandy leaned back in her chair with a quizzical expression on her face. "Bill, what's your motivation for going into this business?"

Bill hesitated. "You've seen my business plan. Isn't it obvious why I want to do this? I think I can make a really good income."

Brandy eyed him thoughtfully. "I think there's more to it than that, Bill."

Bill was starting to become confused – curious, perplexed, wary ...

Finally, he looked into her eyes. "What's your interest in this?" Bill asked. "You've already given me the news about the loan. Why are we still talking?"

"This looks interesting to me," Brandy replied, "and I'm wondering if you're open to bringing me in as a partner."

Bill eyed her shrewdly, without saying a word.

Just then, the waitress arrived to take their order. They quickly made their menu selections and were just as quickly left alone.

Bill was still eyeing Brandy, even as Brandy was looking into his eyes with a smile.

"Why would I want you as a partner?" Bill finally asked.

Brandy touched her water glass and began stroking it. "Because I know where you can get the money you want. And besides," she grinned, "I'm good at marketing."

Bill looked across the table at Brandy. He stroked his water glass ever so lightly.

"So?" Brandy queried.

Finally, Bill made a decision. "I suggest, ah – I suggest that we get together at one of our places and talk this over."

A broad grin crossed over Brandy's beautiful face. "Awesome!"

* * *

Bill arrived at Brandy's Scottsdale townhome at 6:30 pm – right on time. Brandy greeted him at the front door just as he reached for the doorbell. "I sure am glad to see you," she said. "Please – come in."

Bill responded to her broad confident smile with a smile of his own. "This is a great idea. I'm glad to see you too."

Brandy led Bill into the living room.

"Can I offer you some wine?" Brandy asked. "I was able to stab some salmon at the local store – and I have a nice Pinot to go with it."

"Yes," Bill replied, "that sounds really good."

"Please sit down. I'll be right back."

Bill's gaze spanned much of the living room. Appointments in a southwest-style motif were the rule – and some were obviously expensive. Bill's eyes were drawn to the large painting over the fireplace. The painting was a vista of a desert landscape. The vista was from a place high on a mountain looking across a wide expanse of desert and mountains – and it was breathtaking. *She sure has nice taste,* he reflected.

Brandy returned quickly with two glasses of wine and handed one to Bill. "Here's to our discussion," she said with a smile. Their glasses clinked, and they each took a sip.

Bill appreciated a nice wine. But more importantly, he also appreciated a beautiful woman who knew a nice wine. He mentally smacked his lips. "I like this! I really like the subtle flavors in it – I don't often find this in a Pinot." *I need to keep this to the business. No romance – especially after Jennifer,* he mused.

Brandy looked past her glass of wine and smiled. "Thank you. I'm somewhat particular about wine. I think Pinot – a great Pinot, at least – has a nice delicate flavor. And that's what I look for in one of these."

"So," Brandy continued, "let's get down to business."

"Whoa – aren't we going to have some small talk first?"

Brandy looked down sheepishly. "I'm sorry, but I like to be forthright with my business dealings."

"But Brandy, we really don't know anything about each other, and we're already talking about a partnership." Bill paused and looked into her eyes. "I need more time to feel comfortable."

Brandy chuckled as she looked into Bill's eyes. "Isn't it the guy who usually likes to move fast?"

"Yes," Bill laughed, "but aren't we here to talk about business?"

"Okay. Okay," Brandy continued, "instead of talking about partnership; how about we just talk about 'what ifs' – let's just talk about what the business and partnership *could* look like."

"Okay. Let's do it," Bill took a sip of wine. *This seems safer than talking about a 'committed' partnership,* he thought with a mental grimace.

"So, what *does* the business look like? Brandy asked.

Bill shifted in his seat. "Well, I think that the business plan spells out the fundamentals. So, I'll just talk about the things that the business plan doesn't say –"

"Whoa – wait," she interrupted. "I'd like to hear your own words; business plan or not. I want to hear your vision."

Bill took a deep breath. "Okay, I see several things happening. First, I see a U.S. Dollar that is being debased – it seems like they're forever printing more and more of 'em. Secondly, I see Y2K coming –"

Brandy interrupted. "Y2K? What's that?"

"Y2K is a prediction that widespread computer failure will occur when the calendar changes over from 1999 to year 2000 – we call it the 'Y2K computer bug. The problem comes when people can't get their money out of a bank, and food and energy distribution stops. If this happens, the thinking is that people will go nuts and there'll be mass riots."

Brandy nodded. "But is this real? I mean, can this really happen?"

"Yes," Bill replied. "There's a possibility that this could all happen. Personally, I think they'll fix most of the computer problems beforehand. But that's not certain, especially since most software projects fail."

Brandy shook her head. "Wow! Go on."

"So," Bill continued, "the third issue I see is the consequences of either Y2K or a general debasement of the dollar –"

"I realize that debasement is bad," Brandy interjected, "especially for those who are on a fixed income or keep their savings in dollars. But we've lived through inflation before – just look back at the Carter years."

"But this can turn a lot worse than the Carter inflation." Bill was grim. "You might want to read up on 1920's Germany and the Weimar Republic. Hell – their inflation was so bad that you needed a wheelbarrow full of money just to buy a loaf of bread!"

"So?" Brandy prompted.

"So," Bill went on, "I think there could be a huge social or government upheaval because of this. We lose sight of the fact that many governments have been overthrown due to currency debasement alone, and it can happen here too."

"Okay. But how does your proposed business address these issues?"

Bill sighed. And then he said, "That's simple. Gold and silver have been money for 6,000 years. Governments can't print it out of thin air the way they print paper money – so, it's a great hedge against inflation. Quite frankly, it's a hedge against an out of control government; and heaven knows, I think our government is getting out of control."

Bill looked into Brandy's eyes. "Even without all the doom and gloom, I see this as a profitable business with good potential. And if things turn ugly, I see this as a business that will thrive and flourish."

"Oh wow – talk dirty to me." Brandy giggled. "I love a thriving business!"

Bill smiled as he gazed at her. "You seem to be taking this in stride. Doesn't any of this scare you?"

Brandy focused her gaze on Bill. "Why should it? It's out in front of me, and I know what it is – which means I can plan for it and make sure I take care of myself." She looked back at him and said, "It's the events I can't see and can't plan for – now that's what gives me pause!"

Brandy looked up at the clock. "Oh! It's time to put on the salmon. The rest of the meal is about ready!"

Bill followed her into the kitchen. *Damn, she's beautiful,* he thought.

Brandy bustled around the kitchen; grilling the salmon and putting the food on the table. Bill helped out with setting the table.

Finally, Brandy stood over the table with her hands clasped. "Okay – we're ready. Please have a seat."

They sat down to eat and were soon immersed in salmon and small talk.

Chapter 10

Brandy looked at her watch – 8pm. She had put in a long hard day on loan applications; and there was still a large stack waiting for her to process. *Aw hell! These will still be here tomorrow,* she thought. She grabbed her purse and jacket on the way out to the parking garage.

As she walked toward the garage, she reflected on Bill and his business plan. She smiled. *I really like him – and his business plan looks really good!* And then she thought back to Dallas – to her last marriage, and how it ended. She could still feel her ex's fist ...

His fist had knocked her to the floor. She held her chin as she glared up at him – her eyes blazing with fire.

"Damn you, Brandy! You'll do what I tell ya – or I'll mop the floor with ya!"

"Fuck you, Dan!" She fired back. "You lay another hand on me and I'll kill you!"

"Kill me? Kill me? You ain't gonna kill anyone," he sneered.

It was at that moment that she decided to leave. By evening, she was gone – and she never looked back.

Do I even want to get involved with this Bill character? She mused.

She had decidedly mixed feelings when she entered the parking garage. She made her way toward her parking space – it was up an aisle and around a corner. She hated working late; mostly because the garage was cleared out and no one was around. She always felt as though she were ripe for a mugging – *or worse!* She continued walking through the garage as she adjusted her purse – it had a long strap that she wore across her left shoulder. As always, she positioned her hand across the front of the purse as she walked.

Out of the corner of her eye she glimpsed the silhouette of a man, leaning near a concrete pillar of the garage. She wasn't sure, but she thought he may be eyeing her. And then she glanced again out of the corner of her eye, but the silhouette had vanished. She continued walking. Her senses now heightened on a hair trigger, she scanned and assessed everything around her. She felt the man leave his post, and then she sensed the soft impact of footsteps on concrete behind her. Hell, even though he was well behind her, she could almost sense his breathing on her neck!

Shit! This is not good. Her hand nervously rubbed the front of her purse.

She reached into the hidden compartment on the front of her purse. Grasping the grip of her pistol, she felt a bit less anxious, more in control. Her steps were quicker now as she turned the corner heading toward her car. And thinking just as quickly, *damn! He could have an accomplice at the car, or anywhere along my route. I need to confront him right here. Right now!*

She turned the concrete corner, passing by a set of stairs running parallel and next to the wall. She walked quickly by the jagged metal railing attached to the open side of the stairwell – it wobbled at the slightest touch. Just after passing the railing, she took cover behind a nearby concrete wall and drew her pistol from the hidden compartment. She waited with bated breath, surprised how clear and focused she felt. She listened as the footsteps approached, first at a normal pace and then slowing to a crawl.

The footsteps approached the corner. Ever so slowly – closer, and closer. She waited with her pistol in hand, pointing it toward the corner she had just turned. The footsteps were closer now – just around the corner. And then a man in dark leisure clothes came into view. Passing the stairwell, he looked down. And then he proceeded.

"Stop right there or I'll shoot!" Brandy barked.

The man froze in his tracks.

"Put up your hands!" Brandy barked again.

Hesitating, the man raised his arms.

"Higher!" She barked.

The man raised his hands above his head.

Brandy remained behind the wall with her pistol pointing at him. Then her voice barked again, "Who are you? Why are you following me?"

The man turned slowly to face her. His face wore the mask of a defeated man. "Please don't do this," he pleaded. "They'll fire me if they find out I've been caught."

"Huh?" Brandy said in wonderment. "What are you talking about?"

The man stood with his arms in the air. Nervous, tentative, afraid. Brandy watched his body – his muscles seemed to be pulling him to his right, as though he wanted to flee. And then he did flee – or he tried to. The man quickly turned to run in the direction from which he came. But a strange thing happened – he ran into the edge of the stair railing. Brandy watched as the left side of the man's coat was ripped on the jagged edge – and he stumbled as he almost fell over, his knee and elbow scraping the concrete. And then he regained his feet and took off in a sprint – quickly rounding the corner, he disappeared. And all of this took place in a breathless millisecond.

Brandy waited until she could no longer hear his footsteps; then she scanned the area and came out of her cover, her pistol still at ready. She walked toward the jagged railing – the one that the man collided with. As she approached, she saw tattered cloth and a wallet on the ground – she looked around and then stooped to pick it up. *What an inept son of a bitch*, she thought.

Rolling the wallet over in her hand, she finally put it in her purse and proceeded on to her car. She walked to her car while carrying her gun, pointing it down by her side.

She opened the car door and got in, locking the doors behind her. She placed the gun on the passenger's seat; and then, she felt the shakes begin. Starting with her hands and running up her shoulders, and then to her torso, her shakes became more intense. Then came the tears – and still more tears.

Brandy soon regained some of her composure. She started her car and drove out of the garage, proceeding toward her townhome. All the while she watched to see if she was followed.

Arriving home, she pulled into her garage – there was no sign of anyone in the vicinity.

She walked into her living room and sat down on the sofa. *Who was that? And what did he want!*

She pulled out the wallet and opened it. A hundred-or-so dollars, drivers' license, and credit cards. Apparently, Travis Leeson was his name. And then, she came across some business cards:

> Travis Leeson, Special Agent
> Federal Bureau of Investigation
> Maricopa County Branch
> Phoenix, Arizona 85021
>
> Office: (602) 555-6254

What the hell! She thought. *What is this about?*

I don't know if he will help, she reflected. *Hell – I really don't even know the man!* And then she made a decision. She picked up the telephone and dialed a number. "Hi, Bill? Can you come over here?" She paused, listening to Bill. "Well, I know you're busy but this is really important." She paused again. "Okay – I'll see you in 15."

Brandy went into the kitchen and poured herself some Scotch. *Funny thing – I bought the bottle several years ago, but it was still sealed.*

She walked back into the living room and sat down on the sofa. Her shaking hands lifted the glass to her lips. She took a swallow - feeling the bite of the scotch at the back of her throat. Time was moving ever so slowly ...

Ding dong!

Brandy went to the door and looked through the door's peephole. On seeing Bill, she exhaled; feeling her tension rush out of her. She opened the door and let him in.

"What's up?" Bill asked as he strode into the living room.

Then he turned and looked into her eyes. "Brandy. What happened!"

She produced the wallet and handed it to him. "This guy was following me as I was leaving work - walking through the parking garage."

Brandy then related the events of the evening.

Bill scanned through the contents of the wallet and came across the business cards. "Wow! FBI - that's some business he's in!"

Bill looked thoughtfully at the wallet in his hand, and then he looked up at Brandy. "I know this may sound crazy - but I've had a feeling I've been followed too. In fact, I could have sworn that someone tailed me over here."

Brandy sank into the sofa and swallowed a sip of scotch. "Can I get you something to drink?"

"Yes - please. I'll have whatever you're drinking."

Brandy went out to the kitchen. She returned with a drink in tow, and was somewhat surprised that the lights were turned out. She looked over at the window - Bill was peering out through the blinds.

Bill turned and looked at her. "There's a parked car with a man sitting in it - across the street. But I can't make out who it is." He paused for a moment. "Did someone tail you home?"

"I don't think so." Brandy replied. "I kept an eyeball out. I didn't see anyone."

"Then he's probably following me," Bill said, as he turned the lights back on.

"You know," Brandy said, "for some reason, I don't doubt that you've been followed. Though I wonder what it's about."

"Well," Bill replied, "since it looks like we're both wearing a tail, maybe it has something to do with this loan I applied for? Or maybe it has something to do with us meeting after the loan was denied?"

Brandy observed. "If we've been followed, then it's likely we're also bugged – don't you think?"

Bill's eyes became hard as he looked at her. "Shhhh," he said as he pressed his index finger over his mouth.

Bill walked over to the telephone and lifted the receiver. He unscrewed the microphone cover and opened it up – finding the usual components of a telephone mic. He replaced the microphone cover and placed the receiver on its cradle.

Then Bill started walking – softly – around the room; looking for possible places to hide a bug. He stopped at an air conditioning register and peered at the screws holding it in place. The screws and register had been painted along with the rest of the ceiling – the same color; but the screws showed scratches from contact with some kind of a metal object.

Bill walked over to Brandy and whispered, "Do you have a screwdriver?"

Quietly, Brandy walked out to the kitchen and returned, handing a screwdriver to Bill. Brandy looked on as Bill mounted a footstool and unscrewed the register cover. Pulling the cover off, he revealed what appeared to be a small microphone dangling by a couple of wires. Bill left the microphone dangling and stepped down from the stool.

Bill and Brandy paused, just looking at each other. Bill whispered, "Let's get outta here – leave your purse."

Outside, Bill ignored his car and instead walked slowly down the sidewalk. Brandy quickly caught up to him. As they walked, Bill looked around to see if anyone was watching – they were silent as they walked. Soon, they reached a local neighborhood park. Finding a bench in a somewhat secluded section of the park, they sat down – both were still silent.

Bill finally spoke, softly. "Wow! What the hell is going on?"

"I don't know," Brandy replied. "But suddenly, my life is no longer my own."

Bill frowned. "Do you think we have any bugs on us?"

"I don't see how," Brandy replied.

"Yeah – I don't see how, either." Bill said. "I think we need a strategy. What do you think?"

"I think so," Brandy replied. "Do you have any suggestions?"

"Well, first some questions." Bill's voice was grim. "Who's doing this? Why are they doing this? What do they hope to gain? How can we stop them – or will we always have to live under their thumb?"

Brandy felt her expression harden. "I think we ought to start by calling Special Agent Leeson – I'll bet he wants his wallet back," she snickered. "And we may want to have a talk with Marcus."

"Marcus? Who's Marcus?" Bill asked.

"My manager," Brandy replied. "The asshole who denied your loan."

* * *

They began walking and soon arrived back at Brandy's townhome. Brandy pulled out a business card from the wallet and made the call. She began speaking, "Yes. I'm calling Special Agent Leeson. I'm the woman you met in the parking garage, and I have your wallet. Please call me at 602-555-9283 to claim it."

Brandy hung up the receiver, turned, and smiled her first smile of the evening at Bill.

Ring! Ring!

Brandy picked up the receiver. "Yes?" Brandy paused. "Well, you may pick it up at my home. After all, I'm sure you know where I live!" Brandy paused again. "Yes – that's right."

Brandy hung up the phone and turned to Bill. "He said he would be over in a half-hour. He didn't ask for an address; and he didn't ask for directions."

✳ ✳ ✳

Ding dong!

Brandy checked the peephole and then opened the door, finding the same nondescript man she confronted in the garage. In a deliberate fashion, she sized him up – scrutinizing him from head to toe and imprinting him into her mind. She finally said, "Mr. Leeson, I presume?"

"Yes. I'm Leeson," he admitted.

"Will you please come in?" Brandy said.

Brandy led Leeson into the living room. Leeson did not seem surprised to find Bill there.

Bill remained seated on the sofa.

"Hello, Mr. Leeson," Bill said. "Or, should I call you, Special Agent Leeson?"

Leeson mumbled a greeting; and then he turned to face Brandy. "Where's my wallet?"

"I have it right here," she said, brandishing it before him. "But first, I want you to answer some questions."

"Like what?"

"Like, why you were following me?"

"Following you? I was not following you." Leeson sneered. "I was on a stakeout watching someone else – but that person apparently slipped by me."

"Wow," Brandy's voice was dripping with sarcasm. "You lost both your man and your wallet all in the same day. Did you attend the 'Keystone Kops' class at the FBI academy?"

Brandy folded her arms. "C'mon, Mr. FBI, do you really expect me to believe your lame story?"

"Believe what you want," Leeson replied. "Give me my wallet and I'll be on my way."

"Before I give this to you, Mr. Leeson, I have one question." Brandy continued. "How did you know where I live?"

Leeson was cornered now – and he knew it. "Well – ah, ah, um. When – when I saw that you had my wallet, I followed you home."

"No Mr. Leeson," Brandy replied. "I watched for any sign I was being followed. I am certain that no one followed me home."

"With all due respect, Mr. Leeson," Brandy continued, "you made a terrible mistake by stalking me in a deserted parking garage this evening. And I'm not gonna let you off 'til you tell me what you're up to."

At Brandy's last statement, Leeson looked down at the floor. And then he looked at Brandy. With a sullen voice, he said, "Well, ma'am, I'm asking – one more time – that you return my wallet to me."

"We're not finished yet, Mr. Leeson," Brandy replied. "You need to answer for the bugs that were planted in my home."

"And my home as well," Bill chimed in. "In fact, I want to see a court order for all of the surveillance and bugging that you're doing."

"Bu, but, but –"

"Damn it, Leeson," Bill interrupted him, "I want to see your supervisor. And I demand to know by what authority you're so eager to violate my – no, *our* – Constitutionally protected rights!"

"What's your boss' contact information?" Bill snapped.

Leeson was even more sullen, if that was possible. "Give me a piece of paper and a pen, and I will write her contact info down for you."

Brandy quickly handed over a pen and paper. And just as quickly, Leeson scribbled it down and gave it back to her.

Brandy looked at him and smiled. "Now, Mr. Leeson, you may have your wallet – *after* we talk with your supervisor."

* * *

The next morning, Brandy arrived at the office early. She knew that Marcus was frequently mired in his work, and she wanted to talk with him while he was still available. But with last evening's excitement, she was tired and cranky.

Coffee in her hand, Brandy stood at Marcus' office door. *Knock, knock!*

Marcus looked up. "Good morning, Brandy. You're here early. You - you look tired. Did you have a hot date last night?"

Somehow, Marcus' jokes never seemed very funny. And when Brandy didn't laugh, Marcus' smile turned serious.

"I had an interesting evening." She replied. "Last night, I found out that the FBI has had a tail on me."

"Oh?" Marcus leaned back in his chair. "How do you know they were following you?"

"It gets worse than that, Marcus," Brandy continued, "they bugged my fucking home."

Marcus began touching the fingertips of his hands together.

She looked squarely at Marcus. "Did you have anything to do with this?"

Marcus wilted under Brandy's stare. "The FBI has been monitoring Bill Ford. When you and Bill started seeing each other, the FBI began watching you as part of their surveillance on Ford."

"And?" asked Brandy.

"And, what?" said Marcus. "That's all I know!"

"Did the FBI tell you we were seeing each other?"

"Yes."

"And you thought it important enough to invade my privacy?"

Marcus was silent.

"Damn it, Marcus! - What gives you the right to have me followed? Who the fuck do you think you are?"

"I'm sorry, Brandy." Marcus replied. "This was my poor judgment."

"So," Brandy asked, "why were they watching Bill - ah, Ford?"

Marcus cleared his throat. "They found out, ah - that he was involved in the private investment trust. You know, the same one that Ms. Bowman was involved with."

"So," Brandy voice was drenched with sarcasm, "is this all about the 'supremacy' of our Federal Reserve money again? Huh?"

Marcus was silent.

Brandy glared at him. "Marcus, I formally give you my resignation, effective in two weeks. It'll be on your desk within the hour."

Brandy stormed out of the room.

* * *

That evening, Brandy was busily cleaning the kitchen with her thoughts spinning through her mind. *Damn! I like that Bill guy! He's right there for me - and he's so damn smart.* And then she switched gears. *But what about this investment trust? What's his part in it? Is this really as bad as Marcus says it is?*

She was distracted from her thoughts by the front doorbell.

Ding dong!

Brandy opened the door; finding Bill with a sheepish grin on his face.

"Don't you know how to call?" Brandy smiled as she chided him.

Bill grinned and held up a small electronic device.

"What's that?" She asked.

Bill crossed his lips with his index finger, signaling her to silence. "May I come in?" He asked casually.

Brandy stepped away from the door, allowing Bill to enter.

Bill held out his device and began walking through each room, observing a meter on the device as he moved. Brandy followed quietly, watching with interest as he waved it near a telephone, stopped, and removed a device from the telephone handset. He moved on, finding yet another device in her bedroom, and still another in her kitchen. He put the devices in a box and placed the box outside.

Bill then walked out to her car and checked both the garage and her Porsche. Finding a bug in the Porsche, he disposed of it as well.

They walked back into her home.

"Bug sweeper," he held it up for her perusal. "I found some bugs in my house too."

Brandy folded her arms and looked at him with a laugh. "With equipment like that," she joked, "you can come over anytime." *Damn, I like this guy!*

Bill just smiled.

She motioned to the device. "So what's this thing do?"

"It's pretty simple," he replied. "It scans for Radio Frequency emissions. They call it RF." He paused and then continued. "You see, these bugs have to emit an RF signal to transmit the information back to an eavesdropping receiver station; otherwise, they'd be useless. Look at this – this meter gives feedback on the signal strength of any nearby RF device. So, all you need to do is get the device near a bug and, voilà, we've got it!"

He sure has a cute grin, she thought. "Where'd you get it from?"

"I borrowed it from a guy I used to work with. He probably got it from work. Hell, they have several of these just to identify any RF leakage for their cellular network testing."

They both moved over to the sofa.

"So, how'd your visit with your boss go today?"

"With Marcus?" Brandy grimaced. "Shit! I guess it was interesting – but that's the only good thing I can say about it."

Brandy sighed and then continued. "First, they are definitely watching you. Second, they are watching you because of that private investment trust you were involved in. Third, he says that they started watching me when we began seeing each other – but, *really*, I'm not so sure that's true ..."

"And?'

"And I gave him my resignation with two week's notice."

"Wow! Did you burn your bridges?"

Brandy was sheepish. "I'd say so. I didn't call him any names; but I didn't pull any punches either. So, yeah – I probably burned bridges. At least in the banking industry."

Brandy paused and then tilted her head. "So," she said tentatively, "what about this investment trust thing?" She looked at Bill. "What's that about?"

"There's not much to tell." Bill sighed. "I invested some money in a private investment deal. The fund managers invest in global 'opportunities'; usually short-term investments." Bill shifted his position. "They bill it as a big return on your money – as much as several hundred percent per year."

"Wow! Doesn't that sound too good to be true?"

Bill hesitated. "Well, yeah. But I decided to try it anyway."

"Why!"

"I talked with the managers. They said they could achieve these results because they had no government oversight or regulation." Bill shrugged. "And besides, I only invested the minimum amount – $1,294."

"So," Brandy asked slowly, "is it illegal?"

"I don't see how. Hell, the prospectus says they'll only make legal investments. And the U.S. Constitution protects the right of people to enter into private contract." Bill paused before continuing. "And this is, or *was,* a private contract." Bill's voice took on a bitter tone. "But the Feds shut it down. They sent all the fund managers to jail and confiscated all the money." Bill's mouth crooked up in a smirk. "I heard the Feds netted $45 million, maybe more."

Bill looked into Brandy's eyes. "I was in it at the time they pulled the plug. I just left my money in, figuring that was better than letting the Feds know about me. But I guess they found out anyway." Bill paused and then continued. "Hell, I don't know how they got my name. I guess there was a mole in the program. Or maybe – *maybe* my ex had something to do with it," he grimaced. "She used to rag on me a lot. The bitch said I'd be going to jail!"

Bill looked into Brandy's eyes. "Anyway – that's my story."

Brandy's voice was soft. "Thanks for sharing. It sounds as though it was a tough deal."

"Yeah," Bill replied.

"So," she continued, "I'm sorry to be intrusive – you don't have to answer me – but, what happened with your ex? With your marriage?"

"My ex?" Bill looked at her. "We split a couple of years ago; it was the best thing that ever happened to me."

"How come?" Brandy's voice was soft – inviting.

"How come?" Bill's voice was choking up. "In a nutshell, her incessant control and her damn anger. Hell, she was always ragging on me." Bill paused and then continued. "Anyway – it's over."

They both became silent, allowing the silence to settle into the room.

And then Bill's mood shifted. "About these bugs ...," he prompted.

"Yes?"

"I'm pretty sure I found all of them. But there's one caveat that we always need to be aware of. These bug detectors only find bugs that actually *transmit.* Unfortunately, there are some bugs that record information without transmitting – their effectiveness depends on someone retrieving the recorded information. So, we also need to watch for the recording-type bugs as best we can; and also check to see if anyone enters while taking extraordinary steps to hide their entrance."

"Okay," she said. "Anything else?"

"Yes." Bill was thoughtful. "Watch out what you send over email."

"Okay," she said. "Anything else?"

"Yeah. Watch what you say on the telephone."

"Okay. What else?"

"Nothing else," Bill smiled. "That should cover it."

"Cool," her eyes were sparkling. "How about some wine?"

"Oh – yes!" He replied.

With wine glasses charged, Brandy held up her glass. "I propose a toast – a toast to finding a new job."

Bill grinned as their glasses clinked. "To finding a new job."

They sipped their wine.

Brandy eyed Bill, then raised an eyebrow. "So, Bill. Why this gold thing? Why do you want to mint coins?"

"Why? That's simple." Bill smiled. "Because the same government that screwed private investors out of their money, is screwing Americans out of their wealth through inflation." Bill's voice resonated with passion. "And I want to do something about it."

"Wow," she replied. "I guess that covers it."

They sipped their wine as they talked. Most of their conversation covered Brandy's work, the Federal Reserve, and the FBI's surveillance. They talked for some time about the FBI and about the rules put out by the Federal Reserve. Sipping their wine and snuggling, they were happy they could now talk freely, taking solace in the fact that the federal government bugging operation had been shut down.

Brandy noticed their glasses were emptying. "Would you like some more wine?"

Bill frowned. "Yes, I'd like some very much; but if I have any more, I won't be able to drive."

"Well," Brandy chimed in, "why don't you stay here for the night?"

*   *   *   *   *

"So, Ms. Smith," Bill demanded, "by what authority are you conducting surveillance on us?"

Kelly Smith, director of the local office of the FBI, did not even blink. "Mr. Ford, you are very misinformed about our activities. I am head of this office, and I know nothing about any surveillance regarding you or Ms. West –"

"Wait a minute," Brandy interrupted, "I personally confronted this Leeson character – hell, I even have his business card! And you're telling me that he was not following me?"

"Mr. Leeson no longer works here," she said.

"Really? He's gone? What did you do with him?" Bill sneered.

Kelly Smith looked back at Bill and Brandy – her face was deadpan.

Bill pulled out one of the bugs he found and put it on the desk.

Kelly Smith eyed the device. "What is that?"

"You tell me." Bill countered.

"I'm sorry, Mr. Ford. I don't know what that is."

"It's a bug," Bill picked it up and waved it in front of her eyes. "I found it along with several other bugs in and around my home; and Brandy's home too." He paused, looking at her with penetrating eyes. "I had it analyzed, Ms. Smith. It tests positive for materials exclusive to the U.S. government."

"So?" Kelly Smith countered.

Bill could feel his head about to explode. "So these were put into our homes!"

An awkward silence filled the room.

"I'm sorry, Mr. Ford. But I have no information for you."

Bill was exasperated. "What kind of shit is this? Who do you think you are?"

"This meeting is over, Mr. Ford." Then she pushed her chair back and rose to her feet, indicating that the conversation was finished.

Bill and Brandy got up from their chairs.

Bill focused his gaze on Ms. Smith. "You need to know, Ms. Smith, that if I detect any hint of being followed – ever again – I will file suit against you personally."

Kelly Smith looked at Bill and Brandy with a stone face. "May I show you out?"

"No thank you, Ms. Smith." Bill replied. "We can find our way."

As they were opening the door on their way out, Kelly Smith interrupted their exit, "watch yourselves."

Bill and Brandy proceeded out the door.

As they were walking down the hallway, Bill asked, "what did you think of that?"

"Sounds like a threat to me."

"Yep. But what do you think of her?"

"Gawd, Bill. If the rest of the FBI is like her, they are really creepy – and dangerous!"

"Yeah," Bill replied. "Do you want to come over tonight?"

"Sure. What do you have in mind?"

"If you're willing, I'd like to talk about our partnership."

"Wait a minute, now." She joked, "I thought you were the guy that didn't want to move too fast."

"Hey. We can talk without making a commitment, can't we?"

"Do you want me to bring anything?" Brandy smiled.

"Just you," Bill smiled.

* * *

Over several evenings and several bottles of wine, Bill and Brandy spent some considerable time discussing the various aspects of their partnership. Through their discussions, they came to agreement on financing and terms of partnership. Also, they agreed that Bill's primary job would be on product specification, design, and production – for both coin and depository operations, and that Brandy's primary focus would be on sales and marketing.

With Y2K on the horizon, they also agreed they would move to another part of the country – they settled on northern Idaho.

At the end of an evening's discussion, Brandy was seated on the sofa with her head flung back, in an ever-so-relaxed moment. "So," Brandy mused, "when do we make our move?"

Bill moved over next to her and started kissing her neck.

Brandy giggled. "Not *that move.*"

Bill found her lips and they came together in a long, passionate kiss.

"So is that the move you're talking about?" Bill asked.

"(sigh) No – but I already forgot what I was asking." Brandy replied, her eyes sparkling. "Just kiss me."

Bill brought her close and held her body even closer as they kissed yet again. His hands moved under the back of her blouse, gently caressing her skin. And then he slowly moved higher, fondling the back of her brassiere. He ran his hand under the strap, and then he put his fingers on the clasp – it unsnapped. Brandy stopped the kiss and looked at him. "Hey, Mister. What do you have in mind?"

"You," Bill said simply.

"And what makes you think I want you?"

Bill grinned as he presented his arms out to the side, as though performing on stage. And then he said, "Hey. It's me – Bill. I'm the best thing that's ever happened to you."

"I doubt that," she pouted.

"Well, maybe second best thing?"

"Maybe," she said demurely.

Bill's grin was wider still as he said, "C'mon, Brandy – you want me. You know you want me."

Brandy smiled as she looked into his eyes, and then their eyes met. She pulled him close and they kissed again, their passion washing through them even more intensely. "Oh!" Brandy gasped as Bill moved his hand under her blouse, slowly caressing her skin.

She moaned. And as their lips were locked and their tongues probing each other, she moved her hands down to Bill's belt.

... And that evening was special for them both, as they spent it in each others' embrace.

Chapter 11 – Circa 1997/1998

In the absence of the gold standard, there is no way to protect savings from confiscation through inflation. There is no safe store of value. If there were, the government would have to make its holding illegal, as was done in the case of gold. If everyone decided, for example, to convert all his bank deposits to silver or copper or any other good, and thereafter declined to accept checks as payment for goods, bank deposits would lose their purchasing power and government-created bank credit would be worthless as a claim on goods. The financial policy of the welfare state requires that there be no way for the owners of wealth to protect themselves. This is the shabby secret of the welfare statists' tirades against gold. Deficit spending is simply a scheme for the confiscation of wealth. Gold stands in the way of this insidious process. It stands as a protector of prop-

erty rights. If one grasps this, one has no difficulty in understanding the statists' antagonism toward the gold standard.

- - - excerpt from Gold and Economic Freedom by Alan Greenspan, 1966

* * * * *

As executive assistant to the Federal Reserve Chairman, Carol Stapleton seldom lowered herself to the job of typist; but this was one of those times. No one could compose this particular form of memo quite the way that she could. It wasn't the format – heaven knows almost any typist could do that! It was the message and the audience that was important, stated exactly the way it needed to be; with just the right amount of obfuscation and ambiguity – the FOMC[7] would be thankful they understood any part of it! *After all*, she smiled, *we mustn't do anything to ruin the Chairman's reputation!*

Intent on completing the internal memo, the ever-efficient Carol Stapleton's fingers were flying over the keyboard when the telephone rang.

"Office of the Federal Reserve Chairman. May I help you?"

"Hi, Carol. This is Bob Rubin. Is Mr. Chairman available?"

"Let me check, sir. I will have to put you on hold."

"That's fine."

Carol punched a button on the intercom. "Sir, Mr. Rubin on line 2; would like to speak with you."

Carol listened as the intercom came alive. *"Thank you, Carol. I will take the call."*

Carol resumed her typing.

* * *

---

7   FOMC – the Federal Open Market Committee (a committee of Federal Reserve executives) meets on a recurring basis to set monetary policy – interest rates (which is the price of money) and policy implementation.

Soon, Carol's intercom buzzer sounded. She paused from her composition and pressed the button. "Yes sir?"

"Please clear my schedule for the next 3 hours."

"May I remind you, sir, that you have a telephone conference with the Prime Minister of Israel scheduled in one hour?"

"I am aware of that. Please reschedule with my sincerest apologies."

"Yes, sir."

"And please ask Jim Martin and Dave Langford to meet me in my office in 30 minutes."

"Right away, sir."

"And please let them know that this meeting may take some time."

"Yes, sir."

* * *

Tying his necktie, Jim strode into the Chairman's office suite on his way to the Chairman's personal office. "Hi, Carol. How are you today?" He stopped to tuck in his white shirt - catching his sleeve on the pens sticking out of his shirt pocket.

Carol looked up from her composition. "Oh. Hi Jim. I'm doing well." And then Carol continued. "Better hurry. They're already in there."

Jim almost stumbled into the Chairman's office, where he found Treasury Secretary Robert Rubin and Dave Langford - Chairman Greenspan's Chief of Staff - in a heated discussion with the Chairman.

Jim's attention was drawn to Rubin. His face was beet red as he was speaking. "... and she intends to impose regulations on the OTC Derivatives[8] market. I tell you, Alan, I spent a good hour on the phone with Larry Summers[9] – he was pissed. He'd already spent half the morning being assaulted by a room full of bankers. They read him the riot act!" Rubin paused and took a deep breath. "Larry had a conversation with Born. Larry told her that he had 13 bankers in his office, complaining, and *that she needed to immediately stop the movement toward regulation or she would cause the greatest financial collapse ever.*[10] He said to her; "you don't get it! Stop this now!"

"And what did she say?" Chairman Greenspan asked from behind his black-rimmed glasses and his wrinkled, somber face.

"She said she would move ahead."

Jim took a seat and listened. He was good at listening. As Chief Staff Economist reporting directly to Chairman Greenspan, he was experienced at directing the Federal Reserve's stable of economists in their collection of economic data – data that was vital to the formulation of Fed policy. He hated politics – and this conversation smacked of political crap – but he knew

---

8   OTC Derivatives – means Over The Counter Derivatives – derivatives are a class of financial securities that are designed to mitigate (manage and overcome) risk – in other words, a derivative is an insurance policy. Because they are unregulated, the seller may charge much less than the underlying risk exposure; which means that buyers of these contracts may not be fully covered for their risky behavior. Also, the derivatives markets tend to lack transparency – which means fraud can easily be perpetrated, and multiple claims can be made on the same asset without prior knowledge of the counterparties.

9   At this time, Lawrence Summers was serving as Deputy Secretary of the Treasury under Robert Rubin.

10   Introducing regulation (and presumably, transparency) into a market where none existed would change the perceived risk to the contract holders; and could cause them to sell their contracts at a loss – resulting in an unwinding of the derivatives markets. This 'unwinding' would result in a cascade of selling off other financial instruments – stocks, bonds, etc. – causing an economic collapse of epic proportions.

that politics and economics were inexorably tied to each other. And so he deigned to stay engaged.

Chairman Greenspan sat at his desk with his hands folded together – listening. He interrupted the conversation and looked toward Jim, said, "Hi there. We are talking about Brooksley Born, the new head of the CFTC[11]. She claims her agency has the authority to regulate OTC Derivatives."

And then he turned and looked at Rubin. "Does she have that authority?"

Rubin grimaced. "Yes."

"Damn!" The Chairman was clearly dismayed. "Well, she's outside of my chain of command; and yours' too. I think we may need to get Congress in on this."

Rubin's normally handsome face was about to explode. "I've got to tell you, I've received a lot of calls about her. The people I'm hearing from are well-heeled – people who tell me that trillions of dollars are at risk." Rubin leaned forward and looked at Alan in earnest. "Alan, regulated markets are barely profitable. If she comes in and imposes regulations, the derivatives markets will be no more profitable than the other regulated markets – the banks' profits will suffer greatly."

Alan nodded his head in agreement. "Maybe we first should see if we can move her out of the way without going to Congress."

Rubin leaned back in his chair. "What do you have in mind?"

"Let's have a meeting with her. Let's explain it to her."

"Okay. I like that." Rubin stroked his chin. "What do you know about this woman – Brooksley Born?"

"I met her. I invited her for lunch a while back. She was a contender for Attorney General before Janet Reno got the job. Heaven knows we probably would not have had Waco had she been the AG."

---

[11] CFTC is the Commodity Futures Trading Commission. This is an independent agency of the U.S. government that regulates futures and options markets.

"And?"

"Brooksley Born is an attorney and a financial regulator. She's brilliant. But I am not surprised that she thinks these markets need to be regulated. During our lunch, she as much told me she wanted to police against fraud."

Alan shrugged. "Like I said. She's a regulator. She believes in government intervention in the markets."

Left unsaid was the philosophy that both the Chairman and the Secretary lived by – *that free markets are self-regulating and do not require government oversight.*

* * *

Soon after . . .

The limousine wound its way through the streets of Washington, D.C. Inside the limo, Chairman Greenspan and Jim Martin were talking – talking about Brooksley Born.

"So, did Bob happen to mention how far along Brooksley is on her Concept Release?" Jim asked.

"Somewhat. He said that Brooksley was already circulating it to regulators and trade associations. He wants to kill this quickly – and so do I."

"What's so bad about regulating the derivatives markets?" Jim asked.

Alan looked at him and smiled. "Jim, you've been around me long enough to know my answer."

Jim smiled back. "Yes, I know. You believe that completely free markets are the most productive markets; and that markets are inherently self-regulating, requiring no government oversight."

"Correct," Alan noted.

"But," Jim assumed a wry smile, "you've never explained to me how our markets can be 'totally free', as you put it, when we extend our heavy hand in setting an artificial price for money."[12]

---

[12] The Federal Reserve uses various means, such as the Discount Rate and the Fed Funds Rate to set interest rates. In other words, the Fed imposes price

Jim leaned forward. "What this means, Mr. Chairman, is that none of our markets are free, because one side of every transaction consists of money whose value is set by the Fed!"

Alan looked at Jim and smiled. "You have a lot of credibility, which is why I asked you to attend. I urge you to stick to the issues in our meetings; and," he paused, looking at Jim knowingly, "I want you to express your conclusions about imposing regulation in these OTC Derivatives markets."

Jim smiled. "Okay. If need be, I will make myself crystal clear."

*   *   *

The limousine pulled up to the front of Treasury. Alan and Jim stepped out, entered the building, and made their way through the asphalt-tiled corridors; walking by one elaborate old wood doorway after another.

Walking into the conference room, Jim noted that it was typical of federal government meeting chambers – the floor was a quality industrial padded carpet, and the walls were paneled in a medium-tone wood, probably birch. The sun was streaming through the windows.

Jim looked around the room and noted that the main players of the President's Working Group were already seated – Larry Summers, Bob Rubin, and SEC[13] Chairman Arthur Levitt.

Jim noted too that Brooksley Born, Chairwoman of the Commodities Futures Trading Commission was there. Since they had not previously met, he sized her up for the first time. Fifty-ish, with short dark hair, a broad mouth and penetrating

---

fixing on our money. So long as one side of every transaction involves the Fed's money, no transaction takes place in a 'free market'.

[13]   SEC is the Securities and Exchange Commission. This agency holds primary responsibility for enforcing the federal securities laws and regulating the securities industry, the nation's stock and options exchanges, and other electronic securities markets in the United States.

eyes, she was attired in a white blouse and business suit. Her deportment exuded an understated power. *She takes a back seat to no man,* he mused.

Alan greeted Brooksley and sat down beside her. Their manner seemed to be cordial toward each other, but an air of tension permeated the room.

Bob Rubin opened the meeting. "This meeting is called to order." He paused. "The purpose of this meeting is to discuss and provide input to the CFTC's proposed Concept Release for Over The Counter Derivatives."

"Chairwoman Born. Will you please provide an opening statement?"

"Thank you, Mr. Secretary. I will be brief." She paused. Putting on her reading glasses, she began reading from her prepared statement. "Currently, there is no government oversight or regulation of the OTC Derivatives markets. The CFTC possesses sole authority to regulate these markets, but so far has allowed them to function unfettered. We have observed a lack of transparency in these markets; and we believe that fraud is taking place. Because of this, we believe that oversight is necessary to protect the counterparties. But more important than this, we believe that leaving these markets without regulation will promote systemic risk – the risk that the unwinding of these markets could cause the entire economy to collapse."

"The Concept Release that we are proposing is a modest first step. It is intended to gather information about how these markets operate. It is not intended to promote the introduction of regulation into these markets." She paused and looked around at the other attendees. "But for us to continue ignoring these markets means that we risk a collapse of the entire economy. Thank you."

The tension was palpable. *You could cut it with a knife!* Jim thought.

Secretary Rubin replied. "Thank you, Mrs. Born."

Rubin paused and then continued. "Right after you began circulating the Concept Release, we received calls from a dozen or so large banks. These banks are telling us that your move is a threat to a major profit center. They also stated that your action to even contemplate regulation would cause widespread chaos in markets around the world."

Bob placed his hands on the table and leaned forward. "I'm here to tell you, Brooksley – you can't do this!"

Brooksley raised her eyebrows and looked at Rubin. "Oh?"

"Absolutely, Brooksley. You need to stop this now!" Rubin paused. "You can't do this. We just can't have it." Rubin shook his head. "This deregulated market is part of what's brought us this economic boom; and we don't want to change that. The market will take care of everything. And we really don't need regulation of these markets – it would just be counterproductive."

"Well, Bob. I hear you. But I report directly to the President. You have no say over the CFTC or how it exercises its statutory authority."

Rubin sputtered. "Brooksley, your agency doesn't have jurisdiction over these markets."

An ocean of calm, Brooksley looked back into Rubin's eyes. "Oh really? Bob, I have never heard anyone assert that we didn't have statutory jurisdiction. I will be happy to review the legal analysis you're basing your position on."

"Fine, I will gladly provide an analysis from our law department. In fact, I am quite willing to have one of my attorneys come down to see you – I'm sure he can explain the law to you."

Arthur Levitt chimed in. "Brooksley, if you try to undo these existing contracts, we will face a situation of financial turmoil the likes of which we've never before seen."

Jim could feel tensions rising as the meeting wore on.

Alan had been sitting quietly, listening, and facing straight ahead. But the color of his face was crimson when he turned and looked at Brooksley. And unlike the Chairman we all knew, his voice quivered as he began speaking. "This is a serious, serious mistake. It will cause untold damage to the financial services market. You need to stop. You need to not do this." He paused. "This is unwise, and it will cause tremendous damage."

Brooksley appeared to take Greenspan's comments at face value. She nodded but didn't respond.

The meeting continued on for a while – with no let-up in tension. When it adjourned, it was obvious that the unstated mission of the meeting – to convince Brooksley Born to stop what she was doing – had failed.

* * *

Two weeks later, Born instructed her staff to publish the Concept Release. This caused an immediate and unprecedented response from the President's Working Group; and it attracted a visceral response from the financial community at large. Brooksley Born quickly found herself in a crossfire.

Greenspan, Rubin, and Levitt responded immediately with this statement.

DEPARTMENT OF THE TREASURY
OFFICE OF PUBLIC AFFAIRS

May 7, 1998
RR-2426

JOINT STATEMENT BY THE TREASURY SECRETARY, ROBERT E. RUBIN, FEDERAL RESERVE BOARD CHAIRMAN ALAN GREENSPAN AND SECURITIES AND EXCHANGE COMMISSION CHAIRMAN ARTHUR LEVITT

On May 7th, the Commodities Futures Trading Commission ("CFTC") issued a concept release on over-the-counter derivatives. We have grave concerns about this action and its possible consequences. The OTC derivatives market is a large and important global market. We seriously question the scope of CFTC's jurisdiction in this area, and we are very concerned about reports that the CFTC's action may increase the legal uncertainty concerning certain types of OTC derivatives.

The concept release raises important public policy issues that should be dealt with by the entire regulatory community working with Congress, and we are prepared to pursue, as appropriate, legislation that would provide greater certainty concerning the legal status of OTC derivatives.

In addition to the published statement, 'the powers that be' in the Administration also put out information to the mainstream media. The media immediately took the story and ran with it; characterizing the CFTC action as a power grab and further describing Brooksley Born as someone who did not understand the OTC Derivatives markets.

Attacks were focused against the CFTC from all sides, leading to immediate hearings in Congress.

*   *   *

Four hearings were held over the summer. A Department of Agriculture Senate hearing, chaired by Senator Richard Lugar, set the tone for all of these hearings:

Senator Lugar: *"The hearing of the Senate Agricultural Committee is hereby called to order."*

Excerpts from other participants ...

"... today we will receive testimony on over-the-counter derivatives"

"... it is essential that the government not create uncertainty ..."

"... CFTC wants to come into somebody else's yard here ..."

As Brooksley Born was pummeled, the hearing wore on ...

> *Senator Phil Gramm:* "*I see no evidence whatsoever to suggest that this is a troubled market; that fraud is rampant in this market ...*"
>
> *Larry Summers:* "*... the Release has cast the shadow of regulatory uncertainty over a thriving market ...*"
>
> *Arthur Levitt:* "*... the CFTC's action has, and will bring I believe, significant disruption to this important global market ...*"
>
> *Alan Greenspan:* "*... serves no useful purpose, hinders the efficiency of markets, to en ...*"
>
> *Senator Phil Gramm:* "*I feel very strongly that we should not have one agency innovate in this area; and in doing so, create very substantial financial problems.*"
>
> *And then from an unidentified Senator, this question was posed:* "*... my question, again, is what are you trying to protect?*"

Brooksley Born stood firm, saying, "We're trying to protect the money of the American public; which is at risk in these markets."

Ms. Born was head of a small, some would say, insignificant, agency. She was no match against the likes of Robert Rubin, Larry Summers, and Alan Greenspan; and their influence with a Congress already hostile to the CFTC's action.

Congress departed on summer recess without finalizing a resolution ...

*　*　*　*　*

Jim Martin was home watching a movie when he received a telephone call – the call was from no less a personage than Chairman Greenspan himself.

"*Jim?*"

"Yes, sir. What can I do for you?"

"I am sorry. I don't like to call you on a weekend; but especially on Saturday evening."

"That's all right, sir. What's up?"

"We've got a situation. Long Term Capital Management is in the process of melting down."

"Melting down? Isn't that a little strong?"

"Not in this case. They've been losing several hundred million a day."

Jim paused in shock. Mouth open, he ran his hand through his hair. "Wow!"

Alan continued. *"There is something I want you to do."*

"Yes?"

"I want you to provide an analysis of the effects on all of the markets if LTCM[14] collapses."

"Okay. Anything else?"

"Yes. I also want an analysis on the effects to the economy should LTCM collapse."

"Got it. Anything else?"

"Just one more thing. I'd like to know how much capital would be required to keep LTCM in the black. As part of this analysis, you may want to consider a sale of LTCM to some other entity; maybe a bank, or something like that." Alan paused, then continued. *"You'll probably need to get one of your microeconomics specialists - someone who's familiar with the investment industry - to run those numbers."*

"When do you need this?"

Alan paused for a moment. *"We need it in time to save LTCM. So, as soon as you can get it to me."*

"I'll get right on it."

"Thanks."

*   *   *

---

[14] LTCM - Long Term Capital Management. LTCM was a private speculative fund that made extensive use of Derivatives.

Jim was at his desk early Monday when his telephone rang. "Jim Martin."

The Chairman's voice came across the wire. *"What have you got for me?"*

Jim replied, "Well, the current market for OTC derivatives is about $27 Trillion. There are about 15 large banks who are heavily invested in it. And the leverage in this market is about 97%."

Jim listened as the line went silent.

"Mr. Chairman?"

"Yes, Jim. Would you please come on up? And please, bring all your notes."

"I'll be there in ten minutes."

* * *

"So," Alan looked squarely at Jim, "what are the details?"

"Well, sir – I've been in contact with Dale Martin over at the New York Fed. They've been tracking events with LTCM. The word is that LTCM has been bleeding a lot of money; much more than their worst-case mathematical models predicted."

Alan leaned back in his chair, touching his hands together at his fingertips. "Go on."

"So, LTCM specializes in risky arbitrage deals – very lucrative deals in U.S., Japanese, and European bonds. They've leveraged their bets with more than $120 billion in borrowed money – money they've borrowed from banks. They also carry about $1.25 trillion in financial derivatives. As you know, they're considered rather exotic contracts and they're only partly reflected on their balance sheet."

Jim looked at Alan pointedly. "Some of these contracts are highly speculative, and some are designed to insure LTCM's portfolio against whatever risk could be imagined."

"So – what's the core issue causing this?"

"Well, sir. The oncoming Russian default is looking to be a huge problem for LTCM. It has caused a sea change in the markets so that LTCM's models no longer work. The owners of

LTCM are watching their $5 Billion in capital fly out the window."

Just then, the telephone rang.

Alan pressed the speakerphone button. "Yes, Carol?"

"I apologize for interrupting, Mr. Chairman.   Mr. McDonough is on the line and wishes to speak with you."

Bill McDonough was President and CEO of the New York Fed – the same New York Fed that implemented the monetary policy decisions made by the Board of Governors and the FOMC. The New York Fed was also responsible for overseeing the financial markets.

"Put him through please," Alan responded.

"Yes, sir," Carol replied.

And then Jim heard a click on the line.

"Bill?"

"Hi, Alan. How're you doing?"

"I'm doing well, Bill. But I think the question of the moment is, how are *you* doing?"

"Not so well, Alan. This LTCM thing was a big issue. It has now become huge."

"How is that?"

Jim thought he saw Alan's shoulders tighten.

"They're bleeding like crazy, Alan. And their bleeding is causing them to dump their assets onto the market."

"So?" Alan replied. "They knew they were taking risks. Now they need to bear the consequences of their choices – don't you think?"

"For once, I must disagree."

The Chairman responded by raising his eyebrows.

"Alan.   I think their failure will see an unwinding of the $27Trillion derivatives market. But worse – I think it will spread into all of the financial markets."

Alan shifted his stance as he stood over the speakerphone, listening.

"After all," Bill continued, *"much of their leverage is based on money borrowed from banks. If LTCM goes down, then the banks will have to write off the loans. Alan, I see this as causing*

a complete collapse of our financial system. This is the ultimate systemic risk."

Jim watched as Alan stood silently over the telephone - contemplating.

"What do you suggest, Bill?"

"Alan, I've got an idea for a bailout."

"Okay, Bill. I'm listening."

And Jim listened right along with Alan as Bill related his plan. And at the end of Bill's pitch, Alan sat back down at his desk.

"Okay, Bill. I don't like it. It smacks of a bailout." Then Alan's face softened. "But I can't disagree."

* * *

Jim arrived at the meeting early. Not that he had any official reason to attend; but he was fascinated by the oncoming catastrophe and how it would play out. And so, he found a chair well away from the conference table - a place from which he could observe without himself being noticed.

Jim carried a briefcase with him. He placed it on his lap and opened it, withdrawing a leather-bound book. He opened the book to a marked page and began writing in it. He had it open for a while - sometimes writing, but sometimes he would pause and just sit, pondering.

Jim thought about the history of the New York Fed. A major player with a long tradition in the management and implementation of monetary policy. It was within these hallowed walls where fortunes were made, and lost; and where Joe Sixpack's career was written. *Would Joe Sixpack have a job this year? Or would the Federal Reserve withdraw money from circulation and put him out of work?*

But that was not the topic this day. *Today,* Jim mused, *I can watch the unfolding of the resolution to this crisis - how to save the economy of the world from falling into a deep abyss? This is history!*

And so he watched Bill McDonough stand at the entrance to the conference room. His lean face and square jaw assumed a serious posture as he greeted the attendees filing into the room. Leaders, they were; leaders from some of the largest banks in the U.S. and Europe. Goldman Sachs, JP Morgan, Lehman Bros., Bear Stearns, and Merrill Lynch, just to name a few – the men who shaped the world of finance. And through their control of the banking system, they controlled the entire economy.

The throng increased. And with ever more people milling around, the noise, the back-and-forth discussion, also increased. It was as though he were in a nightclub with a million conversations – except there were few women, and the band was not playing.

The last man finally entered the chamber, and the entrance doors closed.

Bill McDonough sat at the head of the conference table; patiently looking from side to side as people talked amongst themselves. Finally, he rapped his gavel on the pad. "This meeting will come to order," he announced. The room became immediately silent.

Bill patiently looked around the room, connecting with his audience. "Ladies and gentlemen. Thank you for coming today."

"I will not mince words. LTCM is in tough straits." He paused. "The Russian default has turned out to be the defining moment for LTCM. It is bleeding capital, and its failure represents a risk to the financial system – a risk so great that it will bring down the entire economy should it fail."

He looked around the room.

"The markets are already spooked and skittish. If LTCM dumps its assets on the market, prices may well collapse; and this would set off a chain reaction that will bankrupt other firms."

"Ladies and gentlemen. I submit that intervention is necessary to save your firms and to save the economy. But – the Federal Reserve and the U.S. government have decided to do nothing to –"

At this statement, a loud murmur arose from the throng. Bill raised his arms and shouted "please let me finish. Please, gentlemen, please!"

The room returned to silence and he continued. " – The Federal Reserve and the U.S. government have decided to do nothing. Instead, they've decided to allow the unfettered free market in over the counter derivatives to work itself out."

Bill McDonough paused to allow his words to sink in. He scanned the room, connecting with the major players before he continued.

"You are a part of the free market, and you have the means to save your firms and to save the economy. Jointly, you can provide the necessary liquidity to save LTCM – doing this will ensure your own survival and continued prosperity. Therefore, I strongly recommend that you take the appropriate action to do so."

With that, Bill McDonough and his aide folded their papers and notes, then walked out of the room.

* * *

McDonough's strategy worked. The participants joined together; each contributing a portion of the purchase price. In this way, the participants were able to sell off LTCM's assets in an orderly fashion, thus avoiding a collapse of the financial system.

Participation was allocated in the following manner:

$300 million: Bankers Trust, Barclays, Chase, Credit Suisse, First Boston, Deutsche Bank, Goldman Sachs, Merrill Lynch, JP Morgan, Morgan Stanley, Salomon Smith Barney, UBS

$125 million: Société Générale

$100 million: Lehman Brothers, Paribas

Bear Stearns declined to participate.

* * *

The hearings concerning Brooksley Born's OTC Derivatives regulations resumed. But now, there was a strong sense that

Congress should do something about the OTC derivatives – that they posed a real risk to the national economy, and to the global economy.

> *"This meeting is called to order ..."*
>
> *"... The United States government is obligated to be on top of the issues ..."*
>
> *"... when and how did the concept of market self-regulation fail us?"*
>
> *"... Americans should be worried, about the gambling of Wall Street elites. That puts at risk every American – it puts at risk our democracy ..."*
>
> *"... how many more failures do you think we'd have to have before some regulation in this area is appropriate? ..."*

But Chairman Greenspan was unwilling to yield:

> *"... I know of no set of supervisory actions we can take, that will prevent people from making dumb mistakes. I know of no piece of legislation that can be passed by the Congress which would require us to prevent them from making dumb mistakes ... I think it's very important for us not to introduce regulation for regulation's sake ..."*

In the end, Congress chose not to allow regulation of the OTC Derivatives market. This meant that OTC derivatives remained an unregulated market – the same kind of market that brought about the great depression of the 1930's:

- No transparency

- No capital reserve requirements

- No prohibition on fraud

- No prohibition on manipulation

- No regulation of intermediaries

Shortly thereafter, Brooksley Born resigned.

Chapter 12 – Circa 1998

The silver dollar was encased in clear GSA[15] plastic – one of many pieces recovered from an old hoard of silver dollars. The hoard was discovered years ago in an old government vault, and this coin was an uncirculated specimen – an 1885-CC Morgan Silver Dollar.

Many people don't know that the United States once operated a mint in Carson City, Dwayne mused. *Yet they minted coins to take advantage of the huge silver deposits in the area. Damn – the old west sure has a lot of story to tell!*

Dwayne examined the coin through his magnifier; taking special care to scrutinize the high points of Liberty's hair and cheek. Then he flipped the case over and examined the coin's reverse. The feathers on the breast were a tell-tale sign of its condition – full breast feathers combined with the absence of wear told the story of this coin. *This was not some flimsy ink-laden paper – this was real money.*

The chimes rang out just as Dwayne finished his examination. He peered through the doorway out into the customer area – Trish was walking through the front entrance wearing a dour expression.

Dwayne knew that expression. He knew that anything more than small talk was dangerous. But he loved her and cared about her; and so he bit anyway. "Did you have a good day at school?"

"Sometimes I wonder if teaching is what I really want to do anymore." She sighed. "Today was a bitch of a day."

"Brrrr – it's cold out there!" She breathed deeply as she shook off the outside cold. She removed her winter coat, and then she continued, "So I walk into my homeroom first thing this morning. Johnny Beckman – I've told you about little Johnny before

---

15   GSA – Government Services Administration.

- well, he's not so little anymore. Anyway, he had completely broken out a window and was hanging his head out shouting at a young girl below. Of course, the principal had sent the girl home because she wasn't wearing a bra and all the boys were gawking at her nipples."

Trish was shaking her head in disbelief. "God help me - please! God help me!"

Dwayne snickered - as much at the story as with Trish's frustration.

"So you think it's funny? Damn you!" She stepped close to him and looked into his eyes, "I go through this shit every day - oversexed, hormone-laden teenagers with no brains! And all you can do is laugh, joke, and snicker at it. You should have seen your son. The way he was gawking at her, I thought they would need a shovel to pick his chin off the floor!"

Trish snickered, and then she sheepishly broke out in laughter.

"So," Trish's eyes were dancing now, "How was your day? Have you had any women come in without a brassiere?"

"Uh hmm. Not that I've noticed." Dwayne's face started to turn red.

"You didn't notice? Are you dead? Are you dying on me?" Trish was grinning ear to ear now.

"C'mon Trish; there's no woman like you!" He brought her into his arms and held her close. They kissed. And then he stepped back as he looked into her eyes. "So, I have an idea. You wanna hear it?"

"Sure."

Dwayne started pacing. "I'm thinking about expanding our business onto the internet. As you know, I've been using the internet for some of my research; and I'm seeing more and more commerce out there. I think there are former store-front businesses that have moved lock, stock, and barrel out to the internet."

Dwayne paced some more.

"I think the business model is compelling. All we need is to put up a website and post advertising on other websites where our customers are most likely to be. From there, we can pull prospective customers to our site. The two biggest hurdles are getting our site out on the web, and hiring an additional person to manage the web traffic – primarily the orders and shipments."

Dwayne stopped and looked directly at Trish. "I'm worried, Trish. Gold and silver have been in decline for a while. And so have the prices on rare coins. With these price declines, our profits are getting squeezed – and this is beginning to spell trouble for us. So I see an internet business as a means of increasing our volume, and thereby increasing our gross profit and operating revenue."

Dwayne's voice was urgent. "It could save our bacon, Trish."

"Well," Trish hesitated. "I kinda like your idea. In fact, I think the internet will grow – and being an early internet adopter should give you a leg up."

"But tell me, dear," she said with raised eyebrows, "what's happening to the price of gold?"

"I'm not sure," Dwayne began pacing. "But I'm amazed at how the price has continued to decline over the past few years – especially the last couple of years. I would have thought it would *increase* with Y2K coming on." Dwayne paused and then continued. "It's hard to find details, but I think the price is being manipulated. It looks like some of the central banks have been leasing gold to other financial players at ridiculously low rates; and these financial players have been turning around and selling the gold into the market." Dwayne turned and looked at Trish. "Obviously, this makes the world stock of gold appear 'larger' than it actually is – with the effect that gold prices decline."

Dwayne frowned and then went on. "It also appears that some of the major players have been shorting the market; and there are rumors that these short positions have been naked."

"Naked?" Trish giggled. "Are they having sex, or something?"

"Something like that," Dwayne said with a wry grin, "except we're the ones getting screwed."

"How's that?" Trish asked.

"Well, the way a short transaction works is that an 'investor' – I use that word advisedly here – borrows gold and sells it into the market. Obviously, the investor will be required to return the borrowed gold at a later time. The investor will most likely sell it short when he believes he can buy the gold back later at a lower price. Then, he can return it to the person who originally loaned the gold." He paused. "But note this: The 'investor' can make a good return only so long as the price is going down."

He paused then said, "But a naked short is different. A naked short is where someone sells gold he doesn't actually possess. In fact, I think you can see how selling a commodity with a naked short will create the appearance of larger supply; thereby driving the market value down even more."

"But isn't that illegal?" Trish countered.

"I'm not sure, but I don't think so. But even if it was, they could probably get the regulators to look the other way. I think this is what's happening – the supply appears to increase, thus driving the gold price lower."

"I've been doing two things to manage our exposure. I've maintained a low inventory – you've gotta know that our supplier has been less than happy with our smaller orders – and, I've been buying 'put' options."

Trish was puzzled, "Put? – put options?"

"Yes." Dwayne was warming up to his favorite topic now. "A 'put' option gives us the option to sell our holdings at a specific price even if the price declines. This means we're protected if the price of gold goes down – because we can still sell it at the 'option price'."

"It costs us a bit and adds to our cost of doing business; but it's better than losing our butts in a declining market."

Trish hesitated. "So, I know that this sounds like a conspiracy-type question (and I hereby declare that I am wearing my tinfoil hat), but do you think that someone is purposely driving the price of gold down?"

"I'm not sure ..."

* * * * *

Josh looked at his watch - 2:55 pm. *Blimey! Manager's meeting in five minutes. I gotta go.* He stood up and walked out of his office, heading toward the elevators. *I wonder what Charles wants to talk about?* He thought. *Hopefully, it's all good!*

On the way, he ruminated about the previous evening's date. *That was a pretty good session, though I wish she'd been more careful with that rope! Damn it was raw - like sandpaper.* He grimaced as he examined the flaky red skin on his left wrist. *From now on, I need her to use silk ties so she doesn't leave marks on me! And my balls - oh my God they still ache!* He smiled to himself as he boarded the elevator. *I wonder what Charles wants?*

Josh walked into Charles' office to find him checking his time piece. "Josh - I'm glad to see you. Please," he motioned, "have a seat."

He opened a box of cigars and offered it to Josh. "Cigar?"

"Yes. Thank you." Josh leaned back in his chair and lit up. He drew on the cigar and then held it out in front of him, perusing it. "These are great. This is Cuban, right?"

"Yes," Charles replied. "And by the way, you've been doing really great work and we appreciate it. So we transferred an additional $10 Million bonus to your numbered Swiss bank account. Of course, this is in addition to your 'official' bonus."

Josh was pleased. "Well, thank you - thanks very much."

"No, Josh. Thank YOU," Charles replied. "Your work has been outstanding."

"Now," Charles continued, "I wanted to talk with you about some changes to your trading operations."

"Very well. What's on your mind?"

"Y2K is coming, and -"

Josh interrupted him. "Y2 what?"

"Oh. I thought you knew about it." Charles continued. "Y2K stands for Year 2000."

"And?" Josh countered.

"Well, there's a possibility that computers around the world will crash and cause financial catastrophe. And if that happens, then there could be shortages of food and energy."

"Okay. So what's that got to do with me?"

Charles smirked as he looked into Josh's eyes. "There's a sub-culture of survival nuts. People who'll stockpile all kinds of things – food, fuel, water, guns – you name it. Anyway, they're liable to stockpile gold and silver too."

"Hmmm. I see your point." Josh frowned. "But can this really happen? Or is it just the ruminations of some nutball?"

"Oh yes – it can happen. In fact, we estimate a probability of 3%." Charles replied. "And if we do have widespread computer failure, then people and businesses will be unable to get their money. Ultimately, this can screw up food and energy distribution – easily to the point where shortages develop. And you know how people are when they're hungry, especially in large cities like London and New York!"

"Hmmm." Josh looked down at his cigar and then raised his head. "So, the bottom line is we need a tight reign on gold and silver prices – especially because of Y2K. Right?"

Charles dragged on his cigar and exhaled. "Correct. We'll need to push more naked shorts than we have up to now. Those bloody survivalists, especially those people in the western U.S., are big on their damn independence. You can bet they'll be hoarding a lot of gold and silver!"

"But what if we can't roll over our short positions?"

"Oh, you can always roll them over. Just sell more shorts into the market until you flush out the weak hands – lots of people will sell when the price falls." Charles leaned back in his chair. "And if that doesn't work, we'll have the regulators raise the margin[16] requirements – then prices will drop like a stone."

---

[16] A margin requirement is the amount of cash an investor must put down to control the asset. The investor borrows the difference between the asset price and his cash payment. If the asset price falls, the investor must put up additional cash or sell the asset. Raising margin requirements usually causes an increase in asset sales, which results in a further decline in asset prices.

Josh frowned. "This sounds like there's no compromise on keeping the prices down."

Charles leaned back, watching wisps of his cigar smoke float into the air. "Let me make it perfectly clear, Josh. The powers that be have decided to drive inflation of the dollar while maintaining the public perception that the dollar is strong. One of the most important ways to maintain this perception is to keep the price of metals low. In short, we've been ordered to keep metals' prices at the current price range, if not drive them lower. And we are to keep this pressure on for the foreseeable future."

Charles drew from his cigar and watched the smoke as he exhaled. "No one knows for sure; but we think they're looking to create a new world currency – and they need to kill the dollar to do it." He paused and tellingly looked at Josh. "A brave new world is coming, and we get to be a big part of it."

Josh was actually not surprised. He had noticed that his contact at the Federal Reserve usually flagged him at just about the time the Fed was pumping more money. So he knew there was a larger plan in the works.

A smirk formed on Charles' face. And then he said, "So please continue to coordinate with the Fed when you 'manage prices'."

The room became silent as Josh pondered what he was hearing. And then he said, "These large short positions will draw a lot of attention. I take it we need not be concerned about regulators checking our transactions?"

"The bloody regulators are of no consequence whatsoever." Charles leaned back and exhaled cigar smoke into the air. "We've paid them off – lock, stock, and barrel."

"Okay." Josh smiled. He was enjoying his cigar; but he wasn't sure about the conversation. "Is there anything else I need to know?"

"Just one other thing," Charles was shaking his finger at Josh. "Silver. Someday, silver is going to be a real problem for us."

"Why?"

Charles' voice quivered. "Because there'll be much more gold than silver above ground. I'd say we'll be seeing this in just a few more years."

Josh had never really considered this before; but it was a fact that silver was being used up at a faster rate than new silver was being mined. *Charles is right. This will certainly be a problem, but it can also be an opportunity!*

Charles smiled and then said, "So what do you think?"

"What do I think?" Josh grinned. "I'll have to think about it."

*   *   *   *   *

That evening, Josh went on another date, with yet another woman ...

"Oh, baby!" Her voice oozed with pleasure. "I love the way you touch me. I love the way you stroke me. And I really like what you do to me!"

Josh looked down at Marcia; her tongue running along her lips as though she was about to eat him. *But she never did*, he mused.

Blimey. Why is it that so many women find it hard to initiate – to be the dominant partner? God help me but I love being tied. I love being teased. I love it when a woman uses me, Josh ruminated as they got it on. *But Marcia, all she wants is basic service. God help me; how damn boring could it be!*

Josh finished and collapsed on top of Marcia. It was so-so, but it would do.

"Oh, baby," she whispered, "are you okay?"

Josh nodded. He laid on top of her for a minute, kissing her. And then he rolled off; looking up at the mirrored ceiling hanging over the bed – gazing at their reflection.

Josh liked his ceiling. In fact, he liked his condo. He had wanted an estate out in the country, but with his London job, he knew he would seldom make it home. So he paid a hefty sum for a condo near work. It came with all of the luxuries: maid and butler service, plush furnishings and appointments, expansive rooms, and plenty of bedroom space for his particular style of toys.

"Josh, what's that?" Marcia said, pointing to a particular wooden rack.

"Oh, nothing dear," Josh responded.

Josh thought back to his time with Cheryl. She loved tying him up on the rack and abusing his body. She would use him for several hours; all the while getting herself off. And then finally, she would bring him to a mind-blowing organism.

How did I ever let her go?

Chapter 13 – Circa 1999

"Blimey!" Dave's eyes were big. "Did you see gold and silver?"

"Of course," Josh replied. "We trade in it every day."

"I know – but that's not what I'm talking about."

"Oh? Then what, pray tell, are you talking about?"

"The volume." Dave's eyes widened.

"Volume? Hmmm ... you mean the volume of gold and silver traded?"

"Yes. Did you notice it's way up?" Dave replied.

"Yes."

"It's been amazing!" Dave continued. "What do you think is causing it?"

Josh turned, stuffed his hands in his pockets, and looked out his office windows at the financial district. "Well, I think that people are afraid of Y2K and they're hoarding gold and silver."

"Y2K? ... Oh yeah, I remember that computer programmer guy down the hall talking about it. He said we might have widespread computer failures and food shortages and petrol shortages. Blimey! He just went on and on like the end of the world was coming!"

"That's right," Josh replied. Some people believe it's coming, and they're stocking up on food and petrol. And some of the people are hoarding gold and silver too."

"What do you think about Y2K? Do you think it's real?" Dave asked.

"I don't know." Josh shrugged. "I suppose it could happen."

"But regardless," Josh continued, "Y2K is perceived to be an issue. Clearly, if we are to keep the price of gold and silver down during the Y2K period, we will need to sell more shorts over the next few months."

Dave thought he noticed Stephanie peeking around the office door, but he continued his conversation. "Are we leasing more from the central banks?"

"No. I checked with Thad at the Fed yesterday. It seems we're on our own for the time being." Josh sighed. "We'll just need to sell some naked shorts and hope that we can roll them over."

"But isn't it illegal to sell gold we don't possess?"

Josh's patience was wearing thin. "No. It's perfectly legal, Dave. It's only illegal if we fail to return it to the leaser. We'll make sure to buy it back when the time comes."

"But, what if we have to pay a higher price to buy it back? If that happens, then our profitability will suffer."

"Well," Josh shrugged, "we'll just sell more shorts to drive the price further down."

And then he gave Dave a condescending look. "You worry too much, Dave."

Dave's expression became quizzical. "You know, this sure seems like we're manipulating the market. I looked at the CFTC rules yesterday. Do you know what it says? It says that manipulating the market is a criminal offense."

Dave's lips became tight, his face drawn. "Blimey – we're breaking the law here."

Dave could swear he'd seen Stephanie out in the hall, peeking around the door.

Josh turned and looked directly at Dave. "Seriously, Dave, everything is on the up and up. There is nothing for you to worry about."

* * *

It was closing time at the office after one of those tough days. Bantering back and forth, Dave and Mike made their way to the *MoonDancer*. Dave pulled open the ornate door and they stepped inside. Standing in the entrance, they took in as much of the crowded room as they could see. The pub was loud and noisy – everyone talking and shouting over everyone else. And with standing room only, groups of people collected together – laughing and socializing.

Dave shouted at Mike. "What a crowd! What's the occasion?"

Mike shouted back. "I don't know."

"Hey, look," Mike motioned out to the middle of the room. "There's Stephanie and Natalie over there."

Dave shouted, "all right! Let's go on over and talk."

Dave and Mike made their way through the crowd.

Natalie's eyes sparkled when she saw their approach. "Alright guys!"

Mike smiled at Natalie as he spoke. "So, what's with the big crowd?"

Stephanie and Natalie both shrugged their shoulders. And then Stephanie shouted, "Everyone is looking for a good time!" She paused as she looked at the two. "I didn't see you at work today. What's going on?"

Dave shouted his reply. "We were working on our gold short positions today – we had to short a lot of gold without having it covered."

Mike chimed in with a shout. "The gold price was really strong yesterday. I thought we lost control. But all we had to do was sell a few hundred more contracts short, and the price tumbled."

"Hell," Mike went on, "to see it drop that fast ... I guess there's a lot of leverage out there!"

"Hear, hear!" Dave held up his mug for a toast. Stephanie, Natalie, and Mike all saluted, and then they gulped in celebration.

Just then, the man standing behind Natalie turned, glared at them, and started shouting. "So you're the bastards manipulating the gold, are ya? Just last week, my mother bought gold on margin; and today she had to liquidate all of it – she lost thousands of pounds." The man continued with a sneer. "How's it feel to be robbing little old ladies of their life's savings?"

The man glowered at Mike. But Mike turned away from the man – ignoring him.

The man stormed forward in a fit of rage. He grabbed Mike by the shoulder and spun him around. Mike shouted his surprise, "what the –" but was interrupted by the man's left hook against his jaw, knocking him to the floor.

Mike stayed on the floor, massaging his jaw as he looked up at the man. The man was glowering over Mike. "You sonofabitch! I oughtta kill ya!" He spat.

The man turned to walk away. But then he shouted "Aw shit" as he spun around and launched his foot, kicking Mike in the head and knocking him unconscious.

The man glared at all of them. Then he turned and made his way through the crowd toward the entrance.

Mike's friends crowded around. Soon, Mike lifted himself off the deck, holding and rubbing his chin and the side of his head. "Blimey! Why do you suppose he did that?" Mike said as he was rubbing the huge welt rising on the side of his face.

"Because he thinks we're stealing from old people," Dave replied. Dave turned and looked to the entrance where the man just departed. "And maybe he's right."

"What do you mean by that, Dave?" Stephanie asked.

"What I mean is that maybe someone has to stand up and report what we're doing to the authorities."

*   *   *   *   *

A few days later . . .

Josh watched as the pallbearers pulled the casket out of the limousine. Carefully, slowly, they carried the casket as they merged with the procession – a procession made up of Dave's family, his loved ones, his co-workers, and his friends. They proceeded carefully over the uneven turf; moving ever closer to the grave site that Dave's family had selected.

There were three stout 4 x 4 posts laid on the ground, crossing over the grave. The pallbearers set the casket down on the posts; directly above the freshly dug grave. Then, a Presbyterian minister stepped forward and began the service.

"David is loved, truly. We all miss him. We all loved him. And we all appreciated his presence, his energy, his exuberance, and his friendliness. David was always there to help others. And he always lived his life by the highest ethical standards. His friend, Clarence, told me of a time that he and David ..." Amid tears, sobs, and an occasional cough, the eulogy went on.

Feeling his sorrow, and feeling the sorrow of others who were sobbing, Josh watched and listened as the service continued. And when the eulogy ended, he watched as the pallbearers placed three strands of rope underneath the casket, and lifted the casket with the ropes. Another aide removed the posts; and then the pallbearers slowly lowered the casket. When the casket reached the bottom, the pallbearers tossed the ropes into the grave.

With red eyes and red streaks from her tears, David's mother came forth, throwing a handful of dirt onto the casket. A procession formed, each person in turn throwing dirt onto the casket. Josh and his staff joined the procession; so that they too could say goodbye.

* * *

Making his way to the parking lot, Josh caught up to Stephanie and fell in step with her. They walked together on the uneven terrain

Josh's face was glum. He had tried to understand Dave's death, but he didn't know how he could – *Dave's death seems so senseless*, he thought. "So," he asked Stephanie, "what really happened?"

Stephanie recounted the story as they walked. "We went out for drinks last Friday night. You know – the *MoonDancer* – the same place we always go? While we were there, a man came out of nowhere. He hit Mike and then kicked Mike in the head. And then the man left the pub." Stephanie paused, holding back her grief. "Soon after, we all split up to make our way home. It was the next morning that I received a call from the police; they wanted to know who might have killed Dave. The only person I could think of was that man; the man who hit Mike. So I gave them a description."

"The police asked me if I'd seen the man holding or packing a gun." She shook her head. "But I didn't, and I told them so."

Stephanie stopped and looked Josh in the eyes. "And that's what I know."

Josh took Stephanie's hand and brought her close to him. They embraced, both of them shedding tears. Finally, Josh and Stephanie let go; and they continued their walk together without speaking. Stephanie reached her car first. She stood and watched as Josh continued on toward his own car. She continued to stand, and they waved to each other as Josh drove off.

Josh mulled over the events of the past week, still not understanding. He reflected that there was much he didn't know. *Why? Why?*

But were he more of a gentleman, he might have solved Dave's murder. A gentleman would have stopped at Stephanie's car, and opened the door for her. A gentleman would then have helped her into the car. And then, a gentleman might have noticed the butt of a pistol protruding from underneath the towel – the towel that lay across the passenger's seat.

But Josh was not always a gentleman, and so he never did learn why Dave was slain.

Chapter 14

Bill and Brandy spent considerable time searching for 'just the right place' to call home. They looked at many different parts of Idaho, and finally settled on a 40-acre parcel with an older-style farmhouse up in the panhandle. The parcel was multipurpose –

some parts were forested, and some parts were flat grassland. Land such as this would allow them to farm, harvest wood, or keep livestock.

Bill was excited. He was born and raised in the Sandpoint area, and he was coming home! He liked Arizona, but he hated the summertime heat. So for Bill, the change was welcome.

A native of Dallas and a lover of the desert southwest, this was Brandy's first experience in the Northwest – and she was instantly taken with her new home. She fell in love with the forest, and she was breathless when she spied the meadow of grass tapering into the distant tree line. Then she was drawn to the homestead area; a quaint rustic farmhouse with a nearby shop (or was it a barn?) nestled in a stand of ponderosa pine, red fir, and western larch. The farmhouse beckoned to her with its steep gabled roof, angled dormers, and brown clapboard siding. Inviting her inside was a covered porch obscured by two trees.

Their move from Arizona went quickly. Brandy's townhome was a rental; and it was easy for her to let go. Bill owned a home that he acquired from his two-year-old divorce. He put it on the market even as he moved to Idaho; believing that it would sell quickly – it did.

Initially, Bill thought they should buy the necessary equipment to set up their own mint. But they soon realized the enormity of the project; and so, they began searching out an independent mint to help with their newly-formed business. The mint they chose was *The Golden Mint* located in nearby Missoula, Montana. They had an initial telephone conversation with Murray Hofstadler, the chief engraver, and found he was very receptive to Bill's design ideas. Bill and Brandy sent a letter to Murray detailing their initial concept of the *Freedom Dollar.*

Dear Mr. Hofstadler,

Brandy and I fully enjoyed talking with you about our project; and we enjoyed listening to your ideas. Your experience and expertise could be a big help toward getting us started.

Following is a description of two coins we'd like to manufacture: The Twenty Dollar Silver Freedom coin; and the One-thousand Dollar Gold Freedom coin.

The Twenty Freedom Dollar silver round consists of 1 troy ounce of .999 fine silver with a reeded edge. The obverse is a picture of Liberty in a chain-mail tunic and holding a sword above her head. A legend at the top says 'Twenty Freedom Dollars'. To the right of the Liberty picture, it says '20'. The year of minting is at the bottom of the obverse. The reverse is a rendering of an eagle in flight, feathers are detailed and prominent. A legend at the bottom of the reverse says 'Trust God'. A legend at the top says 'Twenty Freedom Dollars'. The denomination of this coin is Twenty Freedom Dollars.

The One-thousand Freedom Dollar gold round consists of 1 troy ounce of .999 fine gold with a reeded edge. The obverse is a picture of Liberty in a flowing tunic, and holding a sword above her head. A legend at the top says 'One Thousand Freedom Dollars'. To the right of the Liberty picture, it says '1,000'. The year of minting is at the bottom of the obverse. The reverse is a rendering of an eagle standing proudly on a tree branch, feathers are detailed and prominent. A legend at the bottom of the reverse says 'Trust God'. A legend at the top says 'One Thousand Freedom Dollars'. The denomination of this coin is One Thousand Freedom Dollars.

Please note that the notion of a 'Freedom Dollar' is that of a currency different than a 'U.S. Dollar'. Note further that a free market conversion between the two will be based on the value of the precious metal content of the coin, rather than their relative denominations.

With Best Regards, Bill Ford, Partner

Approximately one week later, Bill received a mailed reply from the mint.

Dear Mr. Ford,

Please find the enclosed drawings of the obverse and reverse for each of your proposed coins.

As drawn, these designs will work well with the size and metal content you've specified. The rim of each coin will provide good protection for the interior of the design; and yet the relief of these coins will be sufficiently high to make them attractive.

The next step in creating these designs is to sculpt each design using clay and plaster. And from the creation of the sculpture, I can create a plaster engraving for your perusal and further enhancement.

With your permission and down payment, I will begin work on the plaster engraving of each of these designs.

Please let me know how you want to proceed.

With Best Regards, Murray Hofstadler, Chief Engraver

Bill and Brandy peered over the drawings; dissecting and analyzing them as best as they could.

"I like these," said Brandy.

"Yeah – so do I," Bill replied. "Also, I think he has covered most of the issues."

"Then," Brandy interjected, "let's get him on the phone and get going on these."

"Okay," said Bill. "We'll also need to plan a trip out there. Soon."

* * *

Soon . . .

The Golden Mint was set back from the road; situated in a park-like setting with pine and fir trees. The main entrance to the building was constructed and appointed with rustic native timber, exuding a warm invitation.

Bill and Brandy walked through the entrance into a plush, nicely appointed main lobby.

The receptionist looked up from her desk and asked, "may I help you?"

"Yes," Bill replied. We're here to see Murray about a new coin design."

"And who shall I say is calling?"

"Ah – Bill Ford and Brandy West."

The receptionist punched some buttons on her telephone, waited, and then said. "Mr. Ford and Ms. West are here to see you." She paused. "I will let them know."

The receptionist looked at them. "He will be out directly. Will you please have a seat?"

* * *

His hands steady, Murray Hofstadler nonetheless felt a rush of excitement as he added some pencil strokes to the drawing he was creating – a drawing of a custom coin. His focus was clear and his short, stubby fingers certain as he made still more and subtle changes to his draft image; all the while his subconscious considered the flow of the blank's metal when struck by a die with this design.

Murray enjoyed working in his peaceful artist's studio off in a corner of the mint. He enjoyed it because he seldom met anyone – and so he was comfortable wearing his graying beard and po-nytail. Unfortunately, he was to meet with customers today. Over the telephone, they seemed open-minded enough to accept him as he was. But many people seemed nice, until they met him ... and then their judgment began.

Murray sighed at the thought of dealing with people. Pausing in his work, Murray took a cloth, wiped his hands, and then proceeded out to meet with his guests.

Murray put on his welcoming facade as he walked into the lobby. "Hi, I'm Murray. And you must be Ms. West and Mr. Ford?"

Bill and Brandy each shook his hand.

"Please call me Bill; and this is Brandy," he said gesturing to her.

"Well, folks," Murray said, "please come on back and I'll show you the plaster engravings I have so far."

Murray led them back to his studio and unveiled the engravings.

Bill and Brandy gasped. As they stepped up to get a close-up view, they began excitedly talking over each other.

Their chatter soon subsided; and then Brandy burst out, "oh my, but these are beautiful!"

Bill was examining the engraving of the gold coin, and how Murray had created the picture of Liberty wearing a tunic. The details of the engraving – such as the flow of the tunic and the fineness of her sword – left Bill with palpable excitement. He turned and looked at Murray. "I *like* it! I *like* both of 'em!"

Brandy wore a broad smile and sparkling eyes. She asked, "What's the next step?"

Murray hesitated, and then replied. "Well, you'll need to look at each of these in detail to make sure they're exactly – and I mean, *exactly* – what you want. Then, I will go through them and clean up any bad sections. And then, we can create a master die for each design and run some test strikes."

"Cool!" Bill and Brandy spoke in unison.

⁂ ⁂ ⁂

A few months later . . .

Brandy was sitting up to her desk, the wash from a bright light illuminating her desktop. She smiled, intently so, as she examined some of the newly minted silver and gold rounds under her ten-power glass. She hefted one in her hand and felt the essence of the coin. Its weight. Its texture. Its intrinsic value – value not determined by the fiat of any government, but instead by rarity. *Who would of thought I'd be in the precious metals and money business,* she mused. And then she felt shivers running up and down her spine.

She looked up and smiled as Bill walked into the office. "I've been contacting some of the local coin shops," she said. "They've a strong interest in buying these, in quantity."

"Great," Bill smiled.

Brandy leaned back in her chair. "So, I'd like to christen our business with the name *Freedom Money.* What do you think?"

Bill put his hand to his chin, and then said, "I like it ... yeah – let's go with it."

And then Bill hesitated. "Ah – I have still another line of business that I'd like to talk over."

"Yes?" Brandy said as she raised her eyebrows.

"Well, I'd like to sell printed receipts for gold and silver that we would keep and store on deposit. That way, people would be able to transact business in paper receipts without having to carry gold or silver coin."

Brandy shifted in her chair as she became immediately interested. "That sounds really cool ..."

* * * * *

Coin dealer extraordinaire, Dwayne worked diligently and invested wisely to establish their website. In pursuing his plan, he found a young software developer who specialized in web development – the young man eagerly took on the challenge of developing and administering the site.

Dwayne wanted to know if the site would attract enough business to make it worthwhile. So, the first site was small and inexpensive – just a few pages describing his products and providing contact information.

With the site now in operation, the volume of internet business started slowly but soon came up to a steady, profitable pace. Although his profit margins remained persistently low, the increased sales volume resulted in a welcome increase in actual profit dollars – and it relieved some of the pressure from the family finances.

They were nearing the turn of the millennium, and business was brisk – especially in sales of one-ounce gold bullion coins. In fact, he could barely keep up with both the customer walk-ins and telephone orders.

And with all of the trade in gold and silver bullion – both coins and bars – prices remained amazingly low. *Strange*, he reflected, *how prices remain so low when the year 2000 is just around the corner. I know that tension is high and people are wary – so why are prices not going up? Especially when people keep telling me how afraid they are!*

The telephone rang again, and again Trish picked it up. Lucky for Dwayne that Trish volunteered to come in and help out. The telephone orders were consuming more and more of his time.

"Revolution Rare Coins" she answered. "May I help you?"

* * *

Dwayne walked into the house after a tough day at work. Prices on gold and silver were down again, although his rare coin business was still holding its own. *Inflation is eating us up,* he thought. *We need to generate more income!*

He walked into the den and sat down in front of the television. He selected the latest edition of the leading business newspaper and began looking through it – oblivious to the incessant drone of the news announcer's monotone voice ... and then he heard:

> *"... And for the latest on **China's permanent most favored nation status** (the words screamed into Dwayne's consciousness), we go to Jim Rhenquist, our correspondent in Washington."*

Dwayne looked at the TV to see the slick, smiling face of Jim Rhenquist.

"Yes, David. Today the House of Representatives voted in favor of giving permanent most favored nation status to China. But it was not without a battle. Majority Whip Rep. Tom Delay (R: Tex.) praised the bill on many fronts."

The apparently live broadcast then cut away to film, showing Representative Delay speaking to the correspondent, Jim Rhenquist.

"While PNTR[17] will help our American economy, this is only one step toward our larger goal: ending Communist rule in China by exposing the Chinese people to American values. Freedom is a contagious virtue. Defeating a foe is a poor substitute for liberating a country from the weight of a repressive ideology. We should today ensure the triumph of liberty by planting the seeds of freedom in China. We should not accept a retrenchment driven by fear and insecurity."

Coming back live, the correspondent continued,

"and Texas Republican Congressman Ron Paul, who has supported the annual NTR[18] bills in past years, had some scathing remarks."

Again, the live broadcast cut away to film; and Ron Paul was seen speaking on the House floor.

"This new 66-page 'free trade' bill is not about free trade at all. It is about empowering and enriching international trade regulators and quasi-governmental entities on the backs of the U.S. taxpayers. Like NAFTA before us, this bill contains provisions which will continue our

---

[17]   PNTR – Permanent Normal Trade Relations.

[18]   NTR – Normal Trade Relations.

country down the ugly path of internationally engineered 'managed trade', rather than that of free trade."

Click! Dwayne turned off the TV and walked out to the kitchen where Trish was preparing dinner. "Shit!"

Trish turned and looked at Dwayne. "What happened?"

"This corrupt government is again screwing the American people. Listen to this!" He paused. "Congress is on the verge of giving permanent most favored nation status to China. This is a country that uses slave labor to make goods that compete with products we manufacture."

Dwayne's face was beet-red. "Mark my words," he spat, "this is the beginning of the end for prosperity in this country!"

"Oh come on dear," Trish responded. "You said that when they passed the World Trade Bill too. Don't you think you're overreacting just a bit?"

"I need a drink!"

* * * * *

With a raucous crowd behind her, the tall, gangly young woman moved in front of the camera. Raising her microphone to her lips, she shook back her blonde mop of hair and took her cue from the cameraman. "This is Sheryl Barclay reporting from downtown Seattle, where you can see behind me a mob. But not just any mob. This is part of a larger movement seeking social justice." She paused to look down. Then referring to some notes, she continued speaking. "These demonstrators are protesting the ministerial meetings of nations' representatives from around the world. These meetings are allegedly to resolve issues of the treaties of the World Trade Organization and the General Agreement on Tariffs and Trade; treaties that many countries – including the United States government – are signatories."

At just that moment, a protester stepped back and bumped violently into Sheryl, pushing her out of the camera's view. She quickly regained her composure and turned to the young man who bumped her. The camera followed her as she called to the protester. "Sir. Sir?" She put her hand on the young man's shoulder. The man turned to face Sheryl, his masked face captured on the camera as he turned. Holding her mic up to the young man, she said, "Sir. Sir! Can you answer some questions?"

The young man paused his shouting and began speaking into the mic, his voice muffled by his ski mask. "We're here today to speak out against what we see as the commodification of all life. Groups like the WTO, governments, corporations, and so on, have basically decided that everything on this planet is here for their use – whether it be animal life, plant life, the soil, and so on, and so on –"

Sheryl interrupted him. "You're dressed in a ski mask. You're expecting trouble, aren't you?"

The man replied, "I'm hoping for trouble."

"Yeah?" Sheryl prompted him further

"Quite frankly. I mean, these businesses – they're not going to bow to people dancing in the streets. They're not going to bow to people dressed as – you know – giant sea turtles or so on. They care about one thing – they care about capital. And unless we put a dent in their pocket, what good, ah – what good –"

Sheryl interjected. "How're you – how're you gonna put a dent in their pocket?"

"Hopefully, by causing property damage," he responded.

As he was talking, the camera captured some demonstrators behind them, smashing glass storefronts and breaking down doors. *Shit,* she thought, *I hope this interview comes through all the noise and destruction!*

The man continued. "By causing economic sabotage. I don't see property damage as being violent. I don't see, um – I don't believe that property and inanimate objects show pain. What I do see, um – the violence I do see is violence happening against the Earth – against the animal nations and the third world. There's no way that any violence perpetrated by us could ever equate to the amount of damage done by the WTO and the federal governments, and groups like the –"

Suddenly, the man jerked away from the camera and sprinted toward a pack of demonstrators. Her mouth agape, Sheryl watched as the pack moved toward a storefront and began throwing rocks at the windows. The camera was already trained on the violence, and so Sheryl jumped between the camera and the mob violence.

Facing the camera, she continued speaking. "As you can see behind me, the demonstrators are becoming increasingly violent and destructive..." She gestured down the street and the camera followed. "... and down the street, we see a line of policemen approaching the protesters. As you can see, the police are ready for battle. I've heard reports that the standard equipment for police in this zone consists of black kevlar helmets with tinted face-shield protection, bulletproof vests, clubs, and M-16 rifles." Sheryl looked earnestly into the camera as she continued speaking. "The demonstrators will be no match for the oppressive police regime, specially equipped as the police are."

As Sheryl stepped out of the view of the camera, the camera continued to record the scene. A scene of imminent violence with the police. For the police moved slowly, inexorably, toward the protesters.

Sheryl continued speaking into her mic. "Brace yourself, as the clash is imminent. Now! Now! Here it is!" She was yelling into her mic as the police, their line still intact, used their clubs and their rifles to knock down protester after protester. And as protesters were put down, still more police came up behind the front wall of police, cuffed the downed protesters, and hauled them to one of several police trucks where they were unceremoniously dumped.

"As you can see," Sheryl was yelling into her mic as the camera continued running, "the police are using their violence – their violent tactics on the demonstrators. First silencing, and then capturing them – Wa! Wa! What is this! I think the demonstrators are retreating – yes they are! Yes, the demonstrators are now in full retreat!"

"And as we move further up the street, we can see the demonstrators continue to evacuate the area in the face of mounting police violence. As you can see, the shop windows are broken out and large quantities of merchandise have been stolen – all of this to protest the World Trade Organization treaty and their meeting here today."

"Wait. Look! Look!" She gestured to the cameraman to train his camera to a storefront up the street. "As we speak, we are watching firsthand three men in ski masks walk out of an electronics store – their arms full of boxes with the latest in electronics equipment."

Abruptly, the cameraman trained the camera toward explosions coming from down the street. Sheryl again jumped in front of the camera and began speaking. "And in this direction, we are hearing explosions. It sounds like gunfire." Sheryl paused as she spied a man quickly walking away from the noise, his head down. She grabbed the man by the shoulder and began shouting into her mic. "Sir! Sir! Can you tell us what you saw?"

The man looked furtively behind him; and then he spoke into the mic. "I was on the other side of the street, over there, on a sit-down demonstration, and the police just walked up. They didn't ask us to leave or nothin'. They just walked up and they sprayed me twice with pepper spray and they were shooting tear gas at us."

"Wow! Can you tell us anything else?"

"Shit. You need to ask them." The man gestured in another direction, near the curb, and the camera followed his gesture; now training his camera lens on a girl pouring water onto a young man's eyes. Sheryl moved quickly over to the girl and began talking. "Excuse me. Excuse me! Are you treating this man for pepper spray?"

The girl looked up at the camera. "The police. Shit! They did it! The police are assaulting us! The police are on the side of the globalists – they are oppressing against the people. I tell everyone to disobey the police. To kill them if they can!"

Sheryl heard still more explosions up the street. "C'mon," she said to the cameraman, "let's go report on those explosions."

And with that, the two of them quickly made their way up the street ...

* * *

Shortly thereafter . . .

With yet another mob behind her, Sheryl stood in front of the camera as she spoke into her mic, "... and in conclusion, this was ultimately a good day for the demonstrators – as only a third of the so-called 'free trade' delegates were able to get through the demonstrators to their meeting. And so, today's meetings were canceled."

This is Sheryl Barclay, signing off for the University of Washington campus news station.

Interlude

The gradients of light danced across log walls, casting shadows hither and yon throughout the ether. Embedded in one wall, a massive stone fireplace faced into the room; casting flickering light onto five leather chairs arranged in a semi-circle. A chair was empty, but the other chairs were occupied by men, their features obscured in the shadows.

Cigar smoke was wafting through the air, creating its own silhouettes as it drifted upward, toward the darkness of the ceiling. And as the log wall also climbed upwards, the logs seemed to vanish into the silhouettes, making a ceiling of indeterminate height.

A tall, dark, slender man with graying temples walked into the room. He did not come here often; but when he was summoned, he knew it was important, and he knew they wouldn't communicate with him in any other way.

He noticed that a chair was empty. He absorbed that curious fact, but allowed no visible emotion. He stood in front of the four shadows with his head slightly bowed. "You summoned me, sir?"

The Leader, a well-dressed and manicured man, waved his cigar in a most expansive manner. "Welcome, Daniel. I trust your travel was enjoyable."

The tall, dark man hesitated; he turned his head to each man in turn. And then addressed his Eminence. "Quite, sir. My passage was quite comfortable."

"Very well, Daniel. We called you here on a simple matter; yet a matter of great importance."

Lord Basil gestured to the empty chair. "Please sit down, Daniel."

More curious than ever, Daniel seated himself.

Lord Basil flourished his cigar through the air. "I will cut to the issue, Daniel. The Council is in need of a war; or maybe seven wars."

Despite himself, Daniel lost his composure. "S-s-seven, my Lord?"

"Yes, my Daniel – yes!" Lord Basil responded in his most robust Oxford English accent.

"Of course, sir." Daniel regained control over his emotions. "Are there any special considerations that I should be aware of, my Lord?"

"Very much so, Daniel. A pre-condition of these 'wars' is that we motivate the American people to take up arms against these countries. You, Daniel, must first arrange for an attack on America; specifically, an attack on the World Trade Center and New York City."

"And then, once the Americans have been aroused, we shall take them to war."

Lord Basil handed a folder to Daniel. "You will find all that is necessary within this folder."

"Of course, sir. Is there anything else in which I can be of service, sir?"

"Not at the present, Daniel. But, the Council wishes to congratulate you on a job well done with the transfer of $4 Trillion from the U.S. to our Asian and Indian partners. And Daniel," Lord Basil smiled, "I wish to add my personal congratulations."

Daniel smiled. "Thank you, sir."

"That is all," said Lord Basil. "You may go."

The tall, dark man stood up, bowed his head, turned, and strode out of the room.

When they were again alone, Julius spoke. "Those seven countries are important. Mostly because their assimilation will send a message to the world that no country may exist without a central bank under our control."

"Yes," Lord Basil chimed in. "It is amazing that those countries have been able to slip outside of our control for so long. Soon, they shall feel the wrath of the American military – *our military.*"

* * *

Daniel arrived at his room after leaving the Council's inner sanctum. Closing the door, he pulled the summary sheet from the folder and began to read it. His brow furrowed as he scanned the paper.

Resource Acquisition Initiative
Target date: September, 11, 2001
Project: World Trade Center Destruction
Objectives:

- Motivate American People for War
- Recover gold/silver stored in WTC basement
- Cover up of tungsten gold bar sales at NYNEX
- Cover up of $2.3 trillion DoD loss[19]

Follow-on Military Action
- Afghanistan
- Iraq
- Iran
- Libya

---

[19] On September 10, 2001, Secretary Rumsfeld announced that the Department of Defense could not account for $2.3 trillion.

- Sudan
- North Korea
- Cuba

Daniel muttered under his breath, "holy shit!" He put the paper back into the folder and made ready for his departure.

Chapter 15 – Circa June, 2001

Josh really enjoyed the Avante style overstuffed leather chair in Charles' office. It was so comfortable that he normally relaxed right into it. But this time he didn't relax. This time, Charles had summoned the department heads from all of the commodities' trading desks. Something was up.

"... so, you have done a really incredible job," Charles was speaking, "and I'm looking forward to seeing how you do with an increase in your staff."

Everyone basked in the glow of Charles' accolades. His warmth and charm were infectious.

"Now," Charles continued, "I want to mention just one more thing."

Glancing around the room, Josh noticed the attendees perked up.

"Ah, yes. All of you, I want you to ensure all your short positions are either closed out or covered by a long. In other words, you should have no outstanding naked shorts for the next few months."

The attendees glanced quizzically at each other and at Charles. And then Josh spoke. "Why? Is there something coming up that we should know about?"

Charles hesitated. "Well, there's not really a lot I can say. And most of it is rumour anyways ... So, just take my instructions to heart."

Josh was even more curious now. "Is there something you need to tell me?"

Charles sighed. "Not much. Just that we've received some information – that there'll be considerable upward pressure on commodity prices over the next two to three months; and this will make naked shorts a dangerous strategy." Charles grimaced and then continued. "It makes no sense to swim against the tide when the incoming wave is a tsunami."

"And?" Josh asked.

"I'm afraid," Charles continued, "that's all I can say."

Charles stood up signaling that the meeting was over.

* * *

Chet, Eddie, Natalie, and Stephanie all filed into Josh's office. Josh was seated at his desk, wearing a frown.

"All right?" Eddie was the first to ask.

Josh was slow to answer. "I just talked with Charles. We're on track for another banner year. Charles and all of executive management are delighted with our performance."

"And?" Eddie just knew that more was going on.

"Well ... he gave me instructions. He told me to close out all of our naked short positions. It's still okay to have shorts; but we need to make sure that we're covered with corresponding long positions."

"Did he say what it was about?"

Josh shook his head. "No – not really. Only ... there's an expectation that shorts will be under considerable pressure. Apparently, they believe that something serious will happen and that it will drive up prices. I think he is concerned that we could lose a lot of money if we are stuck trying to cover naked shorts with higher priced metal.

Chapter 16 – September 7, 2001

Kirk Kincaid was not getting the sleep he needed. Night after night he tossed and turned. And when he dozed, he had dreams – or nightmares – of a high-rise city in destruction. And when he awoke, it was to avoid the imminent pain or death that the nightmare offered. So late afternoon and early evening naps had become Kirk's order of the day.

And at this moment, Kirk was sacked out on the sofa; doing what he couldn't do at night. Sleeping.

Ring! Ring!

Not really awake, Kirk reached over, picked up the telephone, and mumbled into it. "Yeah."

The voice at the other end of the phone sounded urgent. "*Kirk? This is Daniel.*"

Kirk's eyes opened and his brain began to work. "What's up?"

"*We have an emergency and I need you to get some men and equipment down to the world trade center. We have some material that we need to evacuate from there, and we need to get started on it by tomorrow night. I've already sent you instructions via secure courier. You will need to get two trucks with tri-axle flatbed trailers – you know, the kind that has a max payload of 60,000 pounds?*"

Kirk was fully awake by now. "Shit!" Kirk looked at his clock – 4:30 pm. "How do you expect me to get it together that fast? You've got to be joking!"

"*No joke. We've got about two billion dollars in gold stored in the basement of the world trade center. It needs to be moved out by 0800 on Tuesday, the 11th.*"

"Wait – Daniel, this phone is not secure."

"*Not to worry; this line is secure. I had it verified before I called you.*"

"What are we moving?"

"*Gold, Kirk; gold and silver.*"

"Hmmm ..." Kirk ran his hand through his scalp. "How much is there? And where is it going?"

"*There's a shit load of it. You'll be moving it to a Long Island dock. Other people will take care of it from there.*"

"What's the hurry? Why now?"

"*I can't talk about that right now. But when things happen, you'll know soon enough.*" Daniel paused and then continued.

"There are about fifteen-thousand bars; so you're going to need much more security than you're used to."

"I don't know where I'll get that kind of personnel on such short notice. Do you have any ideas?"

Daniel replied. *"I'll take care of it. I'll have them there by twenty-hundred tomorrow. You take care of getting the trucks, a forklift or two, and some men to do the work."*

"Okay. I'll get on it now."

"Thanks."

Kirk's mind spun a myriad of questions. *Why now? What's so important about the eleventh?* He shook his head. *Hell, they never tell me anything anyway.*

Kirk made some quick telephone calls and was able to line up the trucks and men he needed for the job. He told them all to meet him at the world trade center plaza at twenty-hundred hours tomorrow. And despite the short notice, he had no difficulty obtaining commitments. *Money is a great motivator.*

* * *

Walking past two guards and through an eight-inch steel door, Kirk stepped into the vault. Inside, Kirk's gaze took in the endless array of gleaming gold and silver bars, all stacked on pallets, with each pallet occupying a shelf of a massively-constructed metal storage system. *Holy shit!*

Walking up and down the aisles, he noted with satisfaction that the aisle space was sufficient for access by a forklift. He stepped back and looked beyond the gold, beyond the silver, and toward the walls and door of the vault. And he appreciated the vault's integrity – *solid* was the word that came to mind.

But Kirk was not an expert on vaults, and so he did not know that the walls were eight-inch thick poured reinforced concrete; cast in a monolithic pour, and providing a minimum compressive strength of 3000 pounds per square inch after 28 days of aging. He also did not know that the 5/8-inch diameter steel reinforcing bars were laid a maximum of 6 inches on center. Nor did he know that the bars created a cross-hatched steel curtain and that they were sandwiched at half thickness of the concrete. And he surely didn't know that the door was a Class 6 vault door – the strongest specified by the GSA.

At this moment, Kirk was concerned with one issue, and one issue only: moving the precious metals out of the vault and on to his flatbed trailers.

Kirk nodded at the guards as he stepped out of the vault and closed the door. He retraced his steps past an array of vaults and along a corridor toward the industrial-strength elevator. He rode the elevator from the basement's seventy-foot depth up to ground level; where he disembarked and walked toward the commercial entrance to world trade center building number 4.

When he came out on the street, he noticed figures dispersed up and down the complex; each wearing a black uniform and holding an M-16 rifle.

* * *

Kirk was waiting when the trucks pulled up to the front of WTC building 4. Kirk approached the lead truck just as Buck Fuller disembarked from the passenger's side.

"Hey Buck."

"Hey Kirk. Whatcha know?"

"We've got some stuff to move."

Buck looked at Kirk and frowned. "Whatcha got?

"C'mon. I'll show ya."

Kirk and Buck retraced Kirk's previous steps down to the basement and to the vault. They entered the vault; and when Buck looked around, he gave out a long low whistle. "Wow. Just wow."

Kirk smiled. "Think you can get your forklift down here?"

Buck was still aghast. "Yeah – no problem. But where are we taking it all?"

"You'll be driving it down to one of the Long Island piers. I'll get you the address and directions.

"Okay," Buck replied. "I'll unload the forklift and get started."

Soon, Buck was buzzing back and forth between the vault and the trucks; carrying one pallet after another and placing each one on the bed of the truck. Meanwhile, Kirk tabulated the weight that each truck received; making sure that each truck did not go over its maximum payload of 60,000 pounds. The truck drivers were trained not to be curious or inquisitive – they lived up to their training.

* * * * *

September 10, 2001 . . .

The television was turned on in the Jeffrey's den; and the voice emanating from it was incessantly droning – on and on ...

"This is Brett McGee reporting for KTTZ news; on September 10, 2001"

The voice continued to drone.

"... and this just in. Secretary of Defense Donald Rumsfeld made an important announcement today. In his own words, here it is ..."

The reporter then cut to a tape, and Donald Rumsfeld came on the screen.

"... the adversary's closer to home. It's the Pentagon bureaucracy" ...

"... According to some estimates, we cannot track $2.3 trillion dollars in transactions."

... and no one was in the den to hear this report.

Chapter 17 – September 11, 2001

Sleep ... Trish was wishing she could get some. *Damn! Won't this pressure on my head ever go away?*

Her eyes wide open, she rolled over for the umpteenth time, snuggling up to Dwayne. Still sleeping, Dwayne let out a soft snore and cuddled closer.

"Something's not right" she whispered.

Dwayne gave out a snore – but he didn't move.

Trish rolled over and let her foot touch the floor. *Damn it! Even after all these years, getting out of a waterbed is still an exercise in gymnastics,* she thought. Wrapping her bathrobe around her, she walked out into the kitchen. 5:00 am – Omaha time.

She felt tense, anxious; and her gut was roiling, as though something really big was weighing on her. She walked into the family room and turned on the television. Flipping to a cable news channel, she watched for a moment – watched the face, the mouth of the female reporter talking about the President's approval rating. The reporter's mouth was moving, surreal, with her finely-tuned cosmetics and her manufactured voice – running on about things that didn't really matter.

Damn! I'm feeling so sad! ... What's this about?

Click! She turned off the television.

5:10 am ... at least there was coffee to keep her going through the day!

* * * * *

Kirk never really knew the value of the metals they loaded. He only knew that the vault at the world trade center was to be cleared by the morning of September 11 – and it was up to him to do it. And so Kirk and his crew maintained a schedule of one load per truck, per night. They maintained this schedule for several nights, until the night of September 9th. It was on this night that Kirk realized they were not going to meet the schedule unless they doubled-up on deliveries the last two nights.

They doubled up. And at 6:00 am on September 11th, the trucks arrived at the world trade center for their final shipment.

On this day, Kirk was perusing the last of the vault contents when a man dressed in a suit appeared at the vault door. The two guards blocked his entrance; making it necessary for him to converse from the vault entrance. "Excuse me. Excuse me."

Kirk turned. "Yes?"

The man continued. "I heard a rumor that you were cleaning out this vault. What for?"

Kirk frowned as he looked at the man. "Who are you?"

"I'm Jeff. Jeff Farnsworth. I work for the Bank of Nova Scotia. I was down here checking our inventory."

"So, what's going on?" Jeff asked again.

Kirk dropped his arms and relaxed as he walked toward the man. "We were brought on to clear out this vault. They want it clear by this morning."

"This morning? It looks like you'll just make it."

"Yep. I think we'll get out of here at just about 8:00 am – just under the wire."

Jeff's curiosity was piqued even more. "So, who is 'they'? And did they say why they wanted it cleared?"

Kirk hesitated. *Should I tell him? Or should I just brush over this?* Finally, Kirk came to a decision. "Jeff – listen – I really can't say much. But this much I can tell you. If you can do it, you should get all of your stuff out of your vaults by 8:00 am."

Jeff's face turned red. "8:00 am? Just who do you think you are?"

Kirk shrugged and turned away. "Do what you want. Just don't blame me for whatever happens."

Kirk walked away leaving Jeff standing at the vault entrance.

A half-hour later, Kirk heard a couple of lorries – 10-wheeled dump trucks – coming up the old access tunnel. *I guess he took me seriously!* Kirk thought. *But I've got a hunch he won't get it done by the deadline.*

* * * * *

It was a carefree September morning for Eileen Shaw, administrative assistant and legal assistant for Richard Seneca, a Partner in the law firm of Hartley and Mayberry. She had held this position for several years, displaying an efficiency and competence unmatched by many of her peers. On this morning, her destination was the office on the 52nd floor of world trade center building number 2. She was walking smartly in her customary stride – her blond hair bouncing and her skirt hugging her hips as she moved gracefully along the sidewalk. This was a day of clear blue skies and warm temperatures – a day that lifts one's spirits.

Turning the corner into the world trade center complex, she spied two flatbed tractor trailer trucks parked along the road on the side of the building. She could not remember ever seeing trucks parked like that – especially large trucks such as these. *What are they doing?*

Although she was walking at about a thirty degree angle to the trucks, she was nonetheless moving closer to their position. As she closed on the trucks' position, she first noticed a number of men in black garb stationed strategically around the site. And although she was mostly ignorant of firearms, she could see that each man grasped the pistol grip of a black rifle. As she moved closer still, the details of the trucks came into sharper focus. The front truck was hauling a flatbed trailer – the trailer was fully-loaded but the cargo was covered with a tarp. And then her eyes were drawn to the truck in the rear – it was much more interesting. The truck was in the process of being loaded; and unless her eyes were deceiving her, the truck was being loaded with pallets of bars – *(gasp!) are those gold bars?* Of course she was still some distance from the trucks, and the shade obscured the color and glimmer of the bars. But she could have sworn they were a golden color.

She stopped and moved to the wall of the nearest building. Standing against the wall, she watched, looking for whatever clues that might tell her what she was seeing. She saw a forklift as it came up the ramp from the basement. It was carrying a pallet with still more bars. The operator deftly guided the forklift to a spot on the trailer and carefully lowered the pallet. As the pallet settled onto the flatbed, she could clearly discern a downward pressure on the bed. The operator stopped before withdrawing the forks and looked toward her position. She could have sworn he was checking her out.

The man continued to look in her direction. And in response, Eileen felt more and more unnerved by the man's stare; and for that matter, by the entire scenario. *If this is gold they are loading, what would cause them to do so? And why today?* Eileen considered possible answers to this question – the more she thought about it, the more apprehensive she became.

The forklift operator looked back to his work. After removing the forks from the pallet, the forklift turned and headed back down the ramp.

Eileen stood against the building. She tuned into her intuition – her sixth sense – and then a shiver pulsed through her. She sometimes had an episode like this, but never before was it this intense. She came to a place of 'knowing', and she knew that this was a good day to be home. She turned and retraced her steps back the seven or so blocks to the LIRR – the Long Island Railroad. From there, she grabbed the next train back to Hicksville, Long Island.

En route to her home, she heard initial reports that an airliner crashed into one of the world trade center towers.

* * * * *

Meanwhile, at the AB Jorday precious metals trading desk ...

"Blimey! Check out the price of gold!" said Chet.

"What about it?" Eddie retorted, thinking *why is he wasting my time?*

"It's climbing fast. Really fast! It was around $271 a few minutes ago; and now it's up to $280."

"And oil is up too."

"What are the currencies doing?" Eddie asked, now interested.

"The dollar is down sharply. Just in the last few minutes," replied Chet.

"What do you suppose is going on?"

"Hey, Chet. Turn on the tele!" Natalie shouted from her office across the hall.

"Huh?"

Excited, Natalie was now at Chet's doorway. "They just had a plane crash into the world trade center. Turn on the tele."

Chet turned on the television he kept in his office. Everyone in the room let out a gasp as the picture came into focus – showing one of the twin towers with billowing smoke coming out near the top.

Everyone in the office stood around watching the news report. No one said a word.

Finally, Chet piped up. "Blimey! I guess this explains the market action!"

"Well, it sure does." Natalie chimed in. "I just hope those people get –"

"Oh look!" Natalie pointed at the tele. "Oh my God – look at that plane. Look at that bloody plane!"

"Oh my God!" Chet shouted.

Mouths agape, they watched as another airplane came out of nowhere and flew headlong into the second tower.

Eddie was quick on the uptake. "You can't tell me that's just coincidence! There's no way that two planes are gonna fly into two buildings standing side by side within – what – an hour of each other? That's bullshit!"

"Gold is now at $284 an ounce!"

Shortly, the news came over that the U.S. markets would not open that day. Gold finished the day at $287 per ounce, and oil closed much higher. For the next three days, the Federal Reserve pumped $100 Billion per day into the markets and the banking system. And the dollar – a measure of investor confidence in the U.S. – dropped like a stone.

* * * * *

New York (International Press) Crushed Towers Give Up Cache of Gold Ingots

By Nancy Wharl in New York; November 2, 2001

Evidence of a billion dollar cache of gold was discovered at ground zero. The gold was believed to be lost when the two towers fell.

Workers were clearing rubble in a service tunnel underneath one of the collapsed world trade center buildings when they were surrounded by more than 100 armed government agents. Apparently, the agents had been tipped off by the owners where the gold was buried.

In the basement of World Trade Center Building 4, there were a number of vaults; but police have yet to disclose the owners of the gold.

COMEX[20] – the metals trading division of NYMEX – stored a reported 3,800 gold bars in the basement of WTC 4. The bars weigh more than 12 tonnes and are worth more than $100 million. COMEX also held about 800,000 ounces of gold on behalf of other clients – with a value of $220 million. And it stored more than 102 million ounces of silver; worth approximately $430 million. COMEX also held precious metals for Chase Manhattan Bank, the Bank of New York and Hong Kong and Shanghai Banking Corporation.

In addition, the Bank of Nova Scotia kept gold in one of the vaults. They reported a loss of over $200 million.

The gold was discovered on Tuesday. It was apparently being transported through the basement of WTC 4 on the morning of September 11. Recovery workers excavated into a service tunnel and discovered a number of crushed cars; and a lorry – a truck with ten wheels specially equipped to carry heavy loads.

---

[20] COMEX - Commodities Exchange.

The workers built a temporary ramp to gain access to the tunnel. And then a team of police and firefighters arrived to put the gold into Brinks trucks. Other workers were told to leave immediately. "If I tried to go down there they would have shot me," one man said.

No bodies were found in the tunnel; which suggests that those originally transporting the gold were forewarned to leave prior to the collapse of the south tower.

As of this writing, it is not known how much gold and silver was stored in the basement of the World Trade Center.

Part 3 – War

"Gold is my enemy. I am always watching what gold is doing."

— *Paul Volcker, Chairman of the Federal Reserve, Circa 1980*

* * * * *

Chapter 1 – September 11, 2001 (Continued)

THE MAN DROVE along the residential street and pulled up in front of a house. He stepped out of the car, his large but youthful frame struggling through the tiny car door. James Jeffrey looked around, noting that the homes along the street were brightly lit. With the walkway illuminated, he strode up the path and stairs to the front door. He walked into the house, finding his Mom and Dad still awake. They were sitting in the den and discussing the day's events. The television volume was turned way down, yet there was an animated mouth on the screen. The mouth was exaggerated – telling of pain and fear with every new grimace.

Mom and Dad seemed to be almost in shock – emotionally drained. It was at this point when he realized he too was in a similar place – angry, sad, grief-stricken, and ... lost.

When James entered the room, Dwayne and Trish stopped talking and looked up.

And then Dwayne stood up and blurted out, "Are you okay son?"

"I'm fine, Dad; but I can't get over what happened. I spent the day over at Jed's place. Mr. Simpson – Jed's Dad – thinks that when we find out who did it, we'll be going to war."

"That's really perceptive of him, son. Your Mom and I were just talking about it too – that if our government can pin it on any other country, then we'll be going to war for sure."

Trish picked up the conversation. "Oh God. Watching that airplane fly into the tower seemed like a dream. And the towers falling, and all those people dead; I still can't get over it." She began sobbing. "I just can't believe this happened!" She shivered as the tears rolled out. "Dwayne, I'm scared. I'm damned scared of what's coming next!"

"Yeah. I'm scared too."

Dwayne continued. "I'm wondering what really happened. , Because something doesn't add up about this." He paused. "Did you notice how the Air Force didn't scramble fighters to stop the second plane? Did you notice how the Air Force didn't attempt to stop the attack on the Pentagon? And – and did you notice how the towers fell straight down? It was as though the center of the towers gave way; rather than leaning and falling to one side or the other. ... Strange."

"Dad! What in the world are you talking about?"

"I'm just sayin', James. I'm just sayin' that some things about this don't add up!"

*   *   *

"But, Dad!! I want to help our country. I want to kill the rag head scum terrorist assholes. I want to hunt down those bastards and kill 'em."

Dwayne was pacing back and forth. "I understand how you feel, James. I feel the same way. Call me crazy, but I have a hunch that there's more to this terrorist attack than meets the eye."

"C'mon Dad. What is there to know! These rag heads attacked New York and brought down three of our buildings."

"Damn it, James! I'm asking you! Please – PLEASE – wait a few weeks, or months, before you enlist. The Marines, or whatever branch you choose, will still be there. And if this is truly a war we should be in, then it will be obvious to all of us."

"Dad. What are you saying? Are you suggesting that we were not attacked? "

"No, James, it's pretty obvious that we were attacked." Dwayne looked into James' eyes. "The question is, by whom?"

"Aw shit, Dad! Are you going off on one of your conspiracy theories again? I think Mom's right. I think you're a paranoid nut!"

Dwayne's face turned red as he slapped his hand across James' face, knocking him to the floor. He glared down at the boy. Then pointing his finger at James, he said "Don't you ever call me that again!"

James put his hand over his wound, then looked up at his Dad with sadness in his eyes.

Dwayne exhaled as he looked into James' eyes. "I'm sorry, son. I'm so sorry."

James stood up and looked at his Dad. "I'm sorry too, Dad."

"You do what you want, son. After all, it's your life."

* * *

Things were never the same after 9/11. For Dwayne's part, he found his business taking off, and yet his son had left home to enlist in the Marine Corps. And he experienced a new tension among his customers. People who once came in to browse his selection of rare coins were now more interested in bullion bars and coins. Many of his customers now talked of war and terrorist attacks on U.S. soil, whereas they used to talk of family and friends. Times had indeed changed ...

On a day soon after 9/11, Dwayne arrived early at his shop. He had it in mind to gather and analyze financial information from the internet. *Damn!* He thought. *Business has been really brisk. And with both the storefront and internet presence, I'm getting good sales volume. Good enough to more than make up for the low margins on precious metals.*

Dwayne was in the back room checking some transaction data in COMEX gold when the chimes at the entrance rang. He peered through the door to the front of the store, seeing Frank Meeks enter the shop.

Since that first visit eight years ago, Frank had turned out to be a regular customer – coming in somewhat frequently to buy gold and silver bullion. And Dwayne always appreciated the time he spent visiting. As strange as Frank behaved, he had recently completed his Ph.D. in Psychology and was working in a local mental health clinic.

"Hey Dwayne," Frank said. "What do you think about 9/11?"

Dwayne's face turned red. "If I had those assholes in my sights, I would kill 'em – right now! I'd kill 'em all, God damn it! And I'd happily watch them die in a pool of their own blood!"

Frank responded with an outburst of his own. "Shit, Dwayne. What they did was evil – absolutely evil! I can think of nothing they deserve more than the hangman's noose."

Dwayne paused at Frank's comment and looked into his eyes. "I thought you were a pacifist?"

"Yeah ... well," he shrugged. "Just how much shit do you take before you fight back?"

Frank's lips quivered as he continued. "I'm pissed. I don't understand how they did it – it's like our defenses didn't even exist!" Frank paused and then said, "I'm worried, Dwayne – real worried. And my poor wife is scared shitless. She's wondering when the next shoe is going to drop. And frankly, so am I!"

"What do you mean?"

"Look – these attacks shut down air travel for three days. What the hell would the government do if something really big happened? What would they do if some dirtbag terrorist lit off a nuke in New York or Washington?"

"You think that could happen?"

"Yes," Frank snapped. "I absolutely think it can happen. And I think when it happens, they'll implement martial law." Frank's eyes were hard. "I think it's only a matter of time!"

Dwayne felt chills down his spine. "Hmmm... So, what gave you the idea that we could get hit with a nuke? Or worse, that they would institute martial law?"

"Just stuff that I picked up on the internet. You know – on some of these conspiracy websites." He continued. "But you know – sometimes these conspiracy theories seem SO REAL! I can get sucked into them so easy!"

"So, what did they say?"

"Well," Frank continued, "the big items they talk about are the possibility of a nuke or a biological attack. Some of them were saying that a nuke – anywhere in the world – would cause the President to impose martial law. What was really interesting was this one guy was selling some kind of personal radiation detectors. He mentioned that a government agency had just placed a huge order for them. But he wouldn't say who it was."

Dwayne frowned. "So, what kind of people did they seem like?"

"They were very conservative. I can't remember the name of the site. But there was a lot of discussion about 9/11, and a lot of predictions of what was to come."

"So, what did they predict?"

"Well, the predictions that most of the people seemed to agree on were restrictions on our right to privacy, and possibly our right to free speech. And some were talking about a coming police state." Frank was wound up as he continued. "But there were a few that thought the government was involved in 9/11! There was a lot of back and forth talk about it, and a lot of people were downright resentful that anyone would even think it, never mind say it!"

"Hmmm... So, what else did they talk about?"

"Some people were really pushing gold. That's why I've been going there – to learn more about gold and money."

"Gold? Interesting ..."

Damn, Dwayne thought, *I never put much stock in the meaningless conspiracy babble these websites push. But maybe they're on to something. And maybe there's more we need to fear than what's right in front of us. Maybe ...*

"So," Dwayne said thoughtfully, "if a nuke goes off and we wind up under martial law, what are you gonna do?"

"I don't know. I'm thinking about moving – maybe some-place out in the sticks where the martial law troops wouldn't bother me."

"Do you have any ideas on where that would be?"

"I'm not sure ... I'm kinda thinking about northern Idaho. There's not much up there that I know of."

"This is interesting." Dwayne mused. "Here we live in Oma-ha, Nebraska; home of the Strategic Air Command – or whatever they call themselves these days – where the Air Force controls most of the U.S. nuclear arsenal. One of the few places where everyone believes we'd be nuked. And where no one – NO ONE – ever expects to survive a nuclear attack. And now, here we are, talking about how to survive a nuclear bomb and also survive the aftermath that could be martial law!"

"Damn!"

* * *

Frank's visit gave Dwayne a lot to think about. He started looking around at some of the websites, and he found one that was focused mostly on preparation for the end of the world as we know it – they called it TEOTWAWKI. The people on the site talked a lot about 9/11 and other terrorist-type attacks, as well as potential government responses to domestic and interna-tional catastrophe. It seemed as though the site had a strong doom and gloom bias, and yet much of their discussions and predictions seemed to be the thoughts of rational people.

Over time, Dwayne followed the news on these sites and compared it with what he observed in the mainstream media – newspapers, television, etc. And as he noted the differences, he came to the conclusion that the mainstream media was not re-porting on the really important world events.

Some few months later, and after talking with Frank and oth-er customers, Dwayne came to some conclusions – and he made a decision.

* * *

Trish was working at the kitchen sink when she heard the garage door open. Then she heard a car drive into the garage, followed by the garage door closing. *Dwayne is home*, she thought with a smile.

"Hi, Trish." Dwayne greeted her as he walked into the kitchen. "How was your day?"

Trish turned around from the kitchen sink, and her smile faded. The tone of his voice, his posture, his expression, all communicated his thoughtful preoccupation.

He seated himself at the kitchen table and gazed up at her.

"What's going on? Is everything okay?" She asked.

"Yes dear." He smiled a tired smile. "Everything's fine. I've just been doing some thinking."

Dwayne was often thoughtful – that was his nature. But his nature was usually upbeat. Now she wasn't so sure. "About what?"

"Well, about the world, events, and our place in the scheme of things."

She looked at him quizzically. "And?"

Dwayne looked up and into her eyes. "What do you think about moving?"

"Moving? Well, I've always wanted a new home – this house is kind of dated and it doesn't heat very well." She paused and looked at him. "But ... I don't think that's what you're talking about."

She folded her arms and looked at Dwayne. "What are you thinking?"

Dwayne hesitated and then said, "I suggest we close our storefront at the mall and move to the country."

"Huh? What the hell are you talking about?"

"I've been thinking that we should move to the country. Maybe to an area like northern Idaho."

Visibly upset now, Trish sank into her chair.

"No! Not a chance! We've got our friends here. Your family is here. Our business is here. Damn it, Dwayne, this is our home!"

Dwayne was silent as he looked down at the floor. Then he looked up and their eyes met. "May I explain why?"

Looking back into his eyes, Trish took a deep breath and exhaled. "Yes. Please tell me why."

"Well, Frank Meeks – you remember Frank, don't you? Anyway, Frank dropped by a few weeks ago and we got to talking about 9/11. He pointed out some interesting facts that got me to looking further."

"So?"

"So, I've been following the news on a few of these websites and I've found some interesting tidbits. Like, did you know that the U.S. government set us up to enter world war one?"

"Huh?"

"Did you know that the Pearl Harbor attack by the Japanese was known by FDR and his administration several days before it happened?"

"Dwayne. What are you saying?"

"Did you know that the federal government has repeatedly used emergencies – like 9/11 – to push further restrictions on our liberties? And to steal more of our Constitutionally-protected rights?"

"You're nuts, Dwayne! What you're saying is nonsense."

"Will you please listen to me?"

Trish sighed, and then said, "Go ahead."

Dwayne's voice quivered as he spoke. "Frank suggested that a terrorist could light up a nuke in a big city. And that it would cause the government to impose martial law. Just look," he pleaded. "Look at the lockdown on air travel following 9/11, and how they've since pushed through the Patriot Act. Damn it – I think he has a point!"

Trish became silent. She looked down to the floor, watching the shifting of her feet.

Dwayne continued. "We have no way of knowing what's going to happen; but why do we continue to live in Omaha – a primary Russian nuclear missile target? If terrorists wanted to disable our nuclear capability, this is the first place they'd hit!"

"Let me give it some thought," Trish replied...

* * *

A few days later ...

"Hi, Trish. How's my lover?"

Trish's eyes lit up as she turned around from the kitchen sink. She looked into Dwayne's eyes with her most seductive smile. "Hey Buddy, I can usually hear the garage when you come home. But not today – I don't think the garage even opened. So what's this sneaking around you're up to?"

Approaching her, Dwayne looked deep into her eyes. He moved his body close to her, feeling her body against him. Then he kissed her – deeply – longingly – stirring her passion.

Their kiss ended as passionately as it began. And then she smiled while placing her hands on his chest – creating just a hint of separation. "So. Sneaking in here. A long passionate kiss. What, my dear, are you planning?"

Dwayne was enjoying their closeness. "I'm not sneaking around. I was thinking that we could find a nice quiet restaurant for dinner. And maybe spend some time being together."

"Ooooohhh. I like that!" Then, she nodded toward the kitchen table. "There's a letter from James."

Dwayne followed her gaze over to the table. "And ... what does he say?"

"I suggest you read it, dear."

"You're not gonna tell me?"

Trish smiled. "You need the connection with him. Read it."

Dwayne pulled the letter out of the envelope, and began to read.

Dear Mom and Dad, ...

Dwayne read the letter intently; all the while his lips moved as he parsed the words. When he finished, he folded the letter and inserted it into the envelope. He raised his head and looked at Trish. "You're right, I sure do like reading his letters for myself."

"I thought you would," Trish said with a smile.

"So, do you still want to go out for dinner?"

"Yes," she replied. "Let me get my coat."

* * *

That evening over dinner and wine, they came to an agreement and formulated a plan. They would buy some land in northern Idaho and sell out their Omaha property. As a cover story, they would tell their friends they were seeking a more relaxing life in the country. Dwayne figured they could sell out the storefront portion of their rare coin business and continue with their rare coin and precious metals internet business. Their business could use a mail drop as close as possible to their new home – hopefully within 15 miles or so. Dwayne reflected wryly that this was the nature of country living.

Chapter 2 – September 13, 2001

The FOMC – Federal Open Market Committee – met several times a year. Their charter was to set interest rates according to the 'needs' of the economy and the markets – ostensibly to minimize price inflation and maximize employment. But their prime directive was to act as the lender of last resort; in essence, to create money from nothing in order to bail out banks that would otherwise fail.

Seldom did the Committee meet outside their normal schedule. But this time was different. This was September 13th – two days after the attacks of September 11th – and Jim Martin, Chief Economist of the Federal Reserve, was especially curious about the hastily organized meeting and about the way the Committee would handle the aftermath of 9/11.

Jim dialed into the conference bridge. The conference had just begun, and yet the dialogue seemed as dry as ever ... *it sounds as though they might not panic over this,* he reflected.

Chairman Greenspan's voice droned over the speakerphone. And as the Chairman talked, Jim listened and took notes of the proceedings, writing them into his leather-bound book.

"… In summary, as we stood in the early days of September prior to the crisis, we were still in that very precarious balance with regard to which way the economy was going to go.   The shock event of this past week is clearly a negative one. It is negative in the most important sense that it presumably increases the real risk premium for long-term capital investment, for fairly obvious reasons. That is, the longer-term environment for which capital investment decisions currently are being made must be perceived to be less certain and potentially of considerably more concern than one would have felt earlier.   How significant that deterioration is, I think, is exceptionally difficult to judge.   Indeed, one can envision a scenario–it's a low probability scenario …"

As the Chairman continued speaking, Jim imagined that he was watching Alan Greenspan – his patient, measured, and intellectual manner –   expressing himself behind his black-rimmed glasses and his wrinkled features.   *They will, of course, drop interest rates still more; so that they increase the amount of money in circulation,* Jim reflected.   *That seems to be their answer to every crisis that comes along – whether real or imagined.*

Interlude

From the shadows cast by the fire, Lord Basil posed with an air of satisfaction.   He drew from his cigar, letting the smoke waft through the air; and then he waved his hands extravagantly. "Gentlemen. I propose a toast – *le'chaim* – to the success of 9/11, and to all of us, and to our success!"

They replied in unison, "*Le'chaim*" – as they lifted their glasses in salute, and then to their lips.

Success was to be shared by all. And this success was tremendous for its scope and scale. The destruction of the world trade center towers, the reclamation of the precious metals stored in the basement, the collection of billions of dollars in insurance, the cover up of the multi-trillion dollar theft from the U.S. government[21] – and above all, an excuse accepted by virtually all Americans to take America into war.

All of the men leaned back in their plush leather chairs – joyous – reveling in their great achievement.

"Now, gentlemen; we have given our minion, President Bush, the list of countries he is to invade. We shall find out if he is up to the challenge."

They all raised their glasses together. "*Le'chaim!*"

Chapter 3 – Circa 2002

Tall, handsome, with graying temples around his medium-brown hair, Nate stuck his head over the partition wall and into Joe's cube. "Hey Joe. Can you get those software patches into the operations console? This afternoon?"

Joe's head popped up from his computer terminal. He looked up at Nate and said, "Sure. But I gotta tell ya – if we try it this afternoon, we run the risk of screwing up the patch. And you know what that means!"

Nate knew exactly what it meant. If the patch was not inserted correctly, control over network operations would be down for the count. Nate looked back at Joe and paused. "Hmmm ... Can you do it tonight? When the traffic load is way down and we don't need the operations console so much?"

"You bet," Joe replied with a smile. "I'd rather do it then because there's much less hassle."

"Okay," Nate replied. "Leave me an email and let me know how it went."

"Okay."

---

[21] On September 10, 2001 Defense Secretary Rumsfeld announced the loss of $2.3 Trillion by DoD. On September 11, a section of the Pentagon was destroyed. The destroyed section was the exact place where the financial records and audits were taking place. Thus, the attack on the Pentagon had the effect of covering up this crime.

A large, blond, fiftyish man, Joe Miller loved his work – and he was dedicated! Joe worked in a regional network center for the telephone company. As a network engineer who also dabbled in software development, he worked in telecommunications for a former Regional Bell Operating Company.

Joe went about his work but scaled back around 6:00 pm. He hung around the network control center until 8:00 pm, and then proceeded to install and test the new software patch. The installation and test went off without a hitch, so Joe informed Nate via email and went home for the evening.

Joe liked his job ...

* * * * *

"What do you think?" Joe asked as he glanced sideways at Jane. "Is this place worth checking out?"

"Maybe ...," Jane looked at Joe and smiled, "Let's see what they have."

The 'place', as Joe referred to it, was a residential subdivision of new homes. A beautifully landscaped area, it was one of several subdivisions they would visit that day.

Driving under a clear blue sky, Joe turned into the subdivision and drove past a sign to the right of the entrance. The sign read, *'el Chico'.* He followed the real estate signs through a couple of turns to the model homes and parked in front of the sales office. They sat in their luxury automobile for a moment, perusing the neighborhood.

Jane bit her lip. She looked at Joe with a pinched expression. "Can we afford this?"

"Sure we can," Joe replied. "I make good money."

"You make $140k a year, Joe. Yeah – that's good money. But is it enough for this?" She motioned expansively. "In a neighborhood like this?"

Joe looked over at her; his patient eyes resting easy on her attractive, fiftyish features and her petite frame. "Let's go in and find out?"

They stepped out of the car and walked past a sign that whispered '*Custom Homes*'. They disappeared into the sales office.

* * *

Driving around Sacramento's suburbia on a Sunday afternoon, Joe and Jane Miller were seeking that perfect home. The kind of home that would make them feel *fulfilled*. More than just a word, the *fulfillment* they sought was about style, and about image. The relaxed image of a Mexican tile roof and stucco exterior provided a laid back style of casual elegance. And the plush interior appointments of finely-crafted woodwork and stone, combined with floors of ornate Italian tile and red oak, would ensconce them in the elegance they deserved.

And here they were, touring just such a home ...

"Oh. I like this," Jane purred as she ran her hand over the granite countertops, her fingers lightly brushing the hardness of the stone. She paused, looking around the kitchen – the oak cabinets, the wood trim, the brightly-lit countertops, the Italian tiled floor – she took in all of this with a feeling of satiation. She sighed.

Joe looked over at her, smiling. "This is ... nice!"

"Did you see the master bedroom?" She almost squealed.

"I just love that bathtub; it's a full two-person tub!" Joe was feeling lusty as he thought of it.

"Sigh." Jane's voice was filled with passion. "Joe, I love this place. But do you think we can afford it?"

"Sure. I make good money. I work in a good industry. Things are always looking better and better; just look how my raises outstrip the inflation rate. So –"

Jane interrupted him. "Okay, then. Let's get them to build something like this for us."

* * *

Later that evening ...

"Joe. Are you sure we can handle this house payment?"

Joe looked at her in his usual patient manner.

"After all," she continued, "we've got car payments. And we're still putting Leslie through college."

And then she wailed. "I just don't see how we can afford a $3,200 per month house payment!"

Joe walked over and held her in his arms. He raised her chin with the hook of his finger. Looking into her eyes he said, "Hey. You know it costs to buy into the California market."

"I know," she demurred.

"And you know that California real estate is always going up."

"Yeah. I know." Her spirits began to brighten.

"And – hey! Real estate is a great investment." Joe smiled as their eyes met.

"I know." Her eyes crinkled with a smile.

"And you know that my job is solid and that prospects for growth are great. Right?"

She nodded her head 'yes'.

"And Len is out of college, so we need only pay for Leslie."

"And?" she coaxed him some more.

"Look," he continued. We can let the house go up in value – and when it comes time to retire, we can sell out and move to a cheaper state. Maybe Arizona!"

"Or maybe we could move up to Washington?" She fluttered her eyelashes at him with a smile.

"Sure," he replied. "We can do that."

"Okay." She sighed. "Kiss me, Joe." And she raised her lips up to meet his.

*　*　*　*　*

A few months later ...

Perusing their new home from the street, Jane and Joe shivered with anticipation as they held each other close. Jane looked up at Joe and smiled. "I'm so glad you talked me into it," she said.

Joe smiled from ear to ear. "So am I," he said. And then their eyes met. "What do ya think about having a housewarming?"

"Yes. Yes!" Jane replied as she jumped on her toes with excitement.

* * *

The crowd was large, and the housewarming was going in full swing. And Joe was in his element as he worked the backyard grill.

Joe glanced up just as the back door opened – Len emerged from the house, followed by Brenda.

"Hey guys," Joe called out.

"Hi dad," the two replied in unison.

Joe put down the spatula and walked over to them. "So what's goin' on?"

"We're getting married," Len announced.

Joe stopped his advance with an expression of surprise. He looked at one, and then the other, and then back again. "Super! Have you set a date?"

"Yes," Len replied as Brenda nodded her head with excitement. "We're planning on December."

"Great! I'm so happy for both of you." Joe held each of them under an arm and huddled close to them. He whispered, "I hope you both have the most wonderful life together that any couple can have. I love you both."

They split the huddle and then Joe continued. "When are you making the announcement?"

"Soon," Brenda replied. "We want to make sure that no one hears it second-hand."

Joe nodded his understanding. "Well, you better go tell your mother." And then he joked, "Or maybe not ... she'll tell the entire county."

They all laughed. Len and Brenda found the beer and then made the rounds to the other guests. Joe went back to flipping steaks.

"Food's on," he shouted.

* * *

Jane came up to Joe as he was flipping steaks and burgers. "How's the cooking going?" She asked.

"Just look around. Everyone's having a great time."

Then Joe put his grill work on hold and looked at Jane. "Did Len and Brenda tell you yet?"

"About getting married?" Jane asked.

"Yeah. What do you think?"

Jane smiled. "I think it's great. And I told 'em so."

Joe leaned over and whispered. "Do you think he'll do okay with his nursing career? I mean, do you think he'll be able to support a family on that?"

Jane's lips pursed as she glared at Joe. "Damn it. You've been harping on his decision to go into nursing ever since he first told us. It's been four years now, Joe. Get over it."

"Okay. Okay. I was just wondering ..."

"Wondering what?" Jane's face turned red.

"If that job was too feminine for him. I mean –"

Jane interrupted. "Damn it, Joe! Ever since he decided to go into nursing, you've been ragging on him about being a man. Hell, you just about accused him of getting a sex change operation." Jane paused and then continued. "Now what's goin' on?"

"Oh, nothing. Nothing ... "

"Then let it go." She paused and looked sternly at Joe. "Let – it – go!"

Jane turned and walked back into the crowd. Her stern expression immediately transformed into a warm smile as she greeted Mr. and Mrs. Holmsby.

Chapter 4

Ring. Ring! ... Ring. Ring!

Brandy reached over and picked up the telephone. *Gawd how I hate that loud ring.* She put the receiver up to her ear. "Hello?"

"Yes?" Brandy paused. "Yes, we carry those." (pause) "Yes, we carry those too." (pause) "I suggest that we set up a meeting." (pause) "Where are you located?" (pause) "That's fine. How about we meet at Brewer's Deli in Sandpoint?" (pause) "About 12-noon today?" (pause) "Sounds good. In case we don't connect, my cell phone is 208-555-8592. Okay. See you there."

Bill walked in just as she was hanging up the phone. "I'm meeting with a dealer today – new to the area. It looks like most of his business is over the internet. Brewer's Deli at 12 Noon."

And then she smiled at Bill and said, "Wanna go?

* * *

A quaint delicatessen and restaurant, Brewer's stands on the south side of downtown Sandpoint on U.S. 95, close to Lake Pend Oreille. A long time local eatery, Bill remembered it from his earlier days living in the area.

Bill and Brandy entered and immediately connected with the telephone caller – a tall man with light brown hair and a broad smile.

"Please call me Dwayne," he said.

"I'm Bill; and this is my partner, Brandy. Er – ah – she is the person you talked with over the phone."

Brandy's charming smile came forth as she drawled, "How can we help Y'all?"

Dwayne looked back and forth between the two. "I'm looking to stock silver and gold rounds to sell on my internet precious metals site. I'm wondering what kind of price you can give me on quantity purchases?"

Bill produced a silver and gold round, each encased in its own plastic protective sleeve, and placed them on the table. "We currently offer two kinds of coins; a $20 Silver Freedom coin, and a $1,000 Gold Freedom coin."

Brandy picked up the dialog. "We call them *Freedom Dollars*. In large lots, we charge the spot price plus twelve percent."

Brandy continued. "Now, with these pieces, we include a brochure on Freedom Dollars that you can give to your customers. The brochure discusses how these coins can be used in barter transactions; quite possibly in lieu of Federal Reserve Notes. We've been marketing Freedom Dollars this way since their inception – and we've had great success with this approach!"

The spot price was the current price on the COMEX for silver and gold still to be delivered. Bill knew that the price was as good as any dealer could get, especially considering the manufacturing costs of the coins.

Dwayne picked up one of the pieces and looked at it closely. "I think we can do business on these ..."

Then he turned it over to look at the reverse of the coin. "Do you trade in any other product lines?"

"Yes." Brandy's eyes lit up as she produced a one-ounce custom gold coin. "We designed these as a custom run for the Philippines. Their government receives revenue for each coin sold, and we keep whatever profit remains. We've also designed a number of different issues for other countries – usually under the same business model. They've all been successful for us."

"Great! And how much do you charge for them?" Dwayne asked as he flipped the piece over.

"For these, our wholesale price is 30% below retail," Brandy replied. "Remember, these are focused more on the collectors' market, rather than the precious metals market."

"Okay!" Dwayne replied. "But I will need to see what kind of demand exists before I can commit on large quantities, so I'm wondering if I can begin by getting a quantity discount on a smaller first-time purchase?"

"Hmmm ... I think we can find a way to do that," Brandy replied.

* * * * *

Brandy walked into Dwayne's rare coin shop pushing a small-ish four-wheel cart full of Dwayne's new inventory – an inventory of Freedom Dollars and custom pieces authorized by Thailand's government.

Brandy stepped up to the counter and rang the bell. While waiting for Dwayne, she looked around at Dwayne's modest surroundings. The size and scope of the main shop area suggested a rather small rare coin operation – a suggestion that was clearly not true given his much larger inventory and balance sheet.

"Hi, Brandy."

Brandy turned toward the voice and smiled. "Hi, Dwayne. I brought Y'all some stuff. How's business?"

"Damn! That's a big load." Dwayne said. "Did I order all that?"

"Yep," Brandy replied. This is what we talked about on the telephone. Every order you've placed has been larger than the last. As far as we're concerned, your business is growing – and fast!"

"Yes, well ... my transactions seem to be getting more numerous, and the dollar amounts are getting larger too," Dwayne replied.

"So," Dwayne continued, "how're you guys doing?"

"Great." Brandy replied.

Dwayne seemed to lick his chops as he looked at the cart. "How about we go through the invoice and make sure everything is here?"

"Let's do it."

After they finished, Brandy said, "Did you know Y'all can be a wholesaler of both the Freedom Dollars and the custom pieces? That would give you an opportunity to make even more."

"I kinda guessed that. But I've been so busy that I just didn't think about it." Dwayne said. "But now that you've brought it up, I'll see how I can fit that into my business model."

"And also," Brandy's eyes sparkled as she was speaking, "Bill and I have decided to come out with half-ounce and quarter-ounce silver Freedom Dollars."

"Great!" Dwayne smiled, "I've had a lot of people asking for them, so you already have at least one buyer."

Then Dwayne frowned. "So, what do you think of our economic situation?"

Brandy's expression became more serious. "Bill and I were talking about it the other night. We both think that the fundamentals of the economy are looking really bad."

"Not that we'll have a crash today or tomorrow," she mused, "but we see a rather large bubble beginning to form in the real estate market. When you add this to the Fed's previous money-pumping bailouts – Long-Term Capital Management, the dot-com bubble, and 9/11 – and the fact that they're pumping money to bail us out of this recession; well, we think it looks grim.

Brandy continued. "Bill was talking with a friend who is still working in the telecommunications field – Bill left that job back in '96. Anyway, it sounds like the computer and telecommunications industries are in a full-blown depression!" Brandy's eyes grew bigger. "And you know what? They're still sending IT[22] jobs overseas and importing more engineers from other countries. It's killing engineers' salaries and putting them out of work."

Dwayne was stupefied. "You know, Trish and I have talked about these same issues; but I must admit I am shaken – really shaken – to hear this coming from you guys. Especially since you seem to have your wits about you."

The conversation paused. And then Dwayne continued. "So, what do you think will happen?"

"It's hard to say how it will play out. But it appears the Fed is willing to bail out every financial and economic problem that comes along. That alone should tell us we're in for a large debasement of the dollar over these next years."

"But we've been seeing monetary inflation for several years," Dwayne said, "and yet, gold, silver, and interest rates are all extremely low. What gives?"

---

[22] IT is short for Information Technology.

Brandy hesitated, and then she said, "Bill and I think they're manipulating the price of gold and silver – driving the prices down. This allows them to keep interest rates artificially low and it allows them to print larger amounts of money."

"So, where do you think this takes us?"

"Well," Brandy replied, "again, there's no telling for sure, but it could well put us through an Argentina-like collapse down the road. But – and here's a big but – because the dollar is the world's reserve currency, it could remake the entire world in the image of Argentina's collapse!"

"Wasn't Argentina a war zone a while back?"

"It still is." Brandy replied.

Chapter 5 – Circa 2003

Sheryl Barclay's narrow fingers flew over the keyboard as she mentally checked off the arguments that the Congressman mentioned. He was dead-set against the Iraq invasion; and to Sheryl, he had made his reasons crystal clear. *I need to have this speech finished tonight so that he finds it on his desk in the morning,* Sheryl thought. *That way, he can get his corrections out of the way first thing.*

She glanced up at the clock. *Shit! it's 11:30. I'm not gonna be worth a damn if I don't finish this soon!* Her fingers moved even faster over the keyboard.

Recently hired into Congressman Bannister's staff, Sheryl was working well into the evening. Shoulders hunched, she plugged away on the keyboard, glancing infrequently at the notes scratched on a torn piece of paper under the desk lamp. The lamp illuminated her desk; but further out from the desk, the light receded into the shadows, giving just a hint of the walls beyond. Outside her office there was a main hallway providing general access to the office suite; but as was Sheryl's custom, the office suite proper was darkened – the kind of dark that brings out the silhouette of the chairs, the desks, the filing cabinets. But not much more ...

Good! I'm almost done! She thought. *My Communications degree is beginning to pay off,* she mused. *If only I can get a permanent job here with the Congressman!*

Then she heard something. Not knowing what it was, she stopped typing and remained still. She heard only silence. And then, she heard it again – a gentle squeak, as though a door were opening. She remained still, listening and watching. The squeak stopped. She thought she heard rustling, but she wasn't sure.

She reached down under her computer table and quietly pulled out her purse. She felt around in the purse until her hand closed around a spray can. *Pepper spray – this should help,* she thought as she grasped the can. And then she saw a ray of light; probably from a flashlight. The light was moving back and forth, illuminating the walkway through the office suite.

Quiet like a mouse, she tiptoed softly from her desk over to the wall closest to the office entrance. Ever so still, she pressed herself up against the wall and waited – not daring to even breathe.

Was it a security guard? No – they didn't patrol the office suites. They kept their patrol to the corridors. Was it a co-worker? Damn! What would a co-worker be doing with a flashlight? Why not turn on the lights?

She watched the light travel the floor – back and forth – near the entrance to her office. And then the light came up to the entrance and a man's silhouette filled the doorway frame. At that moment Sheryl knew the measure of her resolve. She leaped out of the shadow and sprayed the pepper into the man's face. The man jumped back and let out a horrible scream. "*Arrrgh!* I can't see! I can't see!" The man fell to the floor, writhing in pain.

Sheryl turned on the lights and then stood over the suffering, squirming man. "If you try one damn thing – if you move a muscle or try to escape – I'll call security. You got that?"

"Ya – yes," he hissed in pain.

Sheryl was breathing deeply with the excitement. "Now. Who the hell are you?"

The man's head rolled on the floor as he held his eyes. "I can't see – I can't see. Ca – ca – can you help me out?"

Sheryl's anger was beginning to take over. "Answer my question. Who are you?"

"Mmmm – Mark."

"Mark who?"

"Shannon. Mark Shannon."

"What the hell do you want?"

"Ah, ah – um ..."

Sheryl was still standing over him. "If you don't tell me, I'll spray you again and call security. I'm sure they'll get it out of you."

"You – you wouldn't do that. Would you?"

"In a New York minute, I would! Now talk!"

"Okay. Okay," he wheezed through his clenched mouth. "I – I came to plant a bug."

Sheryl's eyebrows rose. "Bug? What kind of bug?"

"A – a listening device. I was supposed to plant it in Bannister's office."

"Why?"

"I work for the Majority Whip. He – he told me to do it. He wanted information on how many were gonna vote against the Iraq war. He – he knows Bannister's against it. He thought Bannister would be a good source."

"And?" Sheryl was still standing over him.

"And, and – that's it. That's all there is." The man continued to writhe in pain.

"Hmmm." Sheryl paused in thought.

"I think I'll call security," she decided.

"No – no, wait! I'll make you a deal."

"Deal? That's absurd! What do you have that I could possibly want?"

"They – they've got some dirt on Bannister." Mark was beginning to shake off some of the effects.

"Oh?" Sheryl's eyes grew big.

Sheryl watched as a smile broke out on Mark's face. *Damn! I may have to make a deal with this jerk!*

She looked down at him. "Are you wearing contacts?"

"Huh?"

"I'll say it slow. Are you wearing contacts in your eyes?"

"No."

"Good. Because we'd have to take them out first thing."

"Stay here," she commanded. She walked over to her desk and pulled a packet out of her purse. Ripping it open, she extracted a saturated cloth and walked back to the man. She stooped, using the cloth to wipe the pepper off his face and out of his mouth and nose; and then she gave him the cloth and said, "put this decontamination pad over your eyes. It should clear your eyesight quick." Soon, he was sitting up and looking at her.

Sheryl stood back and glared at him. She was now all business. "Tell me what they know about Bannister. What kind of dirt do they have on him?"

Mark talked slowly. "Well, it's simple, really. They – the other side of the aisle – they know that he's banging his Chief of Staff. Loraine is her name, I think."

Sheryl felt her hands shiver and her eyes widen. *So that's what's been going on! Damn! I didn't think about it at the time; but when I look at it now, I can definitely see the signs.* Sheryl gasped. *That time I knocked on the door and then walked right in. Loraine was standing there, stroking her blouse with her hands; smoothing it, I think. But oh – there were other times too! Son of a bitch!*

"Damn!"

The conversation stumbled to an awkward wordlessness.

Mark finally broke the silence. "Hey. I'll bet we can help each other out."

Sheryl crossed her arms and looked at him dubiously. "What do you have in mind?"

"Well, maybe we could feed each other information. What do you think?"

"Hmmm ... I don't know what I can tell you," she responded. "Frankly, I'm not in the habit of betraying my boss!"

"Okay. Okay," Mark was beginning to show his boyish handsome side. "Maybe I can pass you some information? Or, maybe we can just talk? Maybe – maybe we can meet for dinner tomorrow night?"

Mark raised his eyebrows as he looked at her.

"Well," Sheryl lifted her nose up in the air, "I don't know if I want dinner with you."

"Why not?"

"Because you're nothing more than a common thief, that's why." She glared down at the man. "It looks to me like all you do is lurk the Capitol halls in search of anything you can steal. I suppose you check everything to see if it's nailed down," she sneered. And then her brow furrowed. "How much have you stolen in your career?"

"Who, – who me?" Mark turned red. "I ain't stolen nothin'!" He spat.

"You little shit!" She spat back. "You're just a thief. A 'user' of people. Only looking to find what you can use to your advantage – and to hell with everyone else!"

The room became silent.

"Well? Do you want to have dinner with me?" Mark finally asked.

Sheryl looked away from Mark and sniffed. "I'll think about it."

* * *

Sheryl found herself at Rulano's Italian Restaurant – a quiet place tucked far away from the Capitol – sitting across from Mark.

"So, how long have you been working for Bannister?"

"Why do you want to know?"

"I don't know. I just wanted to know how long you've been working as an aide."

"Why do you want to know that?"

Mark was chewing on a breadstick. He hesitated and then spoke. "Hey. Look," he paused, looking into her eyes, "I really just want to know you better."

"Well, why didn't you say so?"

Sheryl watched Mark's face turn red. "I'm sorry. I didn't mean to mess with ya."

Mark smiled. "Yes you did. You meant it."

"Oh. Alright. I was screwing with ya." She smiled.

They looked at each other.

"So," Mark opened, "what do ya think about this Iraq deal? Do you think they've got weapons of mass destruction?"

Sheryl took a nibble out of her breadstick. "I don't know. And I'm not so sure it matters, either."

"Doesn't matter? Why do you say that?"

"Well. Lot's of countries have WMDs – but, unless they attack us, we don't go to war with 'em. So, what makes Iraq different?"

"Hmmm. That's a good question." And then Mark continued, "but if they have WMDs, they can sure use 'em on us; don't ya think?"

"Well, yes," Sheryl replied. "But if you use that logic, shouldn't I be calling the police?"

Mark looked at her quizzically. "Huh?"

"Shouldn't I call the police on you?"

"What are you talking about? I haven't done anything to you. Why would you call them?"

"Well," she looked at him with dancing eyes, "you're obviously a rapist aren't you? And isn't it a matter of time before you use it?"

"Huh?"

She continued. "you have all the equipment, don't you? It's just a matter of time before you use it. Right?" she smiled.

A disbelieving look crossed Mark's face. He paused, and then held up the palm of his hand, as if to say 'STOP'. "Okay. Okay. I see what you're getting at."

The waiter came over and took their order.

Sheryl continued their conversation. "But there's something I don't understand; and maybe you can help me with it?"

Mark stroked the glass with his hand. "What don't you understand?"

"Well ..." Sheryl was thinking. "This Congressman Bannister."

"Yes?"

"Well ..." she paused, thinking. "He decided to change his
vote on the Iraq thing."

"So, why does that matter? Congressmen change their minds
all the time."

"Not this one, Mark. I've worked with him for about a year –
he always sticks to his principles."

"And what are his principles?"

Sheryl looked into her glass. "He's passionately anti-war –
that's what. Hell, he's so anti-war that he always votes against the
defense budget!"

"Wow," Mark replied. "And now he's gonna vote for the Iraq
war?"

"Yes. And I don't understand it!"

They both paused in thought.

"But you know?" She continued. "There's one strange thing
that happened today."

"What's that?"

"This guy came in to see Bannister. He went into Bannister's
office and spent some considerable time with him. Shortly after
the man left, Bannister came out and let us know he was changing his vote."

"Hmmm," Mark paused in thought.

"What was the man's name?"

Sheryl replied. "Daniel, I think. Daniel, ah – Elsbarg? Or
something like that."

Mark looked at her. "Elsbach? Was his name Elsbach?"

"Yeah – maybe. I'm not sure."

"What did he look like?"

"Well. He was tall. Dark. Slender. Graying at the temples."

Mark nodded his understanding.

"Why? Have you heard of this guy?" Sheryl asked.

"More than heard of him." Mark rolled the wine glass in his
hands.

Mark exhaled a sigh. "About three times, I've seen him come to politicians that I've worked for. You know – I used to work for a Senator, and now I work for the majority whip."

Mark continued. "Well, every time he goes in to see my congress critter – no use mincing words here – they change their vote after he leaves. I don't know what it is, but he has some kind of power over 'em."

"And now this with Bannister, a die hard liberal peace monger. Wow!"

Sipping her wine, Sheryl looked across the table at Mark.

Shortly thereafter, the waiter brought out their meals and they spent the remainder of the evening getting to know each other.

Chapter 6 – July, 2003

"Damn! The Fed Funds Rate is now down to 1 percent."

Chairman Greenspan looked up at Jim Martin through his black-framed glasses and smiled. "I would think that would give quite a boost to the economy. Don't you think so?"

Jim paused before answering. "Well, we're surely flooding the economy with cheap money ..."

The wrinkles on Chairman Greenspan's face descended into a frown.

Jim continued. "And surely one would think that boosting the money supply should lead to growth. But did you consider the possibility that driving down interest rates has the effect of weakening the dollar? And have you considered that a weaker dollar will cause more U.S. jobs to move offshore?"

Chairman Greenspan leaned back in his chair, watching Jim intently.

Jim paused again before continuing. "And have you considered the notion that lower interest rates will cause savings and capital to flee the U.S.? Which will cause fewer jobs to be created in the U.S.?

Chairman Greenspan's office became deathly quiet – like a tomb. And like a tomb, Jim felt a shiver as though a granite slab had just slid into place above his head, burying him inside. The Chairman took off his glasses and placed them on the desk in front of him. He seemed to consider each lens in turn.

The Chairman put his glasses on and looked up a Jim. "You raise some good points, Jim."

Chairman Greenspan continued. "I think ... that the price of gold is low, and it is telling us that the value of the dollar has some room to maneuver." His eyebrows raised as he paused. "I think the issue of capital flight has merit. But the U.S. economy long-ago became accustomed to using credit as capital. You know – the credit that we and the banks create? So, the economy is much less dependent on savings as a means of investment." He paused. "And as for jobs moving offshore, I think we will only be doing this for a short time. And so, we should not have any trouble – but this is a gamble we must take if we are to revive the U.S. economy."

The Chairman continued. "As you know, Jim, the U.S. economy, and the world economy, for that matter, have seen a steep drop in economic output. If we are to revive the world economy, we must kick start it with your so-called 'cheap money'." The Chairman smiled with these last words.

The Chairman laid his hands almost flat on top of his desk. "I trust," he said in his measured, patient manner, "that I have answered your questions?"

"Yes, Mr. Chairman. Thank you." And with that, Jim turned and walked out of the office.

As Jim walked through the outer office, he passed a tall, dark, and lanky gentleman seated in the waiting area. Jim nodded to him, then slowed his pace to a crawl. He heard Carol speak into the intercom. "Mr. Chairman. Mr. Elsbach is here to see you."

"Yes, Carol. Please ask him to come in."

Carol turned to the man. "Chairman Greenspan will see you now."

*   *   *   *   *   *

Another day at work, Joe walked into his cube and sat down at his workstation. *Ahhhh - Friday! Maybe, if there's not much going on here, we can head up to the Sierras this afternoon. We'd be able to pitch a tent and bed down before dark.*

Joe smiled to himself. *I should be able to get out of here by 3, get home by 3:30, hook up the boat trailer by 4:00, and be on the road shortly thereafter. We should make camp by 6:30 or 7pm. I'll bet the fish are biting good! I wonder how that new lure -*

Joe looked up as Nate stuck his head into the cube. "Hey Joe. Can you come on down to my office?"

Joe got up from his chair and followed Nate down the hall. *I wonder what he wants? He doesn't usually invite me to talk in his office!* "Hey Nate. What's goin' on?"

Nate walked into his office and Joe followed. Nate had a sober look on his face. "Close the door and have a seat."

Joe sat down and looked across the desk at Nate. "What's with the look? Why so glum?"

Nate leaned forward from his seat; his elbows resting on his desk. "Joe. I'm sorry to bring you bad news."

Nate turned his head away from Joe and continued. "They're laying you off."

Joe looked down at his hands. And then he looked up at Nate. "What? I've been here twenty years! Nate - twenty fucking years!"

"I know. I told them this was a mistake. That we needed you and that you'd done a lot of good work over the years. But, they didn't listen."

"But, but - did they say why?"

Nate looked dejected. "They're laying off a whole lot of people today. New management. You know how it is."

"Shit!"

Joe sat in his chair in silence - *alone* - as though no one else existed. *Twenty years! What the fuck! I wonder what Jane will say? I wonder what kind of job I can get?*

Nate continued. "You'll need to go directly to HR from here. They'll talk with you about your severance package and answer any questions you have."

Nate stood up, signaling the end of their discussion. "I'm sorry, Joe. Really, really sorry. If there's anything I can do, please let me know. It goes without saying, but I will say it anyway – you've been a true pleasure to work with. Don't hesitate to use me as a reference."

Joe stumbled over his tongue as he responded. "Thanks, Nate."

Joe walked out of the office and headed up to Human Resources.

Joe was stunned. More – he was in shock. *After twenty years, I never would've guessed they'd let me go!* Walking up to HR, he passed by a co-worker, John, who worked on the night shift. He was walking abreast with a woman who wore an access badge. Joe didn't know who she was.

And then it hit him. *She's escorting him out of the building. I suppose they'll do that to me, too. I heard that it's standard procedure for people they fire, but not for layoffs ...*

He walked into the HR department and up to the receptionist's desk. The receptionist appeared ready for the day's activities – she did not even blink as she asked Joe's name.

"Miller. Joe Miller," he replied.

The receptionist dialed a number. "Karen? Mr. Miller is here." She paused to listen. "Okay. I'll send him right down."

She turned and nodded to Joe. "Mr. Miller, If you will just take this hallway, it will bring you to Ms. Spender's office. Karen Spender is waiting to see you."

Joe began his journey down the corridor. His journey of – *loneliness! I hate these people ... what the hell are they planning? What's gonna happen?"*

He walked into Karen Spender's office. The woman behind the desk stood up and extended her hand. "Mr. Miller. I'm Karen – Karen Spender."

Joe looked at her warily. "I'm Joe. Joe Miller."

Ms. Spender brought her empty hand down and gestured to him. "Have a seat. Please."

Ms. Spender re-seated herself and placed her elbows on her desk, with her hands folded just below her hard, well-defined chin.

Joe's hands were shaking as he watched her. He waited for her to speak.

"Mr. Miller. I assume you've already talked with Nate?"

"Yes."

"And he informed you that we are letting you go."

"Yes."

"I asked to meet with you so that we can finalize the paperwork prior to your, ah – departure."

Joe sighed. And then he said, "What paperwork is that, Ms. Spender?"

"Ah – we are prepared to offer you a severance package as part of your, ah – retirement."

"Retirement? I am too young to retire, Ms. Spender. Nor can I afford to retire."

"Quite right," she replied. "Well, we are prepared to offer you three months' pay as a severance package; and in return, we want you to sign this document." She held up a document.

Three months! Three months after twenty years of loyalty! "What's it say?" Joe asked.

"Well, ah – it merely says that we terminate our relationship on amicable grounds. And with your signature, ah – you agree not to seek any further settlement from the company."

"And what if I choose not to sign?"

The corner of her mouth crooked up as she looked down at the document. "If you, ah – choose not to sign the document, then we will still terminate our relationship. But you will receive no severance package."

"Do I have time to think about this?"

"No, Mr. Miller. This is your sole opportunity to sign it."

"So you call me in first thing this morning and tell me I'm laid off; and then you present me with this contract and tell me my only opportunity to sign it is now."

"Tell me, Ms. Spender, how long have you known I was to be let go?"

"I'm sorry, Mr. Miller. I do not know the answer to that."

"Are you telling me that you don't know how long you've known?"

She leaned forward on her desk. "Mr. Miller. Joe. I do not know how long they've had the list. I can tell you that I was notified last night."

"Why is the company doing this? Why me? Why now?"

She leaned back and looked across the desk. Then she said, "Because the company isn't doing well." She paused and took a deep breath, then continued. "Hell Joe, you know that the telecom industry is in the middle of a depression. I don't know how you were selected, but I know it's about the economy."

Joe sat across the desk and looked at her intently. Finally, he blurted out in exasperation, "Give me the document. I need to read it before I sign."

Joe scanned the document, and then flipped it over and read the back. He scribbled his signature on it and handed it back to her. She took the document and handed over a check.

Ms. Spender leaned back in her chair, and said, "It's my job to walk with you back to your office and help you collect your things."

Ms. Spender collected a couple of boxes and they walked the corridors back to Joe's cubicle. Ms. Spender stood by while Joe collected his books, pictures, odds and ends ... all the things he had accumulated over the previous twenty years.

He pulled several framed certificates off of the walls – *Outstanding Accomplishment Awards*, each covering a different year of his service. Joe noticed Ms. Spender's seeming embarrassment as he looked at the awards.

When he finished packing the boxes, they loaded them on a cart and she accompanied Joe to the nearest security checkpoint. And then she served the final insult. "Your badge please." It wasn't a request.

As though he were letting go of a long-time close friend, Joe unclipped the badge and handed it to her.

Joe and Ms. Spender walked out to his truck and loaded the boxes. Then he crawled into the cab for the long drive home.

* * *

Joe was driving down Sunrise Blvd. when he approached an intersection with a green light. He momentarily looked to his left and then looked back to the approaching intersection. The light was now red. *What the ...! I only looked away for a second! Hmmm ... was that light really green before?*

Joe sensed he was scattered – unfocused. He felt a headache coming on, and he felt his eyes squinting while they were jumping back and forth. After two more near-accidents, he pulled over to the shoulder. He closed his eyes and allowed himself a moment to rest.

He usually had thoughts running through his mind. But now he felt nothing. And his mind was almost a blank. *Strange!*

Joe turned back onto the road and continued his drive home. He was beginning to feel angry, but he didn't know what to do about it. He continued driving.

* * *

Joe entered the house and closed the door behind him. "Jane?"

"Hey," he heard Jane in the distance, "you got off of work early! Are you all set for the boating trip?"

Jane hopped down the stairs. She saw Joe's expression and halted in mid-stride. "Honey? What happened?"

His voice sounded like a child's. "They laid me off."

"What?"

He looked at her as he reached across his chest to his opposite arm. He clenched his arm as he said, "They laid me off."

"Oh no!"

Joe turned his head as she tried to connect with him. Then, she reached forward and wrapped her arms around him, bringing him close to her. They held each other for some time.

Finally, Jane looked up into Joe's eyes. She smiled. "Let's go fishing."

* * *

Joe's early arrival home gave them plenty of time to get out of the valley before rush hour. They needed only to load up the truck and attach the trailer – activities they had performed countless times before.

They soon departed – leaving the summer heat behind. Up into the Sierras they drove; up, up into the cool of the tall pine and fir trees. On a high section of road, Joe looked out over the expanse of forest – *I've never gotten over how tall the trees grow!* They drove for about 90 minutes and then came upon the turnoff to their favorite campsite – Lake Van Norden. They continued their drive weaving back and forth along the curves of the back roads until they arrived at the lake. Turning into the ranger's checkpoint, they paid the fee and chatted with the Ranger.

"Hi, Joe. Hi, Jane," the Ranger greeted them. "How're you two doing?"

"Fine, Pete. Just fine," Joe replied. "And you?"

"Very well, Joe." The Ranger paused and then continued speaking. "I've got your favorite camping spot open."

"Hey, great!" Joe replied. "Thanks!"

The Ranger then said, "You folks have a nice visit, now."

"Thanks, Pete. And you have a great day too!"

Joe drove over to the campsite and backed in. He turned off the engine and they unloaded their camping gear. Then, while Jane worked on setting up the camp, he towed the boat down to the boat ramp, lowered it into the lake, and tied it up to the dock. Finally, he drove back to the campsite and parked the truck and trailer in the driveway adjoining the campsite.

Joe and Jane worked quickly and had the campsite set up in no time at all. And when they finished, they sat down together. They bantered for a bit and then they said in unison, "Wine?" Laughing, Jane shook her hair and pulled out a bottle. She poured two glasses.

Over the weekend, they relaxed, they fished, and they enjoyed camping and the outdoor cooking. And they talked for hours – about the layoff, the process, and their future. Joe was amazed at how little money was in the three-month severance check – and said so.

They arrived home on Sunday evening. And on Monday, Joe applied for unemployment benefits.

* * * * *

Two years later ...

Jane was sure her head would explode. She had explained it several times, but they just didn't seem to get it. She paused, looking at her clients through protruding eyes. And then she said, "Look, there's already a bid on the house. The bid is $625,000. I know the listing price was $610,000; but submitting a bid of $610,000 will not get you the property. If you want to buy it, you need to outbid the other bidders."

Trevor Townsend looked at his wife, Paula. Paula looked back at him. They both nodded their heads up and down in a gesture of 'yes'.

Trevor turned to Jane. "Okay. We'll offer $630,000."

Paula's face broke out into a smile even as she shivered with excitement.

Jane nodded to the couple and began writing. "Okay, we'll make this offer for $630,000 and see what they do." Jane scratched the pen across the paper in a final flourish. She passed the offer sheet across the table to Trevor and Paula and looked at the two of them while pointing on the sheet. "I need your initials here – and here. And then sign here."

They each signed their initials and signatures, and then Trevor handed it back to Jane.

"So," Jane smiled, "I'll fax this out now. Hopefully, we'll hear something positive before the end of the day."

"Okay," said Trevor. Paula shivered with still more excitement.

Jane shook hands with the young buyers and smiled as she watched them depart, chattering like a couple of hens as they walked out of the office. She enjoyed working with young buyers. They were fun, exuberant, and full of energy; and yet they were ignorant of the home buying process. *I really hate having to educate these kids on this stuff,* she thought.

Jane turned to the fax machine and faxed the counteroffer to the seller's agent. Then finished for the day, at least so far as she knew, she packed up and strode out of her office. *I wonder how Joe's job search went today?* She thought.

Jane opened the door of her late-model Cadillac and slid behind the wheel. With just a hint of hedonism, she ran her hand over the leather seat next to her. *I just love how great these seats feel.* She started the car and moved out of the parking lot and into traffic.

Jane chose to be a housewife and homemaker after their marriage – staying at home and raising their two children. It was an easy decision for her, especially since Joe made such a good salary. But after Joe was laid off, Jane decided to go back to work and build a career; and given that her college major was business, she decided that being a real estate agent would pay off for her. *Hell – it seemed as though California real estate was always going up. There must be some money in it!*

She arrived home and pulled into the driveway next to Joe's truck. *If he doesn't get a job soon, we may need to sell his truck.*

* * *

Joe was coming down the stairs just as she entered the front door. "Hey, lover. How was your day?"

"Oh," she paused for a kiss, "I have a couple who think they can buy a home by bidding less – LESS mind you – than a bid that was already submitted! Some people are just plain dumb!"

"So, what did you tell 'em?"

"Well," she laughed, "I told 'em if they didn't bid more than their competition, they wouldn't get the house. Hell, Joe, I had to tell 'em three times before they got it!"

Joe grinned.

"So," Jane continued, "how was your day?"

Joe's expression turned serious. "Well, still no luck on the job search. I send out resumes' but I never seem to get any callbacks. No interviews. Hell, most of 'em don't even send an acknowledgment. And then there are the replies that say *'we will maintain your resume in our file in case a position with your qualifications becomes available'.* Shit, I hate those bastards!"

They walked out into the kitchen and Jane retrieved a soda from the refrigerator. She popped the top and turned around facing Joe.

"Why the hate?" she countered. "They aren't out to get you. Hell, they don't even know who you are."

"Damn it, Jane. I'm pissed. They laid me off with no notice." Joe paused. "Hell – I send out resumes and I never get a response. I swear they're not really looking to hire anyone. I'll bet they're advertising just to keep their corporate name out there."

"Damn!"

Jane leaned against the counter sipping her soda.

"I talked with Nate today." Joe continued. "You know – my old boss?"

Jane nodded. "What'd he have to say?"

Joe met her eyes and said, "He was laid off."

"What? How long ago?"

"He was laid off a couple of weeks after they let me go."

"Damn! What's goin' on at that place?"

"They told him they were cutting back the entire operation. But Nate has been hearing things from other people." Joe ran his hand down his shirt. "The word out on the street is that the telecom industry is in a depression. Not just a recession – but a full-blown depression." Joe's eyes widened as he spoke. "There's Lucent, Northern Telecom, and a whole lot of other companies that are in big trouble."

Jane nodded and then said, "What do you think we should do?"

"I'm already doing everything I can."

"I know. That's not what I mean. What do you think we need to do from now on?"

"Well, I need to find work so that we have enough income to live on." He paused. "We could sell the house - it's gone up in value quite a bit."

"Yes - but since we're now burning through our retirement fund, this may be the only asset we can count on for retirement - this and social security." Jane paused. "So, I'm not keen on selling this."

"I agree," Joe replied. "Tell you what. If I don't land a job soon, I'll get something flipping burgers - or something like that."

"Well, that will help. But it's pretty small when we have such a large house payment and two car payments. What do you think about selling your truck?"

Joe's face turned red. "That would leave me without transportation. How would I be able to hold a job then?"

An awkward wordlessness came between them.

"Hey," A gleam flashed in Joe's eyes, "how 'bout some wine?"

Jane smiled. "I'd love some."

Interlude

As though alive, the log walls danced in the flickering light of the blazing fire. And with cigar smoke wafting, the air was rife with silhouettes, weaving and winding their way through the ether, projecting an ethereal presence in the room.

In front of the fireplace, five leather chairs were arranged in a semi-circle, each facing into the fire. Five men, each ensconced in a chair, were talking. And while they were talking, each man filled his senses - of taste, of smell - with a very old, very rare brandy.

A tall, lanky man emerged from the shadows and into the center. With dark hair graying at the temples, he nonetheless had the attention of those seated. He nodded to each of the Five.

At the moment in question, the tall, lanky man was speaking. "... and we finally completed the project this past year. GLD[23] has been established and its assets are mostly salted[24] gold bars. And gentlemen, GLD is prepared to lease the 'gold' to other banks for short sales into the gold market. This will saturate the gold market, driving prices down even further."

"In addition, gentlemen, we have sold the excess salted bars into the market, primarily through both COMEX and LBMA."

Julius chimed in. "This is great news, Daniel. Driving down the price of gold creates the psychology that allows us to print more paper money without adversely affecting the paper currency and bond markets."

"Quite, Julius, quite – this is excellent news," responded Lord Basil. "What else do you have to report, Daniel?"

"Well, gentlemen, with regard to countries on our invasion list, it has become clear that the U.S. military will only be able to occupy Iraq and Afghanistan at the present time. They are stretched too thin to attack anywhere else, and the mood of Americans is against further war."

"What about Iran?"

"Iran has a formidable military, my Lord, and the U.S. military does not have enough infantry to hold Iran in addition to the other two countries."

"Hmmm," Lord Basil paused, then he said, "Well, Daniel. That last bit of news is certainly difficult to accept. I'm afraid that we will need to make other plans to take care of them. Maybe ...," he paused, "we should fortify our armies with still more money!"

"Yes, my Lord."

"Otherwise, an excellent report Daniel. You have performed magnificently!"

---

[23] GLD - the three-letter symbol representing the gold exchange traded fund (ETF).

[24] Salted - in the context of 'salted gold bars', means that the gold bar is a fake.

"Thank you, sir. May I be of any other service, my Lord?"

"Ahhhh – possibly, Daniel." Lord Basil paused in thought. Then, "what are you doing about silver?"

"Silver, sir? Why – we are selling it short into the market just as we are gold. But there is some strangeness, too; because the price does not behave like gold."

"It is excellent that you notice this, Daniel. You are correct. The price movement is certainly different." Lord Basil paused. And then he asked, "Do you know why?"

"No, my Lord."

"The answer is simple, Daniel. There is much less above-ground silver than gold. We are already planning a silver ETF[25] for next year. So I suggest, Daniel, that you make some salted silver bars and sell them into our new ETF." Lord Basil smiled.

"At your command, my Lord. I will begin the project right away."

"Excellent. Excellent, Daniel."

"My Lord, is there any other way I can be of service?"

"No. Not at this time." Lord Basil paused, and then said, "You may go."

"Thank you, sir." Daniel turned and walked out of the chamber.

The men had been listening attentively. With Daniel's departure, the men relaxed into their chairs.

"Well, gentlemen," Lord Basil waved his cigar in a flourish. "As the days unfold, we move closer to our objective. The 9/11 recession has passed, even as the Federal Reserve continues to pump ever more money and credit into the economy. And as you can see, it is pumping up the stock markets and housing markets throughout the western world – just as we planned."

---

25   ETF – Exchange Traded Fund is an investment fund traded on stock exchanges, much like stocks. An ETF holds assets such as stocks, commodities, or bonds, and trades close to its net asset value over the course of the trading day. SLV (silver) and GLD (gold) are two such funds.

"And when these markets come crashing down, we shall see the pain and discontent, and the beginnings of a murmur begging us to help them."

From the shadows, the other four men nodded their approval.

"And also as we planned, commodity prices – especially food and energy – are going higher. Higher food prices, particularly, shall sow the seeds of discontent among the rabble. And thus we are planting the seeds of third-world revolution to come five or six years hence."

"Ah yes," Lord Basil continued. "That we control the world's reserve currency means that we can inflict inflation, depression, pain, and suffering on the entire world with just a few keystrokes." Lord Basil smiled with glee.

Chapter 7

New York, November 18, 2004 (International Press) Exchange Traded Fund (ETF) for Gold.

GLD – SPDR's[26] newest exchange traded fund has begun operations today. The fund is structured to allow investors the opportunity to invest in gold without taking delivery of the physical metal.

"This makes investing in gold easier than ever," according to a spokesman for SPDR. "Investors no longer need to deal with the inconvenience and expense of delivery and assaying of their gold. Instead, investors can purchase however many shares as they deem necessary for their portfolio." The spokesman also noted that shares of GLD are fungible – that is, easy to break into small portions.

---

[26] SPDR – A short form of Standard & Poor's depository receipt, an exchange-traded fund (ETF) managed by State Street Global

The custodian for this fund is HSBC[27] bank.

Around the same time, this piece also appeared in the print media:

Rothschild & Sons Ltd. Withdraws from Commodities Trading.

LONDON, April 14, 2004 (International Press) - NM Rothschild & Sons Ltd., announced on Wednesday, that the London-based unit of investment bank Rothschild [ROT.UL], will withdraw from trading commodities in London, including gold. It stated that "... its operations are under review."

This reporter speculates that the risk to gold investors has increased, but without the additional risk premium factored into the price of gold; thus motivating the Rothschild's departure from the gold market.

*   *   *   *   *

Josh rubbed his hands together and said, "Okay boys and girls. It's time to slam gold again."

Josh and his staff – Eddie, Troy, Stephanie, Natalie, and Chet – were gathered in Josh's office, seated on the sofa and upholstered chairs formed in a semicircle. His monthly staff meeting was a ritual. He didn't like it – and he knew his staff didn't care for it either. But it was a way to meet with everyone at the same time.

Looking around at his staff, he noticed that Troy and Natalie were hanging closer together. *A possible romance?*

---

27 HSBC is a British multinational banking and financial company headquartered in London, United Kingdom.

Josh smiled broadly as he spoke. "Well, folks. In terms of dollars, the price of gold is just about where it was ten years ago. We've been enormously successful, and I salute you for the role you've played. There will be bonus checks deposited into your accounts in the near future."

Josh raised his coffee cup. "I offer a toast! A toast to our success!"

Everyone raised his cup and cheered, and then they solemnly sipped.

Josh focused first on Eddie. "How's our gold leasing program going?"

Eddie stopped biting on a fingernail long enough to respond. "I think it's doing good. The central banks have slowed down a bit; but we're leasing more from GLD."

"Great work, Eddie," Josh replied. "Troy. How are the gold shorts doing?"

Troy's eyes lit up as he smiled broadly. "We're keeping the gold shorts in a manageable range, Josh. But we could probably use more help from the other banks."

"Okay," Josh replied, "I will talk with our partners and see if they can pick up some of the slack."

Josh continued. "How about the silver shorts? How are we doing with those?"

Troy's smiled faded. "Silver has been tough. Even as we sell more shorts into the market, the market keeps hitting back. And it's so volatile!" Troy looked pointedly at Josh. "We could lose a lot of money if we get in deep and the market goes the wrong way."

Josh nodded his head in quiet acknowledgment. "I talked with Trevor the other day ..."

"Is that your new boss?" Natalie joked. It was common knowledge that every candidate since Charles had been a failure.

Josh smiled and continued, "Yes - that's him. Anyway, he let me know that we need to do whatever it takes to keep silver under control, even if we have to take a loss."

With that statement, his staff began to chatter back and forth. Taking losses had never before been part of their charter.

And then Josh interrupted as he looked at Troy. "So Troy. You should be selling short as much as you need to keep the price down. In fact, you need to get real aggressive with your short sales. Let's see how many weak hands are holding silver – let's see how much silver we can shake loose from those weak hands."

* * * * *

New York, April, 2006 (International Press) New Exchange Traded Fund (ETF) – Silver.

This month, SLV[28] – SPDR's newest exchange traded fund will begin operations. The fund is structured to allow investors the opportunity to invest in silver without taking delivery of the physical metal.

"We all have a desire for more liquid markets, and this makes investing in silver easier than ever," according to a spokesman for SPDR. "Investors no longer need to deal with the inconvenience and expense of delivery and assaying of their silver. Instead, investors can purchase however many shares as they deem necessary for their portfolio." The spokesman also noted that shares of SLV are fungible – easy to break into small portions.

The custodian for this fund is AB Jorday.

Chapter 8

Joe was smiling. "Hey. It's nice to be working again!"

---

[28] SLV – the three-letter symbol representing the silver exchange traded fund (ETF).

"How about some wine?" Jane said. "I'm bushed after that long day at the office!"

"Sounds great! I'll get some."

Joe retrieved a bottle of wine from storage. A rather delicious Cabernet Sauvignon from Napa Valley, he smacked his lips as he poured two glasses. He placed the glasses on the coffee table, saying "we ought to let these sit and breathe for a bit."

"Come here." Jane beckoned with a smile.

Joe sat down next to her, and their lips met in a long tender kiss.

They separated slowly, gazing into each others' eyes; both were smiling and breathing heavily.

Joe reached for the wine glasses and handed a glass to Jane. He said, "A toast – to jobs that pay the bills."

They sipped. And then they kissed again.

"So now that you've been there a few days," Jane said, "how do you like your new job?"

Joe shrugged. "It's a job. You know – it's different when you're a contractor – they treat you different, and you treat them different. I'd say the politics are a big change – much easier. But at the same time, the company can drop you on a moments' notice."

Jane looked down at her glass, thoughtfully. "You know. I sure am glad you got that contract. I didn't tell you this before, but sales have been slowing down lately. I guess that businesses have been laying off a lot of people and it's starting to have an effect on the housing market."

"I'm glad I got it too." Joe nuzzled up to her and they kissed again. Slowly.

They separated and sipped their wine.

And then Joe paused, holding up his hand. "Hey! I want to show you something. C'mon!"

Joe got up from the sofa and walked toward the den with Jane following. They walked into the den. And then Jane saw it. Standing against the wall was a spanking new flat screen television.

Jane stood and looked at it, and her jaw dropped.

"Well," Joe looked at her with excitement, "what do you think?"

Jane was speechless. Then she blurted out, "Where'd this come from?"

"I bought it. They delivered it today."

Jane turned and looked at him with her jaw agape. "You bought this?"

"Well, yes. I wanted it to be a surprise."

Jane put her hand to her forehead. "Shit, Joe, we have no money for this. What are you thinking!" She paused to collect herself. "Look. You were out of work for almost two years. We've drawn down our retirement fund. We're just getting by on two paychecks. And now you go out and buy a damn television!"

"Joe!" She whispered. "What are you thinking?"

Under her glare, Joe just stood there.

*   *   *   *   *

A year later . . .

Joe guided his new pickup truck through the late evening Sacramento traffic toward home. He had a gleam in his eye, anticipating that Jane would be taken by his newest purchase. *Wait until she sees this!* Joe mentally chortled.

He enjoyed the smooth power of the V-8 as he drove along U.S. 50. He turned it easily as he exited the freeway and then headed south on Sunrise Blvd. *I sure am glad we live south of 50 rather than north - it's a zoo up there.* He turned into his subdivision. Winding through the residential streets, he drove up to the house and pulled into the driveway.

"Ja-ane," he called as he walked into their home.

"I'm in here," he heard her call from the kitchen.

Joe walked into the kitchen and found Jane leaning over the counter reading a newspaper. He walked up behind her and began massaging her shoulders. "Hi, lover. How was your day?"

Jane started to moan and roll her neck under his touch. "Oh wow. Don't stop."

He massaged her for a few minutes, and then bent down to kiss the back of her neck. "Ooooo," she squealed softly.

She turned around and their eyes met. "So, how was your day?"

"Great!," Joe replied. "Work's going well. They talked with me about an extension today."

"Super," Jane nodded.

"And," Joe continued - happiness in his voice, "I went and bought that new truck we talked about."

Jane became serious. "I thought we agreed to talk about it, didn't we?"

"But honey, we *did* talk about it."

"No, Joe. I wanted to talk about it some more."

"But I thought we agreed! Hell. Everything's been going so good for us."

Jane paused and bit on her lip. And then she put her hands on his chest. "Joe."

"Yes?"

"I needed to tell you. Things have not been going so well at work lately."

"What? What do you mean?" Joe stammered.

"What I mean," she replied, "is that houses are not selling as fast as they were."

"But that'll turn around - it always does," Joe pleaded.

"Maybe. And maybe not. One thing I *do* know is that I'm spending more on marketing and promotion than I was before; at least as a percentage of sales." She paused. "So, I'm not getting the income I was before."

Jane's shoulders were hunched over as she looked down to the floor.

Joe's voice was soft. "Well. What do you want me to do about it?"

Jane looked up into Joe's eyes and sighed. "I'm not sure we can do anything about it now."

Chapter 9

And Back in Idaho ...

"Do you know where you're going?" Trish was nearly abreast of Dwayne as they hurried their way through the crowd.

"Yep. I know this place like the back of my hand," Dwayne replied.

"Back of your hand, my foot!" Trish yelled. She began to jog alongside him. "So, where're we supposed to meet him?"

"There's a place where all of the gates come together into a single exit. Everyone gets funneled through it," Dwayne shouted.

Trish was now running to keep up with Dwayne. "Slow down, Dwayne," Trish yelled. "I can barely keep up."

Dwayne shouted a reply. "We've got to hurry or we'll miss him at the gate exit."

They soon reached the airport gate area and watched with bated breath as the passengers filed by. The line seemed endless.

Dwayne was quickly looking back and forth when he heard Trish shouting. "There he is – there he is!"

Dwayne looked at Trish. And then he followed her aim as she pointed into the crowd. *Is that really James? He looks so different!* Dwayne's thoughts paused while he took a few moments to adjust to James' new appearance.

And then he paused again at the sight of another young man behind James. *That must be Stuart,* Dwayne thought.

Dwayne stood back and watched as Trish and James embraced. All three talked for a moment and then made their way through the crowd toward Dwayne.

Dwayne's face grew into a broad smile. "Hello, son," he said simply. They shook hands and then hugged – the kind of bear hug meant only for men. He stepped back from his son. "Boy, have you changed!" And then he acknowledged the other young man and extended his hand. "And you must be Stuart?" They shook hands.

"All right? Oh, ... Ah. Yes sir, I'm Stuart – Stuart Rollins, sir." Stuart's thick British rolled off his tongue as he met Dwayne's eyes. He nodded to Dwayne in a 'reserved' manner.

"I'm so glad to meet you - James told us all about you," Dwayne said with a smile.

Stuart quickly rubbed his hand up and down the side of his trousers. "I'm glad to meet you as well, sir. Thanks for letting me come for a visit."

"Well," Dwayne motioned toward the baggage claim, "we better go and collect your bags."

As they walked toward the baggage claim, Dwayne noticed James' long and easy strides. No longer slouching, he now stood and walked like a man - so different from the James who enlisted in the Marines just four years ago. *My son has grown up!*

They walked at an easy gait as they chatted. "So, have you separated yet? Or are you still their captive?" Dwayne joked.

James smiled. "Oh, I separated when I came through Germany. I'm a free man now - and it feels awesome!" And then James paused. "Dad, I really appreciate your letting Stuart stay with us for a while. He's never been to the U.S. He's gonna enjoy it here!"

And then James looked back at Stuart. "Right, Dude?"

"Alright, mate!" Stuart replied with a smile.

They continued their long strides toward the baggage claim, with Trish still struggling to keep pace.

* * *

James peered through the scope as he acquired his target downrange. The butt of the Barrett M107 rifle was pressed snugly against his shoulder, and his hand grasped the pistol grip - his finger wrapping around the front of the trigger. He took up the slack in the trigger, slowly. And almost without warning. **Boom!** He felt the rifle's butt slam into his shoulder, followed by the odor of freshly fired gunpowder wafting into his nostrils. Still in a firing position, he peered downrange through the scope - confirming the accuracy of his shot.

A semiautomatic rifle, James knew that the rifle operated flawlessly and that the next round was already chambered. James disengaged from the rifle, leaving it in position on the bench rest they used specifically for target practice. He stood up and looked at Stuart with a wry grin. Wiping his hands on his blue jeans, he said, "You wanna try it?"

Stuart smiled as he sat down at the bench rest. "You blokes think this is some kinda special weapon? Two tours in 'stan, I did – and a bloody lot of time looking down the barrel of one of these."

Stuart re-positioned his hearing protection and brought the butt of the rifle into the recess of his shoulder. Then he positioned his cheek on the cheek rest and peered downrange through the eyepiece of the mil-spec. Leupold 4.5x14 scope. A skilled sniper for the British Army, Stuart settled into a relaxed shooting posture. James watched on as he exhaled while taking up the slack in the trigger; and at the point where his exhale stopped and his body became still, he squeezed the trigger.

Boom! Standing off to the side of the rifle, James realized that the side-to-side concussion of the weapon was too much for his ears – no matter what kind of hearing protection he was wearing! James picked up his telescope and moved to the table behind Stuart, placing him outside of the rifle's concussion zone.

Over breakfast just that morning, he had seen his Dad's eyes light up.

"C'mon," he whispered; and the other two followed him into his office. He pulled a long box out of the closet and opened it, picking a rifle out of the box.

"Oh, man!" James' voice was throaty as his face lit up. He held out his hands and said, "Can I see that?"

"Bloody beautiful!" Stuart's eyes too were sparkling.

Eyes still gleaming, Dwayne handed it to James.

"Well?" said Dwayne.

"Awesome!" James said as he turned it over and looked at the different parts. He handed it to Stuart.

"All Right!" Stuart looked up at Dwayne as he was holding it. "This is just like the one I used in 'stan. It's one bloody great piece!"

> Dwayne laughed. "Well, why don't you two try it
> out today?"
> "Oh, wow! Thanks, Dad!" James said.
> "Bloody 'ell," Stuart said

Boom! James came out of his daydream. He watched as Stuart, patient and unfazed, melded his shoulder into the rifle; watched as Stuart exhaled, and relaxed his body. He took up the slack in the trigger.

Boom!

James put the telescope up to his eye and focused in on the target downrange. In just a few rounds, the target was already shredded. *Damn, we really do need a more durable target,* he thought. They were set up at a shooting table/bench that Dwayne had previously constructed. Located near the house, the shooting lane they used was bordered by native timber and followed a path straight out from the bench. The target was placed in front of a medium sized hill, so there was no danger of a stray bullet. James checked the range at 300 meters – about 325 yards.

James was intent on Stuart's shooting, failing to notice the surrounding mountains – mountains chock full of pine and fir trees, and with snow-covered mountain peaks off in the distance.

Boom!

"Nice shooting," James said.

James thought back to when he and his Dad first talked about buying the rifle.

> "... this is a great rifle, son! Accurate! Extremely accurate! The bullet has a flat trajectory that makes it accurate to more than a mile! Son, this here is what we call an 'interesting weapon'!"

An especially 'interesting' weapon, the Barrett M107 was based on previous incarnations of .50 caliber Barrett rifles. A semi-automatic weapon with a ten-round magazine, the rifle fired the .50 caliber Browning Machine Gun (12.7 x 99 mm NATO); a round large enough to take out an automobile, or a small stationary airplane. James knew that the ballistics of the .50 BMG was especially 'interesting' – that the bullet would travel in a relatively flat trajectory at nearly 3,500 feet per second. This helped to make the rifle highly accurate for up to 2,000 meters – an ideal sniper's weapon. But at 28 pounds, it was not a weapon that your average infantry soldier would carry.

Yes, James reflected with a smile, he was delighted indeed to test his father's rifle.

Boom! Stuart squeezed off another round. James peered through his telescope seeking the target downrange. Stuart's shooting had ripped out the middle of it!

Awesome! James shouted.

Boom! Yet another round passed on-center through the already shredded target. And once again, the concussion from the rifle rolled out to the side.

Awesome!

* * *

Dwayne carried some rare coin sheets out to the kitchen table. *You'd think I'd have better lighting in my office*, he thought. *Let's see ... 1885-cc. Now that's a good year!* Just then he heard some banging on the back porch, and then the two shooters walked in.

"Hi, Dad."

"Hi, Mr. Jeffrey."

"So how was the shooting?" Dwayne asked.

"Awesome, Dad. That was so cool!"

Stuart smiled and then chimed in. "Yes, Mr. Jeffrey. That's a nice rifle you've got there. As nice as the rifles they issued us in 'stan."

Dwayne smiled. "I'm glad you like it."

Stuart walked over and looked at the sheet of coins. "Oh, alright! These are bloody awesome. Can I hold it?"

"Go ahead," Dwayne replied.

Stuart picked up the sheet and held it up to the light – a sheet of 12 Morgan Silver Dollars. "Blimey! Are these shiny, or wot?"

He looked at them a bit more. "So. Why is there such an attraction to these coins? What do people find in gold and silver coins?"

Dwayne paused in thought and then replied. "It's real money. It's substantial. And it can't be printed out of thin air."

"Huh?"

"Gold has been used as money for 6,000 years."

Doubt washed over Stuart's face. "Why is that important?"

"Why? Because people know that it will retain its purchasing power. And unlike paper money, you can't just create more of it from nothing."

Stuart thought for a moment. And then he said, "If gold is so good, then why do we use paper money?"

Dwayne's mouth twisted in cynicism. "We use paper money because it benefits the bankers."

"Aw c'mon, Mr. Jeffrey. Isn't that a simplistic answer? Doesn't paper money benefit all of us?"

"No, Stuart. Paper money doesn't benefit us." He paused, looking at Stuart. "Although at first glance it may appear so."

Dwayne cleared his throat and continued. "Paper money allows the bankers to print more and more, while at the same time debasing the currency that you and I hold. With their money printing, our money is worth less over time – the loss of purchasing power we experience is transferred to the bankers and the wealthy. In other words, the bankers steal from the poor and the middle class and give it to the rich. And they use paper money to do it."

"Yeah, but. Isn't paper money good when you want to buy a house?"

"Sure. But why do you ask?"

"Why? Because I have a dream. A dream that someday I'll find a girl I fancy, buy a home, and settle down with my family." Stuart looked at Dwayne with a somewhat pleading expression. "It's important to me – my dreams. I want to live them and see them fulfilled."

Dwayne nodded. "I understand. We all have dreams. And we all want to live 'em."

For just a moment, there was an awkward silence. And then Dwayne piped up. "May I say just one more thing?"

"Aye sir, please continue."

"Well, I didn't want to spoil the mood, but there's one other thing that's important about paper." Dwayne frowned and then continued. "Paper money gives the banks control over the economy. So they can put us into a depression whenever they choose – just by withdrawing credit from the economy. And if they push us into a depression, people lose their homes – and people starve."

"So you see," Dwayne concluded. "when you borrow money from a bank to buy a home, you're putting yourself under their thumb. They get to do with you what they will."

"Bloody 'ell, Mr. Jeffrey. I'll think about that."

* * * * *

"Soups on," Trish shouted. Dwayne walked into their country kitchen and pulled up a chair at the oak kitchen table. The kitchen abounded with a country atmosphere – wallpaper imprinted with hens, oak plank flooring, and country-style furnishings. But Dwayne ignored all of it. Instead, he watched intently as Trish served up a couple of bowls.

Trish brought the bowls to the table, placing one in front of Dwayne.

"Oh man," Dwayne exclaimed. "I just love your chili."

"Eat up," Trish said as she sat down.

Dwayne already had his mouth full.

They were busily eating when Dwayne piped up. "Did you hear about Fed Chairman Greenspan?"

"No," Trish mumbled with her mouth stuffed. "What about him."

"He's retiring."

Trish's eyebrows raised as she put her spoon into the bowl. "Really?" She gulped.

"Yep," Dwayne mumbled with a full mouth. "President Bush has already nominated a new Fed Chairman."

"Who did he nominate?" Trish took a bite.

"Ethan Cohan," Dwayne replied, still with a full mouth.

"Who?"

"Ethan Cohan."

"Never heard of him," she mumbled.

"Me neither. Though I guess we'll find out what he's like."

The conversation paused.

"What does that mean?" Trish asked.

"It means that he's inheriting an economy that's going into recession."

"Why do you say that?"

"Because Greenspan has spent the last couple of years raising interest rates and pulling money out of the economy."

"What's that mean for gold?"

"I'm not sure," Dwayne said, wiping his chin with a napkin. "We've seen a pretty good run up on gold the last few years. I'm guessing that gold prices will continue to rise."

Just as Dwayne shoveled yet another spoonful of chili into his mouth, they both heard James' boots shuffle into the house. "I'm home," he shouted.

Trish turned and called to him. "We're in here, having dinner."

James walked into the kitchen. "Any left for me?"

"Chili," Trish mumbled with her mouth full. "it's over in the pot."

"Awesome! I love chili."

James dished out some chili and sat down at the table.

"Stuart's on the plane, I take it?" Dwayne asked.

"Yep. He's on his way back to England. He flies to Minneapolis and then he picks up a non-stop for London. He'll be there by late morning tomorrow."

Now it was Dwayne talking with his mouth full. "Did he have a good visit?"

"Yep." James looked up from his dish. "He asked me to thank you two again." And then James mimicked Stuart's accent. "I had a bloody mah-vah-las time." James laughed as he said it.

"Great!" Dwayne swallowed a spoonful. "Maybe he'll come over again sometime. If he does, I'd like to talk more about his sniping excursions."

* * * * *

In June, 2006, the Fed Funds rate reached a plateau at 5.25%. The rising interest rates over the previous two years had caused a withdrawal of money and credit from circulation – which resulted in a slowing economy.

Too, the subprime[29] mortgage securities market was now being squeezed. Higher interest rates found their way to home buyers who had purchased homes with variable rate loans; and as interest rates increased, the buyers' ability to make mortgage payments became increasingly difficult. As a result, the investment banks who invested in these securities came under increasing stress.

Cracks in the subprime Mortgage Backed Securities' (MBS)[30] market were beginning to appear. But so far, the cracks were not yet apparent in the economy at large ...

Chapter 10

Joe was in the den watching television; when he heard the front door open and close. "Is that you Jane?" he called.

"It's me." Joe heard a male voice reply.

"Who's me?"

---

[29] In finance, subprime lending (also referred to as **near-prime, non-prime**, and **second-chance lending**) means making loans to people who may have difficulty maintaining the repayment schedule. These loans are characterized by higher interest rates and less favorable terms in order to compensate for higher credit risk.

[30] A **mortgage-backed security** (**MBS**) is an asset-backed security that represents a claim on the cash flow from mortgage loans.

"Len." He heard the voice again.

Len walked into the den. "Hi, Dad."

"Hey, how's it going?" Joe replied with a smile.

"Fine, Dad. Just fine."

"While you're up, can you get me a beer. And get one for yourself too."

Len went out to the kitchen and returned with two beers. He handed one to Joe.

"So," Joe looked at his son and smiled. "To what do I owe the honor of this visit?" He took a swallow.

Len looked down at his beer and began peeling the label. "Mom asked me to come by."

"Yes?"

"She told me that you lost your contract. And you've not been able to find anything else."

"That's true, son. What about it?"

"She's hoping that you and I can talk."

Joe's face took on an expression of curiosity. "Talk? Why would we not be able to talk?"

"Why? Because it's not something we normally talk about."

Joe paused, looking at Len. And then he said, "I'm sure we can talk, Len. What's on your mind?"

"Dad. This economy we're in is not doing well. Since you're out of work, I'm sure you know that."

"Yep, I know it. But I also know that this ain't gonna last. It's gonna get better." Joe took another swallow of beer.

Len nodded. "Well, Mom told me that's what you've been sayin'."

"So," Joe replied. "Isn't that true?"

Len looked into Joe's eyes. "No Dad. The economy's not gonna get better."

"Bullshit," Joe's voice quivered. "These things pass. It always gets better."

"Not this time, Dad."

"Why? Why are you sayin' this?"

"Because, I work with a guy. Yeah, Dad, another guy who's a nurse." Len chuckled. "Anyway, he received a minor in economics. And he says all the fundamentals are pointing to the worst depression in history.”

“He sounds like a wacko doomsayer to me,” Joe's voice quivered even more.

Len waited until Joe calmed down. “Dad. You need to make plans. You need to sell this house before you and Mom lose even more money in it.”

“Aw – c'mon, son. This is California! You know that real estate always recovers. It'll always go up. Hell, everything will get better.”

Len looked into his eyes. “Dad. Not this time,” he whispered.

Joe paused, frowning. And then he asked, “did your friend say why he thinks things are gonna get so bad?”

“Yeah – there's two reasons he gave me. The first is that the enormous world-wide debt will consume the world and cause the dollar to collapse.”

“Hmmm,” Joe paused, absorbing Len’s statement. “And the second reason?”

“He said that when the dollar collapses, it will destroy the entire world economy.”

“And you believe him?”

“Yeah, Dad. I believe him.”

Chapter 11

“You are soooo talented,” Brandy said for the third time since dinner.

Bill smiled. Earlier, Bill produced their latest balance sheet and income statement showing big growth in their business. They tabulated two lines of business – custom minting and Freedom Dollars – and they were both doing extremely well.

“I’d say a lot of the credit goes to you, Brandy,” Bill replied. “Hell, you’re the one who came up with our ‘*marketing through dealer*’ program.”

"I'll drink to that," Brandy raised her glass in a toast, and they clinked their glasses together."

"Hell," Brandy smiled and continued, "I talked with a couple of dealers who told me they're seeing people using Freedom Dollars as a barter currency. I tell ya, Bill, we are on the road to something big here!"

Bill smiled. "I think the barter currency is the biggest thing of all; because a competing currency is the only way to break the hold on the Fed's monopoly." Bill's smile widened still more. "I notice that the Liberty Dollar and the Phoenix Dollar are also doing well."

"I wonder," Brandy's voice dripped of sarcasm, "how the Feds will respond to competition against their *oh-so precious* Federal Reserve Notes?"

"Hell," Bill replied, "everything we're doing is perfectly legal. What can they possibly do to us?"

Brandy turned and looked at him. "Besides shutting down our business and putting us in jail? – Not much."

* * * * *

Liberty Dollars Not Legal Tender, United States Mint Warns Consumers - - - *Justice Determines Use of Liberty Dollar Medallions as Money is a Crime*

Washington, D.C. (September 14, 2006) — The United States Mint urges consumers considering the purchase or use of "Liberty Dollar" medallions, marketed by the National Organization for the Repeal of the Federal Reserve Act and the Internal Revenue Code (NORFED), to be aware that they are not genuine United States Mint bullion coins, and not legal tender. These medallions are privately produced products that are neither backed by, nor affiliated with, the United States Government. Prosecutors with the Department of Justice have determined that the use of these gold and silver NORFED "Liberty Dollar" medallions as circulating money is a Federal crime.

NORFED is headquartered in Evansville, Indiana, and the medallions reportedly are produced by a private mint in Coeur d'Alene, Idaho. NORFED claims that more than $20 million dollars worth of Liberty Dollar coins and notes are in circulation.

Consumers may find advertisements for these medallions confusing and should take note of several issues related to them. The advertisements refer to the product as "real money" and "currency." These medallions might look like real money because they:

- Bear the inscriptions, "Liberty," "Dollars," "Trust in God" (similar to "In God We Trust"), and "USA" (similar to "United States of America"), and an inscription purporting to denote the year of production.

- Depict images that are similar to United States coins, such as the torch on the reverses of the current dime coin, 1986 Statue of Liberty Commemorative Silver Dollar and 1993 Bill of Rights Commemorative Half-Dollar, and the Liberty Head designs on the obverses of United States gold coins from the mid-1800s to the early 1900s.

However, despite their misleading appearance, NORFED "Liberty Dollar" medallions are not genuine United States Mint coins, and they are not legal tender.

The advertisements confusingly refer to NORFED "Liberty Dollar" medallions as "legal" and "constitutional." However, under the Constitution (Article I, section 8, clause 5), Congress has the exclusive power to coin money of the United States and to regulate its value. The United States Mint is the only entity in the United States with the lawful authority to mint and issue legal tender United States coins.

Under 18 U.S.C. § 486, it is a Federal crime to pass, or attempt to pass, any coins of gold or silver intended for use as current money except as authorized by law. According to the NORFED website, "Liberty merchants" are encouraged to accept NORFED "Liberty Dollar" medallions and offer them as change in sales transactions of merchandise or services.

NORFED tells "Liberty associates" that they can earn money by obtaining NORFED "Liberty Dollar" medallions at a discount and then can "spend [them] into circulation."

NORFED's "Liberty Dollar" medallions are specifically marketed to be used as current money in order to limit reliance on, and to compete with the circulating coinage of the United States. Consequently, prosecutors with the United States Department of Justice have concluded that the use of NORFED's "Liberty Dollar" medallions violates 18 U.S.C. § 486, and is a crime.

When contacted, a spokesman for the Federal Reserve in Washington, D.C., said, "There is no law that says goods and services must be paid for with Federal Reserve notes. Parties entering into a transaction can establish any medium of exchange that is agreed upon."

Interlude

The smoke billowed from the tip of the cigar and into the air. Traveling across the room, the smoke cast its wavy silhouette throughout the chamber, even as it melded with the shadows cast from the fire. Despite the warmth of the fire, the room felt cold, dark and emotionless, as though an evil spirit had drained all that was good and right from the room.

Five leather-upholstered chairs were arranged in a semi-circle; all facing toward the fireplace. Each chair was occupied by a man, and each man was obscured in the shadows cast by the fire.

With purposeful strides, a tall, dark, slender man walked into the room. The man walked to the center of the five chairs and remained standing, even as he slightly bowed his head. "You wish to see me, my Lord?"

"Yes, Daniel." Lord Basil was especially business-like. "It has come to our attention that some few people in the U.S. are minting coins and are attempting to promote these coins as money, or currency, if you will. We have reports indicating they are doing this with both gold and silver. We also have reports indicating some of these people keep gold and silver bullion in storage, and issue receipts that give a receipt-holder a claim to a stated quantity of gold or silver."

"Yes, my Lord. This is all true."

"Well," Lord Basil continued, "We, The Council, have decided that these operations must be shut down immediately. And as much gold and silver as possible must be confiscated."

Daniel was taken aback by Lord Basil's intensity. "Yes, my Lord. I will attend to it right away."

Then Lord Basil's manner softened. "Remember, it is our control of money that allows us to control everyone and everything. We must never allow anyone to control their own money."

"Yes, my Lord."

Chapter 12 – Circa 2007

Bill was not big into shopping; but every so often he drove south into Sandpoint. One of his favorite places was a local hardware store known as *Winers*. It was a town fixture, and had been thus for several generations – repeatedly passed down within one family. He stopped into the store whenever he came to town. He liked to chew the fat with some of the locals as he was checking out their new guns or tools.

After his *Winers* stop, he usually dropped by his favorite coffee shop and sipped cappuccino while reading the newspaper. Bill did not take a newspaper at home because the carrier would only deliver it to their mailbox. But their mailbox was a half-mile from their home, and much too difficult a walk on a winter's morning.

On this particular day, Bill was browsing through the editorial page when a casually-dressed man abruptly sat down at his table. He looked across the table at Bill.

Bill was startled as he quickly looked up. With a condescending tone, Bill asked, "May I help you?"

"No." The man's lips replied through his manicured goatee. "But I may be able to help you."

"Oh really?" Bill's gaze was steady as he looked into the man's cold blue eyes.

The man flashed a badge. "I'm Kehoe, with Treasury."

Bill's gaze remained steady, even as his voice was firm. "What do you want?"

"Your coin business, Mr. Ford." The man replied. "We want you to cease and desist your minting operations."

Sometimes, a smile is not just a smile. Sometimes a smile is a pause. And sometimes a smile is angry, or worse. On hearing the man's words, Bill smiled. It was the kind of smile that could kill. Kehoe knew that kind of smile. And knowing this, he unconsciously leaned away from the table; away from Bill.

Bill focused on the man even as he remained under control. "Mr. Kehoe, you have thirty seconds to state your piece."

Kehoe's lips and goatee again moved. "Your coins are being used in commerce. Even though the usage is small, we see it increasing." Kehoe's voice took on a venomous tone. "Mark my words, Mr. Ford, we will not allow any gold or silver coin to compete as legal tender in commerce. Shut down your production, or we will destroy you."

With that, the man stood up from the table. He turned and walked out of the shop.

For some time, Bill sat with his coffee. *Shit! Who are these damn people!*

He finally paid his bill and walked out of the shop. He stood at the entrance and scanned the street, the sidewalks, and the nearby buildings; looking for any sign that he was being watched. But there was no sign.

Time to dust off the bug sweepers, he thought.

He went back to his car and headed north to his home. And as he was driving, he wondered how he and Brandy would handle this.

* * *

Almost immediately after the episode with Kehoe, he made a point of bug sweeping their home, office, cars, and anywhere else they frequented. He also spent considerable time searching for recording-type bugs; and he examined their home and office to find out if anyone had entered undetected. Curiously, he found no sign.

Then he ran a test of their cell phones. He turned off their phones, and then the two of them talked about something innocuous – a dinner date. Nothing. They detected no RF emissions and no sign that their cell phones were bugged, at least while they were turned off.

* * * * *

Autumn in Montana is beautiful. The big Montana sky, the mountains, the crystal clear streams, the leaves changing – all combine to create the rugged beauty and energy of the Bitterroot mountain range of western Montana. And with a pristine setting, the Golden Mint fits in perfectly with Montana's rugged wilderness – standing out like a picture-perfect postcard.

It was early afternoon when Bill and Brandy drove onto the Mint's grounds. They parked in a visitor's space and walked into the lobby.

The receptionist's smile broadened as they came in. "Hi, Bill. Hi, Brandy. How are you folks today?"

"Doing well," Brandy replied. "And you? Are you doing okay?"

"Absolutely," Marlece smiled. "The world is my oyster!"

"Is Murray available?" Brandy asked.

"I think so. Let me give him a ring."

The receptionist punched some buttons on her telephone, waited, and then said. "Mr. Ford and Ms. West are here to see you." She paused. "I will let them know."

The receptionist nodded to them. "He will be right out."

Murray soon came out and greeted them. Bill and Brandy signed in and he led them back to his office.

When they arrived in Murray's office, Bill said, "Thanks for taking some time to talk about the new coin design." Bill handed Murray a piece of paper, and gestured at Murray to look at it.

Murray opened the paper. It read:

Turn off your cell phone.

He looked up just as Brandy had placed her finger up to her lips. "Shhhh," she whispered.

Bill continued talking even as he swept the area for listening devices. When he was certain they could not be overheard, he breathed a sigh of relief and turned to Murray.

"Murray, we need your help."

* * *

Bill and Brandy drove off the road and into the driveway toward Dwayne and Trish's homestead. With trees crowding the sides of the narrow road, Bill guided the SUV up to an openspace area. Here, the driveway split both left and right. To go right would take you on the circular drive with a path directly into the garage. To go left would also take you on the circular drive, with a path to a small guest cottage. Either direction would take you part way around the circle to the front of the Jeffrey's home. Bill turned to the right just as Trish came out the front door and waved.

Situated on 20 forested acres, Trish enjoyed tending her garden and raising her chickens. She especially enjoyed the fresh eggs her chickens gave her – these were so much different than the supermarket eggs she had in her Nebraska suburban home. With rich yellow yokes and firm shells, they tasted great!

She was smiling as they drove up, coming to a stop in the parking area outside the house. "Hey," she shouted. "C'mon in!"

Brandy was especially excited since she did not get to see Trish very often. "Hey – I'm sure glad to see Y'all! Thanks for inviting us." They hugged.

They all walked into the living room just as Dwayne emerged from his study.

"Hi, guys." He said as he gave Brandy a hug.

They'd not been together in a while, so they found much to joke and laugh about.

"... so, Brandy, do you still carry that cannon?" Dwayne joked.

"Sure," she fired back, "all the better to protect me from people like you!"

The laughter went on ...

* * *

Bill was feeling 'stuffed' as he pushed away from the table.

"Thank you, Trish, for an incredible dinner. I think it might take me a few hours to get back on my feet," Bill joked.

"Yes," chimed in Brandy. "Thanks very much. This was wonderful."

Trish smiled as she turned and looked at both of them. "You're so welcome. I have a great time doing this."

"So Dwayne," Bill announced, "I need to talk business with you. Do you have a quiet place to talk?"

"Sure," Dwayne replied, "grab your wine and we'll go back to my office."

Once in Dwayne's office, Bill related his encounter with Agent Kehoe. Dwayne listened soberly, his jaw setting ever more firm.

"I'm sure that the bankers see gold and silver as a threat to their empire," Bill continued. "That's why they contacted me, and THAT is why they've been hitting on NORFED and their Liberty Dollar. In fact, I remember Fed Chairman Volcker stating that 'gold is his enemy' – now that sounds really serious!"

The room became silent as they absorbed the full import of Bill's story.

Dwayne finally asked, "So, what are you going to do?"

"Well, I have a plan," Bill replied, "and Murray – you know Murray Hofstadler, don't you? The engraver at the Golden Mint? Well, he's signed on to help us. But Dwayne, we need your help too."

"I'm all ears." Dwayne smiled.

*   *   *   *   *

Outside of the Golden Mint staff, few people knew that Murray worked as a consultant, rather than a Golden Mint employee. This gave Murray a lot of freedom in both his personal life and professional career. And after talking with Bill and Brandy, Murray agreed to help them with their plan.

He began to implement the plan in earnest. First, by researching properties in far north Boundary County, Idaho; he found a home that was secluded with large acreage. He signed a lease-purchase agreement that retained the current owner as the owner of record. And it allowed him to renovate the property.

The land was situated off a county road – set way back from the road. It was relatively flat, but surrounded by mountains a few miles distant. Because of the nature of the terrain, the land could be used for growing crops or raising animals – a perfect retreat. The home and shop – separated by 100 or so feet – were situated on a cleared section near the middle of the property.

Murray moved into the home and went quickly to work. He engaged a contractor to revamp the shop into a year-round facility, primarily with upgraded wiring, weatherproofing, insulation, and a propane heating system. And he engaged a couple of local men to help install a perimeter detection system – they did all of the heavy labor while Murray planned the system. With the detection system, Murray was following Bill's explicit instructions; knowing that Bill and Brandy's homestead sported a similar set-up, and that Dwayne's homestead would soon be secured in a similar manner.

Everything was taking shape; especially the shop where its now stable internal environment could accommodate electronic equipment and heavy, precisionist machinery.

As the project moved on, Murray began buying and transporting equipment to the site. He brought in several strange pieces of machinery. The men moving the machinery did not ask questions, and Murray did not offer an explanation. Interestingly, he did all this without any apparent contact with Bill or Brandy.

* * * * *

In Liberty Dollars, Federal Government Doesn't Trust

By Maira Keystone
Spokane News
Saturday, November 17, 2007

This past Wednesday, federal agents raided the headquarters of the National Organization for the Repeal of the Federal Reserve and Internal Revenue Codes (NORFED) in Evansville, Indiana. NORFED is an organization that advocates 'sound money' and has been selling a private currency – so-called 'Liberty Dollars' – that it says are backed by silver and gold. The silver and gold are alleged to be stored in Idaho – with a total of more than $20 million in circulation.

The raid occurred just as NORFED officials were preparing to mail out 60,000 'Ron Paul Dollars', the first batch of copper coins, decorated with an image of Ron Paul, and selling for $1 each. NORFED officials stated they had previously shipped about 10,000 silver

Ron Paul dollars, selling for $20 each. Ron Paul is running as a candidate for President and advocates the abolition of the Federal Reserve and the IRS.

In an interview, Bernard von NotHaus, NORFED's founder and executive director, said that the raid netted the Federal Government most of the Ron Paul copper dollars; as well as smaller amounts of silver Ron Paul dollars, gold Ron Paul dollars that sell for about $1,000, and platinum Ron Paul dollars that sell for $2,000 each. NotHaus also stated there was a separate raid of The Sunshine Mint in Coeur d'Alene, Idaho, where agents seized the huge pallets of silver and gold worth more than $1 million and that stand behind the paper certificates issued to its customers.

"They took everything, all of the computers, everything but the desks and chairs," said von NotHaus. "The federal government really is afraid."

The Indianapolis branch of the FBI declined to comment on the raid and referred calls to the U.S. Attorney's office for Western North Carolina in Charlotte. That office's spokeswoman, Suellen Pierce, also declined to comment.

But the affidavit for a search warrant filed last week with the Western District in Asheville was leaked on to the internet.

In the affidavit, the FBI states it is investigating NORFED for federal violations, including "uttering coins of gold, silver, or other metal," "making or possessing likeness of coins," mail fraud, wire fraud, money laundering, and conspiracy. "The goal of NORFED is to undermine the United States government's financial systems by the issuance of a non-governmental competing currency for the purpose of repealing the Federal Reserve and Internal Revenue Code," he states.

The FBI says that the investigation began two years ago. A year ago, the U.S. Mint published a warning against using the Liberty Dollar, prompting a lawsuit by NORFED.

* * * * *

Bill and Brandy heard about the NORFED raid the next morning. Bill immediately did a comprehensive bug sweep of the premises. And then he checked for bugs on their cell phones. He came up empty.

They decided to take a 'walk' on their property.

"So what do you think?" Brandy asked.

"Well," Bill replied, "I think they won't attempt a raid here until they've bugged us."

"But how will we know for sure?" She asked.

Bill was thoughtful. "I think we need to check for bugs frequently – *very frequently*! And then I think we need to watch for any penetration of our computers. But that's easier said than done.

"What do you mean?" She asked.

"Well," Bill replied, "I can see several ways that they could penetrate our computers without detection. But maybe we can use a low-tech method that will tell us if they've been here."

"Yes? What do you have in mind?"

Bill frowned. "What if we placed two pens on the computer in a particular orientation?"

"In which way?" Brandy asked.

"Well," Bill replied, "we can put the red pen across the keyboard, like so ... And we can put the blue pen on top of the case, like this."

"Okay," Brandy replied, "I think I can remember that."

For just a moment, neither said a word.

"Well," Bill mused, "I guess this will be a paradigm shift of our security."

Brandy was perplexed. "Huh?"

Bill smiled at Brandy. And then he said, "Shift happens."

"W-w-why? Why did you stop?" Tim sputtered. "The story's really getting good now!"

"Because I'm hurtin', that's why," the old man replied.

"Your ankle? Where you sprained it?"

"Yeah. It's pretty bad. It's swelling up really bad."

Tim stood up off the floor and walked over to where the old man was sitting. "Here old man. Lemme see it."

The old man rolled up his pant leg and pulled down his stocking, revealing a swollen black 'n blue ankle.

"Damn," Tim said. That's pretty bad." Tim inspected the ankle and then looked up at the old man. "Is there any chance of getting some ice on it?"

"Ice?" The old man cackled. "Hell, sonny. Refrigeration takes power. More power than I can conjure."

"Do you have any medicine? Any anti inflammatory drugs?"

"Nope. I didn't have time to stock any," the old man replied. "And I'm sure you've noticed that all the drugs were wiped out by the gangs."

"Yeah, I know," Tim said. "We've got some – back at the apartment."

Tim scratched his chin and then continued. "Hmmm. Tell you what. Maybe I can get some cold water into an ice bottle so we can cool down that ankle?"

"Well, sonny. I got some water. I keep it in tanks on the other side of that there door."

"Do you have a water bottle?"

"Yep. In the bathroom there yonder."

Tim walked into the bathroom and opened the vanity cupboard. "I got it," he shouted as he reached into the cabinet and pulled out an ice-pack bag. He returned with bag in hand.

"We can put water in it. Then we'll put it outside to cool down," Squirt said.

"Hells bells," the old man interjected. "It'll be all swollen up if I gotta wait that long. That's truth!"

Tim put his hand to his chin. "Maybe we need to go back to the apartment and get some meds. We've got some stuff back there for inflammation."

"Yeah," Squirt chimed in, "but we'll have to travel through these God-forsaken neighborhoods to get it!"

"That's all right," Tim said, feeling his pistol in his pocket. "We can make it. Besides, look at what Jim's done for us. I say we ought to go and get that medicine."

"Wait. Wait," Jim interrupted their conversation. "I don't need nothin' for this. It will heal!"

"Oh really?" Tim replied. "I'd say all that swelling can create a lot of problems. I think you need treatment before it gets any worse."

Tim grabbed his coat and put it on. "If you're going," Squirt chimed in as she too grabbed her coat, "then I'm goin' with you."

Tim sighed. "Okay, Squirt. Let's get going." Tim paused and then addressed Jim. "We'll be back soon."

"Well, you better." The old man broke out in a grin, and said, "Or else you'll miss the rest of the story."

Squirt put her coat on and followed Tim as he opened the door. The two stepped out into the cold pale light of an overcast sky. "Brrrrr," Squirt shivered.

Tim closed the door. "Let's go," he said.

To be continued . . .

Author's note: If you enjoyed this book, please leave a review on Amazon.com. This will help other people to find this story, and it will help me to better promote it. My sincere thanks!

Also, you can receive updates and free stuff via my email list. Please sign up here:

http://davidjewettauthor.com/wordpress/?page_id=346

Or the main page here: DavidJewettAuthor.com

Printed in Great Britain
by Amazon